Paul's love of military history started at an ~~~~~~~ watching films like *Waterloo* and *Zulu* wh~~~~ and the occasional *Commando* comic gav~~~~~ about the men who fought in the great ~~~~~~ twentieth centuries. This fascination led to a motivation to write and his series of novels featuring the brutally courageous Victorian rogue and imposter Jack Lark burst into life in 2013. Since then Paul has continued to write, developing the Jack Lark series to great acclaim.

To find out more about Paul and his novels visit www.paulfrasercollard.com or find him on Twitter @pfcollard.

Praise for Paul Fraser Collard and the Jack Lark series:

'A tour de force'
Simon Turney

'A gripping adventure . . . Jack Lark might not be the hero anyone wants, but he's most definitely the hero *you* need!'
R. S. Ford

'Historical adventure with nuance and a flawed, melancholy hero'
The Times

'Brilliant'
Bernard Cornwell

'Bullets fly, emotions run high and treachery abounds . . . exceptionally entertaining historical action adventure'
Matthew Harffy

'Like all the best vintages Jack Lark has aged to perfection. Scarred, battered and bloody, his story continues to enthral'
Anthony Riches

'A tale of despair, triumph, and disaster amongst the dry diamond workings of the du Toit pan'
Historical Novel Society

'You feel and experience all the emotions and the blood, sweat and tears that Jack does . . . I devoured it in one sitting'
Parmenion Books

'Expect ferocious, bloody action from the first page'
Ben Kane

Paul Fraser Collard

DIAMOND HUNTER

HEADLINE

First published in Great Britain in 2022 by
HEADLINE PUBLISHING GROUP

First published in paperback in Great Britain in 2023

1

Cataloguing in Publication Data is available from the British Library

ISBN 978 1 4722 6353 7

Typeset in Sabon by Avon DataSet Ltd, Alcester, Warwickshire

Printed and bound in Great Britain by Clays Ltd, Elcograf S.p.A.

Headline's policy is to use papers that are natural, renewable and recyclable products
and made from wood grown in well-managed forests and other controlled sources.
The logging and manufacturing processes are expected to conform to the
environmental regulations of the country of origin.

HEADLINE PUBLISHING GROUP
An Hachette UK Company
Carmelite House
50 Victoria Embankment
London EC4Y 0DZ

www.headline.co.uk
www.hachette.co.uk

For Martin Fletcher, Flora Rees and Frankie Edwards

Glossary

---

beak	nose / judge
brass razoo	money
corned	drunk
desk-wallah	clerk
mofussil	country stations and districts away from the chief stations of the region
mollymawk	albatross
pagdi	turban, cloth or scarf wrapped around a hat
sarsaparilla	soft drink made from plants
sawar	cavalry trooper
Shanks's pony	walking
solar topee	light tropical helmet – forerunner of the pith helmet
talwar	curved native sword
Tyburn	site of the King's Gallows from 1196 to 1783
vittles	food

Afrikaans	
bloed geld	blood money

brü	brother (friend)
doos	fool
dopkaas	dick cheese
ek sal jou bliksemse moer donner	I will beat you black and blue
holnaaier	arse-fucker
hou jou bek	shut your trap
jou fokken poes	you fucking cunt
jy prat kak	you are talking crap
poephol	arsehole
rooinekke	rednecks (British)
uitlander	foreigner
veldt	open grassland
verdolt Engelschman	damn Englishman
vrouw	wife
Yissus	Jesus

SOUTH AFRICA, 1871.
JACK'S ROUTE TO
THE DIAMOND FIELDS.

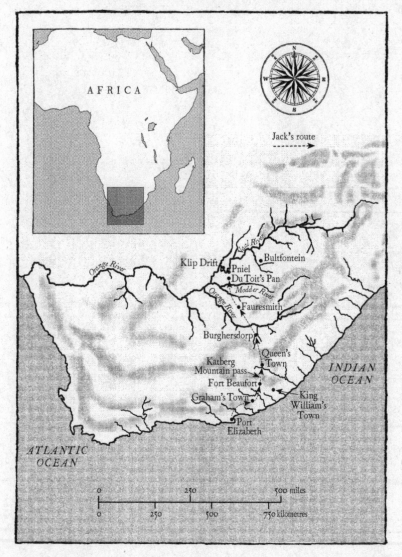

Prologue

Du Toit's Pan, Cape Colony, March 1871

William Kelly reached down into the dirt and picked up a pebble, just as he had a thousand times before. At least, he thought it was nothing more than another damn pebble, as it had been every other time he had laid his shovel on the ground then stooped low to scoop up whatever it was that had caught his eye in the mix of soil and limestone beneath his battered boots.

'Got yourself something there, Bill?'

Kelly looked up to see a familiar face peering down at him over the edge of the pit. 'Just an old bit of rock, Davy-boy, same as all the others.'

David 'Davy' Evans was a Welshman from the valleys. He owned the claim next to the one Kelly worked. The two were friends, if such a thing existed amongst those hunting in the dirt for riches. For people came and people went with frightening regularity. Friendship, like the ownership of the claims themselves, was very temporary in the dry diggings.

'Not found yourself the big one then?' The question came down at him half mocking, half deadly serious. It was the same question that was asked in Du Toit's Pan a hundred times a day. For it was what every digger was there for. The find to end all digging. The find that would be an instant life-changing event. The hope of finding the big one filled their dreams and drove them far beyond sanity, holding them in the diggings long after a wise man would have quit. It was madness, they all knew it. But it was an intoxicating madness nonetheless, and the lure of a life filled with riches sustained them even when their bodies were near broken and their pocketbooks had long since been drained dry.

'Not this time, Davy. Just another damn pebble.'

'Maybe tomorrow.'

'Yep, maybe tomorrow.' It was the digger's traditional answer. For there was always hope. No matter how many picks were blunted or shovels broken. No matter how much cash was left in the money belt cinched tight around Kelly's waist, even here, deep in the dirt of his thirty-foot-square claim; and no matter how many brandies he had sunk down at Turner's Billiard Room. It held him there like a rope around a condemned man's neck, and like that rough line of government-bought hemp, it would hold him until that hope was dead. For the chance of finding the big one was about as likely as finding a nugget of pure gold in a bucketload of dog shit scraped from the macadam of Pall Mall.

'Keep yourself safe, Bill.'

'You too, Davy,' Kelly replied without looking up. He was working his thumb over the nugget of rock he had picked up, rubbing away the coarse grains of dirt that clung to its sides, feeling its shape, letting his fingers decide if there was anything to it.

'Did you hear about that fucking Dutchman, Bill?' Evans

lingered, shouting down the question, the words spoken as if they dirtied his mouth.

'Which one? There's so damn many of the buggers.'

Kelly shared his friend's contempt for all Dutchmen, the Boers who had long ago trekked away from Cape Colony. They were one of the largest contingents amongst the thirty thousand souls who called the diamond fields home now. The Englishman and the Welshman were not alone, but they were a minority amongst the sea of Cape colonists, Americans, Frenchmen, Spaniards, Germans, Italians and others. Most of the disparate nationalities rubbed along pretty well, the petty disputes and arguments that flared up dealt with quickly and fairly enough by the committee that ran the diggings. Only the taciturn and fiercely independent Boers stood apart, setting up their temporary homes in their own encampment, where only their countrymen were welcome. They came in their huge ox wagons with their wives, children and black servants, taking up adjoining claims then invariably finding more diamonds than all the other nationalities put together.

'Van der Whore or some such like that.' Evans shook his head ruefully. 'Got hisself a claim over near the Pniel road.'

'I know him.' Kelly paused his inspection of his rock and squinted at the Welshman, who was silhouetted against the setting sun.

'Found a stone the size of a damned fist. One hundred and twenty carats, they say, maybe more.'

'Is it yellow?'

'Nope.' Evans turned his head and spat out his disgust. 'They say it's as pure white as driven fucking snow.'

For a moment Kelly could not speak as he contemplated the

unfairness of life. 'Fucking Dutchman.' The pithy judgement was all he could summon.

'Fucking Dutchman,' Evans agreed. He wiped his face and mouth with the back of his hand before he spoke again, as if trying to smear away the exhaustion that was written in every pore of his florid complexion. 'Are you going for a drink this evening? Old man Turner's got himself some grog up from Cape Town. Better than the normal piss, they say.'

'Maybe.' Kelly was evasive. But both men knew he would be there. Just as they were both there every night when it got dark. For neither had anywhere else to be.

'Then maybe I'll see you later.' Evans turned and ambled back to his own claim, which ran parallel to the one Kelly had bought for two pounds sterling just three months before.

'Yep, reckon you will.'

Kelly spat into his hand, then worked the rock he still held around his palm, tired, gritty eyes searching for the glint of something, anything, under the layers of dirt. As he uncovered more of the stone, he was finally satisfied that he knew what he held.

'Nothing but another fucking pebble,' he whispered.

The stone was too big to be a diamond. Way too big. And he was too tired to take it over to the table where he sieved through the spoil he dug out of the ground by the bucketful and pick up the chisel to scrape away the stubborn dirt crusted to the rock. It was easier to make the call here and save himself a few ounces of effort.

'Just another fucking pebble,' he repeated, a moment's despair flickering across his mind. The hope, no matter how much of a lie it might be, died hard.

Tossing the rock onto a small heap of similar stones, he reached for the shovel again.

There was still a half-hour of daylight left and the hole wouldn't dig itself.

And he wouldn't find the big one sitting on his arse.

Chapter One

———————◆———————

Port Elizabeth, Algoa Bay, Cape Colony, 9 April 1871

The cloudless sky was the palest blue as the Englishman walked away from the narrow jetty, a salt-stained carpet bag carried easily in his left hand, his right resting on the holstered revolver on his hip. He was not dressed for the cold of that early morning, and he quickly began to shiver. The heavy army boots he wore were snug enough, and he would not give them up no matter the climate, his time as an infantryman making him appreciate their comfort. But he wore long trousers made from a pale brown lightweight cotton, a loose-fitting scarlet Manchester shirt and a rumpled and well-worn jacket with four pockets on the front, along with a number of fabric loops around the waist. In an attempt to stop at least some of the chilly sea breeze from filtering inside the collar of his shirt, he adjusted the bright red neckerchief he wore; he had learned of the many uses for the simple square of cloth from the Texan cavalrymen he had once led. Around his waist was a British army officer's belt with matching holster and ammunition pouch, and on his head a solar topee with a bright red pagdi wrapped tight around it, which could be unwound and used to cover his entire head if needed. It was a good outfit, suitable for a life far from civilisation, but it was also designed to keep its wearer cool under the burning African sun, something that was distinctly absent that morning.

The early mist was lingering in the air, screening much of the port town from his view, but he could see enough to know it barely deserved to be called a port. There was a single large breakwater under construction, but he doubted it would be enough to tame the surging waters that dominated the bay and that had made the journey from the steamer, which was still lying well out to sea, a puke-invoking hell. He did not care to think what that same transfer would have been like if one of the gales that had delayed their arrival by nearly a week had been blowing. He did know that he was heartily glad to have left the steamer behind, that feeling only reinforced by the half-dozen blackened skeletons of ships that littered the beach, each one a memorial to the fate of other seafarers who had not been as fortunate as he. It was a warning he intended to heed. He had spent far too long on board one ship or another. It was high time to get back to where he belonged.

He began to walk away from the jetty, his legs half buckling as he struggled to adjust to being back on firm ground, the earth beneath his heavy boots shifting as if he were still out at sea. It was not easy going. Every square inch was filled with a haphazard arrangement of fishing lines slung this way and that, each one holding dead fish that had been opened, gutted and hung up to dry. The air was filled with the rancid stink of fish guts, the rank odour almost more than he could stand. The town's fishermen had landed a bountiful catch that morning. He saw dozens of snooks, and something that looked to his landlubber's eye to be a solitary pike amidst a forest of mullets, their stomachs slit open to let in the air. There were buckets of spider crabs, the poor creatures climbing over one another in a futile attempt to escape their incarceration, and at least a hundred water-filled pails teeming with crayfish or writhing water snakes, the sight of which was enough to make him cringe. Most plentiful of all were the hottentot fish, the fat, toothy creatures familiar to him after he had dined on not a lot else for the better part of the last few weeks.

The fish entrails had been tossed onto the ground, where they were attracting the attention of great flocks of seabirds. They swarmed overhead, filling the sky as they circled over the catch, diving down then swooping low to snatch up an entrail or a discarded eye before soaring away. One huge bird flew by, momentarily casting him into shadow. He looked up in time to see a mollymawk climbing fast, its enormous ten-foot wingspan powering it away from the smaller birds, which looked weak and fragile in comparison. He hoped the sight of the bird was as good an omen as the sailors claimed. He had a feeling he would need all the luck he could get before long. For he was far from home and about to enter a world where he did not know the rules. Or even whether any rules existed. He had wished for a fresh start, but as he took his first strides into the fringes of the port town, he found himself wondering quite why he had chosen this path amongst all the others that had been open to him.

Leaving the stink of fish behind, he joined the main thoroughfare, which ran from one side of the town to the other, with just a handful of stubby side streets leading off it. Beyond the road was a ridge lined with fine-looking and substantial dwellings, villas and bungalows boasting neatly laid-out gardens and wide, airy verandas. It did not take any knowledge of the place to realise that these would be owned by the more successful merchants and the public officials stationed here in Port Elizabeth. They had done a pretty fair job of securing the best land for their dwellings, the elevated position providing the houses with a fresh breeze along with a spectacular view out to the bay. It also kept them away from the rough working classes who lived lower down. It was clear that this was no shanty town on the frontier of civilisation. He might well be in what felt like the arse end of nowhere, but there was wealth in this far-flung port, and that had to be a good thing. He just needed to find the right way to ensure that some of it found its way into his own well-deserving pockets.

It was still early, yet the street was busy. Men dressed in the rough clothes of those expecting a hard day of graft sauntered past, hands thrust deep in pockets or else carrying cloth-wrapped bundles that likely contained their lunch. A few looked warily at the Englishman, eyes narrowing in instant suspicion at the sight of the revolver snug in its holster on his hip. For he was alone in carrying a weapon on open display, the men heading out to work armed with nothing more dangerous than a pocketknife attached to their belt, or the ubiquitous docker's hook, which looked no different to the ones that had been wielded by the dock workers in the streets of London's East End, where he had been born. Not that he cared about attracting such attention. The men of the town could think what they wanted, even if it meant that they looked at him like he was a sort of madman or outlaw. He had long ago learned never to take anything for granted, and he was on foreign shores, far from anywhere he had known before. He wouldn't dream of venturing into such a place without the loaded Lefaucheux revolver.

He walked on, keeping his pace easy, gradually becoming accustomed to being back on dry land. The port town was laid out along the shoreline, and he headed west, the rising sun on his back. The street was lined with well-built brick and wood buildings, most looking well cared for, with fresh paint and unbroken windows. The majority appeared to cater to the needs of the local populace, selling everything from fish to Cape beer at thruppence a quart. He counted at least five buildings claiming to belong to diamond and precious stone buyers, one even claiming to hail from Mayfair. Another, the busiest of the five, was owned, according to its signage, by a man named De Witt, who promised the best prices in town. Interspersed with the mercantile establishments were some fine public buildings, the offices of the clerks and officials who administered the town. These were in a slightly worse state of repair, clearly suffering from being so close to the shore; the salt-laden air had stripped back the paint to leave bare patches of wood on every facade.

As he walked, he noted a large number of churches, the various faiths vying for attention. An Anglican church stood two doors down from a Methodist chapel. There was a church for Catholics and another for Presbyterians. On the opposite side of the street, he even spied a synagogue for the local Jewish population. Clearly the populace of Port Elizabeth needed the guiding hand of an accumulation of religious institutions to keep them in their place.

Near the end of the thoroughfare, he found a neat-looking building bearing the sign *Dreyer's Phoenix Hotel*. It appeared to be an upmarket establishment, the facade bright and clean, the veranda along the front painted a pleasant shade of yellow. He marked its position for later. He would need somewhere to sleep, and the place looked to be of a better quality than he had expected to find so far from the main cities of Cape Colony. After weeks of travel, he had learned not to be choosy, but it seemed that for once he would have somewhere decent to lay his head that night.

'Good morning.'

The Englishman started as a well-dressed gentleman tipped his tile and offered a greeting as he walked by. He caught the man's eye, noting the raised eyebrow and half-smile playing on his face, but he was gone before the startled Englishman could even think of forming a reply.

'Blow me tight,' he muttered. He had not been ready for the greeting. It put him on his guard. He did not know the rules here, and that left him feeling a strong sense of disquiet, as if the world was watching him. He knew what it was like to be a fugitive, and the sensation that was raising the hackles on his neck at that moment made him feel just the same.

The well-dressed fellow was not the only one to notice the new arrival. A group of black men came past in a tight group, their eyes roving over him, their expressions revealing nothing of their thoughts. All were dressed akin to the white workers he had seen before, and he marked the observation, keen to learn more of these lands. He had seen a fair amount of Africa now, from Egypt in the far north to the dangerous mountainous terrain of Abyssinia and the wilds of the Sudan. In his experience, the local population lived a life apart from the many foreigners who had come to Africa in their droves over the course of the last two hundred years. Here in Port Elizabeth, it appeared that at least some had integrated with the white-faced foreigners, though he reckoned that would be quite different even just a few miles inland, where he expected to find that the local tribes had been ravaged by the ruthless invaders who had come to profit from their land's riches. It would be the same as he had seen in the Sudan, where the towns and villages near the Nile had been stripped almost bare by the ruthless slavers and ivory traders, who thought only of turning a profit, no matter the cost to the people who had lived on the land since time immemorial. Yet no matter what the humanitarian societies of Europe might proclaim, there was nothing that could be done to prevent it. It was the one rule he had learned always applied, no matter his destination. The powerful would prey on the weak. Just as they always had. Just as they always would.

An older woman followed the black workers, her walking stick tapping a fast staccato on the hard-baked dirt that formed the surface of the street.

'Good morning, ma'am.' The Englishman paused to touch a hand to the peak of his solar topee, aping the greeting that had come his way moments before.

The old woman barely glanced his way, the rhythm of her stick unaltered.

'Bollocks to it.' He shook his head and strode on.

The street was beginning to come to an end, the buildings now spaced further apart, the gaps filled with tumbled piles of dry-looking vegetation or human detritus. He was about to turn on his heel and return the way he had come when he heard raised voices, the telltale signs of a confrontation catching his attention and tempting him to walk a little further, his right hand instinctively slipping to his holstered revolver, fingers sliding the buckle open so that the weapon could be drawn in an instant.

The altercation was coming from an empty plot of land sandwiched between two single-storey wooden buildings that were clearly in a state of advanced decay, their wooden facades mottled with rot and damp and streaked with muck, the dark windows barred with planks of wood.

'Listen to me, you *verdolt Engelschman*.'

'I'm not a bloody Englishman, you bloody Dutch idiot.'

'Ag, *mon*, I don't care where you *blerrie* come from. You're all the same to me.'

The Englishman came closer. He was drawn to the argument and the threat of violence like a bluebottle was drawn to a heap of fresh shit. It was a world he understood. Somewhere he felt at home.

'Listen, mate, I don't have anything worth bloody taking, all right. So just piss off and leave me alone.'

'*Hou jou bek*. I don't want your *fokken* money.'

The Englishman stopped when he spied the group of men whose voices he had heard. There were four in total, and it was not hard to see who was who. One man was sitting on his backside, legs stretched out in front him, blood flowing freely over the fingers of his right hand, which was clamped tight to his nose. Facing him were three hard-faced men dressed in baggy corduroy trousers and dirty flannel shirts. Their broad-brimmed felt hats cast their faces into shadow, but the Englishman could see that all three had long, lank hair and rough beards. He did not know what nationality they were, but it was clear they were all cut from the same cloth. And it was clear that the man nursing his busted nose was facing a grim time of it.

'Listen to me, you bloody idiots.' The man on the ground spoke again, the words muffled by the hand cradling his face. If he cared for the claret flowing from his beak, he gave no sign of showing it. 'You've got the wrong bloody man. It wasn't me.'

'It was you, *mon*, and you *fokken* know it.'

The Englishman was sure that the man speaking was the group's leader, something in his stance marking him out. Keen as he was to observe what was to come, he came to a halt a good hundred yards short of the four men. He might have been drawn to the altercation, but that did not mean he had any intention of getting involved. It was certainly tempting to keep moving until he became a part of whatever was to occur, if only to even the unequal odds. There would be something pleasing about releasing the pent-up energy that was the product of too many weeks of boredom incarcerated in polite company on board the steamer. There would be something freeing in being the man he knew he was meant to be. And he did not like what he was seeing. Three against one was not a fair fight, not on any continent. It spoke of bullying and power, two things that stuck in his craw. He had been on the receiving end of both too many times to stand idly by and watch as three men dominated another.

But he had intervened in fights that were not his in the past. Mistakes had been made and lessons had been learned. Yet that did not mean he would just walk away. It was an intriguing set-up, and if nothing else, it might teach him something of the land he was now entering.

He was learning already. For starters, it was easy enough to tell that the men spoke with very different accents. The three heavy set crusty fellows standing around the man on the ground sounded German to his ear, but he had noted that the fellow sitting on his arse had called them Dutch, which sort of made sense. That man himself spoke with an odd accent, one the Englishman could not place. His nasal twang gave each word a strange melody, and it sounded as if he was always asking a question, each sentence ending in a rising inflection that was already grating on the Englishman's nerves.

'Hey, you!'

The Englishman looked up sharply. He had been spotted.

'Are you going to let these Dutch bastards beat me right in front of your bloody eyes, mate?' The man with the bloody face waved his free hand in the air as if to summon the Englishman over.

Three heads turned the Englishman's way. Three bearded faces sneered.

'Is this *poephol* your *blerrie* friend, *mon*?' The question was thrown towards the Englishman.

'No.'

The Dutchman who had asked the question nodded, head moving slowly up and down as if he were giving the answer serious consideration, no matter its simplicity. 'Are you going to stop us teaching this *dopkaas* a lesson?' He indicated the fellow on the ground with his thumb.

'Should I?' The Englishman kept his tone even.

'Not if you know what's *blerrie* good for you.' The answer came back wrapped in an iron threat.

It was enough to make the Englishman half smile. He liked the belligerent tone and the confidence. 'What's he done?'

'If he's not your mate, then I don't see how it's any business of yours.'

The Englishman pulled a wry expression at the reply. 'Fair enough.'

'What the hell!' The man on the ground half rose as he heard his potential saviour deny him the aid he had called for. 'I ain't done nothing, and these Dutch bastards know it. I'm as innocent as the bleeding snow, I swear.'

'*Hou jou bek.*' One of the other Dutchmen snapped the command, taking a step forward, hands bunching into fists.

The man facing a beating complied, shutting his mouth as he was ordered.

'Do you want to *blerrie* watch then, *mon*?'

The Englishman shrugged. It was all the answer he cared to give at that moment. The urge to intervene was growing. Like an itchy mosquito bite, it needed scratching. Yet he held back, standing his ground, contemplating what he would do. He did not know what was going on here, what had caused the man sitting on his arse to face a slating at the hands of the three dour Dutchmen, but he wanted to find out. It might be that the beating was well deserved. Indeed, if he knew what was what, then perhaps he would be happy to deliver it himself. After all, he had never held back in the past. But if the man awaiting his fate was indeed innocent, then the Englishman might still step forward and save him from further violence.

'I suggest you *fok* off.' The command was shouted by the Dutchman doing most of the talking. His patience was clearly starting to wear thin.

'What's that you said?' The Englishman's voice was emotionless.

'I said *fok* off before I stick my boot into your *blerrie poephol.*'

He inclined his head, absorbing the insult. The itch was getting stronger. It was almost impossible to resist the urge to scratch it.

'Look, *mon*, this *dopkaas* stole from us. We saw him do it and now we're going to teach him a lesson. If you've got a problem with that, feel free to come over here and join him. If not, then like I said, *fok* off.'

The Englishman looked from the three men standing to the man on the ground. The explanation was a good one and he sensed that it was true. 'What did he take?'

The leader of the group sighed. 'Does it matter?'

'It matters to me.'

'For *fok's* sake. He took my mother's necklace, all right? We found him trying to sell it to De Witt.' The explanation was given through gritted teeth.

And it was enough.

The Englishman nodded and turned away. He might not like uneven odds, and he himself had been known to steal when it was needed. But he reckoned this was theft for theft's sake. The man about to be beaten dressed too well, and looked too well fed, to have been forced to steal to stay alive. And so he would not intervene and in so doing cause a possible miscarriage of justice. At least that was how he saw it, and for now that was enough. He had vowed to try to keep out of trouble rather than walk willingly straight into it as he had too many times before. And so he made his decision, turning on his heel and showing his back to the three Dutchmen and the man they would likely beat bloody and blue.

'Hey, come on now, mate, you're leaving me in the bloody lurch here.' The man on the ground made a last desperate plea for aid, the plaintive wail following the Englishman as he began to walk away. 'Mate? Come on. Help me out here.'

The Englishman kept walking. His mind was set.

The talkative Dutchman said something else. The Englishman did not catch what it was, and he knew he would not have understood it even if he had, the three men speaking a guttural language quite beyond his comprehension. But he knew it was a jibe, a comment meant to insult, or else to turn him around so that he would be drawn into the violence that was to come. It was followed by a peal of laughter, the three men loud and confident of their power, even with the stranger still close by.

He stopped.

Silence followed. Expectant. Heavy. Filled with foreboding. He could feel four sets of eyes on his back like they were a physical thing, the attention setting his nerves on edge.

The itch remained.

For a moment he stood there letting his breathing settle. Resisting the urge. Then he began to walk again, slow, even paces taking him away from the future he had rejected. He did not look back even as he heard the sound of boots moving and a cry as a heavy fist made the first of many contacts with flesh.

The itch would not be scratched.

Not that day.

Not ever.

For Jack Lark had learned his lesson.

He would no longer repeat the mistakes of his past.

Chapter Two

———◆◆◆———

*J*ack sat at the simple wooden table, washing the dust from his throat with a long draught of warm beer. Belching softly, he sat back in his chair, stretching his legs out in front of him. After he had left the three Dutchmen and their thief to it, he had spent the rest of the morning exploring Port Elizabeth, searching out the stores that would sell what he needed for the next leg of his journey. It was enough knowledge for now. Especially as he did not know what the next leg of the journey really entailed, beyond some vague notions based more on hearsay and hope than fact. Securing a room at Dreyer's Phoenix Hotel had been easy enough, and now he sat in the wide foyer, comfortable in a leather club armchair, a pint of Bass's Indian Pale Ale in front of him as he waited.

The foyer bar was beginning to fill as it got closer to noon. Most people seemed to be drawn to the bill of fare chalked on a board nailed to the wall above the room's only fireplace, and Jack watched as the first heavily stacked plates were ferried from a back room to the hotel's hungry clientele. It was enough to make his stomach growl. He had refrained from breaking his fast on board the steamer that morning, choosing to tackle the journey from ship to shore with an empty stomach. Now he was very hungry, and that hunger was not being helped by the warm beer that was now sloshing around in his belly, or the enticing aroma of hot food.

A woman entered the foyer. She wore the garb of an explorer, or at least someone who spent their time far from polite society, and her face was tanned by the sun. She was dressed in long trousers and a long-sleeved shirt, both made from the same earthy-toned cotton and both sporting a good spattering of sewn-up rents and tears, the tightly tied threads standing out like scars on pale flesh. On her head was a wideawake hat with a long string that drooped beneath her chin. As she entered the foyer, she pushed the hat back from her head, letting the string catch it so that it sat high on her back. The action revealed dark brown hair bound tightly into braids that were tied tidily behind her head with a short black ribbon. On her right hip was a holstered handgun, the weapon smaller than the heavy French revolver that Jack himself wore. In her hands she held a navy umbrella, the tip resting precisely on the ground as she surveyed the room, searching for someone.

Searching for him.

She spotted him quickly enough, then moved briskly towards him, a warm smile spreading across her face. Jack necked the last of his beer, then rose to his feet, moving around the table to pull back another armchair for her.

'Beer? Before luncheon?' she asked.

'It was medicinal.'

She arched an eyebrow.

'I had a dry throat. The dust.'

'Then I would happily have provided you with a tincture.'

Jack grinned. 'Thank you for the generous offer, but it seems to be much improved now. Would you care to eat?'

'Gosh, yes, I'm famished.'

'Me too.' He stood back as she sat, then gently pushed her seat closer to the table. 'It says they have bacon.' He nodded towards the bill of fare.

'Ah, that explains your smile. Or is that from the beer?'

'Both.' He laughed. 'Come on, Anna. Would you really deny a man one beer after he has completed all his chores?'

'Chores indeed. I do not set you chores, Jack.' Anna Baker tutted, but grinned at his foolishness. 'But I am glad to hear you have done what was needed.'

Jack liked her smile. It sat well on her face. She was still too thin; the long and exhausting expedition deep into the wilds of the Sudan with her uncle, Sir Samuel White Baker, the famous explorer turned Egyptian pasha, had sucked every last vestige of fat from them both, and the dark circles under her eyes were those of someone who had been travelling for too long without a proper break. Yet she could still turn heads, and he noticed that a good half of the room's occupants had paused in their drinking or scoffing to watch as she came across to his table.

'Well, whatever you wish to call them, they are all done. I have taken a room for us here, one with a view if you pay credence to the creature behind the desk.'

'Creature?'

'Well, I am not sure what to call him. The buck-toothed bugger couldn't speak clearly. I could barely understand a word he said.'

'You are being cruel.'

'Wait until you see him before you judge me.' Jack took his own seat and turned his attention to the bill of fare. It was hard to resist the lure of bacon and eggs, but he noted a few other options that took his fancy. There were oysters and a half-dozen types of fish on offer, something that came as no surprise given the location. There was also a game pie, along with the more intriguing prospect of springbuck. He gave the decision his full concentration, ignoring the sound of more arrivals filing into what was clearly a popular dining room.

'Hey, you!'

He looked up as a loud voice announced the arrival of a noisier than normal diner. To his surprise, the man was striding, or at least limping, as fast as he could towards the table where Jack and Anna sat, a thunderous expression writ large on his face, purple veins in his neck throbbing.

'You! I see you sitting there, you bloody bastard.'

Anna frowned. 'Is he a friend of yours?'

'No.' Jack sighed. He recognised the fellow well enough as he staggered closer, even though one of the man's eyes was now streaked with red, while the other was surrounded by a sea of puffy blue and purple bruises. Both of his cheeks were scratched and bright crimson, while his upper lip looked at least twice its normal size. From the thick layer of scabs on his chin and around the corners of his mouth, it was clear that he had received one hell of a battering, but it seemed to have done little to lessen his love for a confrontation.

'Well, he clearly thinks he knows you.' Anna found something funny either in the situation or in the expression she saw etched onto Jack's face in reaction to the man's arrival.

Jack sighed. He did not need this. But still he rose, standing four-square as the man blundered on, at least two chairs and a table coming close to being upturned by his clumsy gait.

'I want a bloody word with you, chum. What the hell were

you playing at, letting me get my bloody arse kicked by those Boer bastards?'

'Keep your voice down,' Jack hissed.

'Why?' The reply was belligerent. 'You think no one wants to know that you left me on my own to get a bloody kicking?'

'I think no one wants their lunch interrupted. Me least of all.' Jack took a step away from the table, interposing himself between the man and Anna. 'If you've got something to say, say it, then walk your bloody chalk.' He could feel his temper starting to fray.

'Oh, I've got something to say all right. A fellow like you, wearing a revolver like you're some sort of bloody toy soldier, leaving me to face those three Dutch fuckers all on my lonesome.'

'I won't tell you again to keep your voice down and moderate your damn language. There are ladies present.'

The man glanced at Anna. 'Sorry, miss, and all. But this cobber here, why, he left me in the bloody lurch.'

Anna smiled graciously. 'There is no need to *miss* me. Now, why don't you sit down so we can talk about this like adults?' There was censure in her tone, albeit censure flavoured with honey.

'I'm sorry, miss, but I'd sooner sit in the bloody gutter than with this man. Why, leaving one of his own to be done over—'

'Sit down and shut your damn muzzle.' Jack cut him off in mid flow. 'I don't know what your bloody problem is, but I suggest you speak a hell of a lot quieter.' He was aware that people had stopped whatever they were doing and were now watching the altercation closely, a fine entertainment to accompany their luncheon.

'And you're going to make me, are you? I don't reckon

you've got the bloody stomach for it, mate. Bloody yellow belly, that's what you've got.'

'Sit. Down.' The two words were spoken calmly and slowly, and they left Jack's mouth laced with genuine venom, so that not even the most thick-skulled fool could mistake them for anything but a command that was to be obeyed. And obeyed instantly.

Finally the man understood. He was clasping his hat against his belly, and now he looked down at it, shamefaced. 'You might've bloody helped me, mate,' he said quietly.

'Why?' Jack returned to his own seat, then gestured at a free chair.

The man sat. 'It was three against one.'

'And?'

'Those aren't fair odds, mate. Not in anyone's book.'

Jack shook his head. He was already tiring of the conversation.

'Would one of you kindly tell me what this is all about?' Anna seemed more amused than disgruntled at having the loud-mouthed stranger sit at her table.

'Sorry, miss.'

'I have already told you that you don't have to address me like that. Please call me Anna.' She reached out to place a hand on the man's forearm. 'Now, I can tell you are from Australia.'

'That's right, miss.'

She shook her head, but didn't correct him again.

Jack sat back in his chair as he finally placed the man's odd accent. He hadn't met an Australian before. From what he had seen thus far, he hadn't missed much.

'Now that you're sitting quietly, Jack will buy you a beer.' Anna made the offer without so much as glancing at Jack.

He tried to speak, but she shut him down with a sharp gesture. He had learned not to argue with her. The repercussions could see him consigned to a lonely bed, or worse.

'Now, are you badly hurt?' She turned back to the Australian. 'I can see you have been through the mill.'

He shook his head. 'I'll be okay. I could sure use that beer, though. That'd see me right, I reckon.'

'For God's sake,' Jack muttered, just loudly enough to be heard. But at a frosty glare from Anna, he waved at a nearby waiter, lifting three fingers then pointing at his empty glass.

'My name is Anna. And this is Jack.' Anna raised her eyebrows. 'And you are?'

'Clarke. Joe Clarke.'

'That's better.' She patted his arm, then withdrew her hand. 'So, what brings you to Port Elizabeth, Joe?' She had taken control of the situation, setting it on a calm footing with nothing more than manners and a kind smile.

'I've just come down from the diggings near the Vaal river. I needed a breather. Got too much dust in my throat.' He glared rather pointedly at Jack.

'It's coming.' Jack's tone was about as friendly as a starving wolf greeting a lost lamb. 'If you're just here for a rest, why did those men accuse you of being a thief?' He kept his voice pitched low so that the question would not be overheard.

'They're Boers; they don't have much between the ears, if you know what I mean. And I didn't steal a thing.'

'So they were lying?'

'They were mistaken.' Clarke winced as he shifted in his seat.

'You didn't steal that necklace?'

'No, mate. I *found* that neck-lace.' He pronounced the last word as two separate syllables. 'I didn't know who it bloody belonged to.'

'But you still tried to sell it.'

'Wouldn't you?' He lifted a hand to dab at his mouth as the effort of speaking cracked a fresh scab and set a thin rivulet of blood dribbling down his chin.

'So you're an innocent victim?'

'I bloody am, mate.'

'I don't believe you.'

'Believe whatever you want.'

'Now then.' Anna intervened to put a stop to the belligerent back-and-forth. 'That's enough from both of you.'

Jack heard the warning in her tone. She knew him well enough to spot when his temper was starting to fray, so he did as she said. He knew *her* well enough to heed her when she spoke.

'Joe, you mentioned that you're down from the diggings. Are those the ones at the Pniel river? We've heard they're producing a splendid number of diamonds.'

'No, those are no bloody good, not if you ask me. Fair dinkum, the Pniel's a pretty enough place, and I can see the attraction of having running water and all that. There's plenty of trees for shade and for firewood, and there's folk who think that's reason enough to dig there.' Clarke shook his head. 'But I've been there and I can tell you that there's lean pickings now. Don't get me wrong. Some fella found a thirty-carat shiner not so long ago. But mainly the finds aren't all that great. No, miss, the river diggings, they're no good. For me, it's the dry diggings. There's a fair few to choose from. Some say the best is at Klipdrift, but there's been folk working there for a while now, and getting a claim is one hell of a fight. Cawood's Hope was good for a bit, but I don't know anyone who's still there. It's the same over at Sifonell, where there were some good finds a few months ago, but nothing to speak of since. A few folks are finding stones at Forlorn Hope and Delport's Hope, or at least that's what I hear, but for me, your best bet is going to be the diggings at Du Toit's Pan. We've found some big 'uns there these past few months all right. When I was last there, a fella found one that was well over one hundred carats. There was even talk about a diamond they dug up a few months back that was over three hundred! Can you imagine that? A man could live like a bloody king for a dozen lifetimes on a find like that.' He trailed off as he contemplated a life with such wealth.

'Are you going back there?' Anna did not let him drift too far into reverie. 'To the dry diggings? Du Toit's Pan, did you say?'

'Yes, miss, I am that. I leave next week. Just got to get myself a seat on a wagon heading up there.'

Anna looked pointedly at Jack. A lot was said in that look.

Jack eased forward in his chair. 'We're of a mind to try our hand at the diggings.'

'The pair of you?'

'Yes.'

The Australian sat back, a sickly smile sliding onto his bloodied lips. 'Do you know much about digging then?'

'What's there to know?' Jack did not take kindly to the mocking undertone in the other man's voice. 'It can't be that hard to dig a bloody hole in the ground.'

'Oh, there's plenty to know, mate.' Clarke reached out and picked up one of Anna's hands. He made a play of inspecting it, then dropped it back on the table. 'And neither of you looks like you know which end of the bloody shovel to hold, if you ask me.'

'I didn't ask you.'

'Ha, fair enough.' He fell silent, waiting for them to draw him out.

'So, tell us what we need to know.' Jack forced himself to take the lure, choking down his dislike of the beefy digger.

'Just like that?'

'I'm buying you a beer.'

'Oh, it'll take more than one beer, mate.' Clarke laughed, his face revealing his pleasure at finding he held some cards after all.

'What *will* it take?'

He rubbed his chin with a grubby hand. 'Seems to me you two could use a little advice. So how's about this – I can tell you what you need to know. Help get you set up too, if you like.' He smiled wolfishly. 'And my rates are reasonable.'

'You want us to pay you?'

'I ain't about to do it all for free, mate.'

'Then you can take a running fuck—'

'That's an interesting offer, Joe. Thank you.' Anna cut Jack off. 'But I have a different proposition for you.'

'Anna?' Jack sighed. Anna Baker was not easily swayed once her mind was made up. It was a trait she must have inherited from her uncle, and it had given her the confidence to leave the safety of her family and travel at the side of a man she had only known for a few short months. It was both a boon and a curse. At least from his point of view.

'As well as trying our hand at the diggings, we are of a mind to invest. We have capital.' She reached out and sketched an imaginary circle on the tabletop. 'We just need to find the right partner.'

Clarke was drawn to the very edge of his chair. 'Partner?'

He did his best not to look too keen.

'We provide the funds. Our partner provides the expertise.'

'Anna, this isn't the time,' Jack hissed. She was rushing ahead too quickly for his liking. Their plans were new, and worryingly vague, made on the long journey down from Khartoum. They had first heard of the diamond fields from the master of the ship they had taken to bring them down the east coast of Africa. At first they had thought simply to travel, and as they had started out from Cairo, it had made sense to head south and see what they could find at the tip of the enormous continent. But once they had heard of the fortunes being made from finding diamonds, they had decided to try their luck for themselves. Neither was naive enough to believe that the precious stones were simply lying on the surface of the ground just waiting to be found, as many of the tales would have them believe, but they had come just the same.

'What sort of share were you thinking, miss?'

Anna glanced at Jack, holding his gaze for a second before turning to direct the full force of her personality onto the bloodied Australian. 'For the right partner, we would offer a twenty-five per cent share of our profits. All expenses would be borne by us.'

Clarke licked his lips. 'That's not a great share. Not if you find a big one.'

Jack fought the urge to laugh. The Australian had a hand to play, but he was clearly hopeless at cards, his thoughts obvious to anyone looking at his face.

'It is a very fair offer.' Anna's tone was unaltered.

'It's a fucking great one.' Jack delivered his own pithy verdict. But he respected Anna's opinion, and so he would back her no matter what he thought. He trusted her judgement more than he trusted his own.

'You'd pay all the expenses?' Clarke had clearly given up his attempt at haggling.

'All of them. Starting today.' Anna paused. 'If you accept, of course.'

'And if you don't, you can walk your bloody chalk right here and now,' Jack added.

'Fair dinkum.' Clarke grinned from ear to ear. 'I accept.'

Jack shook his head at the odd expression. But the deal was done.

For better or worse, they had themselves a partner.

Chapter Three

'How much will it cost?'

'For you, *mon*, it's seventy quid.'

'That's a ridiculous price and well you know it.' Jack did not have to fake his astonishment at the figure he was being quoted for hiring a wagon to take them from Port Elizabeth to the dry diggings at Du Toit's Pan.

He was standing in front of Dreyer's Phoenix Hotel. It was proving to be another beautiful day, the sky a beguiling azure blue with not a single cloud in sight, but it was just as chilly as the day before, a brisk breeze whipping off the sea and straight through the town. The main thoroughfare was quiet in the hour after lunch, barely more than a dozen people in sight. The dusty roadway was empty, with just a single wagon trundling slowly towards the port, its load a dozen fat wooden kegs. The driver, an old man with a great shock of bright grey hair, wearing a smart navy canvas jacket, looked to be half asleep, his whip forgotten as his mules ambled along, the wagon moving at barely half the pace of a walking man.

'Then bugger off. There's no shortage of folk looking to go

up to the diggings, and I've only got the one driver and wagon doing the run.'

They had found the wagon master thanks to the Australian, Clarke, who had travelled on his wagons a few months previously. The owner had given his name simply as JW, and he ran his company out of King William's Town. It was clear he knew his business.

'There's just three of us,' Jack pointed out. 'We don't need the whole wagon.'

JW shook his head impatiently. 'It's still seventy quid, *mon*. I don't care if it's just you, or you and all your *blerrie* mates. The rate's the same.'

Jack held his gaze. He believed he could read people well, and he was pretty damn sure that this man was certain of his wagon's value. There was only one sensible route from Port Elizabeth to the diggings, and only a handful of transport companies making the trip. If Clarke was telling the truth, it was a journey of over four hundred miles, too far for them to manage by themselves, even if they could afford to buy the horses and mules they would need. Which they couldn't.

'How many people can you carry?'

'Thirteen, if you're light with the luggage. The more gear you take, the fewer of you I can fit in.'

Jack understood JW's no-nonsense approach easily enough. The truth of it was that the funds they had available for their diamond-hunting expedition were both finite and relatively small. Which meant that if they were going to hire a wagon, they would have to find others to share the cost. It was not a notion he relished. He did not trust other people. At least, not easily.

'How long will the journey take?' he asked.

JW smiled, happy in the knowledge that he had his man. 'First we go to Graham's Town, that's about eighty-five miles from here. Then it's on to Fort Beaufort, then Queen's Town, Burghersdorp and Fauresmith. It'll take thirty days, if we don't run into any trouble.'

'Trouble?'

'We have to cross the Katberg.'

'What's that?'

The wagon master made a scoffing sound. 'You're new here then.' It was a statement, not a question.

'And you're a rude bastard who's committing daylight robbery.'

JW bellowed with laughter. 'Who says Englishmen are always polite.'

'Whoever said that needs to take their head out of their arse.' Jack was warming to the man. 'So what's this Katberg when it's at home?'

'The Katberg is a mountain pass.'

'It's dangerous?'

'Only if you don't know what you're doing.'

'And you do?' Jack raised his eyebrows as he asked the pointed but pertinent question.

'My driver's done the journey a hundred times and I've done it more times myself than I can count. And I'll be there to make sure you don't come to any harm. I've got business up at the diggings and so I'll be tagging along. We'll get you there.'

'Then I'm glad I'm in safe hands.'

'Oh, you are that. At least until you get up to the diggings. After that, you'll be on your own. I'll wish you good luck and leave you to it.'

Jack heard the unspoken warning. But he would not be

deterred. They had set upon this course and he would see it through. 'I reckon we'll be fine. Just get us there in one piece.'

JW made a play of looking him up and down, as if sizing him up for a suit, or maybe a coffin. 'You look like you can handle yourself all right, and you might need to. Folk have been fighting over the diggings at Du Toit's Pan ever since they found the first *blerrie* diamonds up there. Whether it's the Griquas, my lot or your lot, someone is always laying claim to the land up there.'

'And who is your lot?'

'The Boers, man. Those diamond fields are rightly ours, there's no doubt about that. But now your man Keate, or whatever he's called, he's tramping all over the damn place as if it's up to him to decide whose land it is, and that's only made things worse. The Griqua leader, that Waterboer *poephol*, he won't be able to control the diggers now there are so many of them up there. And if your lot take control then it's only a matter of time before they kick everyone out and sell the rights to whichever crony of your damn government is lining the right pockets.'

'How many are there?'

'Nigh on thirty thousand, they say.' JW thrust his hands deep into his pockets. He seemed happy enough to answer Jack's questions. And he had a lot.

'What do the locals think about that many people turning up?'

'The locals?' JW looked surprised at the question. 'It's farmland. Owned by some of my folk. They're getting well paid.'

'But it hasn't always been their land?' Jack probed.

'You mean the blacks?' Both of JW's eyebrows rose. 'It's not their land, not any more. It's been years since they could think of this place as theirs. The Hottentots and the Bushmen were all driven off by the Dutch East India Company decades ago. It's been Boer land ever since. The Griqua still think it's theirs, of course. You won't have to be here long to hear about the claims their leader is making over it. But so long as they don't get in the way, I don't mind them, and there's plenty working up at the diggings. Not that they own the claims, but there's folk willing to pay them for their labour. To be honest, I don't care who owns the bloody land, or who thinks they own it. So long as they leave my wagon in peace, I'll be happy.'

'Fair enough.' Jack tended to agree with that sentiment. He had seen a similar situation in India. The land there had been ravaged by the East India Company, the men from Leadenhall running the country as their own personal fiefdom. The locals had had little say in the matter and he had seen first-hand what could happen should those who had ruled the place for centuries dare to stand up to the Company. From what JW was saying, the area around the diamond fields was claimed by more than one group. He just hoped that the ownership of the valuable diggings did not become the subject of a more open conflict. He would not take up arms for anyone any more. No matter the validity of their claim.

JW half smiled. 'The truth of it, is that this is *our* land, Boer land, no matter what you *uitlanders* think. We've been here for nigh on two hundred years now. Of course, that doesn't mean you *blerrie* English will leave us alone. It seems the Cape Colony isn't enough for you bastards, and I reckon it won't be long before you want to take over the whole of the damn country. We won't let you. We'll fight for this land. But I don't reckon that will stop you. You're persistent *fokkers*,

I'll give you that. We'll have to teach you a lesson at some point.'

Jack was doing his best to take in all the information. He could hear the passion in JW's voice as he spoke of his people's land and their desire to hold on to it. He knew next to nothing of the Boers and he was fascinated by their history. He would have to learn more if he were to thrive here.

'So, with all these claims to the land, is it dangerous up at the diggings?'

JW pulled a face at what he clearly believed to be a naive question. 'Of course it's *blerrie* dangerous. If the digging itself doesn't kill you, or a landslide doesn't bury you alive, then you might get sick. If that doesn't get you, then maybe something else will. It's every man for himself these days, I hear. That's why I keep clear. Leave it to *blerrie* idiots like you to scrabble around in the dirt.'

'If it's that bad, do you think I'll find ten people willing to share the journey?' Jack frowned. He knew little of the diamond fields beyond what he and Anna had heard before they arrived in Port Elizabeth.

'*Ja, mon.* Should be easy enough. There are plenty of fools like you still looking to go to the diggings.'

'Fools?'

JW looked shrewdly at Jack, his eyes scanning his face. 'Looks to me like you've been around the world a bit. Seen a bit of action too.'

'A bit.' Jack resisted the urge to lift a finger to trace the scar that ran across the left side of his face. The weal had faded over the years, but it was still obvious to anyone looking at him. The memory of its taking had not faded; the moment when the Indian sawar had sliced his talwar across Jack's face still haunted him, as did the moment when he hit the ground, bleeding and powerless. That moment had cost him more than the wound to his face.

'But here you are. And just like every other damn *rooinekke*, you think you'll make your fortune at the diggings. You think you'll find the big one.'

'You don't believe we will?'

'There's a reason I supply the *blerrie* wagons.'

'So the stories of the finds up there are just bullshit, are they?'

'Oh no, they're true. But there's thirty thousand folk digging away like little *fokken* bunny rabbits every day, and how many of them make it big?'

'Some.' The answer sounded lame even to Jack's ears.

'Some.' JW repeated the word with scorn. 'You know who makes all the money?'

'I'm sure you're going to tell me.'

'The fellas that buy the diamonds, that's who. And the sensible folk like me who take the money from fools like you.' He laughed deep in his belly at the look he saw on Jack's face. 'I can see you don't believe me. So you'll have to find out for yourself, just like all the other *poephols* I've transported up there.'

'Maybe.' Jack felt himself bristle. For years people had told him what he could and couldn't do. The freedom to choose had come at a high price, and it had taken him a long time to become the man he was that day.

'Agh, I know you won't listen to me.' JW shook his head. 'No one comes this far then turns tail. And who knows? Maybe you will find something and prove me wrong. But then if you do, who's to say you'll keep it. You're not in jolly old England now. There'll be plenty of *holnaaier* waiting to take it from you.'

Jack was struggling to understand the words that peppered JW's speech. But he got the gist of it well enough. 'So who polices the place?'

'No one.' JW grinned broadly. 'The diggers organise a few things themselves, but they do bugger all. No, it's every man for himself up there. So if you do find something, I reckon you should keep it to yourselves. Make sure no one hears of it, or before you know it, they'll be coming round to take it off you.'

Jack made a note of the advice, but he was not concerned. He had fought on more than a dozen battlefields, waging war on everyone from Persian Fars to men dressed in the blue uniforms of the American Union. He did not fear anyone, not now. It was not because he thought he was better than any foe. He knew what he was, what he had become. Survival was down to the whim of fate, not his skills on the battlefield or his ability to kill. In a way, that knowledge had made surviving, and fighting, easier. He could do his best, no more and no less. If it was his turn to die, he knew there was nothing he could do about it, save to face his fate in the same way he had lived his life, fighting to the last and refusing to go meekly.

JW was watching him closely. 'You don't believe me.'

'No. I believe you.' Jack looked him dead in the eye. 'I guess I'm just not easily swayed.'

JW nodded slowly. 'Then I wish you luck, my friend.' He paused to check around him, as if suddenly keen to be away. 'So do you want my *blerrie* wagon or not?'

Jack did not answer immediately. It was not really his decision to make, since it involved spending Anna's money. His own was long gone, used up on the journey south from

Khartoum. What little they had left had to be husbanded carefully, especially as they would need every last penny if they were going to be able to put their plan into action. It was the one fact Anna had failed to mention when she had offered to partner up with the Australian. There was enough money to get them to the diggings, but not much more. But Clarke didn't need to know that. At least not yet.

At last he stuck out a hand. 'I'll take it.'

JW spat on his own hand, then reached out to shake Jack's. 'I knew you would. We leave on Saturday. You'll need to pay me before then.'

Their transport to Du Toit's Pan was arranged.

Only time would tell if JW was right, and if Jack and Anna were indeed fools.

Or if they would be the ones to find riches.

Chapter Four

The wagon rolled out of Port Elizabeth early on Saturday morning, heading away from the coast under a clear blue sky, the weather as temperate and calm as an English summer's day. It was drawn by sixteen huge oxen, each one carrying a wide wooden yoke around its broad neck. The animals were silent, even as they hauled the fully laden wagon the first of what would be many, many miles, their wide backs barely showing the strain, their mouths working constantly as they chewed the cud without pause. They ignored the dense clouds of flies that surrounded them as they dragged their hopeful load across veldt, forest and mountain pass, enduring stoically so that twelve men and one woman could seek their fortune amongst the dust and rocks of the dry diggings.

The long journey to Du Toit's Pan had begun.

Jack sat as comfortably as he could, resting his back against the side of the wagon, getting used to balancing himself as it rolled and pitched and started to pick up speed. Anna sat at his side, her body jolting from side to side in time with his own, so that they swayed in unison, pressed close together. It was hard not to feel a moment's excitement. He had been to many places in his life, from the scorching mofussil of India to the noisy streets of Boston, yet he could not recall a time when he'd felt as free as he did in that moment.

Not that he was comfortable. The jolting was fierce and constant, the flat back of the wagon pitching up and down more violently than the deck of a ship in the teeth of a gale. Everything shook, the judders reverberating up and down his spine so that it felt like the devil was dancing a jig in the small of his back and setting his teeth on edge. It was hard to see how he could stand the discomfort for hours on end, but he was an infantryman at heart, and he had covered enough miles in army-issue boots to know that any ride, no matter how uncomfortable, was preferable to relying on his own two feet.

Yet it was not just the shuddering that started to test his patience, even in the first hours of the long journey. The wagon was twenty feet long and just over five feet wide, its flat bed covered with a high-arched framework that was open now but could be covered with canvas if the weather deteriorated. With thirteen passengers and all their gear, there was not enough room to move once they had all found their allotted place, which JW had thoughtfully marked out in pencil on the wagon's floor, the dimensions barely enough to accommodate a midget, let alone a fully grown man. The rest of the space was taken up by their goods and possessions, packed in a mismatched collection of wooden crates and casks, carpet bags, haversacks, tin boxes and portmanteaus. Surrounding these were dozens of rolled blankets, alongside spare clothing and bolts of cloth stuffed into tightly tied cotton sacks. More gear was attached to the wagon itself. Cooking pans, canteens, buckets, kettles and billy cans had been tied on any old how. Coarse hessian sacks of onions, potatoes, hardtack and thick ship's biscuits had been lashed to the sides, while all manner of hunting paraphernalia, from fishing rods to leather gun cases, hung from hooks or nails driven into the framework overhead.

Jack and Anna had spent a full day in one of Port Elizabeth's stores as they purchased all they would need to see them through the first months in the diggings. It was no Fortnum's, but the supplier knew what the would-be diamond hunters needed and had provided them with small sacks of tea, coffee, pepper, salt, curry powder and sugar, along with short, stubby tins of butter and condensed milk. Larger sacks contained a month's worth of rice, flour and beans, while paper parcels bound with string contained vittles from pickled fish to dried meats, either the famous biltong that Jack adored, or more traditional dried sausage and salami. The rest of the wagon's passengers had packed much the same provisions, although some had added crates filled with bottled beer, which Jack eyed jealously, or barrels of Cape smoke brandy.

Then there was the bewildering array of weaponry, from outdated percussion-cap rifled muskets to single- and double-barrelled hunting rifles, some muzzle loaders, other more modern breech loaders. With the rifles came ammunition packed into tin cases soldered shut, along with the cleaning paraphernalia that would be needed to keep the guns in working condition for the months ahead. Alongside the weapons were all sorts of personal effects; one of the passengers had even packed a concertina, which was tied to one of the wagon's struts so that it wheezed and puffed whenever the vehicle jolted hard, which it seemed to do with back-straining regularity. The rest of the space was filled with the bedding and tents they would all need once they had managed to stake a claim, along with the tools to dig it, the picks, shovels, coils of rope and crowbars far cheaper to buy in Port Elizabeth than they would be at the diggings.

Jack's carpet bag was safely stored by his boots, his revolver cleaned and ready, no matter that JW had promised them no trouble on the route up from the Cape. Anna had her own case, which she had meticulously filled with medicines from one of the stores near the waterfront. She had learned her medical skills the hard way, her journey into the Sudan with her uncle providing plenty of bitter opportunity to practise on the sick and the dying. Her uncle's second wife, the formidable Florence Baker, had proven a good teacher, and to Jack's mind, Anna was now at least the equal of any regimental surgeon he had had the misfortune to come across in his army career. Not that he knew much about treating the sick himself, and he had little to no idea what most of the packets and vials contained, but he did know that Anna had Dr Collis Browne's chlorodyne for the treatment of diarrhoea, along with enough doses of quinine to protect them from malaria for at least a year. She had sulphate, zinc and rose water, a mixture of the three said to be a successful treatment for ophthalmia, something they had heard was common in the diggings, plagued as they were with flies. She had purchased multiple jars of both Holloway's ointment and carbolic ointment, a dozen bars of soap and an array of bandages, slings and dressings. She had also insisted on a good number of jars of sarsaparilla and a roll of surgeon's knives that had intrigued and terrified Jack in equal measure, his mind revolted by the thought of the razor-sharp blades and vicious-looking saws working on flesh and bone. At the same time, he was fascinated to know more of quite how she would use such a bewildering array of medicines.

The rest of their possessions were scattered here and there in their allotted space, some tied to something else with twine, others simply rammed into any gap that could be found. It made for a chaotic, noisy journey, the groans and screeches of the wagon's wheels underscoring the clash of pots and pans and the dull thump of tins and boxes coming together. Overlaying these constants were the crack of the driver's whip and his cries for the bullocks to get on. Yet despite all this, Jack was finding something rather comforting about the chaos and cacophony. The ox-pulled wagon hauling them to Du Toit's Pan reminded him of the wagons he had escorted on another long journey, from the cotton plantations of Louisiana down through Texas, then across the Rio Grande and to the Mexican coast, where traders had waited to ship their cargo to the mills of Europe. Back then, he had enjoyed the freedom of being on horseback, something he reckoned he would surely miss this time around, his choice limited to Shanks's pony or the uncomfortable ride aboard JW's wagon. What he wouldn't miss was the danger that had come with escorting the valuable cotton south. The journey across the border from the southern states into Mexico had cost many men their lives. If JW was correct, the drive to the diggings would be much less fraught, if a little less comfortable.

'Get on, damn you!'

The driver's whip snapped out, the tip zipping through the air and hitting the back of the lead bullock with a precise snap. JW's driver was called Fred, and he hailed from the port of Liverpool, a place he claimed to have left two dozen years before on a sailing packet destined for India. That voyage had

been cut short, according to Fred's dramatic tale, by a storm
that had sunk the vessel and left him as the lone survivor,
shipwrecked on a forgotten beach a dozen miles from Port
Elizabeth. Jack had no clue whether that tale had even an iota
of truth behind it, but he was the last person to cast aspersions
on a man's past. He could see that Fred knew his business, the
long whip he used to drive the oxen flicking back and forth
with the casual precision of a man who had repeated the same
action so many times that it had become a part of him. The
wagoner was dressed in a flamboyant style, matching the
colourful tale he had shared with the passengers within a
minute of meeting them that morning, his bright scarlet trousers
paired with a mustard cotton shirt and paisley cravat. On his
head he wore a black top hat decorated with a tall ostrich
feather so old that most of its colour had long been bleached
out by the sun. He sat high on the wagon's driving seat, his
backside jumping up and down as if he was bouncing with a
barely contained excitement.

A second, smaller wagon was following in their wake,
driven by JW himself and containing his personal possessions
as well as his wife, a plump, smiley lady called Iris, who had
not uttered a word since she had been given a perfunctory
introduction to the latest souls her husband was to convey to
the diamond fields. Even Anna had failed to draw a single
syllable from her, the most pleasant compliment greeted with
nothing more than a simpleton's smile.

'This is unbearable.' Anna hissed the words half under her
breath as the wagon bucked over a badly rutted section of road,
her shoulder bouncing off Jack's own every few seconds.

'You'll get used to it,' he replied. 'And it beats walking all
the way there.'

'You would say that. I swear you would ride behind the devil himself to avoid straining yourself.'

'Maybe.' Jack grinned, hiding his own discomfort as best he could.

'I think you have it right. This is unacceptable.' The statement came from a man sitting to Anna's left. He was dressed in a tweed suit over a white shirt and black necktie, and his accent came straight from the high roads of Hampshire. He was a portly fellow, who looked more used to sitting at a table in a fine restaurant than to slumming it on a trail far from civilisation. His bulbous nose and cheeks bore the red veins and blotchy bluish stains of a long-term drinker, and his flushed cheeks glowed brightly above a rather scruffy salt-and-pepper beard.

'Thank you, Mr Goodfellow. It is nice to hear that someone agrees with me,' Anna replied, at the same time pinching Jack's side to quench his smile.

Jack snorted, not caring that he would appear rude in front of his countryman. He did not think much of the fat man who had been the first to pay for a space on JW's wagon. Goodfellow had given every impression of being little more than a well-meaning buffoon. He had spoken at length to Anna of his past, a life that as far as Jack could be bothered to recall had been incredibly dull until, for a reason not yet explained, he had upped sticks and left his comfortable country existence behind, swapping it for a passage on a packet out to Cape Colony.

'Please, call me George.' Goodfellow preened as Anna smiled at him.

'And you must call me Anna.' She was all grace, even though she was wincing as the wagon seemed to kick a good foot into the air as it crossed yet another rut in the road.

'I shall indeed, Anna.'

'Does that go for all of us?' the man opposite chimed in.

Jack looked at him sharply. As much as he might have wished it to be different, there would be no avoiding conversation with those close to them in the wagon, the cramped conditions forcing them to sit cheek by jowl with no hint of privacy. The man who had joined the conversation unbidden had the thin, pinched face of a city boy, with a wispy moustache, sallow cheeks and a pallid, unhealthy complexion that spoke of life far from fresh air. Jack judged him to be still short of his twentieth year. His accent made it clear that he hailed from London, but thus far Jack had not taken the time to find out which part of the great metropolis he had once called home. All he did know of the lad was that his name was Flanagan, and that he had paid his fare with a collection of small-denomination coins so grimy they looked like they had once been buried in soil. He was dressed in the anonymous corduroy trousers and plain flannel shirt worn by so many of the men they had seen since they had arrived in Cape Colony. Neither fitted his sparse frame that well, so that it looked like he was dressed in hand-me-downs from an elder brother, an effect completed by the incongruously large trilby hat that he wore well tipped back on his pea-shaped head.

'Of course.' Anna tried to sound gay, but the effect was spoiled when she gasped with a moment's pain as Jack's elbow dug into her side.

'Then I am much obliged to you, Anna.' Flanagan knuckled his forehead, a sly smirk on his face that belied the respectful gesture. He did not offer his own forename. 'So, are you two married or what?'

'None of your business, chum.' Jack leaned forward. He

didn't like Flanagan, every instinct telling him that the lad was a chancer. 'I'd recommend keeping your beak out of other folk's business if we are to get along.'

Anna looked sharply at him as he sat back, his warning delivered. She clearly sensed his distrust, but said nothing.

'All right, mate, just being friendly and all.' Flanagan shrugged, then turned his head away, casting his gaze over the side of the wagon.

'I would say you are quite right not to trust that one.' It was Goodfellow who spoke, whispering the words just loudly enough for Jack to hear. 'He looks like he doesn't have a brass razoo to his name.'

'We should refuse to trust him just because he is poor?'

Goodfellow puffed out his cheeks as if Anna's words had punched him in the gut. 'Now, now, Anna, please. I am not that much of a snob. Well, perhaps I am, but I would still not trust that fellow if he were as rich as Croesus.'

'What of you, George?' Jack eased forward to look at his countryman, using the man's first name with a mocking tone to his voice. 'I take it you have the fullest of pocketbooks?'

Goodfellow grinned, amused by the blunt question. 'A gentleman does not enquire of such things.'

Jack barked a short, harsh laugh. 'I'm not a fucking gentleman, chum, and I'll ask what I fucking please. It's up to you if you choose to answer.'

'Come now.' Goodfellow was chortling, as if delighted by Jack's choice turn of phrase. 'You carry yourself as an officer. Do not tell me you have not served in a position of command.'

Jack furrowed his brow. He did not like being read. 'Did you serve then?'

'Good God, no. I leave that to fellows like you. I am

something more of a planner, if you like, a desk-wallah rather than a man of action.' The glib reply was followed by a rather high-pitched titter.

Jack noted the choice of words. 'But you were in India?' It was clear there was more to the man than he had first thought.

'For a time.' Goodfellow nodded in appreciation of Jack's perception. 'After the Mutiny. Yourself?'

'Before. And during.'

Both of his eyebrows rose. 'You were there in fifty-seven?'

'Yes.'

'Where?'

'Delhi.' As soon as the word left Jack's lips, he tasted a moment's chill. He had been in Delhi when it had fallen to the mutinous members of the 3rd Bengal Light Cavalry. And he had returned with the British relief force. First to sit outside and stare at its walls throughout the long, dreadful months of the Indian summer, then in the front ranks as the British finally launched an assault on the city.

Goodfellow was looking at him closely, or at least as closely as the bucking wagon would allow. 'You have my sympathy. And my admiration.'

'And I want neither.' Jack glanced away. Memories were starting to stir. Memories he kept shackled and buried.

Anna reached out a hand, laying it on his. He had told her everything. From his stealing of an officer's scarlet coatee before the dreadful fighting in the Crimea to the horror of Solferino. Nothing had been left out. She knew it all. Good and bad. There were no secrets between them.

'So what brings you here, George?' She asked the question as much to spare Jack as to actually find out more from Goodfellow.

'I'm afraid to say I was something of a gambler, and not a very good one. Somehow I managed to lose rather a lot of money, and it transpired that it might be a capital idea to leave England, at least for a while.' Goodfellow smirked as he made the revelation. 'Coming here seemed a good way of rebuilding the family finances and avoiding a few rather frightening fellows who were demanding payment somewhat forcefully. When I have that in hand, I will return home.'

Jack was surprised by the confession. But Goodfellow was being too glib, and he reckoned there was plenty he had left unsaid. Yet he held his tongue. He would not push for more, just as he would not want anyone to probe into his own past.

Goodfellow fell silent. It gave Jack the chance to look around at the faces of the other men who were accompanying them to the diggings. The Australian Clarke was there, of course, their new partner almost buried on the far side of the wagon beneath a maroon carpet bag half the size of a full-grown man. Then there were the four Boers sitting together towards the rear of the vehicle. All were young, not one more than thirty years of age, and they shared the lean, muscled build of men used to a hard day's graft. They kept themselves to themselves; Jack had not spoken to them beyond the exchanges necessary to arrange their carriage, and as far as he could tell, none of the other passengers had engaged with them either. The rest of the passengers were all from Cape Colony: a pair of English brothers called Thomas and Arnold Thompson, who claimed to hail originally from the port town of Chatham in Kent, along with two other men, the four of them approaching Jack as a group when they had heard there were places available on the wagon. All were old enough to have salt in their beards and grey at their temples, and looked well used to manual labour, possessing the sort of thick fingers and heavy shoulders that were only gained through a lifetime of hard physical work. All four also sported the ample girth of men in their middle years who had spent too long sitting on their fat backsides. But they seemed a decent enough bunch, and they had loaded enough Cape brandy onto the wagon to keep them going for a year at least. Jack just hoped they would share it.

The wagon rolled on, the noises blurring together as the miles passed by.

After the second hour, all thirteen passengers had fallen into some kind of stupor, any attempt at conversation replaced with silence as they rocked back and forth, bruised and buffeted by a hundred collisions with the wagon, its contents or each other. It was a time for sitting back and just enduring, and so Jack closed his eyes, letting his body soak up the incessant battering while his mind emptied. After all, he had been a foot soldier. He knew what it was to walk day after day.

This was better.

Just.

Chapter Five

━━━◆━━━

'*D*o you still like the stars, Jack?'

Jack did not answer immediately. He was lying on his back looking up at the sky, Anna at his side. The heavens were alive, the inky sky filled with pinpricks of light in such a multitude that he could not recall seeing its like.

Like the rest of the passengers, they were enjoying the second of the night's rests, which had been called some time just after midnight. It was five days since they had left Port Elizabeth, and they were getting used to the routine, even if they were still frustrated by the slow pace of the ox-driven wagon and no amount of familiarity could allow them to become accustomed to the discomfort. It had got bad enough for Jack to break his creed and walk as much as he could, the aches and strains of long days spent on foot preferable to enduring hours of back-breaking vibrations riding in the wagon. He was not alone: all thirteen passengers spent much of the day walking. As if in some sort of silent pact, they had formed three distinct groups, the Boers and the Cape colonists keeping themselves to themselves in two separate cliques, while Jack and Anna spent most of their time with Clarke and

Goodfellow. Flanagan didn't join any of them, the silent Londoner roaming far ahead of the wagons, as if eager to reach the diggings first.

'I think they are magnificent.' Anna spoke again when Jack did not reply. 'And nothing like we see at home.'

'I don't think I ever even saw the stars before I went to the Crimea.' Jack reached out to take hold of her hand.

'I expect you were too busy being a rascal and a rogue.' She chuckled at the notion of a younger Jack.

Jack did not match her gaiety. There was nothing funny in his past. It had been a struggle, his earliest memory one of working in his mother's gin palace, collecting empty glasses and dodging clips around the ear from her dubious clientele as he took their still half-full glasses away just as she had instructed.

'I remember being taken to Box Hill when I was perhaps five or six. We stayed until it was dark. My father showed me the constellations.'

'You don't talk about him much.' Jack knew her uncle well enough, but Anna had barely mentioned her father, Sir Sam's younger brother.

'He was a good man.'

'That's it?' Jack did not like the banal answer. He wanted to know more.

'What is there to say? He did what he was told and lived the same life his own father had lived, just as his grandfather had before him. He abhorred the idea of change, and so he did nothing new, ever. He ate the same food, went to the same places; he even inherited the same opinions. He was his father's son and that was enough for him.'

'Sounds like he had it cushy to me. But how on earth did a man like that then create a creature like you?' He squeezed her hand to make sure there was no offence in the question.

'I rather think I was something of a disappointment to him. I was too wilful, or at least that is what I remember. I have a vivid memory of standing in his study when I was three or four years old while he berated me for playing with the servants' children. I'd got my dress muddy, I think, and he was not happy with me. I still remember his expression.' Anna sighed. 'He died when I was ten, and that was when my mother and I went to live with my uncle.' She pulled an odd expression that sat uncomfortably between regret and relief. 'He was very different, but of course you know that.'

'You can say that again.' Jack had worked for Sir Sam and seen the man's mercurial style at first hand.

'I was fortunate, I think. My uncle encouraged me to think for myself and to challenge others. I do not think my husband was best pleased when he realised what he had been saddled with.'

'He was still a lucky bugger.' Jack knew Anna's life's story, just as she knew his. 'As am I.'

'Oh, beware the charmer.' Anna shook her head at the flattery.

Jack laughed, then gasped as she poked him hard in the ribs. 'We need to get some rest. JW will want to be on the road again before too much longer.'

The days had settled into a pattern. They mainly travelled at night, as it was easier on the oxen, starting out late in the afternoon, around four, with a break around nine and another at midnight. They would then plod on through the small hours before camping just after dawn. Jack would have liked to keep moving for longer, but JW would not even discuss it, and he had enough sense to leave the man to it.

JW and his wife kept a distance from their passengers, a self-enforced separation, as if the wagon owner was unwilling to get to know the men and women he was transporting across the veldt. Fred was a different kettle of fish completely, spending the long daylight hours moving from group to group, regaling them all with the same tales, seemingly intent on making sure each passenger knew every last detail of his colourful past.

The daytime tended to drag, or at least it did for Jack. The passengers would all sleep for a few hours, but none of them found it easy, even after having walked for hours through the night. A few of them would strike out on their own, rifles primed and loaded as they sought to supplement the rations they had purchased in Port Elizabeth. Jack refrained from going with them. Hunting lessons had been scarce in the grimy back streets of London. He had been on a single hunt with Anna's uncle. That short exposure had coloured his notion of shooting animals, even for food, and he preferred to follow Goodfellow's lead and simply buy some of the day's bag from those with a stomach for murdering the wild animals and birds that populated the veldt.

The hunters did a fair job of it. In the main they shot doves and partridge, the gamy birds making for a good stew when mixed with potatoes, onion, peas and bacon from their supplies, even if they risked breaking a tooth on an errant bit of shot left in the bird's flesh. Once or twice there had been hares to add to the pot, and Jack heard tales of bushbucks and springbucks being sighted, although none had yet been brought down. At one remote farmstead, the group had found a farmer willing to sell some of his sheep, the old man and his wife familiar with the travellers coming through their land and happy to make a few shillings from the hungry wayfarers. The group had shared the sheep between them, the meat added to the items bought in Port Elizabeth, but they were still munching their way through their supplies at an alarming rate. Worse, they were ploughing through their supplies of tea, something that had Jack threatening to impose rationing.

'How long until we move?' Anna rolled onto her side as she spoke.

'Not long.' Jack did not take his eyes from the heavens. He reckoned it was a good half-hour after midnight. He would have to haul his backside up before too long, and the idea did not sit well. He was comfortable where he was, even if the woollen blanket he was lying on was making his back itch.

'I'm cold.' She shivered.

He stretched out an arm, pulling her closer so that she lay against his side, her own arm snaking out across his stomach.

'You think this will work out?' She nestled in, pressing tight, stealing his warmth.

'I have no idea,' Jack answered with blunt honesty. 'It if doesn't, then we move on.'

'But we will need money.'

'We can find money.' His answer was certain. He was a boy from the rookeries of East London. He had been born poor and he had found riches before losing them. Money came and went, but he knew he would always find enough, by fair means or foul.

It was answer enough for Anna. She rested her head on his chest. 'I never thought my life would come to this.'

'No, neither did I.' Jack snorted softly at the comment. The lure of the Queen's shilling had pulled him away from his mother's gin palace. The ordinary life of a British redcoat was meant to have been his, his years of soldiering spent idling at one garrison town or another, until he was sent to fight whatever foe he was ordered to face, wherever on the globe that might be. But he had been cursed with ambition and the desire to find a better life than the one he had been born into. And so his long charade had begun. At first it had been based on deceit, names and lives stolen to fuel his ambition. Somewhere along the way, though, he had started to face the world as himself, the skills and experience he had earned on the bloodiest fields of battle leading him to places he had never dreamed he would see. And there he had learned what it meant to finally be himself. The path to that place had cost him dearly, but now, lying under the stars with Anna at his side, he could not help but think it might all have been worth it.

'I wonder what my mother would say if she could see me now.' Anna broke into his train of thought.

'You don't think she would be proud of you? She should be.'

'I think she would be mortified. If you listen carefully, I think you can hear her turning in her grave.'

'What did she want for you?'

'What she gave me. An education, or at least as much of one as I was allowed. She believed that to learn too much was to be destined to be a spinster, and she could think of nothing worse. She was thrilled when I was betrothed. It was exactly what she wanted. First marriage and a husband. Then children. A household. She had it all planned out for me.'

'Sounds like you had it all.' Jack tried to sound glib.

'I did.' Anna sighed. 'But no one ever asked me if it was what I wanted. That was my destiny, and who could possibly have thought I would want something different. I mean, who would not want to be the lady of a grand house in the country, with servants at her beck and call and a succession of gracious visitors and family to entertain?'

Jack grunted. He had known women forced to sell their bodies to feed themselves and their bastard babies. The life Anna described was far beyond the aspirations of nearly everyone he had ever come across. And yet he did not think her foolish, or conceited, or just plain bottle-head stupid, for leaving it all behind. So many of the decisions he had made over the years had been in order to fight fate. Anna was no different. She had walked away from the life she had been allotted to find something else. Something that would allow her to be herself. They came from very different worlds, yet they were the same.

'Do you think I'm daft?'

'Yes.'

She poked him sharply for the swift reply, then huffed. 'When Martin died, I had to find a new life.'

'And your uncle took you back in.' Jack felt a short stab of jealousy at the mention of her husband's name. It was bearable to think of him as an entity, a notional *husband*, but when she used his forename, it gave him life. And that made Jack uncomfortable.

'For which I shall always be grateful.' She paused, settling against him. 'Do you think he despises me now?'

'No.' Jack was certain of the answer. He and Sir Samuel White Baker had never seen eye to eye, Sir Sam too ambitious and driven for Jack to ever fit comfortably at his side, his willingness to expend other men's lives to achieve his goals something Jack refused to condone. But he was sure that Sir Sam would not think badly of his niece for leaving with Jack instead of joining his expedition to open the Nile Basin to

Egyptian rule and trade. He was too much of a maverick to condemn someone for following a similar path to his own, even if it took Anna far from his side.

'I hope he does not.'

'Florence would not allow him to think ill of you.'

Anna laughed gently at the idea. 'She is a formidable woman.'

'As are you.' Jack moved his head to rest it against Anna's. He meant what he said. Anna was Florence's equal, even though she had been born with every comfort while Sir Sam's second wife had been stolen away from a Hungarian slave market. The two were not related by anything other than marriage, but they were cut from the same cloth.

'Thank you, Jack.' Anna pushed her head up so that she could look him in the eye. 'Thank you for everything.'

He heard the meaning in her words and he shook his head. 'No. You have nothing to thank me for.' He smiled. 'We are in this together. For better or worse.'

It was enough for her to return his smile. 'I hope you will still say that if we do find a fortune in diamonds and all those young floozies come chasing after you, fluttering their eyelashes and offering you nights of untold delights.'

'Young floozies, you say?' He tried to look serious, as if truly contemplating such a future.

'Don't even think about it, Jack. My knowledge of anatomy is good enough to know what to chop off. Why, I even have the tools to do it and keep you alive afterwards.'

'Cockless Jack.' Jack laughed out loud as he conjured the title. He had been a British officer, a maharajah's general, an assassin and a fugitive in his time. But he had never contemplated a life without his prick.

His laughter set Anna off. 'Consider yourself forewarned, Jack Lark.'

Before he could reply, the sounds of an altercation came from the opposite side of the wagon. Raised voices, then the first shouts of quick anger and the snap of insults thrown back and forth, followed by the scuff of boots across the ground as others were drawn to the fracas.

'Shit.' Jack gently moved Anna's arm away, pushing himself to his feet with a groan as the action set off the pain in his spine, the persistent backache so much worse after hours of walking and periods riding in the jarring wagon. But it was not enough to stop him straightening up, then offering a hand to Anna to help her up too. It never occurred to him to leave her behind.

'They've been drinking.' She brushed down the seat of her trousers.

'Probably. Ready?' He gave her a moment to prepare.

She sucked down a deep breath. 'Ready.'

Jack did not wait for more. The voices were getting louder. Whoever had been angered was making one hell of a fuss.

It took them no more than a dozen paces to round the wagon and see what was going on. The four Boers were squared up, facing three of the Cape colonists. The fourth was lying on his back, blood smothering his face like a mask.

'What the hell is happening?' Jack shouted as he came closer. It was not his fight, but it was his future that would be thrown into jeopardy if something happened to force JW to turn around. He would not allow that to happen.

'Keep out of it.' One of the colonists turned to snap at him.

It did not deter him, and he came closer, Anna just behind him. He could see Clarke and Goodfellow lurking on the far side of the wagon, watching what was going on while making sure they kept a safe distance from the fracas. JW and Fred were standing by as if readying themselves to pick up the pieces of whatever occurred, while JW's wife was sitting at a campfire a good dozen yards away, her face set in a cherubic smile as she stared at the flames, seemingly blithely unaware of what was going on.

As Jack approached, the colonist who had been knocked to the ground slowly got to his feet, his hand lifting to smear the blood from his face.

'Those fucking Dutchmen tried to take our gear.' One of the colonist brothers, Thomas Thompson, raised a thick finger, jabbing it directly at the four Boers with enough force to set his fair-sized gut wobbling. 'They're thieving fucking bastards.'

'*Jy prat kak.*' One of the Boers stepped forward, thrusting his chest out. He was tall, well over six foot, and lean to the point of being skinny. There was not a scrap of flesh on his face, the skin drawn tight to reveal an angular bone structure, and his eyes were set deep in his skull.

'Stand back.' Jack moved between the two groups, hand raised towards the Boer.

'He's full of *kak*.' The Boer came closer, glaring at the colonist. 'He's drunk too much of his own *fokken* brandy.'

'Shut your fucking mouth, mate, before I shut it for you.' Thomas took a step forward. 'If you weren't trying to take our stuff, why did you knock my brother on his arse?'

'Because he came at me with a whole passel of accusations.' The Boer showed no sign of backing off. 'And I'll knock you down next, *poephol*, if you don't walk away.'

'That's enough!' Jack snapped.

'*Ek sal jou bliksemse moer donner!*' The Boer ignored Jack and spat the threat towards the colonist.

'I'll beat *you* black and fucking blue, you Dutch whoreson.' Thomas clearly understood what had been said to him.

'Enough! If either of you takes another fucking step, it'll be me knocking you down on your damn arse, you hear me?' This time Jack bellowed the command, both hands thrust out towards the two men, physically interposing himself between them. He glared at each in turn, making sure they understood that he meant what he said. 'Now back the fuck down.'

'He's a fucking thief.' Thomas pointed at the Boer.

'And you're a noisy fucking drunk. Now get yourself the fuck off while you still can.' Jack glared at him, holding the man's gaze until finally the colonist looked away. 'Sit down and get some rest. We'll be moving out soon.'

'Something should be done about those fuckers,' Thomas muttered, but he did as he was told, taking another of the colonists by the elbow and steering him back to the blankets the group had spread on the ground.

Jack waited for one more long moment to make sure the four were moving away, then turned to face the Boer, who was still standing his ground. 'You too, chum.'

'Who made you chief here?' The Boer lifted his chin.

'I did. If you have a problem with that, then let's you and I talk about it tomorrow.'

The Boer snorted. '*Verdolt Engelschman.*'

'Stow it, chum.' Jack didn't speak the man's language, but he understood well enough. 'Your name is de Klerk, right?'

For a moment the Boer's mouth twisted as if he was about to spit. Then it settled into something calmer and more pleasant. 'It is.'

'Then I suggest you go and sit back down, Mr de Klerk.' Jack waited, looking the other man dead in the eye.

Finally, almost reluctantly, de Klerk nodded. 'Fine.'

'Thank you.' Jack was doing his best to be polite. It was not his strongest skill, but it seemed to be working. 'Now, I don't know what happened here, but I know how it's going to end, and it's with you and your pals simmering down. Do you understand me?' He kept his gaze level, waiting for de Klerk's reaction.

'Fair enough.' The Boer inched his head towards Jack. 'But the next time a man calls me a thief, he'll get more than a bloody nose.' His face contorted into something that on another day and in another situation might have approximated to a smile. 'Do *you* understand *me*?'

'Fair enough.' Jack borrowed the other man's turn of phrase. 'And if I find out that one of you stole so much as a single farthing, I'll give *you* more than a bloody nose.' He smiled as he saw the corners of de Klerk's mouth twitch.

'I'm glad we understand each other, *brü*.' De Klerk turned away, gesturing for his fellow Boers to follow him.

'Well done, Jack.' Anna came to Jack's side and squeezed his arm.

Jack simply grunted. He had done little. And he knew it would take more negotiation to prevent the two groups from causing trouble in the following days.

They had a long way still to go. Only time would tell if they would all reach their destination in one piece.

Chapter Six

The Katberg pass stretched out in front of them for what looked to be several miles. Low flat-topped mountains rose from the surrounding terrain, filling the horizon, their tops dusted white with snow, the majestic monolithic peaks casting long shadows over the stony, dusty ground of the trail that snaked through the lonely landscape.

Jack walked easily, eyes roving over the path they would have to take, glad that the early-evening light was just about good enough for him to get a look at the route ahead. A brisk breeze blew directly into his face, and above his head, grey and black clouds raced across the sky at pace.

Thus far they had largely covered a wide expanse of veldt, the land given over to sheep farming, although they had all enjoyed the antics of the odd-looking animals at the few ostrich farms they had passed. Ostrich feathers were highly sought after across Europe, the fashion for the bright decorations making the farmers in this remote land a small fortune. In the last few days they had crossed dozens of miles of grassland decorated with the odd wooded hill or winding river. It was as pleasant and picturesque as any country he had seen, greener than he had expected, and it had made for an easy, languid journey. Now that would change. Fred had warned of the precipitous path ahead, the rough winding trail over the Katberg mountain the greatest challenge, and the greatest danger, they would face on the entire journey.

The path that led onto the mountain was not much to look at, little more than a narrow mud and gravel track the width of the wagon. It cut through the grass and scrub that surrounded it, twisting back and forth and always heading uphill, the gradient shallow but enough to pull at the calves of those who had chosen to walk. Occasionally the terrain would break, and the open views were breathtaking, the rolling countryside stretching away for a dozen miles, the greens and browns of the trees and grasses warm against the dusty yellows and ochres of the soil. The scenery was certainly spectacular, but to Jack's eye it bore little comparison to the wilds of Abyssinia, the land here far less forbidding than the hellish landscape the British Army had been ordered to traverse to bring the Abyssinian Emperor Tewodros to account for daring to flout British power. The memories of that long journey filled his mind as he ground out the yards, boots crunching on the gravel beneath. Then, as now, he had covered the miles on foot, but back then his companion had been the mild-mannered Watson, and instead of the comfortable clothing he had chosen with care for just such a journey as this, he had been wearing native dress. Not for the first time, he was grateful for the sturdy boots on his feet. He might not enjoy trekking all night, but at least he was doing it in comfort.

'This is the life, eh, Jack?'

He turned to see Goodfellow coming up to walk beside him. The man's face was flushed with exertion. Unlike most of the others, he spent the majority of his time sitting in the wagon, preferring to spare his chubby frame the exhausting trek. On the few occasions he did walk, he favoured a long dark-wood cane topped with an ivory handle, the tip covered with the same material. He had the habit of tapping the end down with every step, and the constant pitter-pattering sound of ivory on hard-baked sand and gravel was fast becoming possibly the most annoying noise Jack had ever heard.

'Is it?' Jack was in no mood for chit-chat. Goodfellow had already proven himself to be somewhat irritating, and no more so than at that moment. In an attempt to divert the man, Jack looked for Anna, hoping he could beckon her over to him so that she could take up the conversation. To his dismay, she was walking too far away, her attention focused on Clarke, who from his gestures was explaining some complex technique they would need for turning the soil once they finally reached the diggings. In desperation, he looked for Flanagan, the young Englishman's limited conversation preferable to what would surely be far too long in the bombastic Goodfellow's company but, as ever, the Londoner was nowhere to be seen. Flanagan did a good job of keeping himself to himself, something that Jack found himself envying often and never more so than in that particular moment.

'Come now, Jack. Look around you. Is this not beautiful?' Goodfellow raised his cane, using it to gesture towards the surrounding landscape. 'Very much like Hampshire, I would say. Would you agree?'

Jack sighed. The man would not be easily deterred. 'I have no idea. I prefer London.' He kept his reply as brief as he could, lying with practised ease. The truth was that his last stay in London had been miserable and had ended in disaster. The great metropolis had nearly swallowed him whole. All he now recalled was the feeling of being suffocated there, the grime and the dirt worming deep under his skin. He had craved a return to a place such as the one he was now in. But to admit that to a man like Goodfellow was more than he could bear. And so he lied. He was good at lying.

'London has its merits. But I confess I am a country man at heart.' Goodfellow either didn't hear or simply ignored any hint of Jack's desire to avoid the conversation. 'I must say, I miss my home. It is odd, is it not, to be so very far from where everything is familiar.'

Jack glanced at him sharply. To his eye, Goodfellow looked the sort of man more used to sitting by the fire with a glass of brandy in his hand than a fellow who enjoyed the outdoor pursuits of the countryside. But he heard the longing in his voice as he spoke of home – a notion he himself was not familiar with – and so he sucked down his crabbiness and offered a more polite and willing response. 'Where are you from?'

'Hampshire. Nether Wallop. Do you know it?'

'I can't say I do.'

'I'm not surprised. It really is in the arse end of nowhere.'

The bald remark caught Jack's attention. It was the first interesting thing Goodfellow had said in their short acquaintance.

'I lied, Jack,' Goodfellow continued. 'I hate London. It stinks and it is full of men like you.'

'Like me?'

'Men who scare me.' He laughed at his own admission. 'I am not brave, Jack, and I rather think I was blessed with a face that is asking to be punched. It makes me fearful of men like you. Men who growl and scowl and hide behind their scars.'

Jack walked on in silence. The breeze was getting stronger and he could feel grit being blown into his face with enough force to sting. He did not deny what Goodfellow had said. He knew how he looked. And it was not just due to his scar.

'It must make life interesting,' Goodfellow mused. 'Terrifying people, I mean. I suspect it puts you at an advantage. I cannot think many men look at you and feel sure of themselves.' He glanced at Jack, as if wary of speaking so freely. 'I rather suspect people look at me and see little more than a chubby buffoon who drinks too much. That puts me at a disadvantage in life, but I cannot help it, and so I rub along as best I can, even if doing so leaves me quaking in my boots with my bowels in turmoil.'

Jack knew he should probably offer a polite rebuttal of Goodfellow's claims of inadequacy. But to do so would be to lie again, and so he held his tongue.

'Do you have me pegged as a buffoon, Jack?' Goodfellow pressed.

'Yes.' The answer was short and blunt. Jack glanced at his fellow Englishman. Despite Goodfellow's self-effacing admissions, he still looked rather crestfallen.

'I cannot say I blame you, I really can't. It is the truth, if I am honest. I like a drink, and I know I am not blessed with the good looks and charm of Adonis. I have learned that I shall not attract a mate, so I have become certain that I shall face this life quite alone.' He paused, reaching out to clasp Jack's arm as they walked side by side. 'But I am not a fool, Jack. I would like you to know that.'

'I will try to remember.' Jack paid the claim no heed. He would make up his own mind if he had to. In truth, he would prefer that their acquaintance came to an end as soon as they reached the diggings. He had no need of friends. Buffoons or not.

'For that, I thank you.' Goodfellow tipped his tile, then looked away. 'I say, this breeze is picking up a bit.'

Jack knew when a man was changing the direction of a conversation. It was the truth, though. The gale was indeed picking up. It was enough to stir dust devils into the air, and he could feel it pushing against his chest, so that he had to work harder to maintain his pace.

He was not the only one to notice. The four Boers had chosen to remain in the wagon, and now one of them stood up and gave a loud whoop of excitement. He was clearly enjoying the thrill of being buffeted by the gusts that were quickly growing in force.

'Damn fool,' Goodfellow muttered.

'Hey! Sit down!' Fred called over his shoulder.

'Just drive the *blerrie* wagon, *mon*.' The Boer was having none of it. He stood on his tiptoes, arms thrown wide as the brisk wind scoured across his face.

Fred spat in frustration, then flicked his whip across the back of the lead bullock to urge it to pick up the pace.

'He told you to sit the fuck down.'

Jack turned in time to see the man from Cape Colony, Thomas, shouting an instruction of his own. The four colonists were walking just behind the wagon. The trail was steep enough to make them lean forward as they marched up the slope, and to a man, they were already sweating hard.

'*Hou jou bek!*' retorted the Boer.

Jack shook his head at the start of another pointless fight between the two camps. Distrust and dislike between the Boers and the Cape colonists was deeply entrenched, and neither side needed much of an invitation to start a slanging match. Thus far, none of the verbal altercations had come to anything serious, but Jack had seen enough to know that it was just a matter of time before one escalated and there would be a brawl. Both sides wanted a fight. And so they would fight. It was how it was. He just hoped it didn't get out of hand or delay them.

'Fucking Dutch cunt,' Thomas sneered, speaking loudly so that everyone heard his verdict.

'What's that you say?' This time it was de Klerk, the Boer Jack had prevented from fighting the Cape colonists just a few days before. He had come to his feet next to his countryman, glaring down at Thomas, hands already balling into fists.

'You heard the man. Sit the fuck down.'

'You telling us what to do?'

Around them, the wind was beginning to howl. Dirt and dust were kicking up with a vengeance, filling the air with a fine yellow cloud. It was blowing with enough force to have slowed the wagon to barely a crawl. The colonists strode forward, closing the distance. The two brothers walked side by side. They could not have looked more alike, both beefy of body with wide bellies, the red lines and purple blotches of heavy drinkers on their faces. Yet both had hefty shoulders to match their fat, and fists like great hams, fingers and thumbs thickened by hard work.

Thomas did not hesitate. He came up to the back of the wagon, face stern and furious. As soon as he was close enough, he reached up, both hands taking firm hold of the nearest Boer's ankle. His grip tightened. Then he yanked hard.

The Boer's fall was spectacular. Jack watched as his leg was pulled beyond the open back of the wagon. His standing leg slipped from underneath him, and he went down like he had been shot, arms windmilling.

Thomas tugged even harder, hauling away with enough force to pull the man's legs far beyond the back of the wagon, then he pushed up sharply, so that the Boer came down arse first. As he started to fall, he was powerless to do anything but howl in shock. That howl ended abruptly as the back of his head hit the lip of the wagon with a sickening crunch and he crashed to the ground. He didn't move, just lay there in a heap, legs and arms in a jumble.

For one long-drawn-out moment, not one man spoke, the only sound the roar of the wind as it increased in power, rushing down the track like an express train thundering through a small-town station.

Then all hell was let loose.

The three remaining Boers jumped down from the wagon, de Klerk leading the way. As soon as their boots hit the dirt, Thomas and his cronies swarmed forward. There was little space on the trail, and a sheer drop on either side as the ground fell away. The confrontation that Jack had known was coming would take place in a narrow corridor behind the wagon.

'Shit.' He was turning his head from group to group, watching both sides react. Each was clearly relishing the chance to bring the other to account for the hundred slights and snarls that had filled the journey thus far. He knew what was to come unless someone intervened to stop it.

He took the first half-step forward, already sucking down a deep breath in preparation for bellowing at the two groups and demanding they stand down.

He was stopped in his tracks.

To his surprise, it was Goodfellow who was reaching out to hold him back, a restraining arm held across his chest. 'Let them have it, Jack. It's better this way.'

Jack made as if to throw Goodfellow's arm to one side. But something stopped him. Instinct. Fear. Sanity. Or just experience. He was not certain what made him stand there, his muscles quivering with a barely controlled tension. No matter what drove his decision, though, he did not take another step.

De Klerk came forward first, his fellows taking up position at the back of the wagon, angry faces watching the four colonists to their front.

Thomas stepped towards him alone, his companions suddenly reluctant to face the three much younger and harder Boers, even with superior numbers on their side.

De Klerk moved fast. He came at the colonist, fists swinging. But Thomas was no coward, and he held his ground, feet braced like a pugilist taking the ring, crouching as he settled his weight ready for what was to come. It was bravely done, to Jack's eyes at least.

The two came together. De Klerk was much the quicker, and he punched first, driving his right fist into Thomas's ample gut. Thomas bent double, breath spewing out of his gaping mouth with an audible whoosh, his flailing right hand swiping past de Klerk's nose.

De Klerk came again, left hand jabbing, the fast-moving fist catching the colonist on the side of his head. It landed with enough force to knock Thomas to one side, his balance thrown off by the twin blows. De Klerk did not give him time to recover. He stepped forward, both hands reaching out to shove the colonist, toppling him over so that he came down with all the grace of a sack of shit thrown from the night-soil man's wagon.

He landed no more than a yard from the drop on the far side of the trail.

'Get up!' De Klerk was not done. He came to stand over

Thomas even as he lay winded on the ground, his breath coming in huge gulps and sobs. 'Get up, *poephol*, before I kick you over the *fokken* edge.'

Thomas writhed. He was plainly hurting, his body shuddering as it absorbed the pain of the twin blows and the brutal impact with the rocky ground.

'Get the *fok* up, *mon*, I'm not done with you.' De Klerk came closer, his heavy boots no more than a foot from Thomas's head. For a moment, Jack thought the Boer would lash out and kick the fallen colonist over the edge of the trail. But instead, he stood there, fists at his sides, giving Thomas just enough space to get back to his feet and face him.

But Thomas had other ideas. Even as he squirmed on the ground, his hand slid to his belt, and to the knife sheathed on his left hip.

Jack saw his plan.

'Stop!' he shouted, thrusting past Goodfellow's restraining arm, which still hovered across his chest.

He was too far away, and too irrelevant, to be heeded.

Thomas slipped the knife from its sheath, the metal of the blade glinting in the sun. Then he lumbered to his feet, blowing hard, turning to face his foe.

The wind was howling now, filling the trail with noise. Dust was driving hard into the face of every man.

Yet every one of them still saw the knife.

For a fat man, Thomas moved quickly. No sooner was he on his feet than he was slashing the blade in a vicious, glittering arc aimed directly at de Klerk's gut.

De Klerk reacted fast, stepping away until his back hit the rear of the wagon. In the confined space, there was nowhere else for him to go. In desperation, he sucked in his gut, bending away from the knife. The movement was enough, the blade sliding past no more than a hair's breadth away from his belly.

Thomas cried out in frustration as his first wild swipe missed its target. But as soon as he found his balance, he came forward again, shouting in triumph as he saw he had his foe cornered. He lunged at the Boer, the second stab sharp and controlled.

But de Klerk was young and he was fast. With his eyes fixed on the blade, he jerked to the left, dodging out of the way. He kept moving, dancing back the other way as a third stab came hard on the heels of the second, gasping with the effort even as Thomas bellowed in rage at failing to land a telling blow.

And then de Klerk tripped.

The rock was no bigger than a man's hand, but it was enough. The side of the Boer's boot caught it, his ankle turned and he went over. As he fell, he reached out to try and grab hold of the wagon, but he missed and went down hard.

Thomas was on him in an instant, with no thought of mercy or of holding back as the Boer had done.

Jack lunged forward. He did not know why. Not fully. It was not his fight. Ever since one fateful day not far from the Nile river when he had intervened in a skirmish without thought for the fighting's cause, or care for the consequences of his actions, he had refused to intervene in anything that did not concern him, limiting his actions to protecting himself and Anna. Yet now he rushed to the aid of a Boer he did not know, a Boer who hated all Englishmen.

The wind was howling like a banshee released from hell as he darted across the trail. It stormed down the track, whipping up dust, striking the small group of men who stood watching as a fist fight turned into a fight to the death.

Thomas's lips were pulled back in a snarl, his arm readying for the next strike. Sprawled in the dirt, de Klerk would be powerless to avoid the blow that was coming for him. The blade moved almost quicker than the eye could track. It came forward hard and fast, tip rushing towards the Boer's chest.

De Klerk threw out an arm. But he was on his side, and his desperate attempt to ward off the attack was doomed to fail, the angle all wrong.

The blade was coming for him.

Then Jack struck.

He threw himself at Thomas, boots scrabbling on the dusty ground then powering him forward so that he hit the colonist with his full weight. Clasping hold around the man's waist, he drove them both over the edge of the trail, the blade that would have surely killed a man thrown into the dust-filled air.

The two of them landed brutally hard, arms and legs intertwined. They rolled immediately, the angle of the slope pulling them downwards, limbs flailing helplessly as they tumbled down the gradient. Down and down they went, both crying out as they turned over and over, the sound leaving their open mouths on a rush of air as the wind was driven from their lungs by impact after impact.

The wild, careering tumble ended abruptly when they hit a raised line of rocks a couple of dozen yards below the trail. Beyond was a cliff face and another perilous drop.

Neither man moved.

Jack groaned. He tried to transfer his weight, but his body would not obey. Everything ached. Once, he would have been able to spring to his feet, his only thought to batter the man he had knocked down. But that was before. When he was younger. Now he could do nothing but lie there absorbing the pain as he sucked down lungfuls of air, spasms of agony running up and down his spine before shooting down into both legs.

'Fuck me,' he gasped. He felt old. Tired. Broken.

Slowly, gingerly he rolled onto one side. To his relief, Thomas was in no better shape, struggling to get air back into his own tortured lungs. And then Jack glimpsed de Klerk.

The Boer was charging down the slope, arms spread to keep his balance. In one hand he held Thomas's knife. He came on fast, legs working furiously to hold him upright, the yards disappearing in the blink of an eye.

'Stay away.' Jack tried to snap the order, but it came out as little more than the croak of an old man. He tried to get to his feet, willing his body to respond. But he was hurting and slow, and he could do nothing as de Klerk came to a breathless halt, looming over the two men, the naked blade turning in his hand as he readied himself to strike at the now defenceless Thomas.

The sound of the gunshot was shocking. It rang out, echoing off the mountains and filling the ears of every man who stood watching the fight.

'That's enough. Next time I'll shoot you down.'

Jack scrabbled to his feet, just about finding his balance despite the trembling in his muscles that almost made his legs give way beneath him. Anna was standing no more than ten feet away from de Klerk, wideawake hat hanging down her back, her braided hair flying this way and that as the wind pummelled over her, the revolver he had bought for her held in both hands and aimed directly at the Boer, a thin trail of smoke whipping away on the fierce wind.

'Now, Mr de Klerk. Step away, if you please, and place that knife on the ground.' Her instructions came out wrapped in iron.

De Klerk hesitated. He glanced at Thomas, assessing distances. Anna had come halfway down the slope. It made for an awkward downhill shot. One that might miss.

Or one that might not.

'I said step away,' she repeated, jerking the revolver. 'Now.'

De Klerk licked his lips. Then he did as she ordered.

'Are you all right, Jack?' Anna asked as he staggered up the slope towards her.

'I'm fine.' His voice was hoarse.

'Any bones broken?' She did not take her eyes from the Boer.

'No.' He spoke through gritted teeth. He didn't think anything was busted, but his back was in agony.

'Good.' She didn't look at him. 'Did you know that line of rocks was there?' she asked out of the side of her mouth.

'No.' He glanced at her to see her lips pulled thin.

'Fool.'

'Always.'

She flashed the merest hint of a smile at his answer, then gave the Boer her full attention. 'Now, Mr de Klerk, are we done here?' She had to shout so that she was heard over the roar of the wind.

De Klerk glanced one last time at Thomas, who still lay sprawled where he had fallen. '*Ja*.' He spat out the single word as if it tasted of shit.

'Good.' Anna gave him a warm smile before she slowly lowered the gun, though she continued to watch him carefully. Only when she was sure he wasn't going to try and renew his attack on the colonist did she slip the weapon back into the holster on her right hip. 'Now, let's see to that poor fellow who cracked his head. Jack, can you fetch my medicine bag, please.'

She did not wait to see if he obeyed. Instead, she turned and began walking back up the slope, leaving Jack to follow dutifully in her wake.

As soon as he reached the trail, he went to the front of the wagon to do as he had been instructed. It was only as he moved towards the rear, where Anna was tending to the fallen man, that he realised that de Klerk had followed him.

'Would she have shot me?' the Boer asked.

'Yes.' Jack grimaced as he replied. 'She would.' He felt bruised all over, and his back was killing him. He was in no mood to chat.

'That would have been a shame after you saved me, *brü*.'

Jack grunted by way of reply. He was not sure why he had saved de Klerk, why he had broken his new creed of not intervening. But he would not dwell on it. Things happened. Sometimes they were within your control. Sometimes they were not. Either way, there was no point letting your thoughts linger. What was done was done. And the future would take care of itself, with or without his soul-searching.

'Don't go thinking that I owe you.' De Klerk spoke slowly and clearly, making sure Jack understood. 'It's not all hearts and roses between us, *mon*, or any *kak* like that. You did what you did and you have my thanks. But that's it. Nothing more.' He held Jack's gaze, making sure the message was both delivered and understood, before he turned and walked away.

Jack paid the comment no heed. He was no longer a soldier facing the danger of the battlefield. There would be no chance for the Boer to repay the debt. Not now. Not ever.

No chance at all.

Chapter Seven

———◆———

Eighteen miles from Du Toit's Pan, 30 May 1871

J ack stood by and watched as the Boers removed every scrap of their gear and supplies from the wagon. They were making a thorough job of it, the two men up on the vehicle taking their time as they checked for anything left behind, both seemingly impervious to the attention they were being given by the Cape colonists, who were watching their every move with eyes hooded with suspicion.

'Are you really leaving us now?' he asked the tall, gaunt Boer at his side.

'*Ja.*' De Klerk kept his answer brief. He was standing guard over the pile of belongings, his rifle held in his hands as if he expected to be rushed by those watching as the group of Boers prepared to strike out on their own.

'It's your call.' Jack wanted to know more of the Boers' decision. There was still at least eighteen miles between them and the diggings at Du Toit's Pan. 'Care to tell me why?'

'No.'

'Fair enough.' He tried not to huff. It was time for another tack. 'Can I see your rifle?'

De Klerk stared back in lieu of an answer, distrust written into every inch of his expression.

'I just want a look, chum. I've not seen one like it.' The request was genuine. The Boer's rifle had a distinctive top-opening breech. When it was hinged forward to open the chamber, the curled lever resembled an animal's tail, giving the weapon the nickname 'monkey tail'. Jack had heard of the rifle and its manufacturer, Westley Richards, but he had never seen or held one.

The Boer grunted, but he handed the rifle over.

Jack took it carefully. It reminded him of the Snider he had used in the Sudan, although it was shorter, the barrel perhaps around twenty-four inches long. He could see the advantage of the smaller size, which would make the rifle easier to handle on horseback. The monkey tail was a breech loader, like the Snider, and he took time to check the mechanism. The cartridge looked to be fired by a percussion cap, something that would make the weapon robust and easy to find ammunition for, unlike his own Lefaucheux, which fired more modern pinfire cartridges. These had proven difficult to source, and he had failed to find any beyond those he had bought in Khartoum.

'It looks good.' He hefted the rifle then handed it back to the Boer. 'Had it long?'

'Since I was eight.' De Klerk handled the weapon with the familiar ease of a man who had used it for a decade or more.

'That young?' Jack raised his eyebrows.

'*Ja*. We had to hit a hen's egg at one hundred yards before we were allowed to take it out.'

He nodded thoughtfully. De Klerk's claim meant the Boers

would all be accurate shots. That was worth noting.

'I hope you don't have cause to use it for anything else but shooting game,' he said pointedly.

'Me too, *brü*.' De Klerk glanced towards the four Cape colonists.

Jack followed his gaze, reading him easily. 'Are they the reason you boys are leaving?'

'Maybe. Maybe we just want to get there first.'

'You think we should do the same?'

'Up to you. But for sure, the quicker the better for us.'

'Have you got family there?' Jack was trying to understand the lure of a faster arrival.

'*Ja*.'

'I see.' De Klerk's replies had set off a train of thought in his head. Perhaps there would be an advantage to be gained by getting in ahead of the Cape colonists. There was certainly an appeal in the idea of striking out, leaving the wagon to follow. 'Thank you.'

De Klerk grunted, his attention fully back on the men from Cape Colony.

But Jack had learned enough. And he came to a quick decision.

It was time to get on with what they had come so far to do.

It was time to head out on their own.

'Are you ready?'

'As I'll ever be.' Anna grimaced, then shifted her weight from foot to foot as she tried to settle the haversack on her back into a more comfortable position.

Jack appreciated the effort. 'We can stop for regular breaks.' He offered a half-smile. 'It's not a forced march.'

'I am glad to hear it, Jack. Be sure not to treat me as one of your soldiers.'

'Yes, ma'am.' He turned to their companions. 'You all ready?'

'Absolutely, Jack.' Goodfellow nodded firmly. He looked like a street tinker, his ample frame layered with pots and pans hanging from his own heavy haversack, while he also carried two carpet bags, one in either hand. On one hip was a sturdy keg of brandy; the other was hidden behind two canteens.

'Me too, Jack. All shipshape and Bristol fashion, as you bloody Englishmen say,' Clarke chirped. He was standing next to Goodfellow, his own luggage limited to his large maroon carpet bag. Jack had arranged for JW to deliver the rest of their gear to them when he arrived a few days later; there was no way they could carry it all themselves, none of them as strong and hale as the four Boers. Goodfellow had damned his eyes for being a fool, Jack's fellow Englishman certain that JW would simply sell the precious commodities to the nearest merchant the moment he arrived at the diggings. It was why Goodfellow was carrying a load larger than the rest, the items he deemed essential now strapped about him. But Jack had seen the best and the worst of men, and he judged that the wagoner would stand true to his word. He hoped he was right. Otherwise they would have to face the first weeks in the diggings without the tools they needed to start work on any claim, and with nothing to eat beyond the hardtack and biltong he had made sure each of them carried in their bag.

'Good. And you?' He turned to the last of their merry little band. He had been as surprised as anyone when Flanagan had asked to come with them. The Londoner had said little to any of them in the weeks since they had left Port Elizabeth, but as

soon as he heard that the group planned to strike out on their
own towards Du Toit's Pan, he had been keen to join them.

'I'm ready, Jack-o.' Flanagan looked Jack in the eye as he
replied, a rare thing for the younger man to do.

'That all you want to take?' Jack gestured towards the small
haversack at Flanagan's feet.

'It's all I've got, chum. All I need too.'

Jack smiled at the remark. It might have come out of his
own mouth. He was not one for possessions, save for his
weapons. It seemed Flanagan was cut from the same cloth.

'You can buy more when you're rich.' Jack made the
comment with a wry smile.

'When I'm rich, I won't be buying anything I can't eat, drink
or f—' Flanagan cut himself off abruptly as he glanced at Anna,
the faintest flush colouring his cheeks.

Jack laughed at the younger man's discomfort. Anna had
been around him for long enough not to be embarrassed by the
odd ribald remark.

'Sounds like a good plan to me.' He grinned as he said it,
immediately side-stepping as Anna went to land a slap on his
arm.

He looked around his small band of companions, assessing
each one in turn. All seemed ready to go. Raring even.

The pace of the journey up from Port Elizabeth had been
slow and grating for all them. Excruciatingly so. It had taken
forty-four days to that point. Forty-four tiresome, irksome,
boring days. They had crossed the Modder river in the dark the
previous night, which had taken several hours, as JW had
insisted the wagons be emptied before they took them across.
The delay had seemed to go on for ever, and when Jack had
suggested to Anna that they follow the Boers' lead by covering

the remaining miles on foot in a single day if they could, she had seized on the idea.

Not that everyone had shared the same desire to go it alone. None of the four Cape colonists had been keen, and they would remain with the wagon, saving their strength for the months of digging that were surely to come.

The Boers and the colonists had kept to themselves after the knife fight. Or at least the colonists had had the sense to steer a wide berth around the Boers, one of whom sported a thick swathe of bandages around his damaged noggin. Anna had cleaned and treated the wound, and checked it every day. She had told Jack that as far as she could tell, there was no lasting damage to the man's head, a testament to the thick and resolute skulls of the young. Not that Jack cared. Once they reached the diggings, he planned to avoid them all.

'Right, gentlemen,' Anna called out to the small group. 'If we have finished chit-chatting, shall we go?' She glowered at Jack as she made the remark, making a point of blaming him for the delay, but the smile on her face somewhat lessened its force.

A murmur of assent confirmed that they were all ready.

'Then follow me.'

Jack grinned as she sang out the instruction, one he had given more times than he could recall. This time, he was happy enough to be a follower.

Especially when his leader was as attractive as Anna.

They got their first glimpse of the diggings just before the light failed. In the distance was a thinly wooded hill lined with white tents. From a mile or so away, it reminded Jack of the British Army's encampment at Upper Sooroo in Abyssinia, and he felt the same odd sense of dislocation at seeing the presence of mankind in the wilderness. But here there was one difference. Where the army's encampment had had the order of a military establishment, the tents at Du Toit's Pan were spread across the low-lying hillside in a haphazard arrangement that would have driven any self-respecting commissariat officer to despair.

'And so it begins again,' he muttered under his breath. The feeling of discombobulation was strong. It was always like this for him. A long journey was coming to an end and a new start was imminent. He could sense Fate sitting on his shoulder. She was laughing at him, as she always did whenever he formulated a plan of his own. For she controlled his destiny, just as she had since the moment he had stolen an officer's rank and taken it for his own. And now here he was, about to start what he hoped would be the first step towards a new life. There were many more steps to come if he was to get to the future he wanted. He just hoped Fate would let him find it this time.

'We made it, Jack.'

He turned to see the glow of excitement on Anna's face as she pointed ahead. 'I never doubted we would.'

'Do you still think this is the right thing to do?'

'It's too late for that.' He was curt. There was no point second-guessing. They had made their decision a long time before. 'We're here now. We leave doubt behind and make the best of whatever we find.'

'Yes, Jack.' Some of Anna's excitement was fading. 'You are right, of course.'

'It is a good plan.'

'Yes, it is.' She took a moment to compose herself, breathing deeply.

'We make enough to set ourselves up. Then we quit.' Jack

went over the scheme they had formulated together, first on a Nile dahabiya as they headed upstream to Khartoum, and then on the steamer on the long journey down the east coast of the African continent. It was a simple one, deliberately so. In his experience, the more complicated the agenda, the more likelihood it would go awry. They would dig until their funds ran out or they found enough diamonds to pay for the next stage of their travels. They had not spoken a single word about what would follow the money running out, but both knew Anna could go home whenever she needed, her family wealthy and welcoming enough to be sure to pay for her return, no matter where she was. Jack had no such option, but he reckoned he would face that future with a happier heart knowing that Anna would be all right. He would be alone once more, shifting for himself as he had done countless times before. He would survive. He always had.

'So where shall we go next?' She posed the question with a smile.

Jack was pleased to hear it, the return to their favourite topic a sign that any uncertainty she had felt was passing. He had lost count of the hours they had spent talking of their future travels, and he was happy to do so again.

'Wherever you want.'

'America?'

He grimaced, just as he always did when she talked of travelling across the Atlantic, and just as she knew he would, the barb deliberately aimed. He had spent too long in the United States. He had fought there. And he had lost there. 'I was thinking we could start somewhere closer to home. Hungary, perhaps? I hear a man can make some interesting purchases there.' He made the reference to the slave market where Sir Sam had found his second wife, Florence, with a smirk on his face.

Anna snorted. 'Don't even think about it. You are stuck with me now. You do know that, don't you?'

'Stuck?' Jack laughed at her choice of word. 'I'm not stuck with you, love.' He composed his face to be as serious as he could make it. 'We go on together. For now and always.'

His tone was enough to make Anna laugh. It was a good sound, warm, and it spoke of contentment, no matter that they were so far from their homeland. 'That's enough for me, Jack.'

'Good. It's all you're going to get.' He stepped quickly sideways as her jabbing finger came for him, dodging it easily.

'You are a rogue and a scoundrel, Jack Lark.' She chuckled as she castigated him.

'So I've been told. Now, save your breath. It might look like we're close, but it's still a fair way away.'

They were walking in a compact group, him and Anna in the van, while Clarke, Goodfellow and Flanagan followed behind, each seemingly in their own world. Ahead was a broad expanse of veldt filled with stunted grasses and scrub, along with a scattering of thorn bushes. The occasional mimosa tree broke up the barren terrain, but other than those, they were in wide-open terrain, the sky pale blue and enormous overhead. Jack had journeyed on the American prairies and on the great plains of Europe, but he could never recall a time when he had felt quite so small and insignificant as he did that day. The surroundings were somehow larger than anything he had experienced before, as if the gods had stretched the horizon so that it was impossibly far away, while he could not remember being under a sky quite so large as the one above their heads that afternoon.

'Look!' Anna hooted with glee as a herd of small, pale deer bounded across their path. 'Springbuck.' The tiny animals were moving fast, each one dancing and fleet of foot. 'Aren't they beautiful?'

Jack said nothing.

'It is a good omen, Jack.' She was mesmerised by the animals. They moved as one, the sense of each individual somehow lost in the herd.

'Maybe, love, maybe.' He had no time for superstitions, placing his faith in his own abilities and the revolver on his hip.

But still, he was pleased that Anna sounded so happy.

Now that *was* a good omen, and one he was glad to hear.

Chapter Eight

Jack led his small party into the outskirts of the encampment around Du Toit's Pan. By unspoken agreement, they had closed ranks as they came into the town that sprawled around the diggings, though 'tent city' was perhaps a more apt description for the bewildering array of temporary accommodation that smothered the slopes of the hillside rising up out of the veldt. He could see tents of every shape and size, as well as dozens upon dozens of wagons, some no different to the one that had brought them all the way from Port Elizabeth, others at least double the size, while some were barely big enough for a man of very short stature to lie down flat. Many were set up as small homesteads, surrounded by cooking sheds or ovens, or corrugated-iron stores likely filled with digging equipment. These extra features cast the scene in a more domestic form, and it looked like many of the tents and wagons had been there for some time, the stained canvas and deeply dug-in wheels pointing to a life that had become a great deal less temporary.

Beyond the first ranks of tents were a handful of buildings of a larger size and at least some degree of permanence. There were one or two marquees of the type Jack had become used to seeing deployed as a headquarters or senior officer's domain within the British Army. Alongside these were at least two houses made from corrugated iron, and even one that looked to have been built of brick. The signs of a proper town emerging from the temporary homes gave him some idea of how long the digging had been going on, and he had a sinking feeling in his gut that they were perhaps arriving too late.

His small group walked on in silence, not one of them finding anything to say. They passed the first of the tents, most still empty even as the sun was setting. A few faces turned their way briefly, a complete lack of interest in every expression. Jack understood why. The five of them were anonymous here, their arrival completely unremarkable. It suited him well enough.

For the first time, he noticed a number of animal pens in and around the tents. As before, there was no sense of organisation, the animals living cheek by jowl with the diggers. Bullocks were everywhere, the great beasts standing stoic and silent. Other pens held small flocks of sheep, the air filled with the constant bleat of the docile animals marking time before they were led to the slaughterman. Elsewhere there were lonely mules, either kept in small pens or else simply left tethered to stakes buried in the ground. There were a handful of horses, but far fewer than perhaps he would have expected to see. It pointed to the diggers not being ones for travel, their lives now restricted to the dusty ground in which they searched for a fortune.

The pan itself was hidden from view. There was no sign of the diggings, or any of the claims he had heard so much about. Far beyond the encampment, he could see another shallow hill, where great herds of cattle grazed on the scrubby grass, moving slowly back and forth as they searched for food amidst the sparse vegetation. All were skinny, their bones clearly visible even from a distance.

'Look at that!' It was Anna who pointed ahead. A great plume of dust rose from the area beyond the furthest tents. It hung in the air, grey and filthy like powder smoke lingering after a battalion volley. 'The diggings?'

Jack nodded. 'Must be. Let's go take a look-see.'

He led them on, following something that approximated to a path through the tents and wagons. A dog barked at them, the animal tied to a stake by a length of chain just about long enough for it to defend the nearby wagon. Jack watched it lunge and snap in frustration as it failed to reach them, its mouth foaming with spit. He could smell the aroma of woodsmoke and cooking, the agreeable smells underscored with something far less pleasant, the miasma of piss and shit tainting the air. Along with the familiar stink of an encampment, another odd smell lingered. To him it smelled like the factories that had sprung up in the East End after he had first quit its dark and dingy streets, and which he had seen first-hand when he had returned there after his time in the United States, something artificial and chemical that caught on the breeze. It smelled of industry. Of some sort of processing, or at least that was what he could taste, along with the more familiar feel of grit on his tongue and dust on his face.

They walked on, silent and calm, but with something he could only describe as some form of trepidation hanging over them all, one that was no easier to carry for being shared. He glanced back, seeing the same look of unease on his companions' faces, mouths set firm while brows were furrowed. Anna's head turned slowly from side to side as she took in her new surroundings, ones that were surely as alien to her as they were to him.

It was only as he looked away from her that he saw they were passing the last of the tents.

And he gasped.

The ground was flatter and more open now that the diggers' temporary lodgings were behind them. Ahead, rocks and boulders littered the ground, each one of a size and weight too large for them to have been shifted by manpower alone. Further on were great mounds of earth and gravel piled up in every direction, a testament to months upon months of digging. Jack could not begin to contemplate how many man hours of labour it would take to shift such an enormous amount of dirt. Hanging above them all was the same cloud of dust Anna had already spotted. It lingered in the air, thicker than even a London particular, casting a sickly yellowish tinge over everything, so that it felt like they were entering another realm that was not quite of this earth.

Then they saw the pan itself and all five stopped on a sixpence.

The open area was huge, a great rectangle of land a good quarter of a mile wide. The pan itself was formed of a bowl-shaped depression in the dirt that might once have been filled with vegetation or water. Now, though, it looked like nothing Jack had ever seen before.

Every inch of ground was claimed, the land divided into neat little parcels around thirty feet square by pegs, rope and small pennants. Some looked fresh, to his naive eye at least, bearing but a few scars from the tools the diggers used to scrape away the friable ground near the surface. Others were forbidding, great gouges and pits hacked from the earth. From his vantage point on the periphery, he could see that some of the diggers had chosen to sink vertical shafts deep into the soil, with toeholds gouged into the face so that they could clamber up and down without the need for ladders or scaffolding. The only evidence of the work going on down in the bowels of the claim were the jerry-rigged A-frames and supports that stood over the pits, bewildering arrangements of ropes and pulleys used to send empty buckets down to the men working below, or to haul up the spoil as it was dug.

Others had employed a different tactic, digging down in stages, their claims sunk to varying levels so that it looked like a lunatic had decided to excavate a flight of wide steps in the middle of the pan. Other claims looked to have been tunnelled out, the entrances sloping down from the surface into darkness. There was something rather unpleasant about these forbidding entrances cut into the ground, and Jack felt a cold hand on the back of his neck as he contemplated being the one to crawl down into the blackness, the earth pressing down on top of him. It was enough to make his stomach lurch, and he made a vow to himself that whatever anyone suggested, they would never dig in that way.

'Where on earth do we start?' It was Anna who broke the silence.

'We need to purchase our claims first.' Clarke was beaming as he took in the diggings. Of all of them, he was the only one who had seen them before. He had done his best to describe them to the others, but the picture he had painted had done little to illustrate the sheer scale of the enterprise. 'They're all the same size and you can have as many as you want so long as you can afford it. I reckon the three of us should start with just the one. We can get more if we want to later.'

'Are there any left?' Jack waved an arm to encompass the vast expanse.

'There always are.' Clarke sucked down a long, slow breath as he contemplated the sight in front of them.

'Why?' Jack asked.

'Some diggers quit.'

'Why?'

'What are you, a bloody toddler?' Clarke snapped at the repeated question. Then he sighed. 'They quit because they don't find enough to keep going.'

Jack grunted. It was as he'd expected, but that did not make it any more palatable.

'But we're going to be different.'

He looked across to see Anna looking at him as she spoke. She must have seen his thoughts reflected on his face.

'Absolutely,' Goodfellow chimed in. 'And I have some news for you. Mr Flanagan and I have decided to pool our resources and work together.'

Jack looked at his fellow Englishman sharply. He was genuinely surprised. The two were chalk and cheese. 'When did that happen?'

'We have discussed it at length.' Goodfellow looked pleased to see Jack's reaction. 'This is not a place to work alone. Besides, it makes sense. You are a three. Now we are a two. With luck, we can secure adjacent claims.' He paused, his expression becoming serious. 'I fancy this is a place where it will pay to keep one's friends at hand.'

Jack did not gainsay the statement.

'I think that is a perfect idea. Perhaps we can look to share some resources.' Anna answered for them both.

'Capital.' Goodfellow puffed his cheeks, then looked across

to Flanagan. 'My partner and I will be happy to pool whatever we can.' Clearly he believed he was the mouthpiece for the newly formed partnership.

Flanagan scowled at the notion. 'I don't know about that, chum. I reckon we need to stand on our own two feet.'

Goodfellow puffed his cheeks out again as he absorbed the remark. 'I think we will find it will pay to be neighbourly.'

'You won't be saying that when we pull out the big one.' Flanagan looked sharply at the older man. 'And if you offer to share that then I'll cut off your ball sack and give them that instead.'

'Well, I never!' Goodfellow spluttered.

'We would never dream of wishing to share your good fortune.' Anna interceded before the fledgling partnership dissolved in front of her. 'But there may be times when we can be of assistance to one another – and I am sure we can all agree to that.'

Jack tuned out the conversation, instead directing his attention towards the diggings. To his eye, the pan looked more like an anthill disturbed into action by a predator than it did anything made by man. Few of the claims were being worked by an individual shifting for himself. The majority looked to be occupied by three or four hardy souls, while a few had as many as a dozen diggers and sorters, the sweaty, dirt-streaked faces of white men and women present alongside hundreds of black workers. And the effort was not reserved for adults alone. He saw great numbers of children spread across the claims, some tiny, others almost grown.

The mismatched collection of men, women and children were hard at work, each one moving with purpose. Some dug at the ground, attacking it with pick or shovel, while others disappeared from sight as they clambered down into the pits they had already excavated. But it was also becoming clear that the actual digging was just a part of the process of searching for the diamonds that were supposedly buried in the ground. At least half the figures he could see were working with great oblong sieves, each one about three feet wide by two deep, suspended on ropes from a simple frame made of two posts. The operators were shovelling in fresh soil, then swinging the sieves rapidly back and forth on the ropes, the spoil collected in great oblong trays underneath. As far as he could tell, it was sieved twice, through mesh of different sizes, before finally being dumped onto roughly made tables, where more workers, mainly women or older children, were waiting to spread it out with fat wooden scrapers. Even from so far away, Jack could see how the sorters dived into the debris scattered across the table, scrabbling through the dirt for the finds that had brought them to this dusty wilderness. There was a keen intent to their work; even so late in the day, he could see that they were sharp and focused, their tired fingers and gritty eyes still eager to find that last stone. Inspection done, the dust and rock was swept from the table before the next load was placed down.

'Jack?'

He started as Anna called out to him in a tone that told him it was not the first time she had asked for his attention.

'Shall we go? We should establish a base for the night. We can look to purchase our claims in the morning.'

'Yes, fine.' He tore his eyes from the diggings. From his initial inspection, it was clear he had a lot to learn. The skills he had practised on dozens of battlefields meant nothing here.

In the dry diggings of Du Toit's Pan, he would be just another hopeful fool with a shovel.

Chapter Nine

The group of five walked into the large open space at the centre of the diggers' town. It was mid-morning and the place was empty, the area clearly reserved for a special purpose. It was surrounded by the more substantial buildings of the town, but most were quiet, the few people abroad clearly in a hurry, as if they had no time to waste.

They had spent the night without shelter and with nothing for comfort other than the few things they had each brought with them. Any thought that there would be a welcome for the new arrivals had died an early death, the only lodgings full and not one soul willing to offer them a place to rest. They had been able to buy a decent enough dinner from a billiard room that ran a dining room on the side, but the prices were exorbitant, the venders charging rates that would make even the owners of Brown's blush.

But they had survived, none of them overly concerned by a night under the stars after the long journey up from Port Elizabeth. Yet the sunrise had brought with it new worries and now Jack was up close, he was not impressed with what he saw. He stood next to his four companions, his head turning in a slow circle as he contemplated his new surroundings. He could not recall its like, and he had been as far from civilisation as it was possible to be. The town was not squalid, unlike some of the places he had passed through, nor was it poor and unkempt. But it was clear that not one of its denizens cared a jot for it. It was a town only for as long as the diggings were being worked. A convenience. Nothing more. When they were done, it would be abandoned in a heartbeat.

From his vantage point, he could see a large marquee tent that, from the number of damaged people passing in and out, seemed to be some kind of hospital. A much more popular tent boasted a simple sign, the place claiming to be part theatre, part liquor bar. Around these two tents were some of the wooden or corrugated-iron buildings he had seen when he had first arrived. Most appeared to be some kind of store or another, all selling the few commodities the diggers needed to maintain their quest for riches. A couple had been given over to canteens to cater for those too tired or incapable to cook for themselves. Then there were at least two butchers that he could see, both quiet, a blacksmith, and half a dozen traders pertaining to carpentry. Some of the rest were dedicated to transport, and he was pleased to see a hand-painted sign advertising the services of JW Transport of King William's Town. On its other side was a tent guarded by two beefy-looking fellows. He guessed this would be the office of one of the many diamond merchants who flocked to the diggings to buy from the men who had prised the stones from the grip of the earth. Clearly this one was doing enough business to warrant a pair of sentries, although from his first cursory glance, he doubted either would put up much resistance if anyone decided to force entry. He marked the thought down. He was there to find diamonds. If he couldn't hack them from the ground, that didn't mean he necessarily had to go away empty-handed.

'Jack. Do you see that?'

He turned to see Goodfellow pointing towards a commotion near one of the few buildings to boast a second storey. It was a roughly made affair, with a simple veranda running around its ground floor, while the upper level boasted a small balcony that overlooked the space where they now stood. The windows were little more than openings hacked into the facade, while the door consisted of a few grey sheets sewn together. It was outside these that a small group of men had gathered. Even from a distance, it was clear they were not happy, their raised voices just about carrying to the five companions, while their wild gestures and dramatic flourishes could only denote anger.

'Come on,' Jack called to his companions as he started towards the altercation. He wanted to see what was what. He did not wait to see if they followed. He knew they would.

It did not take long to get close. From the flushed red faces and building commotion, it was clear to Jack that someone had gotten their drawers in a twist, and he wanted to know why.

'The Dutch bastards!'

He came to a halt in time to see one man throw his hat to the floor in disgust. The group did not look like much, not to his eye. There were perhaps twelve of them present. All were dressed in the worn-out clothes of diggers, the ubiquitous corduroy trousers and faded flannel shirts bleached by the sun and shrouded in dust. None were young, all sporting a fair amount of grey in their beards or in the hair on their head, if they had any.

Jack turned to one of the men on the periphery of the crowd. 'What's going on?' The fellow was old enough to have lost most of his hair, and his body was short and round, like a fat ball of butter. He was wearing a grey flannel undershirt, stained with sweat and salt, while the braces that should have been holding his trousers aloft were hanging down towards the dirt.

For a moment, he thought he would be ignored, the man he had accosted flashing him little more than a suspicious glance.

'Bloody Boers are at it again.' The answer came out of the side of the man's mouth as he concentrated his attention on the angry crowd in front of him.

'At what?' Jack tugged his elbow.

The man turned sharply, a retort forming on his lips. And there it stayed, as he thought better of whatever sharp words he had thought to throw at the stranger.

'They jumped a dozen claims at Bultfontein.'

Jack had seen the way the man's eyes had widened a fraction as he had taken in the scar on his face. It was not an uncommon reaction. He knew how he looked at first glance. He liked how he looked at first glance.

'Where's that?' He let go of the man's elbow as he saw he had the fellow's full attention.

'It's a farm a few miles over thataways.' The man gestured towards the far side of the town.

Jack had more questions. But he held them in check as he noticed another group heading their way. They looked different to the diggers who had thronged together in anger. Where the latter wore heavy, thick-soled boots, these newcomers wore a lighter, shorter boot not quite ankle high. Most sported a double-breasted jacket made from some sort of faded yellowy-brown fabric. All had wide-brimmed hats on their heads, so that there was an odd uniformity to their weathered clothing. Jack knew he was looking at a group of Boers, the men remarkably similar to the four who had shared the wagon up from Port Elizabeth.

'Fucking Dutchies.' The man next to Jack spat a thick wad of dirty green phlegm to the ground as he identified the men striding towards them.

Jack could feel the tension in the air as the Boers came closer. Yet the angry shouts and accusations died away, an eerie silence replacing the calls for action. His hand instinctively crept to the holstered revolver he still wore, his fingers sliding over the clasp, ready to snap it open. The shouting might have quietened down, but in his experience that did not mean anything, and he resolved to be prepared for whatever might happen.

'Get behind me,' he whispered to Anna, his left hand reaching across to guide her.

She did as she was told without a murmur.

He scanned the men around him, looking for anyone else readying a weapon. To his surprise, he alone was carrying a handgun, the rest of the crowd unarmed. The lack of firepower made him pause. He did not know the rules here, or what was expected when angry mob met angry mob.

He was not the only one sensing that he might be reading the situation badly. Anna reached forward and took his hand, which was hovering over his holster, then guided it away.

'You boys got a problem?' One of the Boers stepped forward. He was clearly their leader. His beard was fully grey, as was the tangled mop of hair on his head. He was tanned and weathered, and there were deep wrinkles around his pale blue eyes, evidence of a lifetime spent outdoors.

'They say you jumped the claims at Bultfontein.' The accusation came from deep in the crowd.

'Says who?' The Boer stood easy, hands on hips as he addressed the crowd.

'People who was there.'

He nodded. 'And they're right. We took those claims. If any of you good folk have a problem with that, then you're welcome to come talk to me about it.' His English was good, but he spoke with a thick accent that coloured the words, making them sound short and clipped.

Again Jack looked around him, studying the faces of the crowd. He was expecting to see a growing anger as the Boer leader happily confessed to doing exactly what he was being accused of. He saw nothing of the sort, the expressions on the diggers' faces more calculating than furious.

'Bultfontein was open for claim. Same as here.' The Boer spoke calmly and evenly, pitching his voice loudly enough so that all could hear. 'We'll pay the same ten shillings a month per claim as we do here. Same rights for all, too. Anyone wanting a claim can buy one.'

He paused, taking a moment to run his eye over the crowd. Then he turned, beckoning to his followers.

The crowd murmured as the Boers walked away. But the anger had subsided, the issue settled quickly and easily.

Jack noted it all. He had a lot to learn; the confrontation here showed just how little he understood of life in the diggings. There had been no threat of violence or strong men looking to take power. It was surprising, refreshing even.

Already the crowd was beginning to disperse, the men returning to their own claims. Jack and his four companions were left standing there, a rock in a stream of people.

'It looks like that's the place we need.' Goodfellow plucked at Jack's sleeve, pointing towards what looked to be some sort of office, based in a building fabricated from corrugated iron.

Jack agreed. It was time to make their arrival official.

It was gloomy inside the office, and it took several long moments for his eyes to adjust after the bright morning sunlight outside. Not far from the door was a plank of wood thrown across a pair of trestles to form a makeshift desk. It was covered with numerous heaps of paper, mostly forms to Jack's eye, but also an odd-looking assortment of letters and a neat stack of newspapers called *The Diamond News*, along with half a dozen inkwells and as many steel pens. In the middle of the desk was a thick iron cash box.

'Can I help you good folk?'

The man seated behind the desk greeted the group the moment they walked inside. He was not much to look at. He was fat, his bulbous belly resting against the plank, and was dressed in a simple shirt that might once have been blue but was now a pale grey that matched his hair, or at least what was left of it. The remains clung bravely to the sides of his skull, the dome completely bare save for a fine fluff. Perhaps to make up for the lack of hair on his head, he had tried to grow a beard, but had succeeded in producing something that might on a good day be passed off as a goatee with matching moustache, but on that morning looked more like the first scruffy hairs of adolescence under a boy's arms.

'Yes.' Jack stepped towards him. 'We're here to purchase a claim. Two, if possible.'

'I see.' The clerk seemed tired already. Clearly the single request had exhausted him. 'Two, you say?'

'If we can.'

'Oh, you can have as many as you like,' he muttered under his breath. Exhaling loudly, he twisted awkwardly in his seat and reached for a stack of papers a foot from his podgy right hand. He took a moment to rifle through them, ink-stained finger flicking with practised ease. Then, with a loud tut, he selected one sheet of paper and then another.

'These will do you. Two claims adjacent on the far side of the diggings.' He looked down his nose as he scanned the forms, eyes narrowing at the squiggles of tight handwriting that covered them, then tossed them towards Jack.

Jack bit his tongue at the clerk's sloppiness. As tempting as it was to snap at the man, it would achieve nothing save to potentially delay the purchase of their first claims.

Placing the forms on the table in front of him, he started to read, taking his time, his finger running along the pencil marks on the simple sheet of paper. He sensed Anna leaning forward to do the same, and he was glad that she did. He could read and write, one of the few legacies his mother had left him that he appreciated, but he was slow, and he was grateful for a second pair of eyes on the official documents.

Not that there was much for them to read. The legal title to the claims was written in a fine, flowery script, with gaps left for names to be inserted. The last owner's name had been erased, but he could just about make out that he had been one William Kelly. But he could also see the faint marks and scrubbed-out letters of at least two names that had gone before. Clearly they were not to be the first owners of these small patches of land.

'Both claims are thirty foot square. Market price is ten pounds plus one shilling to register it in your name. Then you pay ten shillings a month for the digging licence.' The clerk rattled off the details without looking at any of them, the lines clearly ones he had spoken a hundred times before.

Jack turned to look at Clarke. 'That sound right?'

Clarke shrugged. 'About right, mate, yes.'

'About?' Jack frowned. Clarke was supposed to be the expert on the process.

'They're all the same, mate.' The Australian laughed at his reaction. 'Just pay the man.'

'Fine.' Jack did not take kindly to being told what to do, especially when it involved spending a chunk of their remaining funds, but he turned to face the clerk all the same. 'We'll take them.'

'Write your name in the gap, then sign at the bottom.' The clerk tossed a pencil over. 'Then it's yours.'

Jack picked up the pencil. For a moment he pictured himself reaching forward and stabbing the point directly into the clerk's right eye to see if that would engender a more polite response. But instead, he simply pulled the first claim towards him and dutifully wrote his name down carefully before signing as he had been told.

He had yet to pay the clerk, but he had filled out the simple paperwork.

The claim was theirs.

Chapter Ten

'What do you think?'

'It doesn't look like much.' Jack answered Anna's question honestly as they contemplated the claim they had bought. The two of them were alone. Goodfellow and Flanagan were nearby, inspecting their own claim, but Clarke had left them to it, preferring to go off to discover the fate of the mates he had left behind.

The thirty-foot square had been dug down to a depth of no more than four feet across two thirds of its surface area, and there were two parallel shafts close together, both about five feet deep, the depth a man working alone could reach before he needed help.

'It looks like a bloody grave.'

'At least it's one big enough for us both.' Anna sighed. 'I wonder what happened to the previous owner.'

'I don't care what happened to him. So long as we don't dig the poor bugger up.' Jack grunted at his own gallows humour, then jumped down into the depression dug into the surface of the claim. His boots hit the compacted earth with a thud, and he felt the reverberation of the impact judder up through his legs and into his hips. 'Bugger me, but it's hard.' It was difficult to remain upbeat, and his back was already aching at the thought of the toil that was to come when he started attempting to dig into what seemed to be rock-hard soil.

He bent low and scraped up a handful of dirt, his fingers forced to scrabble to make an impression on the impossibly hard surface. He held it tight, squeezing it then rubbing it between his hands. The cursory examination told him nothing, his knowledge of soil inadequate to say the least. He let the handful pour slowly away through his fingers. Once broken up, it was dusty and dry, the fine pale dirt mixed with small pebbles. From where he was standing, he could see a number of much larger rocks peppered across the site that were clearly too big to be moved.

From his conversations with Clarke, he had learned that some of the luckier diggers had found diamonds in the upper-most layer of the friable soil, but it was already clear that whoever had owned the claim before them had searched that thoroughly. The best and biggest stones were said to be buried under a layer of what Clarke had said was mainly limestone. The Australian had claimed that to find those stones required just the small matter of digging down a couple of feet. It appeared that the previous owner had only got down that far in two places, and that was enough to give Jack hope. One thing was clear. They would need to work hard. From what he had already seen on other claims, some diggers were going way down, far below the surface, some thirty to forty feet or more, but as he squatted in the dust, he could not begin to see how he could do that working with just Clarke and Anna to assist. It would take months of back-breaking toil to get to even half that depth, with only a shovel and pick at his disposal.

'Are you sure this is a good idea?' He was unable to keep a hint of doubt from creeping into his tone.

'It's a bit late to ask that now.' Anna tried to sound light-hearted, but her expression was downcast. 'We need to hold to the plan, Jack. We work this claim. We find enough stones. We sell them, then we move on.'

'Yes, ma'am.' He knuckled his forehead as any good servant would when receiving instructions from their mistress. She made it sound wonderfully simple, but he knew it would not be. Not in any way, shape or form.

She laughed. 'I am pleased to see you remember your place.'

Jack contemplated the figure standing above him. 'If only your uncle could see you now.'

'He would damn me for a fool.'

'Maybe he would be right.' He looked down and scuffed a toe into the soil. It barely left a mark. He turned around slowly, eyes panning over every inch of the claim, taking in the land that he had bought. He saw nothing new, save for a spoil heap over in one corner. Other than the two shafts, it was the only real feature on the claim, and so he wandered over towards it.

'No. He would be wrong.' Anna jumped down into the pit and started to investigate the soil for herself, bending over at the waist then scratching at the ground around her boots.

'It wouldn't be the first time,' Jack replied without taking his eyes from the heap of spoil. He had argued with Sir Sam more than once, believing the expedition's leader to be taking the wrong approach as he tried to force the flotilla further and further down the Nile. It had earned him nothing more than a rapid dismissal.

His thoughts of the hardships endured at Sir Sam's orders disappeared as he spied something glittering in the soil that had been excavated from the ground. He approached the spoil heap and squatted on his haunches. The mismatched pile of pebbles and mud was not much to look it. It must have been discarded by whoever who had worked the claim before them. That would only have happened once it had been sieved at least twice and checked over for anything that might have been missed. It was little more than valueless crud that was not worth looking at, not really, except for that tantalising glint that had him scrabbling at the soil like a child attacking the sand at Camber.

He knew the process that had created the spoil heap well enough, Clarke's lessons on the journey up from Port Elizabeth describing it at great length. The dirt was hacked from the ground, then broken down into something that could be hauled away by bucket. The newly removed dirt was sieved, first to remove the larger stones that could damage the equipment that would follow, then through the finer mesh of a second sieve. Next, the stones and rocks large enough to be of interest were removed from the sieve and dumped onto the sorting table. They had already decided that this would be Anna's domain, while the digging and sieving would be down to Jack and Clarke. She would spread out the dirt with a scraper, then pick through the mix of limestone, rubies, carbon, chalk, green trap, ilmenite, peridot, talc, and maybe, just maybe, the one object every digger was there to find: diamonds. Only when every load had been thoroughly checked would it be dumped onto the spoil heap and the whole process repeated.

The object that had caught his eye, whatever it was, was bright enough to make his heart beat a little bit faster. It was almost completely buried, and so he started to pick at the earth around it with his nails. The spoil heap was as hard as rock, the discarded soil long since baked hard by the sun, but quarter-inch by quarter-inch, he forced a narrow trough around the object.

'Have you found something, Jack?' Anna had spotted what he was doing and was immediately intrigued.

'I'm not sure,' he answered distractedly, his attention focused on his task.

'Do you think—'

'Hush.' He cut her off in mid flow. He had his fingers on the prize. His heartbeat was beginning to race. It couldn't be this easy. Not here. Not where every man had the keenest eye for anything that glittered. He reckoned the diggers might be broken-down souls, battered and bruised by months of digging, but they would have missed nothing. And yet the object was there. Glittering. Silent. Just waiting to be found.

It came away, and he held it up, his breath catching in his chest.

'What is it?'

Ignoring Anna's eager question, he turned it around and around in his hand. He had never seen its like before. Its dark surface was shiny, and it was both heavy and dense. He felt the irregular shape on his palm. If he did not know better, he would say some odd fellow had spent at least a month polishing a tiny lump of coal. He did not know what it was, but he knew what it was not.

'Here.' He tossed it up to Anna, who snatched it from the air.

She looked it over, a momentary flash of excitement fading fast.

'What do you think it is?' Jack asked as he straightened up then arched his back, stretching away the ache.

'Carbon.'

He grunted in agreement. Clarke had told them there was plenty of carbon to be found on the claims. It was near worthless, although he was aware of one buyer for it at the diggings. At best it would fetch five shillings per ounce. Not much reward, for sure, but better than nothing. The claims were also said to produce a fair amount of deep red garnets that the diggers called rubies, and even some green stones like emeralds. None were worth even a fraction of the price of a single diamond. Those prices were ingrained in their brains now, the subject of hours of conversation on the wagon. A seven-and-a-half-carat diamond would be worth something close to one hundred and fifty pounds. Such an amount would be a fitting reward for the toil it took to hack the stone from the ground. Most of the finds were much smaller, less than a single carat, but they would still produce enough income for a digger to keep at it as they tried to find the big one. For that was the dream shared by every digger.

Tales of such finds were talked of incessantly. A thirty-carat diamond would be worth two and a half thousand pounds, a veritable fortune to the men at the diggings, who worked from dawn to dusk in their threadbare clothes fuelled by little more than rice, beans and hope. And if the hope of a thirty-carat diamond was not sufficient, there was more. These were the finds that were spoken of in reverential tones, diamonds so large they commanded an almost unimaginable price. Clarke spoke often of one found by a friend of his, an enormous ninety carats that he stated had been worth some ten thousand pounds. Jack had no idea if the tale was true, but it was enough to inspire awe. And enough to inspire a steady stream of new arrivals to come to the dry diggings on a quest to find their own fortune.

'Keep it.' Anna held up the lump of carbon as if it were some sort of trophy. 'It's our first find. It might bring us luck.'

Jack shook his head at the superstitious folly. 'Well, let's hope.' It was all the acknowledgement he would give to the notion of needing luck. 'But one thing is for certain. We need to find something to sell quick sharp. We barely have a brass farthing to our name any more.'

'We will.' Anna brought the rock to her lips, giving it the briefest of kisses before tossing it towards Jack. 'Here, catch,' she called.

Jack lost sight of the dark shape as it came towards him, and he fumbled the catch, dropping the rock to the ground. He bent down to retrieve it, moving sharply to cover his embarrassment.

'Shit,' he hissed as the movement jarred his back. He snatched the rock from the ground even as he winced with the sudden pain. For a moment he was tempted to throw it away, but instead he put it in his pocket.

'Poor Jack.' Anna saw his pained expression. 'Your back?'

'Yes. Sweet Jesus.' He spoke through gritted teeth.

'Well, that's no good. We haven't even started yet.'

'Tell me about it.' He rubbed the small of his back, then shook his head. There was no point complaining. Not now.

'We can hire some workers. Clarke says there are plenty of folk here looking for engagement,' suggested Anna.

'No.' Jack sucked down a deep breath as he walked to the far side of the claim. 'We'd burn through what little money we have left, and then what would we do?'

'But we might find something quicker if we employ others to help us dig.'

He snorted. Anna had been bitten by the diamond bug. 'We

might. Or we might not. Or we might find one and have some sneaky bastard slip it into their arsehole before we ever even see it.'

It was Anna's turn to grimace. 'I am sure there are other places they could hide it.'

Jack shook his head at such naivety. 'There's nowhere as safe as shoving something where the sun don't shine.'

'Spoken like a true gentleman.' She laughed.

Jack could not help smiling. He liked to make Anna laugh. He scrambled up the side of the claim and back onto the higher ground.

'So it's going to be just the three of us.' Anna climbed out too, then reached down to dust some soil from her trousers.

'If that bloody Australian stays around.' Jack had not grown fond of Clarke, despite so many hours spent in his company. He had met enough chancers over the years to know one when he saw one, and there was something decidedly shifty about the Australian.

'You don't think he will stick with us?'

'No. At least not for long. He'll want his own claim again, or he'll find another partner. He's not the sort to work for someone else, and he won't put the effort in for just a quarter share. He'll want more than that. We were a free ticket to get him up here, nothing more.'

'You have a low opinion of people, Jack,' Anna chided him.

'It's just what I've seen, that's all.'

'Maybe he will prove you wrong.'

'Maybe.' But Jack was not convinced.

'Well, if you think he will leave, then we had best learn all we can before he does.'

'We had.' Jack could only agree. 'And then it will be just me and you, love.' He grinned at the idea. He could think of no one better to share the adventure with than the niece of one of Britain's most famous explorers.

'For now, and for always.' Anna spoke the words quietly before laying her head against Jack's chest.

'Yes.' Jack did not need to say more. But a dark thought that had been lurking in the bowels of his mind made its presence felt. He might wish with every fibre of his being that they could be together, but he knew it was not in his power to make it come to pass. That honour belonged to Fate and Fate alone. And she had never been a kind mistress. Not to him.

Not ever.

Chapter Eleven

Jack used the handle of a broken shovel to poke the fire into life, wincing as it chafed against the blisters on his hand. It had been a hard first week, and his hands had been rubbed raw by the hours spent using a pick or shovel on their claim. He had tried wrapping them in bandages to spare himself some of the pain, but nothing he did lasted through the first hour, and so he had just suffered. Anna treated them every night with carbolic ointment to stop them festering. Judging by the state of the other diggers they had seen, even the slightest scratch could soon become an open sore; nearly every man they came across was covered with small, oozing wounds or huge greeny-blue boils. She believed the inevitable cuts and scratches were made worse by the lime dust that was ever present in the diggings, and she was doing her best to keep all their wounds clean.

'Morning, mate.'

Jack looked up to see Clarke emerging from his tent. 'You're still here, then?'

'I'm not going anywhere.' Clarke scoffed at Jack's greeting. 'Least not till I'm good and bloody ready.'

Jack bit his tongue. The Australian never failed to nettle him, even with just his presence. He did not really know why, but he put it down to the man's accent, the way every sentence finished as though it was a question worming its way into his brain until he was almost ready to throttle Clarke within a minute of his starting to speak. Instead of committing an early-morning murder, he looked at a tiny, dusty black bird with half-white feathers on its wings. The small creature was standing on the tip of their tent pole, singing for all it was worth.

'Is there tea on yet, Jack?'

'No, not yet.' Jack fought the urge to sigh as Goodfellow hove into view. As he did every morning, the Englishman was brandishing a toasting fork in one hand and a half-eaten loaf of bread in the other.

'Capital. Then we shall have toast first and tea second.' Goodfellow slumped onto a low stool on the other side of the fire and pulled a short knife from his pocket, which he used to hack enthusiastically at his loaf. 'At least I have some butter left.' He reached into a pocket and produced a paper-wrapped bundle that he opened carefully before placing it by his boot. 'Come on then, Jack. Let's get that fire going properly, shall we? A bit more kindling should do the trick.'

Jack bit back a sharp retort. He was a boy from a metropolis, but he knew how to light a fire.

'Ah, new blood!' Goodfellow clapped as something caught his attention.

Jack looked up to see a gaggle of men walking past their part of the encampment. Their newly arrived status was obvious to anyone who cared to look, their dust-free, clean appearance marking them out. Sometimes as many as two hundred people arrived at the diggings in a single day. The

encampment was growing fast, and new stores, and even a
hotel, had started trading that week.

'Oh dear, my poor fellow. Here, sit down and rest.'

Jack tore his gaze from the new arrivals to see that Flanagan
had come to join them. The Londoner was holding his head
and looked just about ready to puke.

'Good night, was it?' Jack asked him. One of the taverns
had attracted a travelling concert party the night before. Jack
and Anna had not gone, preferring to hold on to as much of
their dwindling supply of money as they could, but Goodfellow
and Flanagan had.

Flanagan said nothing, instead sitting down next to
Goodfellow before burying his head in his hands.

'I rather think my young friend overindulged a little,'
Goodfellow answered for his partner.

'Can't he take his beer?' Jack teased. He was in a crabby
mood himself that morning, but it was helping to see the
younger man suffering.

'Stow it,' came the muffled reply from behind Flanagan's
hands.

Jack laughed. 'You need a good dose of soot, lad. Or some
eels.'

'I think I'm going to puke.' Flanagan lifted his head long
enough to scowl at him before hiding it away again.

'Come on, a good mug of tea, some of Goodfellow's toast
and you'll be as right as rain,' Jack said cheerfully. 'Surely this
isn't the first time you've got corned?'

'I wish.' Flanagan raised his head again, a wan but proud
smile on his face. 'If you'd drunk as much as I did last night, I
doubt you'd be so fucking chipper this morning.'

'What did you drink? A whole pint of ale?' Jack laughed

again as he poked the sickly young bear.

'Jack, leave the poor boy alone.' Anna pushed past the flaps to their tent and emerged into the morning light. 'A good drink of water will see you right, Master Flanagan. Be sure to purify it first, mind.'

'Thank you, miss.'

Jack watched the formal byplay between the two. Flanagan was obviously a rogue, but he never failed to be polite when speaking to Anna.

'I wouldn't drink the water, chum.' He offered his own advice. 'Although you are from south of the river, aren't you, so maybe you'll be all right. You're all queer coves down there.' Flanagan hailed from Southwark. It was barely a few miles from Whitechapel, but it might as well have been a hundred, and Jack had only been there once or twice in all the time he had lived in London.

'Did you live in Southwark all your life?' Anna asked. 'Hurry up, Jack, get the fire going,' she ordered as she waited for Flanagan to reply.

Flanagan hesitated. He had revealed little of his former life. 'Yes, miss.' He rubbed his head as he spoke.

'With your family?'

'With my ma, miss. Until she passed.'

'What happened to you then?' Anna smiled as she tried to draw the young man out.

'I was in the workhouse, for a bit anyways.'

Jack nodded. He had known orphans who had been taken to the local workhouse. It was not a fate he would wish on anyone, the life they endured on the charity of the parish brutal and harsh. If Flanagan had not stayed there for long, Jack didn't blame him one jot.

'What did you do then?' he asked.

'This and that. There was a group of us. We looked after one another, you know how it is.'

Jack did. He was well aware of the gangs of urchins who would rob and steal to feed themselves. None lasted long. 'Then what happened?'

'We got nabbed. Some old bastard of a beak sent us to Botany Bay.'

Jack grunted. It was a familiar story. The boys who fended for themselves either died or were arrested. When that happened, a sentence of transportation usually followed, the young miscreants sent to the distant penal colonies in Australia.

'So how did you find yourself here?'

'I got away.' Flanagan looked shifty as he answered.

Jack did not probe any deeper. Transportation was a grim fate. He would not blame Flanagan for whatever he had had to do to earn his freedom.

'I stowed away on another ship. Stayed on it for nearly four years. The master was a decent bloke. Let me work.' The young man's bloodshot eyes scanned his meagre audience. 'I jumped ship 'bout a year ago.'

'And now here you are.' Anna brought the tale to a conclusion to spare Flanagan any more questions. 'We are glad you are here, Mr Flanagan.' She dipped her head as she beamed at him.

'Indeed we are!' Goodfellow chimed in. He had said nothing for a while, concentrating on slicing his bread. 'Come on, Jack, do something about this bloody fire. It's as cold as a spinster's heart.'

'Excuse me, miss.'

Jack was spared any more fire-building advice as a young

woman came close and asked for Anna's attention. A child was with her, holding tight to her mother's skirts, her grubby face half buried and hidden away.

'Can I help you?' Anna rose out of her seat, her face creasing with concern.

'It's my little one, miss. She's got the trots something bad. They said you might be able to help us.' The woman did not look well herself. Her skin was pale, and huge dark bags hung under her eyes.

'Yes, of course.' Anna was already turning to go back into the tent for her medicine chest when Jack reached up to clasp her around the arm and hold her in place.

'Who is "they" when they are at home?' He stood as he fired the question at the new arrival.

'Old Arbuthnot. He was telling everyone that this nice lady had helped him.'

Jack scowled. Anna had tended to the old man two days earlier, when she had spotted the running sores on his face. It appeared her reputation was spreading fast. Too fast for his liking.

'We're not here to help any Tom, Dick or bloody Harry that wanders along, love.'

'Jack!' Anna was having none of it, and she pulled her arm out of his grip. 'Of course I'll help you.' She cocked her head as she studied the woman. 'I'll get some sarsaparilla for you too. You look done in.'

'You should go easy.' Jack spoke softly, the words for Anna alone.

'These people need my help, Jack.'

He opened his mouth to say more, but he could see the defiance on her face. He would not stop her from helping the woman and her child, just as he knew he would not stop her helping any waif or stray who came to her. It was who she was. But he would make sure she knew the price she might be paying. 'What if we need those medicines, Anna? We can't afford to buy more until we start finding something we can sell.' Their first week in the claim had not been productive. It was still very early days, but it was not a good omen, and they were both worried.

But Anna was not swayed by his argument.

'These people need my help, Jack. None of them know how to take care of themselves. These damned diggings are consuming them. We have the medicines and I will not husband them for a day that may or may not come when they are needed now. I do not care what it costs.'

'You know what you're doing.' Jack ceded ground fast. 'But hold some back just in case we need it ourselves. Otherwise you must do whatever you see fit.'

'Thank you, Jack.' Anna reached out to clasp his hand for a moment, then ducked low and went inside the tent.

Jack stepped back. He would not stand in her way.

Not now, and not ever.

Chapter Twelve

Jack lowered the pick, resting it against his leg, and studied his right hand. A fat new blister glistened in the centre of his palm. It was about the size of a sixpence and it throbbed incessantly, red raw, burning, and bloated with fluid inside.

'Bugger.' Poking the painful lump of flesh elicited the curse, the stab of pain flaring bright. It hurt enough for him to lift his hand to his mouth, teeth bared, and then he bit into the nugget, pulling apart his own flesh. As soon as the taste of bitter liquid touched his lips, he pulled away, breath hissing from his mouth.

A quick glance told him his simple doctoring had worked, the skin at least now flattened even if the burning sensation was stronger. Spitting on his hand, he picked up the pick and went back to work. A blister was no excuse to linger. His rudimentary attempt to lessen the pain was preferable to showing it to Anna, who would insist on slathering it with some lotion or potion that he knew from bitter experience would hurt more than simply gripping the pickaxe and getting on with it. She could treat it at the end of the day, but for now it could be ignored.

He swung hard, the tip of the pick striking the ground with a satisfying crack, sending a few splinters of sun-hardened earth skittering away as the thin crevasse he was working on widened another fraction of an inch. He was learning to be patient, he knew it would take hours of toil to open up the new seam. As he eased back into the regular motion of working the ground, Jack let his mind empty, not even the searing pain in his palm enough to divert him. The rhythm came quickly now, his body as familiar with the action as it had once been with the rigid routine of reloading a musket. Yet now his enemy was the ground, his mind plotting a route below the surface as it once had planned a way to outflank an entrenched enemy.

But that was not to say there was no danger.

Jack heard the sound of a wagon on the move. It was a regular racket around the claims, diggers always moving supplies or equipment between the Pan's centre to their working claims. They consumed all manner of timber in myriad fashions, from reinforcing the sides of a deepening shaft, to constructing rudimentary frames, towers and rigging to pull buckets from a pit hacked deep. There was a constant need for picks, pails, shovels and sieves, all of which broke frequently from constant use. Few would want to haul such items to the claims on their aching backs, and so wagons picked their way back and forth, the drivers avoiding the hundreds of pits and shafts that were scattered throughout the working ground. It was not an easy task and, in many places, there was just no way of knowing where optimistic diggers had worked horizontally out from their claim, the borders between them either ignored or forgotten once a shaft was driven deep under the surface. Jack had already seen at least four wagons sink deep into ground that had collapsed around their wheels as they had driven over a hidden gallery. It was just one of the dangers faced by the diggers. In their first week, Jack and Anna had stood by and watched as the corpse of an Irishman was pulled from the earth and stones, just two days after his shaft had collapsed under the weight of a wagon bearing barrels of water.

So it was with an anxious eye that Jack followed the path of what he saw was a small, two-wheeled bounder, his attention fixed on the driver as he worked the donkey pulling the dog-cart forward, his long whip snapping out to direct the beast around the far corner of Flanagan's and Goodfellow's claim. The cart was small compared to many of the other wagons, but that did not make it any less of a danger to the diggers working down in the bowels of the earth.

'Hey, take care there!' Jack shouted the warning to the driver as the man tried to negotiate a turn that took his nearside wheel dangerously close to the edge of a shaft that Jack knew their neighbours had started working on only a day previously. It had been begun by the claim's previous owner and it ran deep, at least fifteen feet down into the dry soil. He knew Flanagan and Goodfellow were working in the depths together, the shaft wide enough for one man to dig whilst the other shovelled the spoil into tin buckets.

His warning was ignored, the driver long immune to the shouting that marked every journey he took through the diggings. The small cart came on, the driver craning his neck forward to see just how close he was cutting the turn, even as he flicked his whip against the ears of his donkey. The right-hand side wheel caught the edge of the pit, a cascade of soil falling into the workings, an avalanche of dirt and stone that would surely have struck the men working so far below ground, their first notion of sudden danger the stinging impact of gravel raining down on their heads.

Jack lowered his pickaxe, an icy hand of dread tickling the back of his neck.

The dog-cart's driver tried to correct his course, even going so far as to half-stand, half-crouch, as he hauled on the reins. The cart lurched to the left, the donkey reacting to the whip and twisting off course. It almost worked.

'Shit.' There was just time for Jack to hiss the word before the right wheel of the dog-cart slipped over the edge of the pit.

For one terrible drawn-out moment the cart seemed to stop moving, the right-hand wheel hanging in space. Then the whole thing disappeared over the edge. It went quickly, the wagon crashing end-first into the pit, great chunks of soil torn from the edges as it fell.

Jack was moving even before he heard the driver's despairing cry. Dropping his pick, he ran across his own claim.

'Anna! Look lively now.' The words came quickly as he darted across to her. But Anna was already on her feet, the sieve she had been using discarded in a heartbeat.

He grabbed her hand and together they ran onto their neighbour's claim. Ahead, the air was filled with the terrified shrieks of the donkey. The poor beast had been powerless to hold fast against the combined weight of the dog-cart and its driver.

'There!' Jack saw a bloodied hand emerge over the edge of the pit. He charged towards it, sliding to a halt on his knees, then reached forward to grab hold. A sharp pain shot through his back as he took up the man's weight, then he was tumbling backwards as he dragged Flanagan up and over the lip of the pit.

'Fucking hell!' The younger man gasped as he sprawled on the ground. He was covered in dust and grime, and a thin river of blood tracked down the side of his face, carving a path through the muck.

Jack did not let his fellow Londoner lie. Jumping to his feet, he grasped the front of Flanagan's shirt and shook him hard as he fired a question into the lad's face. 'Where's Goodfellow?'

'He's still down there!' Flanagan pointed to the pit.

Jack followed the direction of Flanagan's finger, but he could see nothing. With his heart in his mouth, he crept closer to the edge of the pit, neck craning forward as he tried to look down into its depths without getting too close to the friable soil at its edge. He would do no one any good if he followed the cart over the edge.

He got close enough to be able to look down into the gloom. There was no sign of either the driver or of Goodfellow himself.

'Shit.' The dog-cart was not huge, but the force of it landing on your head fifteen feet down in the earth was more than enough to kill.

Anna crouched over Flanagan, fingers reaching out to run over his scalp as she quickly checked for the source of the blood on his face.

'This is just a scratch. We've got to get Goodfellow out.' As soon as she had given her verdict, she pulled Flanagan to his feet and pushed him back towards the edge of the pit.

'I'm not going back down there.' Flanagan wiped the back of his hand across his lips, smearing away dust and debris before his own fingers searched for the wound on his head. 'Besides, I'm bloody injured, aren't I just.'

'You're fine,' Jack growled, then grabbed Flanagan's elbow and steered him forward to inspect the pit.

They were greeted by a tangle of twisted reins and broken wood. The cart itself was at the bottom of the shaft, lying on its broken right wheel. On top of it, the donkey lay sprawled, the poor beast kicking this way and that as it tried to get up, an act made futile by a front leg that was clearly broken, the lower half of the limb twisted at an obscene angle. There was no sight of the cart's driver. Or Goodfellow.

'Jack. I'll get help.' Anna reached out to touch Jack's arm before she turned and ran towards the claim on the far side of the one Goodfellow and Flanagan worked.

Jack watched her go. They knew the owner of the claim by sight, if not by name, and they had seen at least four men digging there most days. Now those diggers would have to be pressed into a makeshift rescue party. But it would take time for even someone as persuasive as Anna to organise them and get them moving. And time was in short supply, every minute surely precious. If Goodfellow or the cart's driver was badly hurt, they could be dead before Anna returned. So, something had to be done.

And done immediately.

He turned to Flanagan, his mind racing. 'Have you got a gun up here?' He fired the question at Flanagan.

'No!' Flanagan pulled a face. 'Who the fuck are you going to shoot?'

'That poor bloody animal!' Jack pointed at the donkey that was still writhing on top of the ruined cart, its plaintive wails coming without pause as it continued its desperate bid to stand.

Jack sighed. His own revolver was back on his own claim. It would take time to get it. Time he did not have.

'Fine.' Jack gripped the short knife in his pocket. 'Right,

come on.' He dropped down onto his knees, twisting around as he prepared to clamber down into the shaft.

'You're a fucking lunatic, mate. I'm not going back down there.' Flanagan took a step away from the edge. 'We need to wait for some other bods to get here.'

'For fuck's sake.' Jack pushed himself back to his feet, face set like thunder.

'I said—'

Jack gave Flanagan no time to complete his sentence. Instead, he grabbed the front of the lad's grime-streaked shirt and turned a half-circle, reversing their positions.

'Now get down there before I push you over the fucking edge.' He gave his command in a tone wrapped in iron.

'I'm not—'

Jack jerked his arms forward as Flanagan made to complain again, as if about to push the young Londoner over the edge. He stopped just short of doing so, pulling Flanagan sharply back towards him.

'Don't bloody push it. Your mate is down there, and he needs our help. And we're going to give it to him. You get me?'

'Alright, chum.' Flanagan's face was pale as he gave in. 'Keep your fucking hair on.' Still, he turned around, going down onto his knees as he prepared to do as he had been told. 'Fucking lunatic.'

'Just get on with it.' Jack had no patience for the lad's mutterings.

Flanagan slipped easily over the edge, his boots reaching down to the toeholds hacked into the face of the shaft. A moment later he was descending, his head disappearing from sight.

Jack took a moment to glance around, eager to see if Anna

was on her way back with help. He saw nothing and no one. And so, he followed Flanagan over the edge.

Unlike the younger Londoner, Jack moved slowly and carefully, holding his weight on his arms until he could force the tips of his boots into the narrow clefts cut into the side of the shaft. Only when he was sure that he had a firm grip did he begin to lower himself down into the gloom.

The smell of the earth was rich in his nostrils, the aroma laced with the taint of damp. He went down gradually, making sure of each foothold and handhold. It would do no one any good if he rushed and fell. If he did, he would surely break his leg or his back. Then there would be another casualty to be rescued and the two men already down in the depths of the pit would see their own hopes of safety dashed.

He reached the lowest sets of holds then looked down. It was a drop of barely three feet. Nothing to fear on a normal day and a jump he would usually have made without thought. But this was no ordinary day and now the ground of the pit was littered with debris and he could easily turn an ankle or worse.

Yet time was slipping away, and he had long ago learned to put fear to one side and just do what had to be done. No matter that he was in a hole in the ground and not on a battlefield, the rule held good.

'Fuck it.' He hissed the words then dropped.

He hit the ground a heartbeat later, stumbling forward, his right leg giving way as his boot hit a fallen rock. For one horrible moment, he thought his ankle would snap, but by some miracle it held and he found his footing.

He was down. And he was safe. For now.

There was little room to move and he found himself pressed

close to Flanagan who was clearly waiting for his arrival before he moved so much as a single inch.

'Do you see either of them?' Jack hissed the question, breath rasping after the effort of the climb.

'I see that poor sod!' Flanagan jerked his head in lieu of pointing.

Jack followed his gaze. He saw the cart's driver immediately. The fellow could not have been much older than Flanagan himself, a young face staring back at Jack beneath a shock of curly blond hair, and covered with one of the thinnest beards Jack had seen. It was a beard the man would never grow. His neck was clearly broken, his head and its unruly curls twisted at an impossible angle whilst sightless eyes looked up at his would-be rescuers, his tongue lolling out over his lips.

'What about Goodfellow?'

'Do you see him?' The sarcastic answer came back at Jack.

'He must be underneath the cart.' Jack took a deep breath as he made the ominous verdict. 'Goodfellow! Do you hear us, man?'

But the pit was silent, save for the soft whimpers of the donkey. The animal was tiring. 'Right.' Jack paused, fishing his pocketknife out then pressing it into Flanagan's hand. 'Deal with that poor creature first.'

'What?' Flanagan looked at Jack in alarm. 'You want me to kill it?'

'No, I want you to dance with it. Of course I want you to kill it. It's broken its leg and it needs to be put out of its misery.'

Flanagan looked back at Jack with wide eyes. 'I ain't killed anything before,' he confessed. 'Least of all a fucking donkey.'

'Well, it's high time you started.'

'How do I do it?'

'Cut its neck. That should do it.' Jack gave the grim instruction.

'Can't you—'

'No, you're closer. And I need to look for Goodfellow in all this shite. Unless you'd rather crawl under there?' Jack pointed towards the twisted remains of the cart.

'No. Fine. I'll do it.' Flanagan's Adam's apple bobbed up and down. 'Just cut its throat, you say?'

'Yes. Push deep and hard, else you'll get the blade stuck.'

'Right.' Flanagan's eyes betrayed his horror. Yet, to his credit, he still did as he was told, clambering up on top of the wrecked cart as he started to pick a careful and slow path towards the badly injured animal that had finally fallen silent. It lay still now, its suffering marked only by the occasional whinny of distress.

In the half light, Jack could finally see more of what lay ahead. The cart filled nearly all the space at the bottom of the shaft. It had landed on its rear end. The force of the impact had broken it in two. The two halves formed a sort of triangle and, from what Jack could tell, Goodfellow could only be trapped somewhere underneath. His hopes of finding the man alive were fading by the minute.

First inspection complete, Jack crouched down, peering ahead. It was dark at the bottom of the shaft, but he could see enough to spy a way underneath the cart. Staying low he eased forward, sliding down first onto his knees then onto his belly.

He saw Goodfellow almost at once.

The Englishman was lying on his back with his head twisted awkwardly to one side, eyes closed.

Jack's heart stopped beating. He squinted, looking for signs of life. He saw none.

Goodfellow was lying as still as a corpse.

Jack sucked down a breath. He was no stranger to death. But something shifted. Grief. Sorrow. Sadness. He did not know which.

Then Goodfellow's eyes opened.

And he was staring straight at Jack.

'You're alive then?' Jack felt a wave of relief. He had half expected to find Goodfellow crushed beneath the cart. Yet there he was, lying underneath the pyramid of the broken cart, as if just resting in a space created specifically for that purpose, not a mark on him.

Goodfellow did not speak straight away. Instead, he swallowed with obvious difficulty. It was then that Jack saw the fear etched onto the man's face. Or perhaps terror was a better description.

'Anything broken?' Jack asked.

This time, Goodfellow gave a very slow shake of his head.

'Then you are one lucky bugger.'

Goodfellow did not answer. Instead, he moved his head ever so carefully and looked down towards his own midriff.

'What is it?' Jack asked.

Goodfellow's head came back up. It moved even slower than before. 'There is a shard of broken wood.' The words were whispered, spoken slowly and carefully. 'It is a couple of inches from my groin.'

Jack could not help smiling as he began to understand Goodfellow's predicament.

'What's that you say?'

'There is a shard of wood pointed directly at my nether regions.' Goodfellow's fear was real and his voice shook as he spoke. 'It looks horribly sharp.'

'Where?' Jack inched forward.

'Down here!' For the first time, there was panic in Goodfellow's voice as his eyes jerked around in their sockets, trying to direct Jack's gaze with them alone.

Jack's eyes travelled down Goodfellow's prostrate body. At first, he couldn't see the threat to his fellow Englishman's manhood. Then he saw a spike of wood that had broken off from the side of the cart. It was angled away from the debris, the dreadfully sharp tip about three inches above Goodfellow's groin. If the cart fell any lower, then Goodfellow's balls would almost certainly be punctured.

'Shit.' Jack hissed the word as he realised that was exactly what could be about to happen. 'Flanagan!' He shouted for his reluctant companion.

'What now?' The reply came shouted back at him from above. Flanagan was already on top of the cart as he picked a slow and careful path towards the wounded donkey.

'Don't move another bloody inch!' Jack shouted the instruction, alive to the risk his decision had created.

Goodfellow's eyes widened in sudden horror. 'Where is he?'

'Going to sort out that poor donkey.'

A dreadful realisation reached Goodfellow's mind. 'God-dammit. Flanagan, don't move!' he screamed as the whole cart gave a sudden lurch above them and dropped another inch.

'Make up your fucking mind,' Flanagan sung out. 'Do you want me to kill this fucking thing, or what?'

'No!' Both men shouted in unison.

'Stay there.' Jack gave a final command. He paused then, waiting to see if Flanagan did as he was told. Only when he was sure that his instructions were being obeyed did he crawl forward.

His head was now directly beneath the side of the cart. If it fell, his skull would be crushed. It was not a pleasant thought and it stuck with him as he gingerly wormed along on his belly towards Goodfellow, using just his toes to push himself forward.

'Jack?' Goodfellow whispered as Jack came ever closer.

'What?' Jack's fear kept his answer short and sharp. The upper half of his body was fully underneath the cart now. The spike of wood that would maim his countryman was just ahead.

'Thank you.' Goodfellow spoke the simple words earnestly. 'I mean it. I do not think there is another man in this world who would risk their life for me.'

'Then lucky for you I'm here.' Jack stopped moving. With exaggerated care, he rolled half onto his side to free up enough space to ease his arm forward.

As he reached for the spike of wood, the cart lurched once more.

A dreadful cold rush of terror seared through Jack, every muscle tensing in expectation of the world coming crashing down on top of him, his body crushed into oblivion in the span of his next heartbeat.

It never came. The cart settled. Death was not coming. Not at that moment.

'Jack?'

'Yes.' Jack spoke the single word with difficulty.

'Can you hurry, please?'

Jack did not reply, but he saw the spike of wood was now no more than an inch above Goodfellow's privates.

He did not need to be told twice. Reaching forward, Jack took firm but careful hold of the shard of wood that had broken away from the cart. It was still fixed to the main axle, so he worked it carefully back and forth, holding his breath as he did so.

It came away with a crack like a gunshot.

Both men winced and flinched at the same second.

The cart was deadly still.

'I think you owe me one.' Jack laid the spike carefully on the ground.

'Indeed I do.' Relief coloured Goodfellow's words. 'Indeed I do.'

High above them came the first shouts as Anna returned with enough diggers to offer assistance. Instructions were shouted down and ropes passed to make the cart fast and ready to be hauled out.

It would take time, but with Flanagan already tying the ropes to the cart, they were all safe.

For now, at least.

Chapter Thirteen

Du Toit's Pan, Cape Colony, 29 June 1871

Jack ducked out of the tent, pulling his woollen scarf tight around his neck. It was cold, ball-achingly, toe-freezingly, arsehole-clenchingly cold, and the bitter air rasped as he dragged it into his lungs, while a great cloud of mist billowed out of his mouth as he entered the icy domain outside his tent flap.

They had been at the diggings for a month. Enough time for there to be a routine to their lives. A back-breaking routine that left them both exhausted at the end of every day.

Hoar frost lined the land, the canvas of the tent Jack shared with Anna crusted with a thick white layer. Even the tools left nearby were dusted with it, like sugar on Turkish delight. It added a sense of serenity to the morning scene, nature hiding away the ever-present dust and grime under a coating of white. But it would only last until the first hour of sunshine had cast the frost into oblivion. Then the muddy greys and browns would dominate once again, while the clean, chilly air of morning would become tainted with the dry taste of dirt.

Jack stamped his feet, forcing feeling into his frozen toes, then strode towards the bucket of water he had left outside the previous night. The surface was frozen, but the thin layer of ice was easily broken by the base of the kettle as he thrust it downwards.

'Holy Mother of God.' He could not help exclaiming as the ice-cold water splashed over his fingers as he waited for the kettle to fill. But it was not enough for him to withdraw his hand. His need for tea was stronger than his need to escape the water's freezing touch.

Water drawn, he moved slowly to the fire, or at least what had been a fire the previous night. Just as he did every morning, he squatted low, then reached into one of the pockets on his jacket for matches. The kindling was kept in a hessian sack near the fire, the dried bullock dung it would ignite bought every few days by the bucketful from the children who roamed the diggings gathering then selling the fuel, which was all that was available to burn. Wood was scarce and highly in demand for the sieves, props and cradles needed to dig the claims. It was too valuable to burn.

'Another fine day, Jack.'

Jack looked up and grunted as he saw who had come to disturb his morning routine. 'Did you get lost, Clarke?'

'I'm just saying g'day, mate.'

Clarke paused as he surveyed Jack's small encampment. It was not much to look at, the tent pitched amidst a hundred others. They were a good ten minutes' walk from their claim, but he could not get them any closer, every inch of land already occupied.

'You still not found much?' Clarke spoke abruptly, stopping to blow warm air onto his hands.

'No.' Jack was concentrating on piling up bullock shit rather than talking to the walking, talking gobby shit standing nearby. He had learned he needed to leave small gaps for air to circulate around the balls of dung. Get it wrong and the fire would not catch, and precious kindling would be wasted. Giving the fire his full attention was also preferable to seeing the look of pity he knew would be plastered across the Australian's face. Their supposed partner had moved on just a fortnight after their arrival, the lure of working his own claim too much to resist, just as Jack had predicted. Not that he really blamed Clarke for ending the partnership.

A quarter share of fuck all was fuck all. And fuck all never paid for anything.

'Keep at it, mate. You never know what you might find. There's always a chance, right?'

Jack held back another reply and lit the fire. Clarke was gloating. He knew that Jack and Anna had found nothing beyond a few bucketfuls of carbon and a dozen tiny rubies. It was not enough to pay their expenses, not by a long way, and they were eating through the little money they had left. There were no other funds available. The diggings were supposed to finance their further travels. But now it looked more likely that they would dig until the funds they had were gone. Although they still hadn't talked about what would happen then, Jack had already decided what he would do. He would see Anna safely to civilisation, and then he would walk. Alone. Just as he always had done. She had the family and the connections to make a new life for herself. She might not be happy, or even content, with that life. But she would be safe, and for him that would be enough. As to his own future, he didn't give it a thought. He would find something.

The first ray of sunlight broke through the early-morning mist. It would not take long for the damp and ice to burn away. Jack knew that by his second mug of tea, the frost would be nearly gone and the sky would be clear blue from horizon to horizon. After just one hour of digging, that serene blue would be tinted grey by the dust cast up by thousands of picks and shovels. By noon, it would barely be visible at all, the world thrown into a yellow-tinged shadow by the diggers, who would work until the sun set and its light was once again shut off from the world.

A fat fly buzzed towards his lip and he swatted it away without even looking, his attention fixed on the tin kettle he was placing carefully over the first flames as they began to flicker up from the freshly lit dung.

Clarke noticed his flailing arm. 'Uh oh, the little bastards are waking up.'

'You're still here then?' Jack muttered. He had no plans to offer the Australian a cup of warming tea or a seat at his fire.

The flies were just another bane of the diggers' lives. They were everywhere, a plague almost as bad as the dust. They filled the air, finding a way into even the most tightly laced tent. And they were aggressive, not at all like the sleepy bluebottles that were so common back home. The seemingly suicidal creatures in the diggings thought nothing of plunging at eyes and mouths, or throwing themselves into a death dive the moment an ounce of food was revealed. Their loud, angry buzz was just as persistent a sound in the diggings as the scrape of shovels or the impact of heavy picks on rock-hard soil.

'You're grouchy this morning, mate. Anna not letting you have your way again?' Clarke guffawed at his own comment.

'Wanker.' Jack mouthed the single word under his breath.

But he would not seek a confrontation, and so he held his tongue. Clarke would soon tire if deprived of an audience.

'Did you see the newspaper yesterday?' The Australian was in no hurry to move on.

'No,' Jack lied. Everyone read the weekly *Diamond News*. It was published over at Klipdrift and was filled with stories of diamonds found and those who had found them, alongside news of the diamond buyers and merchants who were coming to the pan. This week's paper had been delivered the day before, and Jack and Anna had scoured it that evening just as they always did, its arrival a highlight of their week. It had reported that the previous week at Du Toit's Pan, a diamond of over one hundred and eighteen carats had been dug up, along with another over ninety. There had been other finds of between thirty and eighty carats, with similar stories coming from the adjoining diggings at De Beers and Bultfontein. It made their own failure to find anything even harder to bear.

'Uh oh, watch your back, Jack.'

Jack sighed, turning to discover what had caught Clarke's attention, expecting to see nothing much of anything at all. He was wrong.

For the Australian was not the only one wandering by that morning.

'All right there, Dutchies, you got yourselves lost?' Clarke's words were friendly, but his tone was not.

Jack straightened up, ignoring the twinge in his back and the creak in his knees. He saw the Boers at once. There were just the two of them. One of whom he recognised.

Clarke was right to be wary. The Boers in the encampment – and there were many – kept themselves largely to themselves. By some unspoken agreement, the area had been divided into two distinct sections, one for the Dutchmen and their heavy wagons, and one for everyone else. It was rare for a couple of Boers to be ambling through the wrong part of the camp, and Jack smelled trouble.

'Morning.' He tried to be friendly, or at least an approximation of it.

'Lark.' De Klerk returned the greeting curtly.

'Who's your friend?' Jack tried to take the initiative.

'My cousin.'

Jack looked at the second Dutchman. There was a family resemblance, the Boer as thin and bony as de Klerk, his horsey face covered with a patchy beard that was clearly going to take years to fill out.

'Good morning.' He nodded the man's way. He was rewarded with nothing but a mute stare.

De Klerk paid Jack's attempt to dictate the conversation no heed. Instead he glared at Clarke. 'Do you men happen to know anything about some stolen water barrels?'

Jack heard the anger in the simple question. He understood it at once. Water was scarce in the dry diggings. There was a pair of artificial rainwater holes dug deep in the encampment, but the brackish water they yielded was barely fit for washing clothes. Just outside the diggings were more wells. All were busy, with queues of women, children and servants stretching away from them from dawn until dusk. None of the wells were productive. Each offered little more than a thimbleful of water a minute, so that filling a single bucket took an age. Even that effort was barely worth it, the muddy water tainted with the stink of ancient soil.

There was one good well. It was fed from an underground spring and it yielded clean, fresh water by the bucketful. It was a godsend, a gift from the heavens in the barren, dry diggings.

And it was owned by the Boers.

'I've heard nothing about that, mate.' Clarke's answer was immediate. 'How about you, Jack?'

Jack did not take kindly to being dragged into the discussion. If the Boers had had barrels of water stolen, he could well understand why they would be searching the encampment for the culprit, but that did not make it his concern.

'No.' He kept his answer short and to the point.

De Klerk snorted. 'Of course you haven't.'

'You think we're lying to you, Dutchie?' Clarke retorted.

The Boer just shrugged.

'Wherever your water is, it's not here.' Jack sought to bring the pointless conversation to an early conclusion. He knew why the matter was bringing out de Klerk's anger. The Boer who ran the well sold the water at threepence for two buckets' worth. He was making a small fortune on his near monopoly. The only other option for the thirsty diggers was to take a six-mile wagon trip to a local farm, where there was another spring. There were men who would make the journey each week, taking barrels that they would fill, then sell back at the diggings, but their prices were hardly any lower than those charged by the Boer. The nearest river was the Vaal, some twenty-five miles away. No one was making that trip, the time it would necessitate away from their claims making it out of the question for the diamond-fixated diggers.

'You sure about that, *mon*? We saw some fellow skulking around our wagons last night. It could have been you.' De Klerk cocked his head as if trying to match Jack to his memory of the figure he had seen.

Jack fought the urge to snap. 'It wasn't me, friend. And

if you saw someone there but didn't stop them pinching your damn barrels, then more fool you.' He could not resist throwing the barb. He meant it, too. If the Boers were foolish enough to allow themselves to be robbed, then he had no sympathy.

De Klerk changed tack. 'You found anything yet?'

'Maybe.' Jack had no intention of engaging in chit-chat. He could hear the water in his kettle starting to boil. The Boer was keeping him from his tea.

'We heard you found nothing but dust, *brü*.' De Klerk spoke mockingly.

'Then people talk too much.'

'So it's not true, then?'

'We're still here, aren't we?'

The Boer grunted at the reply. He made a play of looking around him, but took care to ignore Clarke, who was still standing there, arms crossed defensively across his chest.

'You look like someone in need of money.' There was condescension in the remark, along with a trace of arrogance.

'I didn't steal your water, chum.' Jack could not help the tiredness seeping into his voice. 'You're beating around the wrong fucking bush here. I suggest you piss off and find your thief elsewhere.'

De Klerk considered the answer, looking around one more time, then nodded. 'Take care, *brü*.' He spoke softly, so that Jack alone could hear, then turned and walked away, his companion trailing dutifully in his wake.

'Cocksuckers.'

Jack ignored Clarke's verdict and returned to his tea.

'They think they run the bloody place.' The Australian snorted with distaste.

'They do.' Jack carefully picked out a few pinches of tea leaves from a sack near the fire, then dropped them into two tin mugs.

'Didn't stop them having their bloody water nicked, did it?' Clarke was scathing.

His tone was enough for Jack to look up. 'You know something about it?'

'Of course I bloody do. There's nothing happens around here I don't know about.'

'Go on.' The words tasted sour in Jack's mouth as he encouraged the Australian to say more.

'You know the fellow who took it.'

'I do?'

Clarke's face spread into a sickening smile as he preened before revealing his news. 'It was that skinny mate of yours, Flanagan. He sold it this morning before sun-up.'

Jack absorbed the news. He had seen Flanagan a fair bit over the course of the last month; he was working the claim adjacent to his and Anna's after all. He and Goodfellow appeared to be finding a steady stream of small diamonds and a good number of rubies and carbon, but clearly they had not done well enough for Flanagan to forgo a bit of petty thievery to supplement his income.

'The bloke's an idiot then,' he said.

'You think?' Clarke clearly did not agree. 'Seems like a good bit of business to me.' He sniffed loudly.

Jack did not bother to answer. Flanagan was clearly a fool. Life was hard enough in the diggings without adding danger by stealing from the Boers.

'I'll leave you to your precious tea.' Clarke finally tired of what had been a mainly one-sided conversation. 'And you'll let me know when you want me to show you how it's done, won't you?'

The barbed comment brought Jack up sharp. 'What's that you say?'

Clarke laughed. 'It's a genuine offer, mate. Think of it as a thank you for bringing me here.'

Jack had no words to reply. But the Australian was not done.

'I'm thinking of taking a few days off digging anyhow. Found a five-carat stone two days ago. I've got money in my pocket for once and I intend to spend it wisely.'

'Good for you.' Jack tried hard to hide the bitterness in his tone. It was not a big stone, not by any means, but it would be enough to keep Clarke in beer for a couple of weeks, and it would give him confidence that his claim was not worthless. Not like the one Jack and Anna had bought.

'Just let me know if you want any more lessons, all right?' Clarke smiled smugly.

'We don't need them.' Jack's answer was short. 'We're fine.'

'Are you sure?'

'See you later, Clarke.'

He turned back to his tea and reached for the cloth he would use to hold the kettle as he removed it from the flames. But even as he started to pour the scalding liquid, he thought on Clarke's offer. His answer had been quick and it had been true. He would not ask for help.

He was his own man now and he would stay that way.

No matter what it cost.

Chapter Fourteen

The sun was nearing its zenith in a sky of hazy blue that stretched from one distant horizon to the other. Jack was working bare-chested, his body sheeted in sweat as he swung the pick in a measured rhythm, the same motion repeated over and over. He was moving easily now that constant repetition had ingrained the swing deep into the memory of his muscles. The tip of the pick hit hard, shattering the rocky soil, the impact marked with a crack like a pistol shot. Dirt and dust flew up, a momentary fountain that lasted for no more than a single heartbeat before it pattered gently back to the ground. The pick was already moving away even as the debris landed, Jack swinging it high over his shoulder before bringing it back down sharply. The force of the next impact jarred, but he barely felt it now, his arms and back hardened by weeks of toil. That did not mean there was no pain. At the end of the day, his back and shoulders felt like they had been trampled by a bull elephant, and the pit of his spine shot fiery lances of pain down into his legs with enough force to leave him trembling. But the pain had to be ignored, no matter how bad it got, and despite the fact that he would both start and finish the day moving like an aged cripple. Anna did her best, but there was no tincture for a lifetime's strain.

The pick swung down again, a rock the size of a child's fist sent skittering away. He was digging a new shaft. His third. At first he had tried to dig across the claim, keeping the level as consistent as he could, taking it down inch by inch, removing the soil by the bucketful. That had yielded nothing but a handful of carbon. And so he had changed his tactic, sinking his first shaft in the dead centre of the claim. Initially he had believed he had hit upon the perfect solution, the narrow channel yielding a couple of tiny diamonds the very first day, but there had been nothing more since. By the time the shaft was six feet deep, it had stopped producing anything at all. So he had tried again, digging another shaft three feet to the left of the first. He had been sure it would deliver a better result – more of the small diamonds and perhaps even something bigger. He had been proved to be utterly and completely wrong, the second shaft yielding nothing at all. He had gone deeper, cutting toeholds in the side of the shaft so that he could clamber down. He had worked in the pit every day, his life reduced to digging in the dark, the walls of the shaft inches from his face, nose and eyes clogged with dust, the taste and stink of dirt in his mouth. The buckets of spoil had to be carried up by hand, and each one had been full of nothing but dirt.

He had started the third shaft that morning.

The pick swung one last time. Enough ground had been broken, the sun-baked surface now ravaged and ruined. Placing the pickaxe on the ground and taking up the shovel was done without much thought, Jack working like some sort of new-fangled automaton. His mind was empty. There were no thoughts now, not of pain, not of time, not of hope of what might be found or what would happen if this shaft proved as much of a waste of effort as the other two. There was nothing save for what was needed to grab the nearest iron bucket and start shovelling the broken soil inside.

He dug hard, quickly finding the rhythm. Then his shovel hit a larger than average rock and stuck fast. His work with the pick had done nothing to loosen it from the grip of the ground.

The first flare of hope came swift and sure. He could not help it. It started deep in his toes and stirred through his gut before racing into his heart. It did not stop to think that this same event had happened a hundred times before and would likely happen again a thousand times more. It was fed by tales from *The Diamond News* and from the talk of every evening. For this was how the big ones were nearly always found. A tired digger bending down to retrieve another rock, or perhaps a worker at the sieve pulling out an usual stone from the tray.

He bent down, prising the rock from the soil then scooping it up before holding it in front of eyes that were red raw and dry from the dust kicked up from the digging. It did not look like much, this recalcitrant rock. It was uneven and covered with a crust of brown that broke off easily enough as he used his thumb to pick at it.

The soil fell away. It revealed a lump of carbon. Nothing more.

'Fuck it.'

A new emotion surged through him. Raw. Powerful, irresistible. Frustration and tiredness mixing together to create a volatile cocktail of such strength that it overwhelmed everything else.

'Fuck it. Fuck it. Fuck it.' The curses came fast, the words releasing something deep inside him. He let the rock fall from his grip like it was burning him, and it dropped back into the dirt around his boots.

'Jack?' Anna rose from her place at the sieve, face creasing with concern.

Jack said nothing. He was staring up at the sky, trying to control the rage that was burning in his belly. It was so unfair. He worked as hard as any of the diggers, harder even, toiling from dawn until dusk and pouring his strength into the small square of dirt he had bought, like a drunk pissing away his night's worth of drink into a ditch.

And yet it was all for naught.

'Jack?' She came closer, wiping her hands on her filthy apron.

Jack looked at her. Really looked at her. She had been changed by the countless hours she had spent at the two sieves, picking through the dirt in the hope that she would find something other than mere dust. Her fingers were hooked like claws, nails ripped and torn, the skin around them raw and bloody. Her hair was no longer braided and clean. It stuck out around her head like a dark cloud, the tangled tresses tightly intertwined like the nest of a hard-working sparrow. But it was not her hands, or her hair, where he saw the most change. It was there in her red-rimmed eyes, filling the puffy grey pouches underneath and etched into every pore of her face. The claim was sucking the life out of her, just as it was pushing him to breaking point. He had faced the stoic, silent Persian Fars at the Battle of Khoosh-ab and he had not shirked from the violence of the mutinous sepoys as they rampaged through the streets of Delhi, their great mutiny beginning in an orgy of blood and violence. He had charged into the Hornets' Nest at Shiloh and he had walked towards the Great Redoubt at the Alma while all around him were slain. He had been one of the first into the breach at Delhi and he had run from the Austrian cavalry on the slopes around Solferino as they rode down the exhausted French legionnaires. He had even faced his death in a ruined hacienda in Mexico, fighting to the last as all had fallen around him. And he had walked up the slopes at Bull Run, following the path of those who had already been slaughtered by the Confederate reinforcements on that blood-soaked ground. Yet nothing, no enemy, no battle, no campaign, had ever tested him like this thirty square feet of plain dirt.

The meagre patch of ground was besting him.

Breaking him.

Killing him.

'Look at it, Anna.' He pointed to the start of the shaft. He had barely broken the soil. 'I can't do it any more. I just can't.' The words leaked out of him.

Anna moved towards him, walking as if on eggshells. 'Take a break,' she said gently.

'I don't want a fucking break,' Jack howled, then turned away, raw emotions flooding through him like water breaking through a dam. 'I've had enough of this.'

'Shall I make a cup of tea?'

'For God's sake, Anna, don't you see?' He turned back to face her, taking hold of both her arms and shaking her, as if trying to wake her from some sort of stupor. 'We're killing ourselves here. And for what? I'll tell you for what. For fuck all!'

Anna pulled away. For a moment, her cheeks coloured as her own temper surged. But unlike him, she swallowed it down. 'You need a rest, that's all. You've been working too hard. We both have.'

'No. I'm done.' The words came out as little more than a whisper.

Anna stood there looking back at him, a strand of matted hair stuck across her forehead with sweat, a streak of dirt crusted to one cheek.

Jack tried to meet her gaze.

He couldn't.

He had failed.

He was not a warrior, as he had once believed. He was not a leader, his failure to command leaving him unable to control his own mind. Now he was not even a soldier, his life reduced to that of a common navvy.

Once he had been an officer, even if a counterfeit one. He had revelled in his stolen role, finding himself becoming the man he had always wanted to be. And he had been a killer. He had been good at that too. He knew how to be brutal, learning that to survive on the battlefield meant fighting with everything he had without any notion of mercy or surrender.

But he had tired of being both a soldier and a killer. He had wanted to be something more. Something just for himself. Something real. Something good.

And that had led him here with Anna to a life digging in the dirt. Yet now even that was beyond him.

For he was done.

Spent.

Broken.

He looked down at the few feet of trampled dirt around his boots, then up at the face of the woman he was coming to love more than any other.

He came to a decision. Anna offered him something better than even the largest diamond they could hope to find. Something he had never expected to find again.

'We're done here.' He meant it. The dream was over. Hope

was gone. It was time to move on. It was time to be someone new.

For *them* to be something new.

'Are you sure?' Anna asked, voice small.

'Yes.' He paused. 'Will you come with me?'

'Yes. Of course.' She found a smile. It was thin, wan even, but it suited her. 'Always.'

Jack did not know why she had chosen to stay with him no matter what. But he was glad that she had. His life was changing and for once it had a single, firm footing. He had Anna.

'Shall we sell this piece of shit and go someplace else?' It was not much of a plan, but it was all he had left. They had barely any money and he had no real idea how they would manage. But they would survive. They would find a way. *He* would find a way.

'Are you sure you want to quit?' Anna asked.

'You want to stay?'

For a moment, there was no answer. Then, 'What will we do? Where will we go?'

'You have a choice here, Anna. You don't have to come with me.'

'So I could go back to England while you go on to God knows where?' Her mouth tightened.

'Your family would take you in.' He gently voiced the thoughts he had allowed to take root in his mind. He did not want her to go. But he would offer the option, no matter that she might take it and leave him.

'They would.' Anna nodded gravely as she considered then affirmed his notion. 'But I would never ask them to. Not now.'

'Why?' he probed.

'Because we may not have unearthed a diamond, but I think I still have found something here.' She offered a thin smile.

'What's that?'

'I found you.'

'Me?' Jack could not hold back the exclamation. 'I was already with you.'

'You were different then.' Anna held his gaze. 'You were always distant, as if you were holding something back. It was as if you expected me to leave at any moment.'

Jack did not reply. He did not have the words.

'I could have left you, I think. When you were holding back on me. But that's done now. It was before we spent all this time together.' A lick of anger coloured her words now and her chin lifted, defiance writ large in her expression. 'Before I came to love you.'

Jack opened his mouth to reply. No words came out.

'So no, I won't leave you. I won't go home on my own. You don't get to drop me.' Her eyes were wide with hurt. 'Like I said, you're stuck with me, I'm afraid.'

Jack looked down at the dirt that had defeated the thief, the assassin, the killer, the warrior, the commander. He could feel Fate's presence in that moment. She had slipped back unnoticed into his life, just as she had so many times before. She was present, he knew that. He could sense her. Yet for the first time, she was silent.

The choice was his, and his alone. His future hung on what he said next.

'Fair enough.' As he uttered the words, he felt Fate's hands close on him, like the tightening of the hangman's noose around his neck. He had made his decision. What happened next was not his to control.

Anna looked at him, expression quizzical. 'So we stay together, no matter what happens?'

'Yes.'

'Then gather your gear, soldier. It's time we got going.' Anna took what looked to be a very deep breath. Jack could almost see the shackles of their life in the diggings fall away. He felt it himself, a sudden sense of freedom, of a burden being taken off his aching shoulders.

'Yes, ma'am.' He sketched a salute, then bent down to gather up the tools he would no longer need. They could still be sold; tools were always in demand in the dry diggings. They would need every penny they could get.

As he stepped away from the hole he had been trying to hack into the remorseless soil, he felt the rock he had discarded earlier crunch under his dusty boot, breaking into smaller pieces.

He was about to walk away, but his eyes dropped to the dirt, the habit too ingrained to ignore.

That was when he saw it.

He had been wrong. Completely and utterly wrong.

For the glint of a diamond caught the midday sun.

Chapter Fifteen

'Just leave it behind. We don't need it.' Jack was watching as Anna tried to fit a blanket into an already bulging knapsack.

The two of them were in their small tent, packing up everything they had accumulated during their time in the diggings. There was not a huge amount of gear, but it was still too much for them to carry, and so they had resolved to sell whatever they could not fit into the two knapsacks to one of the traders who made their money supplying the diggers with everything from hemp and shovels to grog and victuals.

'What about this?' Jack held up a spare dress Anna had barely worn. He rolled his eyes as he saw that she was still trying to force the blanket home.

'Sell it,' she replied instantly.

He did not need to be told twice, and tossed the dress onto the growing pile of items to be sold. They planned to travel light and with as much ready money in their pockets as possible. Selling the diamond would come later, and until that happened, they would have to make do with whatever they could lay their hands on. The thought struck him as funny as he stuffed a single shirt into his knapsack, throwing the others onto the heap of discards. He had a king's ransom in the pocket of his jacket, and yet they would have to scrimp and save and sell anything they could just to buy two seats on a wagon for the trip back to Port Elizabeth.

'I appreciate you want to be away, but there is no sense getting rid of things we will need.' Anna had spotted the face he had pulled, and now spoke sharply as she continued her efforts to ram the blanket home.

'I don't want to stay a minute longer than we have to,' he admitted freely. He did not like to dwell on the feelings that had erupted just before he had trodden on the stone that had changed their lives. Those raw emotions had been powerful, intoxicating even. He had felt something similar before. That had been in the heat of battle, his mind lost to an overwhelming urge to fight and to kill. This time the feelings had hit him in the peaceful confines of a digger's claim. Yet there was a similarity that he would do his very best to ignore. Confronting his demons had never done him any good. They had power, real power, and he could not win, not against them all.

'We won't dally,' Anna reassured him. 'And we will walk all the way to Port Elizabeth if we have to.'

Jack grunted. He had no desire to walk, but he would if necessary. They would get a better price for the diamond in Port Elizabeth, the bigger dealers there sure to pay more than the keen-eyed merchants who were prepared to rough it in the diggings just so they could buy stones from those who wanted to sell them there and then.

'Yes, we will.' He could not help flashing a glance at the tent flap, the nagging feeling that someone could be eavesdropping ever present now. They had agreed not to tell a soul what they had found. They had cleaned the diamond back at the claim, Anna working hard to work it free from the clasp of centuries of grime. Even then it did not look like much, not really, but both knew what they had found. And what it was worth. It had to be close to one hundred carats. If the prices in *The Diamond News* were any sort of guide, it was worth over ten thousand pounds, perhaps more to the more affluent dealers in Port Elizabeth.

It was what they had come so far to find.

'Are you really taking that?' Anna was pointing to the salt-stained carpet bag that had sat untouched in the corner of the tent ever since they had arrived.

Jack did not answer at once. He stared at the bag he had carried for so many miles, and which contained his weapons. The Lefaucheux had not been cleaned for weeks, the heavy revolver forgotten as the days of digging stole away his appetite for anything other than rest.

'Yes,' he said eventually. He would not give up the handgun. Not that Anna would ask him to. She understood what it meant to him.

'We can put some of my medicines in there, if there is room?'

'Fine.' Jack did not mind the suggestion. The revolver could be buried away under anything, so long as it was still there. He wondered whether it was time to take it from the bag and clean and load it. With the diamond in his pocket, the weight of the Lefaucheux on his hip would be reassuring. But he knew that to carry the gun would be to draw attention, and that would not do. They wanted to make a swift and clean exit. There was no need for goodbyes in the diggings. People came and went with alarming regularity. They would not be missed.

But they had been spotted.

'What's going on with you two?'

Jack and Anna looked at one another as they recognised the voice at once.

'You left your claim in one hell of a hurry.' Clarke spoke to them from the other side of the tent flap. 'Is everything all right?'

'All is quite well.' Anna answered for both of them. 'Thank you for your concern.' She glanced across at Jack, her face creasing with apprehension.

'Are you sure? No one leaves their claim in the middle of the bloody day. Unless . . .' Clarke paused, leaving the thought unfinished. But not for long. 'Did you find something, then? I saw you. It sure looked to me like you found something.'

Jack and Anna shared another look. Anna's eyes narrowed and her lips moved, the words mouthed slowly and silently.

Shall we tell him?

Jack shook his head. They could trust no one. Especially Clarke. The Australian had not stuck around to honour his commitment to their partnership and Jack felt no need to tell him anything. All obligations had dissolved the day Clarke walked away and left them to it.

Anna stared back at him. Clearly she had understood his answer. But she was still hesitating.

Jack spoke. 'Fuck off, Clarke. Don't poke that ugly beak of yours into business that doesn't concern you.'

'All right, mate, don't get your balls out. I'm just checking you're all right, that's all,'

'Thank you, Joe.' Anna's eyes widened, giving Jack a very clear warning to shut up. 'But as I said, all is fine. Jack had a bit of a turn, that's all. Don't tell anyone, will you? You know how crabby he gets.' She slowly shook her head at Jack as she continued. 'He doesn't want anyone to know he isn't as young as he used to be.'

'Fair enough. You all tuckered out, Jack?'

'I'm fine,' Jack growled, his eyes locked on Anna.

'Sure you are, mate. Sure you are.' Clarke chuckled. 'Maybe you're not cut out for this. I've seen it before, big hard guys who quit after a few weeks of real work. They don't have the strength for it, not day after day. No, it takes a real toughie to stick it here.'

Jack shut his eyes as Clarke chuntered away. It took all his self-control not to rip the tent flap open and knock the mouthy Australian onto his arse to show just how tuckered he really was.

'Thank you for your concern, Joe.' Anna lifted a finger and held it towards Jack as she read his thoughts easily enough. 'But we are fine. You should go back to work. You never know, today might be the day.'

'You never know.' There was a pause, then the sound of feet moving on the ground.

Anna's shoulders slumped with relief that Clarke was finally leaving them alone.

But she was mistaken.

The tent flap was snatched back suddenly. Both of them started, the sudden motion making them jump.

'Cut the crap.' Clarke's head slipped into the tent, lip curled with a mixture of anger and jealousy. He had not bought the lie. 'What did you find?'

Jack recovered first and lunged towards him, hands balling into fists. Anna grabbed his arm.

'It is none of your business, Joe.' She kept her hand in place, holding Jack back.

'So you did find something. I bloody knew it. And you weren't going to tell me?'

'We want to keep it quiet,' she tried to explain.

'It's a big one then.' Clarke licked his lips, then glanced at Jack, a sudden flicker of fear crossing his face as he belatedly realised he might have overstepped the mark. Men had been killed for less when there was a large diamond involved.

'You need to shut your fucking muzzle and piss off right now.' Jack would not be silenced any longer. 'If you so much as breathe a word of this, I'll rip your heart out and make you eat it, you get me?'

'All right, calm down, mate.' Clarke's face visibly paled as Jack snarled his threat. But he did not retreat. 'How big is it?'

'Your heart? Fucking tiny.'

'No, the stone you found.'

'I'm not telling you again—'

Anna cut Jack off with a sharp gesture. 'Not so big, Joe. Thirty carats, perhaps a little more. Certainly nothing to get excited about.'

'Bullshit.' Clarke made his thoughts clear, even if he did glance anxiously towards Jack as he spoke. 'Folk don't quit with thirty carats in their pocket. What is it really?'

'I'm telling you the truth, Joe.' Anna's eyes narrowed a fraction, the silent warning delivered. 'Now I would be extremely grateful if you would leave us in peace.'

'Come on, love.' Clarke tried to grin. The expression didn't reach his eyes, which remained cold, hard and calculating. 'I set you up here, didn't I just. You can tell me.'

'I would be grateful if you'd leave us now.' Anna repeated the same request in as calm a tone as before, but Jack could see that the tension was getting to her.

Clarke refused to back away. 'Now look here—'

He never finished his sentence. Jack had heard enough. Brushing Anna's hand aside, he reached past her, grabbing the front of Clarke's shirt and forcing him back out of the tent.

'You heard what she said.' He pulled the Australian towards him, thrusting his own head forward as he did so, leaving their faces no more than an inch apart. 'And I'm going to spell it out for you, as it seems to be hard for you to get it into your noggin.' He paused, moving another half-step closer, so that their noses almost touched. 'Leave us the fuck alone.' He delivered the words staccato, each one carefully enunciated, then pushed hard, sending Clarke stumbling away.

'What the hell has got into you, mate?' Clarke sneered as he found his footing.

'I told you. Go away.' Jack took another step forward, his heart hammering in his chest. The urge to fight was growing.

'I thought I was your mate?'

'You thought wrong.'

Clarke opened his mouth to say more, then paused as the words failed to form. He looked to the ground, his head moving slowly from side to side as he composed himself. When he glanced up at Jack again, there was genuine pain in his expression, or at least a fair imitation of it. 'So you found a big one and now you're running.'

'We're not running.' Jack pulled a face at the choice of word.

'No? It sure looks like it to me.'

'Think what you want, but I'd still advise you to bugger off quick sharp.' Jack had had enough of talking.

'He's right.' Anna came out of the tent, moving past Jack and putting herself between him and the Australian. 'You should go, Joe. It would be best all round.'

'Best for who?' The retort was sharp and full of hurt. But then Clarke sighed, before nodding his assent. 'Fair enough. You want me gone, so I'll go.' He paused, fixing his gaze on Anna. 'I'm glad you found something, Anna, truly. It sure must be a big one to have you on your toes so quickly.' He looked at her quizzically, still trying to prise out the information he wanted.

'We're grateful for all your help, Joe.' She smiled in a half-hearted attempt to mollify him. 'You have our thanks.'

'A man can't eat a thank you.' For a moment it seemed like Clarke would say more, but then he scuffed his heel into the friable ground beneath his boot and turned to leave.

'Good luck to you, Anna.' He nodded as he made his farewell.

'And good luck to you, Joe.'

He looked at Jack. Neither man said a word, both their faces blank and wooden.

Jack said nothing as he ushered Anna back into the tent. He hoped Clarke would heed the warning to leave them be. Every instinct was screaming at him to get the hell away, as quickly as they could.

He could smell trouble coming.

And as ever, it would surely be coming his way.

Chapter Sixteen

'Are you ready, Jack?' Anna shrugged her shoulders to settle the knapsack more comfortably on her back. She carried her umbrella in one hand and her case of medicines in the other.

'Give me a minute.' Jack spoke without looking at her, his eyes focused on the task of loading the Lefaucheux. The weapon was dusty and it needed to be cleaned more thoroughly than the cursory wipe he had given it. But he was loading it regardless, the encounter with Clarke changing his mind. There was fear in the act, he knew that, but he had once been caught with a revolver unloaded. That had been on the Grand Trunk Road, which traversed the great swathe of mofussil between Bombay and Delhi. That he had survived that day had largely been down to luck and the timely arrival of the 2nd Punjab Cavalry. He would not risk the same fate befalling them on the way to Port Elizabeth.

Squatting on the ground, he slid the pinfire cartridges through the hinged gate on the right-hand side of the revolver's sturdy metal frame. The gate was opened by pinching the two small levers together then lifting it away from the body of the weapon. When fired, the empty cartridges would be ejected through the same opening by the ejector rod that ran along the length of the stubby barrel. The Lefaucheux was nothing like the Navy Colt that had served him for so long, or the Beaumont–Adams that he had taken with him into the wilds of the Sudan, but he rather liked it. It reminded him of the Henry Repeater that had saved his life so many times when he had been in the warring United States. There was a modernity to the weapon that resonated deep inside him. It was the weapon of the experienced soldier, a tool that had been made to kill, as reliably as possible.

He just hoped it would not be needed. Not that day. Not ever.

'Can you believe it, Jack?'

'Can I believe what?' He kept his eyes on the revolver.

'That we did it. That we did what we came here for.'

He glanced up, flashing a fleeting grin. 'It was never in doubt, was it?'

Anna pulled a face. She knew the truth, had seen him when the despair had taken hold. Yet she had not mentioned it. Not once. 'No, never!' She laughed, spirits high.

Jack laughed with her, then stood, sliding the now loaded revolver into the holster that sat on his right hip. Glancing up, he noticed a bank of ominous dark clouds spreading across the horizon. They were puffy and the colour of copper, and they were coming on fast, casting the land into shadow. He had been in the diggings long enough to recognise the warning signs of a thunderstorm when he saw them.

The diggers were well used to the storms that swept across the veldt with a savage bite. They were quite unlike anything Jack had experienced before, even in the tempestuous wilds of

India. Most of the men took the sensible precaution of placing an empty glass bottle on top of their iron tent pole, in an attempt to spare them should their meagre accommodation be struck by the lightning that always accompanied the thunder, and which attacked the ground with a velocity that made a searing hot roundshot seem like a pea fired from a child's toy gun. There was a constant debate regarding which was the more dangerous, the lightning or the lethal landslides that followed every deluge. The diggers were enthusiastic in their attempts to hack diamonds from the ground, but only a few really knew what they were doing. So shafts collapsed with every storm. And diggers died. Whether struck by lightning or buried alive, their passing was just as final, and just as grim.

'I want to be off before that arrives.' He nodded towards the building storm, making sure Anna had seen it. 'We will still likely get caught up in it, but I don't care, do you?'

'No. I agree. I just want to get away from here.'

All they had to do now was go to the office to settle their account and sell their claim, then arrange for a trader to come and agree a price for the belongings they would be leaving behind. It would not take long, the clerks and traders very familiar with those departing the diggings in a hurry.

Then they would be free to go wherever they chose.

'Jack?'

Jack had turned away to gather up his knapsack and carpet bag, so he did not see the new arrivals until Anna called for his attention. He looked up to see that a small group of Boers had come to visit. He did not know why. And he did not want to know why. He just wanted them gone.

'Can I help you?' He straightened slowly, lowering his baggage to the ground, keeping his hands free. He sensed danger.

'We're looking for your friend.' De Klerk was amongst the group, and it was he who spoke.

Jack also spied de Klerk's bony cousin in the party, which amounted to four dour-faced men. The older two he did not know, but it was clear that they had all been cut from the same dusty, drab cloth. All were tanned – or perhaps 'weathered' was a better description for the craggy mahogany-coloured skin that could just about be seen behind the long hair and beards that smothered every man's face, save for that of de Klerk's wispy-chopped cousin – and all were dressed alike.

'Jack doesn't have any friends.' Anna answered blithely on his behalf. She came to stand at his side, her face hidden under her wideawake hat. If she was fearful of the band of Boers, there was no sign of it in her voice, the words coming out even and pleasant.

'The one called Flanagan,' de Klerk grunted.

'He's not here, mate. And before you ask, I have no idea where he might be.' Jack spoke brusquely. He had no intention of revealing anything more to the Boers even though the hackles on his neck were rising. Clarke had told him that Flanagan had been known to possess light fingers and had already lifted some of the Boers' precious water. But that was not something he would share. Especially with the Boers. 'He's no friend of mine. Like she said,' he nodded at Anna without moving his eyes away from the Boers, 'I don't have any friends.'

'What do you want with him?' Anna asked.

Jack reached out to place a warning hand on her arm. He did not want the discussion to go on for a second longer than it needed to.

'He's been stealing our water,' de Klerk replied.

'Do you have proof?' Anna fired back, even though Jack

squeezed her arm in an attempt to quieten her.

'He was seen.' De Klerk glanced towards one of the two older men. 'Oom Joost saw him.'

Jack looked closely at the man de Klerk had indicated. He reckoned Joost was perhaps in his early fifties. His thick, bushy beard was more salt than pepper, his eyes shrouded by heavy grey brows. His gaze was intense and piercing. He carried himself like a much younger man, and he had a certain air about him, something rarer than mere strength or brawn. Jack could see that he was a leader, a commander even. It was clear in the confident set of his shoulders and the composed look on his face. The other older man did not have it, nor did either of the two younger Boers. It marked Oom Joost out as clearly as any braid or insignia of rank.

'How can he be so sure? A lot of men look alike here.' Anna was not done. She even took a step forward. 'He could be mistaken.'

'He is sure.'

'But come, Mr de Klerk.' Anna's brow was furrowing as she argued the case for a man she barely knew. 'Mistaken identities are common, especially in a place such as this.'

De Klerk was spared another answer as Oom Joost turned to look at him. A staccato stream of Afrikaans followed, the instructions, or whatever they might be, delivered swiftly. From the man's thunderous expression, it was clear the older Boer was already tiring of the exchange.

'We want him.' De Klerk's expression was unchanged, but his own words came out clipped, his tone more belligerent now. 'And we *will* find him, so if you know where he is, why don't you save us all some time and just tell us.'

'He's not here.' Jack squeezed Anna's arm tighter, pulling

her backwards before she could speak again. 'So I suggest you boys move along.'

Anna shook off his hand. She was not one to be silenced. 'What are you going to do with him should you find him?'

De Klerk gave a faint shake of his head, clearly not happy at being addressed in such a tone by a woman. 'He is a thief.'

'And?'

'He will be punished.'

'By you?'

De Klerk shrugged, but still glanced at his elder, who was shifting from foot to foot as the conversation dragged on.

'If you wish to accuse a man of a crime, you must take it to the authorities.' Anna's chin lifted as she spoke, her cheeks colouring as she demanded a more proper solution to the Boers' claim. 'There are men here who will look into your accusation and make sure that anyone who is stealing is brought to account.'

De Klerk's head shake became more vigorous. He ignored Anna and instead spoke to his elder in Afrikaans.

And that was enough. The Boers began to move on, turning their backs on Anna and Jack.

'You must take this to the appropriate authorities, Mr de Klerk.' Anna was not done. She even took a few paces after the group, haranguing them as they moved away.

She would have been ignored, not one of the group bothering to listen to her words. Except at that moment, two Englishmen came into view around the side of a nearby tent, carrying wooden fruit boxes filled with supplies.

Jack saw them first. He saw Goodfellow, the amiable fellow who had shared the wagon with them on the journey from Port Elizabeth.

And he saw Flanagan.

'Shit.' He hissed the word under his breath, then reached forward to haul Anna behind him. No good would come from what was about to unfurl. At least not for anyone who was not a Boer.

'Ha! There!' De Klerk's cousin spotted the pair just moments after Jack had seen then himself. He stopped and pointed, an accusatory finger aimed straight at Flanagan.

'Stay here.' Jack could only hope that this time Anna would heed him. He stepped forward, thinking to put himself between the Boers and the two unsuspecting arrivals, who continued walking, both looking down as they carried their weighty burdens towards their own tent, which was not much more than a few yards away from where Jack and Anna had set up their temporary home.

'Hey, you there! Stay where you are!' It was de Klerk who began shouting at the pair, who finally became aware of the trouble they were strolling towards.

'Don't get involved, you hear me,' Jack hissed to Anna, as he spotted Flanagan's eyes widen in alarm. The urge to run was written in every pore of the younger man's face.

'What's this, Jack?' Goodfellow looked from the four hefty Boers to Jack and Anna, then back again.

'Your partner has been spotted pinching water.' Jack was hurrying to place himself in a position where he could prevent whatever the Boers had planned. Only when he was roughly in front of Flanagan and Goodfellow did he turn to face the group for a second time. The four Dutchmen had not been idle. They'd had further to go than he had, but they were moving rapidly and were even now fanning out in a rough C shape facing the three Englishmen. There was not much space this

deep within the encampment, the surrounding camp paraphernalia giving little room for manoeuvre. The Boers were
hemmed in by Jack and Anna's tent and the scruffy grey bell
tent belonging to their neighbours, a small group of diggers
from Cape Town who, like pretty much every other denizen of
the diggings, were up working their claim. There was no one
else around.

'I never pinched nothing.' Flanagan's face was creasing with
growing concern, and he stopped to place his supplies on the
ground, freeing himself ready to run.

'Yes you bloody well did.' Goodfellow muttered the words
under his breath, just loud enough for Jack to hear.

He glanced towards the Boers, hoping they were far enough
away not to have overheard. But it did not bode well.

'You're a bloody idiot, lad.' He pitched his own voice to
carry only as far as his countrymen.

'It was just some bloody water.' Flanagan stood straight,
but his eyes were darting around like a cornered rat seeking to
escape the catcher's net.

Jack knew the young man was on the point of bolting. That
would not help any of them. He had seen the way the Boers
dealt with those who had wronged them, the beating that had
been dealt to Clarke back in Port Elizabeth a fair indication of
the fate that was in store for the dolt who had been foolish
enough to steal their water. He had little sympathy. If Flanagan
had to take a slating for his stupidity, it was a price he was
more than willing for the idiot to pay. Just so long as it brought
the matter to a swift and final conclusion so that he and Anna
could get away.

He took a couple of paces forward, covering the ground in
great loping strides, and grabbed the young man's arm.

Flanagan threw him a look that was something between anger and panic.

'What the fuck are you doing?' He tried to pull his arm away.

Jack held tight. 'Let's just sort this out, chum.' His was a simple solution to the situation they found themselves in. Flanagan would face the music for his thievery and take the beating that was coming his way. He would live. He might even learn. Then the matter would be closed and they could all go about their business.

'No fucking way.' Flanagan threw his shoulder backwards in a futile attempt to get free.

'Just stay there.' Jack gritted his teeth and held on. He glanced towards the Boers. They were coming on fast, stepping over tent ropes and around crates of supplies as they closed on the thief who had taken their precious water.

'Fuck you.' Flanagan lashed out, punching his palm into Jack's chest, fighting to free himself.

Jack grunted as he absorbed the hefty blow, but he held firm.

'Jack?'

He ignored Goodfellow even when the other man pulled at his sleeve, trying to attract his attention.

'Let him go, Jack,' Goodfellow urged.

'It's better this is dealt with.' Jack spoke through gritted teeth as he held on to the floundering Flanagan, who was twisting this way and that as he tried to escape. 'He's young,' he gasped, fighting to keep his grip. 'A few bruises will heal quick.'

'I don't think they want to beat him.' Goodfellow's voice was laced with dread.

'What's that?' Jack had no breath for more.

'Let him go! Look lively now.' Goodfellow's tone became more demanding. He even went so far as to reach out to prise Jack's fingers free.

'What the hell?' Jack felt his grip start to loosen. Then he saw the rope being carried by de Klerk's cousin, and finally he understood why Goodfellow had taken Flanagan's side so quickly.

It was not just a rope. One end had been tied into a noose.

Flanagan was not facing a beating.

He was facing a lynching.

Chapter Seventeen

The first clap of thunder tore the heavens asunder. It echoed across the veldt like the opening salvo of a barrage from a grand battery, the roar going on and on, the wave of sound reverberating through the air and momentarily stunning every man and animal in the diggings into silence.

Then it began to rain.

This was not English rain. It did not start with the smattering of a few gentle droplets. It did not open with a fine, misty drizzle or even a drenching downpour.

This was South African rain, and it hammered from the sky like piss from a bull.

'Run, you fool.' Jack let go of Flanagan the second he saw the noose, snapping the command, a sudden rush of dread adding ice to his tone.

Lightning flashed, the darkening sky turning white for the span of a single racing heartbeat.

'Run!' Jack repeated. He was already turning to face the Boers. There was no time to see if Flanagan obeyed, but he was determined to at least give the young Londoner a chance.

'There he goes!' De Klerk's cousin spotted the movement,

immediately shouting out in alarm. It was all the confirmation Jack needed. Flanagan was doing as he had been told and running for his life.

'Leave him alone!' He spread his arms wide, bellowing the command, drawing everyone's attention towards him. More thunder followed his cry, the gods above echoing his instruction with a cacophony of sound. The rain came without pause now, flaying the dusty ground into slime and drumming on the felt hats of those who sought to kill and the bare heads of those who sought to save a thief's life.

All four of the Boers were rushing towards him, the two younger and more agile men quickly altering their course so that they pursued their quarry. Jack let them go. He could no more stop them than he could stay dry as the heavens emptied onto the dry earth, but he had given Flanagan his chance. For now, he could do little more.

The pair of older Boers stopped in front of him. Both their faces bore the same sullen, distrustful expression. Neither spoke. They just stood there in the rain, clothing turning from grey to black as it absorbed the deluge being poured over them from above, their eyes boring into the lone Englishman who had dared to deny them an easy capture of the man who had stolen their water.

Jack stood his ground. He noted Goodfellow moving over to join Anna, both watching, both waiting to see what would happen next. He tried to stand easy, showing the Boers that he did not care for their ire, that he did not fear them, or the tempest that had broken around them. But he failed, the rain and the thunder stealing away his insouciance. And so he faced the two Dutchmen ramrod straight, like a soldier on parade. And he held that pose, ignoring the cold as his sodden clothing pressed down onto his flesh and water ran across his skin.

The leader of the Boers, the man de Klerk had called Oom Joost, took one step towards him. He rolled his neck, loosening the muscles like a prizefighter entering the ring, then looked Jack up and down.

'Why are you letting him go?' He asked the question in English coloured with a thick, guttural accent.

Jack considered the man in front of him. There was not a shred of doubt in Joost's level gaze. Just certainty in his own judgement. Certainty in his ability to fight if need be.

'Because he's one of mine.' Jack did not shirk from the remorseless gaze boring into his skull. He did not fear Joost. He had killed harder men than the Boer.

'He is a thief.'

'He is.' Jack offered a tight-lipped smile as he agreed. 'But then again, aren't we all?'

The Boer blinked as he absorbed the reply. Then he nodded. 'Yes. But he was foolish enough to steal from me. For that he has to pay.'

Joost said nothing more, instead turning his back on Jack and returning to join his fellow Boer, waiting for his younger comrades to bring Flanagan back.

Jack watched them. He did not know what would happen next. But one thing was certain. He would not allow the Boers to take Flanagan away. No matter what it took. He had told the truth. Flanagan was one of his own.

Above his head, the heavens were darkening. Huge copper-coloured clouds spread across the sky, the great formations tinged with the blues and blacks of a fresh bruise. Thunder came almost without pause now, the sound rolling on and on until it was drowned out by the cataclysmic clash of an enormous bolt of lightning.

He heard the Boers who had given chase coming back. Loud voices called to their brethren. Confident. Cocky. Sure.

And there was laughter.

The two men had run hard and they had run fast. And they had taken their quarry.

Jack could hear in their tone that they believed Flanagan's fate was now sealed. Or at least they were celebrating as if that were the case.

But they had discounted Jack Lark. And he was not yet done. Not by a long shot.

'So be it.' He spoke the words under his breath as he turned to watch the pair bring Flanagan in, the skinny lad frogmarched towards the waiting Boers, his feet barely touching the ground, the toes of his boots cutting a trench in the muck that lay like mush on the ground now that the rain had churned it into so much slurry.

'Jack!' Anna left Goodfellow's side. 'We must stop them!' Her voice was barely audible over the storm that raged on without pause, the skies reverberating with fire and thunder.

'Stay there! I'll do it!' He waved a hand in her direction in a vain attempt to ward her away. It was a gesture he knew she would not obey.

'Leave the lad alone!' He bellowed the demand towards the two Boers dragging Flanagan to his fate. Neither de Klerk nor his cousin paid him any heed. 'Leave . . .'

His words trailed off as a deafening peal of thunder shook the ground, and instead he began to move, breaking into a run then jumping a tent rope, just about avoiding a pair of tin buckets that he only spotted in his path at the last moment. He did not shout again. He would neither be heard nor heeded. It would take something more dramatic to stop the Boers from killing a man for the theft of some water.

De Klerk was the closer of the two men hauling Flanagan, and so he was the first to see Jack approaching. His jaw clenched, his mouth twisting with determination as he held the squirming Londoner tighter.

Jack began sprinting, eyes flickering left and right, assessing distances, planning, plotting. The two older Boers were rushing forward, but they were still a good dozen yards away. That left Jack two men to fight at first. He had faced worse odds. He hadn't always won, but he made his plan nonetheless, altering his route slightly so that he would come at de Klerk's open side.

De Klerk and his cousin came to a halt. Neither relinquished their hold.

Jack saw all three faces looking towards him, all streaked with rain, two coloured by anger, one paling with open fear.

He hit them at full speed, swinging his arms wide as if attempting a ferocious bear hug and driving them backwards, his hands locking tight on both Boers' arms, his head ramming into the slight gap between de Klerk and Flanagan.

All four men went down like so many sacks of horseshit, arms and legs jumbled, cries of surprise changing to short, sharp exhalations as they hit the ground, which was still rock hard under the top layer of mush.

Pain flashed through Jack's body, the impact jarring every bone, even though much of the collision was absorbed by those underneath him. Then he was up, pushing down hard with his arms to lever himself to his feet, careless of the body – he did not know which one – he used to force himself upright.

'Come on!' Reaching down, he grabbed for Flanagan's wrist, hauling his countryman out of the jumbled mess of bodies.

De Klerk saw what he was about. Even though he must have been hurting, he fought back, snatching at Flanagan's leg and pulling at him in an attempt to keep him on the ground.

For a moment, the two engaged in a human tug-of-war, Jack leaning back as he tried to free Flanagan, de Klerk straining hard as he lay on his back, tugging with as much force as he could muster. But Jack had the better angle, and he stepped backwards, forcing the young man free from the Boer's grip, breaking him out of the jumble of bodies.

'Fucking hit him!' He spun Flanagan around, turning him to face de Klerk's cousin, shouting the only command he could think of in that moment. There was no time left for Flanagan to run. Already the two Boers were starting to get up, and he needed them to stay on the ground if he was to give his fellow Englishman any sort of chance to escape.

Stooping low, he thrust out a hand, pushing it hard into de Klerk's chest. 'Stay down!'

Out of the corner of his eye, he saw Flanagan attempting to do the same to de Klerk's cousin. He failed badly, the Boer twisting easily around the weak prod, then bundling to his feet, hands grasping for Flanagan, who recoiled and tripped, hitting the ground on his backside.

'For fuck's sake.' Jack had time to mutter under his breath before he stamped sideways, careless of his boots hitting the now sprawling Flanagan, his only thought to batter de Klerk's skinny-arse cousin to the ground. But the younger man was too quick and too lithe, darting away, then squaring up to face him.

Jack did not hesitate. He stepped forward, butting his forehead into the very centre of the Boer's face, the blow delivered with the snap and precision learned in childhood scraps in the back alleys of Whitechapel.

The headbutt took the younger man completely off guard. It drove him backwards, face colouring with a rush of claret-coloured blood that spurted from both nostrils as Jack's forehead crushed his nose almost flat.

Jack gave him no time to recover. Darting forward, he punched hard and straight, right fist swinging then landing on the same spot as his headbutt, a wet, smacking sound coming loud as his hand connected with the bloody morass that was all that remained of the skinny man's nose.

It was too much for the Boer. Eyes fluttering, he swayed on his feet for a full second before he crumpled, his body appearing to fold over itself as he slumped to the ground.

There was no time for Jack to admire his handiwork. De Klerk had spotted an opening, and he did not delay. He came at Jack even as he was recovering from the punch that had turned out the other Boer's lights.

Jack felt a hammer blow in the very small of his back. It landed right on the spot that had been turned into a red-hot maw by weeks of incessant digging, and it was delivered with enough force to send a spur of pain searing down both legs, up his spine and beyond into his neck. Back arching, he staggered forward, vision greying from the thunderbolt of agony that coursed through his veins. It took all he had to stay on his feet, his legs turned instantly into so much mush, and he was powerless to do anything but absorb the sharp jab de Klerk slammed into his gut. The blow drove the air from his lungs, bending him double, the sudden jerking motion sending a white-hot needle through his skull. It also left him defenceless, his body stooped over like an old man trying to totter towards his chair.

De Klerk needed no second invitation. Clasping both hands

together, he hammered them down onto the back of Jack's head, a blow that would have felled an ox.

Once Jack might have been able to take it. Once he had been as tough and as hard as any man. But he was past his fortieth year now and his body had been badly abused over the decades, the strain of soldiering and fighting leaving him weaker than he had ever been, and certainly way short of the strength he would have needed to remain standing after the pile-driver blow de Klerk had just delivered.

With his body reacting to the pain in his back, his arms failed to move, and he hit the ground chin first. Only the fact that the rain had turned the top of the ground into slurry saved him from a worse impact, but the contact was still enough to send his senses reeling, and for a moment he saw nothing but black.

'*Jou fokken poes.*' The Boer bellowed in triumph as he felled his foe, then he grabbed him by the hair and lifted his head out of the mire. Jack had no notion what insult had just been spat into his face, but he recognised the twist of rage on de Klerk's lips. He was about to get a slating the like of which he had not been dealt for years.

He could do nothing as de Klerk slammed his head downwards, his face hitting the ground with enough force this time for him to feel blood begin to run down his chin from lips crushed back against his teeth.

De Klerk did not let him lie.

The first kick came hard and fast, connecting with the side of his torso and driving into his ribs with so much force that he felt his body turning on its side. Another kick came an instant later, his now exposed midriff taking the full impact.

Pain engulfed him, filling his head and swamping his senses, so that he no longer existed in the real world, but somewhere else, somewhere darker, somewhere there was nothing but pain. That pain only intensified as more kicks followed, his body unable to do anything save roll back and forth on the claggy ground. He was dimly aware of other boots pounding into him, the blows coming from every direction, rain and mud sloughing over him to mix with the blood that was pouring from his face.

'Stop!'

The command came from somewhere far off in the distance, he did not know where. It was ignored, another flurry of kicks battering into his abused flesh. One caught him full in the face with enough force to throw his head back as if his neck were little more than a spring. He felt a booted foot stomp down onto his side, at least one of his assailants choosing to stamp rather than kick.

The pain was fading, the individual blows lost amongst the onslaught. There was nothing save for the constant thump of boots on his body.

'I said stop, goddammit.' The voice came again. Faint, distant. He was too far gone to know who was speaking, or why.

The kicking continued without pause. Blow after blow. Brutal and without mercy. A beating that would not end until a man was lying dead in the muck.

A thunderbolt of lightning flashed across the sky, a moment of shocking power that tore the world apart for no more than the span of a fleeting heartbeat.

Then there was a gunshot.

And the world, and everything in it, stopped.

Chapter Eighteen

Jack lay face down in the filth. He could feel the damp of the ground on his skin and he could sense the rain drumming on his back, the hundreds of tiny impacts blurring into one. Yet none of it registered in a mind filled with pain. There was neither room for sensation nor space to comprehend the gunshot he had heard. All that mattered was that the kicking had stopped.

'Get up!'

The words were muffled, as if spoken far, far away. They were followed by the roar of thunder and the crack of lightning, the twin sounds blending into one cataclysmic racket. He sensed hands pulling at him, but he was a dead weight, a corpse still with breath, and he did little but loll back and forth like a beached whale, his muscles unable to control his battered flesh. The voice itself barely registered, the words shrouded in fog.

'Get up, for God's sake. Please. She needs you.'

More muted words came at him. Begging. Urging. Pleading. With them came someone's hands, pulling, pushing, grasping, yet still he did not understand why he was being summoned.

Nothing made sense. He just wanted to lie there letting the rain soak into his body. He had room for nothing save the pain that tormented him and robbed him of his sense of self. He could not see anything beyond the muddy slush in front of his eyes or fully comprehend the words directed at him. His body was beginning to shake uncontrollably and he could not summon the strength to do anything but lie there helpless.

'Jesus Christ, help me! Do you bloody well hear me, Lark? You've got to help Anna. She needs you, goddammit.'

The words were the first to pierce the fog that filled his soul.

They registered, sparking a flame. Reigniting life.

The world came rushing back to him, overwhelming senses that had been battered into a grey netherworld. Cold rain. The smell of mud. The taste of blood on broken lips. The feeling of bruised and battered flesh.

And fear. Soul-chilling fear.

A single thought came alive in the centre of his mind. Screaming out. Demanding he move.

Somehow he knew that Anna had been shot. It made sense. The sudden gunshot. The end of the kicking. Something had happened to stop it, and all he could picture was the moment when a heavy bullet struck her down. A perfect image flashed unbidden before his mind's eye with all the clarity of a photograph. Her broken body lying in the dirt. Blood puddling around her. Her eyes glazing over. He had seen that moment of death in a dozen stares. The instant when life fled. The second when he was cast adrift.

Fate was stealing her from him, just as she had stolen away all the others.

Anna was gone.

Anna was dead.

He opened his eyes, focusing his vision on the person trying to heave him to his feet. It was Goodfellow, his face flushed with effort.

'Get up, Jack, I beg you! Quickly now.' The plea was followed by the crack of a bolt of lightning, then a long rumble of angry thunder, the storm in the heavens raging on.

Jack tried his best to obey Goodfellow's entreaties, his body reacting to the rush of fear surging through him. He pushed down with a hand in an attempt to lever himself up. But it slipped sideways, his palm unable to do anything but slide in the slurry. He tried again, summoning the strength from he did not know where, his hand moving feverishly back and forth as he fought for purchase on the rain-slick ground.

'That's it, Jack, up you get now.' Goodfellow was hauling away for all he was worth, both hands clamped around a single arm, his words offering breathless encouragement.

Jack scrabbled in the muck. From somewhere deep inside came a wave of determination. He would not stay down. He would not give in to the flickers of despair that he could feel deep in his gut. First one hand then the other found some form of grip, and he pushed down, forcing his chest up and out of the mud. Groaning with pain, he slid a knee forward, getting it underneath him and taking his weight. He tried to get up then, but the pain in his back unmanned him and he cried out, the sound torn from somewhere deep inside. Shaking, he held his position, willing the agony to go away, holding tight to the world around him lest he slip into the darkness that was threatening to engulf his senses. He concentrated on the feel of blood, warm on his face, the rain drumming on his head, cold mud on his hands. He held on to every sensation, using them to tether him to the murky light that surrounded him, fighting away the gloom that was coming for him relentlessly, engulfing, powerful, strong.

'Come on, Jack. She needs you.' Goodfellow was flapping, plucking at Jack's sleeve, trying to keep him moving, all the while pleading with him to stand.

It was enough.

'Where is she?' Jack hissed the words as he rose like a ghoul from a grave, his feet sliding back and forth as they struggled to help him upright on the slippery surface. 'Where's Anna?'

'That's the way.' Goodfellow was reaching out to help him. Now he turned him around, pointing away into the gloom. 'There, you see. There she is, Jack.'

Shapes and figures emerged from the murk. The rain was still coming down without pause, the turgid, swollen storm clouds shutting out the sun and casting the ground into shade and shadow.

He saw her.

She was kneeling in the muck, khaki shirt blackened by the water it had absorbed. She was clasping both hands to her face, hiding, unable to face the world.

Relief flooded through him with enough force to almost send him tumbling back to the ground.

Anna was alive.

He still had her. He still had the purpose he needed.

He stood still, swaying on his feet, letting the frosty taste of fear leave him. He had been wrong. She had not been shot. She had not been taken.

But she had been broken. Something had happened. The notion was enough to halt the flow of relief and replace it with something darker, something colder.

Anna was not dead, and yet she had been brought to her knees.

He could not recall seeing anyone more forlorn. Lost. Alone.

Lightning flashed, bright and scalding, filling the sky, a moment's daylight amidst the gloom.

It revealed the rain-drenched world that surrounded them.

And he saw the body for the first time.

De Klerk's cousin lay flat on his back. Sightless eyes stared up at the sky, rainwater mixing with blood to form murky rivers that flowed from a face already taking on the waxy sheen of death. He lay in a pool of blood – there was so much blood – a great lake staining the mud in a gruesome circle all around the fallen man's body.

His chest had been torn half open at the breast, a pulsating gory mass showing where the bullet had hit him straight in the heart. As Jack watched, another wave of blood came rushing out of the gruesome tear in the flesh. Another followed, and then another, the failing heart pumping out its life force. Each pulse was weaker than the one before, the heart's power failing as the end of life came close.

Jack stood there, his mind slowly absorbing the details, rain streaming down his face. He could see the two older Boers rushing to the body, the grey-bearded pair losing their precious dignity as they ran forward in desperate haste. De Klerk was already at his cousin's side, on his knees, leaning forward, hands pushing into the dreadful wound in a futile attempt to somehow stem the flow of blood.

And he saw the Lefaucheux. The heavy black revolver lying in the mud not far from Anna's knees.

He had no idea when the weapon had been removed from

the holster on his belt. It could only have happened when the
Boers had been giving him the kicking, the weapon surely
booted far from its owner lest it somehow turn the tables in the
uneven fight. He could only surmise that Anna had picked it
up, and that it had been she who had demanded the beating
stop.

And it had been she who had just killed a man.

'Get her away, Jack.' Goodfellow looked like a prisoner
faced with a choice of the hangman's noose or the executioner's
axe. He thrust his face in front of Jack's own, eyes wide in
panic. 'Get her away, you hear me.'

Jack blinked hard. He understood. Anna had likely killed a
man in front of witnesses. Now it was her life that was hanging
in the balance.

'Yes.' He formed the single word, lurching into motion the
moment it left his lips.

He left Goodfellow behind, staggering towards Anna, the
world around him still somehow distant. He had enough
strength to see his path to her side, nothing more.

'Anna.' He called out to her, not registering that he was
speaking in a voice no louder than a whisper.

The distance between them closed with excruciating slowness. Try as he might, he could not move faster, the ground
crawling past at a snail's pace no matter how hard he strained.
He could hear the shouts of the Boers as they tried to save the
young man, begging for his soul to remain in the ripped and
torn flesh. He knew they were wasting their breath. The lad
was dead, quite dead, or at least he would be very soon. No
amount of pleading would change anything. Not with a wound
like that.

'Anna!' He called out again, louder this time, his boots

sliding across the filthy ground, his voice cutting through the noise of the storm that continued unabated.

She looked up, registering his presence at last. Her face was contorted into an expression of despair, grief and shock writ large. With her hair plastered to her scalp and her clothes hanging heavy and wet, she looked like a forgotten child left out to play when the rain had come.

'I killed him.'

She spoke the words clearly, calmly even. She was looking at him as she did, so that he could see the utter devastation in her eyes. For years she had strived to save lives, even in the most difficult and dangerous circumstances. She had helped others to live when she could have left them to die.

Yet now she had killed.

And it had broken her.

'Come on.' He covered the last yards between them, his arms reaching out to take hold of her.

She recoiled as he touched her, her body lurching up and away as if he repulsed her.

'It's all right.' Jack would not be denied. He moved closer, hands held out, voice as gentle as he could make it. His own pain was there, scalding and hot, but it was meaningless now and he forced it away. Whatever he felt, it was as nothing to the agony Anna was experiencing at that moment.

'It's all right.' He repeated the trite phrase, taking hold of her again, bringing her towards him.

This time she came into his arms. Yet she was as stiff as de Klerk's cousin would shortly be, the rigor mortis of horror clasping her tight.

He heard the first shouts then. Deep voices bellowing in rage and grief. Anger unleashed.

'Come on.' He turned her, holding her tight then leading her away.

He did not know where they would go, but at that moment it did not matter. All that counted was getting her away from the scene of the murder.

For that was what it was.

And he held a murderess in his arms.

Chapter Nineteen

'She's asleep?'

'Yes.' Goodfellow whispered his confirmation like a parent who had finally soothed a newborn to rest.

'Good.' Jack eased himself to the ground at Anna's side.

They were in Goodfellow's tent. None of the three had spoken until Jack had broken the silence with his question. The two men had busied themselves with Anna, first removing her soaking outer garments, then wrapping her tightly in blankets before laying her shivering body down. She had not uttered a single sound the whole time, her face devoid of all expression, eyes glazed with shock. They had finally closed, and now she lay like a corpse, Jack sitting next to her like a faithful hound.

Goodfellow had been a godsend. He had gathered their gear as Jack hauled Anna away, the knapsacks, carpet bag and Anna's medicines safely stored in a corrugated-iron hut outside his tent. Now he was sheltering the two of them, keeping them out of sight. It had also been Goodfellow who had told the rest of the sorry tale, the Englishman able to watch the whole sordid affair as it played out. He had lost sight of Flanagan almost immediately. The young Londoner had fled the ruckus caused in his name without a second thought for those who had intervened to save him. The Boers had been too busy to give chase, their attention focused first on administering Jack's kicking then directed towards the Boer Anna had shot down.

For her aim had been true, the single shot from Jack's revolver killing the young Boer stone dead. Goodfellow was certain of it.

There was little more to tell.

Jack, Anna and Goodfellow had slipped away in the confusion that had followed the gunshot, the trio saved as much by the storm as by any actions of their own, their departure hidden in the gloom.

'So what happens next?' Goodfellow asked quietly. Like Jack, he was soaked to the bone, and he started to remove his sodden clothing on the far side of the tent, giving Jack and Anna as much space as he could in its cramped confines.

Jack left the question to hang. He concentrated instead on removing his boots, the heavy army-issue footwear caked with mud. The rain still fell without pause, drumming against the canvas as a constant reminder of the world beyond the tent flaps. A world that was now much more dangerous than it had been just an hour previously.

'Jack?' Goodfellow prompted.

'I don't know, all right.' Jack's voice was still hushed, but no less venomous for the lack of volume.

'Jesus Christ!' He hissed the blasphemy as the effort of pulling the first boot from his foot jarred his back. Every inch of him hurt, but as far as he could tell, nothing was broken. That would have to do.

'You can stay here.'

He pulled a face. 'Don't be bottlehead stupid. They saw you

there. They know you work a claim with Flanagan. This'll be the first place they bloody come.' He shook his head at his own curt reply. 'But thank you.'

'Then where will you go?' Goodfellow removed his trousers.

'I don't know.' Jack glanced at his countryman, who was standing there in his undershirt and drawers, his great hairy belly poking out.

'I don't think Anna can go anywhere for now.' If Goodfellow was embarrassed to be seen in his undergarments, he gave no sign of it. He removed his undershirt, then wrung it out, water dripping onto the ground sheet by his feet.

'No.' Jack said no more as he took off his second boot. Placing them on the ground, he took another blanket from the pile Goodfellow had provided and used it to dry his damp feet. He had been an infantryman for too long to neglect either his feet or his boots. Both would be dried and cleaned before he did anything else.

'I do not think she meant to kill that man.' Goodfellow clearly needed to talk. He eased himself to the ground, his bulky frame moving awkwardly, breath whooshing out as his ample stomach folded over itself. 'I think she just wanted to make it stop. She would not let them kick you to death.' He pulled a blanket from the pile and wrapped it around his shoulders, pulling it tight under his chin.

'It was a bloody good shot.' Jack shook his head slowly. Anna knew how to shoot; her uncle had seen to that. But it was still hard to imagine her picking out the Boer's heart and drilling it so cleanly with her first effort. Fate had been playing with them that day. Just as she always did.

'She was trying to protect you.'

The remark made Jack sigh. Goodfellow was speaking the

truth. Anna had seen him being kicked and beaten, and so she had intervened. That made it his fault. Not hers. His.

The events that had led to him lying on the filthy ground, the Boers' boots pounding into him, were replaying themselves over and over in his mind. Even as he sat there, he thought of what he should have done, of handing Flanagan over to the Boers and letting them take their justice, no matter if it meant them stringing the thief from the nearest pit frame.

But Anna would never have stood idle when a young man was being executed in front of her eyes. And if Jack had stopped her, his life would still have changed. All he would have done was destroy his relationship with her; she would never have stayed with a man who had stood by and let another die. Whatever choice he had made would have sent him on a new path, one not of his own choosing.

Fate would not just let him be.

'You need to leave the diggings.' Goodfellow was burrowing into a haversack as he spoke.

'I know.' Jack watched as his countryman brought out a bottle of Cape brandy. He did not speak as Goodfellow pulled out the cork with a loud popping sound and took a long, slow sip. Only when he was done did he hold out the bottle.

'Thank you.' Jack drank deeply, holding the brandy in his mouth, letting it burn then swallowing it slowly, feeling it slide down his gullet.

'If I can help . . .' Goodfellow left the thought unfinished.

Jack handed the bottle back. He did not know if it was the brandy or something darker inside his soul, but the first touch of an idea was brewing.

'You can.' He paused, letting the idea run around his mind. 'Just ask, my friend.'

'I want you to tell people you were there. Tell them what happened.' Jack fixed his gaze on Goodfellow, his stare boring deep into the Englishman's skull. 'I want you to tell them I did it.'

'What's that?' Goodfellow blanched, clearly surprised.

'Tell them I killed that poor bastard.'

'How the hell did you do that when you were lying on the ground getting ten bells kicked out of you?'

'Just tell them. Keep Anna out of it.'

'I see.' Goodfellow grasped Jack's plan. 'What if others have heard the truth of it?'

'They won't have.' Jack's mind was still fogged with pain, but he knew what he was about. 'Those Boers won't be spreading this around. Their damn pride won't let them admit that a woman killed one of theirs, and an Englishwoman at that. They will keep the truth to themselves, or at least they won't tell anyone who isn't a bloody Dutchie what really happened. So just tell folk it was me that killed him.'

'And what happens then?' Goodfellow spoke slowly and clearly.

'They leave Anna the fuck alone.' Jack's answer was short, sharp and pithy.

'But what happens to you?' Goodfellow reworded his question to convey its true meaning.

'That doesn't matter.'

'They might kill you.'

'They can try.'

Goodfellow barked a short, humourless laugh. 'If that is what you want me to do, then that is what I shall do, Jack. I understand your motive. It is a noble thing you are proposing. If I can help, I will.' He smiled sadly. 'We must protect Anna, after all.'

'Thank you.' Jack heard something meaningful in Goodfellow's tone. There was a hidden truth there, one that crept into his mind. Goodfellow liked Anna more than he had known. But it did not hurt to understand that, nor did he feel even a tiny stab of jealousy. Not now. Not with Anna in such trouble. They both needed Goodfellow's help. That was all that mattered.

'And what happens to her when you are kicking your heels from the end of a hemp rope?' Goodfellow drank deeply from the bottle before handing it back to Jack.

Jack did not answer for a moment. His plan was still fresh. It needed fleshing out. 'Will you take care of her?' he asked at last. He was offering something the man had likely only dreamed of. Anna would be safe with Goodfellow. He would protect her, Jack was certain of that now.

'What if they come looking for her?' There was an undertone of fear in the reply. 'Some of them were there. They will know it was her that shot him.'

'They won't want to blame it on a woman. They think women are there just to breed and to cook.' Jack had learned a little of the Boers in his time around them. Not once had he spoken to one of their women. His opinion was based on that and that alone. 'If we tell everyone it was me, I doubt they'll admit it was a woman that killed one of their own. No, they'll come for me. That will suit them nicely. They can get their revenge without the shame of the truth getting out.'

'How can you be so sure?'

He smiled thinly. 'I'm not. But if they string me up, I reckon both of you will be safe.'

The notion did not frighten him. He knew what it was to face death. On one occasion he had given in, accepting his fate like a docile sheep led to the butcher. At other times he had fought, refusing to surrender no matter what. The idea that the Boers might try to kill him was nothing new. Not to him.

'You'd care to wager your life on that?' Goodfellow laughed at the wry remark, then reached out to take his brandy out of Jack's grasp. 'I am not sure I approve of your plan, Jack. But I will do as you ask. I think you know why.'

Jack was spared an immediate answer as Anna stirred. He reached out to her, laying a comforting hand on her shoulder, then tucking the blanket tighter around her. The shivering had stopped, but her skin was pallid and her breathing shallow. It was as if she were retreating deep inside herself, the world shut out.

'We still need to move. We cannot stay here.' He spoke once he was sure she had settled. 'When she wakes, we'll go some-place else.'

'I know where you can go. There is an empty tent I know of. Its owner is sick and in the diggers' hospital. From what I hear, he will not be returning soon, if at all, poor fellow. You can stay there.'

'Good.' Jack kept his eyes on Anna's face as he agreed to Goodfellow's plan. Every few moments, her features moved, a slight spasm as if she were wincing while she slept. He could imagine what images were filling her mind as she tried to hide from the world, what torment was flitting across her thoughts as she slept. He knew what it was to have demons. He corralled his own deep in his mind, hiding them away. They emerged into his dreams as nightmares and into his thoughts whenever he let his guard down. He never knew when they would push against his barriers, when they would surge free and consume him. When that happened, there was nothing he could do but accept them, no matter how much they unmanned him. It took time to regain control, and he feared that one day he would fail and be unable to return them to their jail. He did not know what would happen then. Now Anna would have to learn to create her own barriers, building defences to hold the memories of that stormy night at bay.

There was nothing more to be said. The plan was set.

He would take the blame for a murder he had not committed. That notion was enough to make him smile. He had killed so many times.

There was an irony that he might meet his end for a death that had not arrived at his hand.

Chapter Twenty

———◆———

'Help me, Jack.'

'What is it?' Jack was on his feet the moment Anna said his name.

'I need the latrine.'

'Come on then, quickly now.' He moved sharply, coming to her side and lifting her to her feet before helping her across the tent, the two of them bent double like a pair of old crones. He paid no heed to the stale smell that emanated from her, the mix of musty sweat and acrid vomit now familiar. This was not the first time he had had to take her out, and he doubted it would be the last, the dreadful bout of diarrhoea starting around midnight. In her current state, there was no way he could take her to the camp latrines, the huge open trenches too far away and too public, and so he had dug a pit behind their own tent, screening it from sight with blankets.

'That's it, love, nearly there.' He reached out to pull back the tent flaps, holding her fast, his arm around her waist, as he helped her outside. It was easily done. She was light, and seemed to be getting lighter by the hour.

She staggered into the sunshine, then immediately bent

double and groaned, her free hand clasping her belly.

'Come on now.' Jack could do little more than hold her upright and half carry, half drag her to the pit he had dug. No sooner had she made it there than a stream of slurry came spewing out of her in a thin, watery torrent. He did his best to offer comfort, rubbing her back, his hand moving in small circles just as it had a dozen times before in the last few hours. There was nothing left in her belly save for the grim, foul-smelling liquid, but it was still coming out of her with alarming regularity.

They had left Goodfellow the previous day, scurrying through the encampment at twilight towards the tent he had suggested they borrow. It was on the far side of the diggings, furthest from the claims, and proved to be meagre shelter. It stank, and was riddled with enough fleas for Jack to hear their tiny feet scratching as they crawled over the groundsheet. But it was forgotten and ignored, and that would suit him nicely enough as he decided what was to be done next.

Goodfellow's plan would have worked out just fine, as not once did anyone come to question their arrival, or their right to be there. But Jack had woken in the middle of the night to find that Anna was sick.

Very sick.

'Done?' He asked the question as gently as he could. He was rewarded with a hasty nod. She did not look at him.

'Come on then.' He did his best to clean her up, using one of the last rags he had left, then held her fast as he turned her around. He glanced at the result of her motions, the yellow-brown liquid stinking to high heaven. There was not much of it this time; certainly less than before. He hoped that the reducing quantity was a good sign, that whatever disease had taken hold of her was passing.

He escorted her back into the tent, and she sank to the ground gratefully, immediately curling up so her knees were pressed tight into her chest. Jack could find no words of comfort; everything that could be said had already been said. He just eased himself down onto the ground sheet next to her, taking a moment to tuck the blankets around her shivering body in a vain attempt to ease her suffering.

'Thank you.' The words came out in a whisper so faint he could barely hear them. 'You are being kind.'

'My pleasure.' Reaching out his hand, he smoothed back her hair from her face. It felt lank and greasy under his touch, and it was stuck fast to her clammy skin, so that he was forced to pick it free before he could move it off her forehead. He watched for a reaction, but there was none, her eyes shut tight as she fought against the pain deep in her guts.

'Is there anything I can get you?' he asked. A light shake of the head was all the answer he received.

He sat back, resting his weight on his arms as he tried to take the strain off his spine. To say his back ached was an understatement, but he had to ignore it, just as he had to pay no attention to the fear that was swirling around deep in his belly.

A fear that Anna would be taken from him.

He did not know what was ailing her. The illness, whatever it was, had taken her from the moment he had first laid her down in the tent. At first he had put it down to shock, her distress at having killed a man causing some form of physical reaction in her body. He had seen it before. Even the strongest man could be brought low by battle, the terror of the fight more than he could bear. He had seen men fall to the ground, their entire being consumed with terror. Others had run, either at the first gunshot fired at them in anger, or after hours spent enduring the worst the enemy could throw at them. The horror of war could strike down the most capable and the strongest.

But as the hours had passed, so his concern had increased. Not only was Anna shivering and shitting, but now her skin was fiery red and blotchy, especially around her neck, and he could see at least a dozen tiny red pimples on her chest and back. They disappeared when he pushed them, but he was sure they were spreading across her pale skin at an alarming rate. She seemed to be fading in front of his eyes, taking on a grey pallor that reminded him more of a corpse than a living being, and he could feel the heat emanating from her even though he was a good foot away. Despite that heat, she complained only of being cold, and so he had swaddled her in Goodfellow's blankets, piling them on top of her, his ability to care for her reduced to that and little more. Anna was the physician, the one who knew what was to be done, but thus far she had given little direction save asking to be left to rest and to be made to drink as and when she could.

It left Jack feeling impotence like nothing he had experienced before. Try as he might, he could not shift the image he had seen in the moments after the Boer had been shot. The clear picture in his mind of Anna lying there, eyes glazed, life force lost.

'Are you there, Jack?'

The question made him start awake. He had been dozing, waiting for he knew not what, when Anna had spoken.

'How are you feeling?' He was instantly fully alert, every sense tuned to her, hope flaring that somehow the worst was past.

She shook her head, wincing as she did so. 'Not good.'

Jack grunted at the understatement, reaching out to rest his hand again her forehead. 'You're burning up.' He paused as she grimaced at some secret pain. 'Tell me what to do.'

'I need my bag.'

'I'll get it.'

'Where is it?'

'Back with the rest of our gear outside Goodfellow's tent. He's looking after it for us,' Jack explained. 'I'll go now. It won't take long.'

'No!' Anna's voice was surprisingly strong. 'They'll be after us. They will know where Goodfellow's tent is. They will know he helped us.'

'I won't let them see me.' He tried to shrug off her concerns. 'You need the medicine, Anna. You are not well.'

She did not reply at once. Her breathing was shallow and she was clearly struggling to stay conscious.

'It's going to be all right.' He reached out, stroking her hair, his fingers as gentle as he could make them. 'You rest and I'll find your bag.'

'And that will make everything better, will it?' Her voice wavered as she replied.

Jack stopped his stroking. She had spoken in little more than a whisper, but the lack of volume did nothing to hide the bitterness to her tone. 'You need to get better, love.'

'Why?'

He sucked down a deep breath. Anna was sick, that was true, but this was something else, something darker. And he understood it, for it was with him always. She had looked into the shadowy corners of hell and had been scarred by what she had seen.

'Because you *have* to. I need you, Anna.'

'What have I done, Jack?' Sunken, reddened eyes stared up at him. Her gaze was intense, boring into his. Yet he did not shirk from it, even as she bared her soul in a way he could never do.

'You saved my life, love.' He leaned forward, kissing her gently on her forehead. 'That's what you did, Anna, you saved me.' He repeated the words, hoping they would sink in. 'If you hadn't done what you did, I would be lying in a cold grave now. They wouldn't have stopped, you know that, don't you? They would have carried on beating me until I was dead.'

It was true. If Anna had not fired that single shot, she would now be quite alone, and Jack would have found out what waited for him when Fate untied the frayed string that held his life together.

'I killed him, Jack. I took his life. He was so young, so very young. And now he is dead because of what I did.' She shivered as she faced up to what had happened. He admired her courage.

'Yes. You killed him.' He would not spare her or try to mollify her. It was time for the truth. A truth she had to accept and absorb else it would destroy her. 'He died and I lived.'

Her body convulsed with a great tremor, as if the thought of that moment was so horrific, she was trying to reject it. Her arms curled tighter around herself, holding in the pain.

'Would you rather I had died?' He asked the question as gently as he could. He did not know if he was being kind or cruel by speaking so plainly. But he knew the words had to be said. They could not be sugar-coated. Not if Anna was to heal.

'No.' It was the voice of a child.

'So you did what had to be done. Nothing more, nothing less. Had I been standing in your shoes, I would have done the same without hesitation. We fight for those we love, Anna. We have to.'

'It had to be done?' A moment's fire entered her tone. 'That man had to die, did he? His life had to end just like that?'

'If I was to live, yes.'

This time Anna did not answer him. She was shutting down again, what little strength she had found fading fast.

'It is just how it had to be. Sometimes . . .' he paused, trying to find the right words, 'sometimes you have to fight to protect what is yours.' He spoke quietly, once again reaching out to soothe her. 'Sometimes you have no choice.'

'There is always a choice.'

'No!' For the first time, Jack snapped back at her. 'You had no choice. You could not reason with those men; you could not tell them to stop or summon someone to make sure there was justice. It doesn't work like that here. You had to take action. And so you did what you had to do.'

'And a man died.' The words were a hoarse whisper, nothing more.

'Yes. A man died.'

'And I killed him.'

'You did. Just as you had to.' Jack held her head then, cupping her damp face, the hot, clammy skin held fast. 'You did what you had to do. Nothing more.'

'So speaks the soldier.'

He did not reply. He was not a soldier, not any more. He did not hide behind orders or the safety of a uniform. Yet he was still a killer. And he would have killed to save her. Just as he still would.

'How many men have you killed, Jack?' she hissed. There was anger in her tone now. Anger coloured with shame.

'Too many.' He replied with honesty. His body was cold and battered, but his own suffering meant nothing, not while they talked of death. His demons were pulling against their chains, hungry for the freedom of release.

'How many, Jack? Ten? Twenty? A hundred?'

He found he could not answer her. He swallowed with difficulty, and all the while his demons were straining and fighting to escape from the darkest recesses of his mind.

'Did they all deserve it? Did they all deserve to die? Was there always no choice?'

'I don't know. But I do know this.' He voice vibrated with barely contained emotion. 'Sometimes it comes down to you or them. And so you do whatever it takes for it to be them. Then you learn to live with it. And that's what you have to do, Anna. You have to live with this. What is done is done, and what was done was done for the right reason. There is nothing else to it.'

'How do I move on?' There was real pain in her voice now.

'You just do.' It was all the answer he had for her.

'I don't think I can.' A great shudder ran through her as she replied. Then she lay still once again.

The silence stretched thin. Jack had no words to console her, no advice that would offer comfort beyond just being there. Anna would have to win the battle for her soul by herself.

'I'm so cold, Jack. So very cold.' She broke the silence, her teeth chattering.

Jack reached out for the blankets, tucking them tighter then laying his hand on her shoulder. 'I've got you.'

There was nothing else to be said.

Chapter Twenty-one

The market had only just opened, but it was already busy, the wives, children and servants of the diggers thronging around the stalls in the very centre of the encampment. Everything they needed was on sale, men with an eye for a profit eager to sell whatever the small community needed. Fortunes were being made, the men trying to find the precious diamonds forced to pay eye-watering prices for the essentials they needed to remain working at the pan.

Jack picked his way through the crowd. He was not the only man present, but he was certainly in the minority. Diggers would not waste precious daylight shopping for supplies unless they had to, not when the big one was waiting for them somewhere under that dry, friable soil.

A smallholder bellowed something at Jack, slapping his hand against the fresh carcass of a wildebeest, his words lost in the tumult of a dozen other merchants competing for the crowd's attention. The rest of the man's stall looked like a small abattoir, the skinned bodies of three springbuck lying on the countertop, while six fat ducks hung from a line of twine tied to one of the posts. A good half of the counter was given over to biltong, the dried meat that was a staple food of the diggers; most would have at least some tucked into a pocket ready to be gnawed on when hunger struck.

Jack ignored the man's attempt to lure him in, concentrating instead on going with the flow of the crowd, not pushing past but moving with those around him as he made for the one apothecary supplying the pan with medicines, most of which were made to his own recipe. A rare few had been imported from Europe, and these carried a price tag to match the distance they had travelled. Not that Jack cared for the price. He would spend every last penny he had to get what Anna needed.

He passed a greengrocer, the man's stall the back of a wagon, his vegetables and fruit laid out as neatly as the best costermonger's barrow. Potatoes of every size, enormous carrots, fat beetroot, and cabbages the size of roundshot lay in heaps next to lines of apples, both red and green, bulbous bright yellow lemons and plump oranges. There were other vegetables and fruit on display that he did not recognise, and all seemed larger and somehow more vibrant than those he had seen on the costermongers' barrows in the East End of London. Beside the greengrocer was a wide-bed wagon laden with wool and animal hides, the proprietor standing high above the crowd, his assistant left to pull out the wares that his master was selling to the handful of customers below. Another smaller wagon came next, its owner a small, frail woman with grey hair and whiskery cheeks who sat on a stool, her sharp tongue lashing the two young black boys she employed to wave fans over her cakes and confectionery to drive away the multitude of flies drawn to the sweet treats.

Jack walked on, ignoring the delicacies as he did his best to keep his head down, the ubiquitous broad-brimmed felt hat he had borrowed in place of his solar topee pulled low over his eyes. He kept a close watch on two Boers moving in the opposite direction, their loud voices and braying laughs sounding clearly even over the murmur of the crowd and the shouts of the merchants. Neither looked familiar, but that did not discount them as a threat, and he walked a new course so that should they look his way, they would see only the back of his hatted head. He did not know whether the story of the Boer's murder had filtered through the diggings, but he was sure that the other Boers here would have been told. They might come from a dozen different families, but they would stick together and look out for one of their own. He did not doubt for one moment that enough of the sad tale had permeated through the Boer encampment to make it dangerous for him to be abroad.

'Jack?'

'Shit.' There was time for Jack to hiss the oath under his breath as he recognised the voice before Clarke reached out to pluck at his sleeve.

'What the hell are you playing at?' the Australian murmured, face aghast at seeing his former partner out and about. 'You should be keeping your bloody head down, mate.' He urged Jack to duck down, and even went so far as to pull him behind him so that he would be screened from the crowd around them.

'Look, Anna's sick and I need to get her something that will make her better.' Jack gave a short and sharp explanation.

'She'd better be bloody dying if you're taking such a damn-fool risk as wandering around here like you don't have a bloody care in the world.' Clarke's eyes scanned the vicinity as though he expected to be rushed by a band of angry Boers at any moment.

'What did you hear?' Jack steered him out of the press of the crowd, pulling him down the side of the wool merchant's wagon and into some degree of cover.

'That either you or Anna shot a Boer stone dead. In cold blood too.'

Jack grunted. The tale was simple enough. And accurate.

'That bastard de Klerk is searching for you, as is every other bloody Boer in the diggings. They want you dead, I reckon.'

Jack sighed. Not a lot happened at the pan, and so it was no surprise the story was on everyone's lips. That thought was enough to make him copy the anxious Australian and glance around him, expecting to see every pair of eyes looking his way. And yet he saw nothing untoward. It was oddly calm, the denizens of the diggings going about their daily tasks just as they had done the day before and the day before that. In Jack's world, everything had changed, his existence thrown into turmoil and his life now in danger, yet to everyone else who called the pan home, the cogs were turning just as they always had.

'You'd better find what you need, then get the hell out of here, if you know what's good for you.' Clarke was not done offering instructions.

'I will.' Jack tried not to bristle at the pointless advice. He had not been dawdling and had no intention of staying any longer than was needed to get Anna the medicines she had instructed him to find. He did not know what any of them looked like, and so would have to trust to the market's physician not to fob him off.

The extra medicines were only needed thanks to Anna's generosity. She had used up nearly all of her stocks treating those around her. Now that she needed them for herself, there were barely any left. It was a blessing that she had been able to write down the names of the medicines Jack would have to purchase. That simple act had taken an age, and her once neat, precise writing had been reduced to an illiterate's scrawl. He just hoped that the pills and potions would do something to aid her recovery. To his eye she was getting worse, the flesh seeming to melt off her at an alarming rate. The pimples on her chest and back were multiplying, and her motions, what there was of them, were a ghastly, greasy cream colour.

'I can't help you; you know that, right?'

'What's that you say?' Jack wasn't sure he'd heard Clarke correctly.

'I can't help you,' Clarke repeated. 'I would if I could, mate, but you know how it is.'

'Oh, I know how it is.' On a different day Jack might have laughed at the expression he saw on Clarke's face. The Australian was clearly anxious to get away and take himself as far from the Englishman as he could.

'Good, I knew you would understand.' Clarke was already starting to back away. 'You don't look overly concerned, Jack. I'd be shitting myself if I was in your shoes.'

'I'm sure you would.' Jack fought the urge to snort with derision. But the Australian was quite correct. He was not bothered about being a wanted man. He had been a fugitive before, and the man who had been coming after him then was far more dangerous than all the Boers put together. That did not mean he was taking the threat lightly – he was no fool – but for the moment, all he cared about was getting the medicines and taking them back to Anna. He would turn his attention to the future when she was recovered. Not before.

He looked across the market, plotting a path through the throng, his only thought getting to the apothecary.

And then he saw de Klerk.

The Boer was no more than ten yards away. He looked knackered, his face ashen, eyes bloodshot and raw. Either he had been on one almighty bender, or Anna was not the only one struggling to deal with the events that had left a young man lying dead.

Before Jack could look away, de Klerk caught his eye.

The two men stared at one another, each holding the other's gaze.

'Make yourself scarce.' Jack spoke to Clarke out of the corner of his mouth. 'Now.' He did not move his eyes away from de Klerk.

'I'm gone.' Clarke too had spotted the Boer. He turned and began scampering away, clearly wanting no part in what was to come.

Jack held his ground. He would not run like a pickpocket caught with his hands on a gentleman's handkerchief.

De Klerk was coming straight towards him, easing his way past a pair of gossiping women, his gaze fixed on Jack as if he expected his quarry to make a break for it at any moment.

Jack stood as still as a statue. Waiting.

'*Yissus*, you're either brave or a *doos* to be standing there.' De Klerk addressed him as he came close.

'We need to talk.' Jack did not fear the confrontation.

'*Hou jou bek!*' Spittle was flung from the Boer's lips, such was the force with which he spoke. 'You have nothing to say that I want to hear.'

Jack grunted as he saw how the conversation was likely to play out. He could see heads turning their way, those closest to the pair hearing enough to know that a confrontation was brewing. 'Let's go somewhere a little more private, shall we?' He did not wait to see how de Klerk would react, and turned away from the market, certain the angry young man would follow.

He was right. The Boer held his tongue as Jack led him towards a line of parked merchants' wagons not far from the market. Without hesitation, he walked between two of them, taking de Klerk into the shadows and away from any nosy parkers keen to listen in on what was about to be said.

'So, what the *fok* do you think we have to talk about?' De Klerk fired the question the moment Jack turned around to face him.

Jack shook his head at the Boer's tone. 'Look, chum. I know you're brassed off. You have every right to be. But it was him or me, you boys know that.'

'*Jy prat kak.*' De Klerk's face twisted with fury as he spat the words.

'Speak fucking English.' For the first time, Jack revealed a taste of his own anger.

'Fine.' De Klerk thrust his face forward. 'You're talking shit, and you know it. That bitch of yours shot Hennie like he was a *fokken* dog.'

'Be careful,' Jack snarled. In another place, any man who called Anna a bitch would now be sitting on his backside nursing a broken jaw. But this was not a normal situation and so he checked the urge to lash out. He had to.

De Klerk looked away, his jaw clenching tight. Clearly Jack was not the only one just about holding on to his temper.

'You owe me.' Jack delivered the words deadpan. It was time to call in a debt. A demand that he had never thought he would need to issue.

'I told you we don't hold with *kak* like that. What you did is down to you, not me. I owe you nothing.'

'Bullshit. I saved your damn life. Now you need to pay me back.'

'You want me to let her go free?' De Klerk struggled to get the words out, such was his distaste.

'Yes.'

'*Fok* you, that's not how this goes.'

'You need to make it happen.'

'No chance. Not even if I wanted to. Oom Joost wants her strung up for what she did. He'll make *that* happen.'

'Then you need to stop him.'

'No.' De Klerk sucked down a deep breath. 'Ask for something else.'

Jack opened his mouth to argue, but the words did not come. It was time for his alternative plan, the one he had asked Goodfellow to set in motion. One that might be more palatable to de Klerk and that would save Anna from the threat of the Boers for ever.

'Fine.' He spoke firmly. 'Then tell your friends you saw me do it.'

'What the *fok*?' De Klerk was taken by surprise. 'I saw her shoot him.'

'Did anyone else?'

The Boer snorted as he understood what Jack was asking. 'I don't know.'

'It was pissing down and you boys were all doing your best to give me a good shoeing. So tell them you saw me shoot him from where I was on the ground.'

'No chance.' De Klerk shook his head. 'They know you were done in. There's no way in hell you could have shot him in the state you were in. Besides, even if they did believe me, they would just want the both of you dead.'

Jack felt the burn of frustration. His idea was falling on deaf ears. And he had no other plan. All that was left was for him to attempt to flee the diggings before the Boers came for them. Anna was too sick to move, but he would have to try, regardless of the agony it might inflict on her. Even if it killed her, trying to get her to safety was preferable to waiting for the Boers to come for them. Not that he would see her hang, no matter how it all played out. He would die before that happened, standing and fighting for her life no matter how many men came against them.

'There is another way.'

'What?' De Klerk's words took him by surprise. His mind had been filling with the notion of the fight that now seemed inevitable.

'*Bloed geld.*'

Jack bit at the lure. 'What's that?'

'Blood money.'

'You want paying off?'

'I've seen it done. If you pay enough, Oom Joost might let you live.'

The idea burned into Jack's mind. He had known men pay to earn their freedom. It was common in London, those with the means to buy off a magistrate able to avoid all but the most serious of crimes; even then, they could still find a path that would keep them from the gallows. If rich folk could do it, why not him?

'We found a diamond.' He spoke slowly, making sure de Klerk heard every word. 'I'll give you that in exchange for letting this go.' He made the offer without hesitation. Even if it was indeed worth ten thousand pounds, Anna's life was worth more. Much more.

'How big?'

'Big enough.' He saw de Klerk pull a face at the vague answer. 'One hundred carats.'

It was the Boer's turn to be surprised. 'That's worth a pretty penny.'

'You think it's enough?'

De Klerk shrugged. 'Maybe.' He paused. 'Maybe Oom will just kill you anyway, I don't know. The only way to find out is to give him the diamond and beg him to leave you alone. If you do that, well, who knows. But I don't see you have any other choice. Go to your claim, tomorrow morning before dawn. We will be waiting for you. Bring the diamond and we will see if Oom will let you live.'

Jack saw the fire burning in the Boer's gaze. He wanted blood, that much was obvious. But the diamond was a powerful lure. One that might just be enough to buy their freedom.

'Fine. I'll be there.' The choice was easy to make. Because it wasn't a choice, not really.

He would take the diamond back to the ground where it had been found.

And see if the Boers would let him walk away.

Chapter Twenty-two

'Where are you going?'

Jack stopped in his tracks. He was preparing to leave the fetid air of the tent for his meeting with the Boers and he had been certain that Anna was deeply asleep. Clearly he had been wrong.

It was still well before dawn and far too dark for him to see her face, which suited him just fine. He did not want to be reminded of what was at stake, or what he might be leaving behind, perhaps for ever.

'I need the latrine,' he whispered.

'That's not like you.' He heard blankets rustle as she moved.

'I'm getting old, love.' He tried to be glib.

'So where are you really going?' Even in her sickened state, she had recognised the lie when she heard it.

He sighed. 'I'm going to sort out this thing with the Boers once and for all.'

'How?'

'I'm giving them the diamond.' He squatted beside her and reached out to lay a hand on her head. 'They call it blood money – "blud gilt" or something. De Klerk thinks it will work.'

'Do you trust him?'

'No.' He stroked her dirty locks. 'But he owes me for saving his life on the trail and I don't think he is lying – at least I hope he isn't. But I don't know if the diamond will be enough. He could just be playing me for a fool.' He smiled wryly. 'Still, it's worth a try.'

Anna did not reply. He could hear the air rasping as she fought to breathe. Even the simple effort of staying alive was taxing her now, the virulent illness stealing away her vitality. The medicines he had purchased from the apothecary after his confrontation with de Klerk had done nothing to alter the course of the disease.

'Then this will be done, finished.' He filled the silence. Offering her a future. 'And we can get you better before we move on.'

'Where?' The whispered reply came almost immediately.

'It doesn't matter.' It was true. Staying alive would be enough for now.

'What if I don't get better?' The words were delivered slowly, as if speaking them caused Anna a great deal of pain.

'You will.' He spoke with all the certainty he could muster.

'You make it sound simple.' She gasped as she shifted beneath the blankets.

'It is. I will get you better. No matter what.'

'And what if it is my fate to die here?'

A shudder of dread sank deep into his gut at her words. He had fought against Fate more times than he could recall. Never had he won. 'I won't let it happen.'

'It is what I deserve.'

'What did you say?' She had spoken so softly that he was not sure he had heard her correctly.

'I deserve this. For killing him. I deserve to die for what I did.'

'You're talking nonsense.' His reply was swift and sharp. 'You're sick, that's all.'

'I'm dying.'

'No!' Jack rose to his feet, uttering the single word with every ounce of force in his soul. 'I will not let that happen.' He spoke through gritted teeth, spitting out the words with venom. 'You will not die.'

Anna fell silent. Then she rolled away from him, facing the wall of the tent, groaning with pain.

She did not speak again.

'I'll be back soon.' He screwed his eyes shut as he fought to wipe away the image she had conjured. He would not lose her. Not like he had lost all the others. Yet he could almost hear Fate laughing at him in the silence that filled the tent. For deep down inside, he knew there was nothing he could do. The futility and the impotence that knowledge inspired was almost more than he could bear, and somewhere in his head a scream began. It went on and on, filling his soul, drowning out the voice that tried to rail against such a future.

For Fate would have her way and there was nothing he could do to prevent it.

Jack rested on his haunches. Watching. Waiting.

It was still dark, just the faintest tinge of grey on the distant horizon foreshadowing the arrival of dawn. It was the last hour of the night, the time for the stars to fade, for the living to wake to face another day, and for men like Jack Lark to sit in the shadows and battle the darkness in their own soul.

He was still there as the sky started brightening and turning to the palest of pale yellows, the first hint of the warmth that would soon return to the world. He was shivering as he waited, the chill of that early-morning air enough to force his body into action. But he paid the cold no heed, just as he no longer had the vision to see the beauty in that moment. For his mind was in turmoil, fear and trepidation fuelling something deep in his being, something that on another day might grow into uncontrollable rage or the insatiable urge to kill, but on that frosty morning was turning into something far darker.

He knew with utter certainty that if Anna died, he would break. The chains and shackles that held the creatures of his nightmare in check would shatter, and he would be left with nothing but hate and fury and fire. The part of him that had held fast for so long would be finished. The dam inside him would break, and in the flood that would follow, there would be nothing left for him to cling to. Like a drowning man succumbing to the moment when he could hold his breath no longer and the first salty rush of water forced its way inside his mouth, choking, deadly, he would be done.

Everything he had been and everything he could be would come to an end.

He did not know what would be left behind if that happened.

His hand fell to the loaded Lefaucheux on his hip. The urge to draw the weapon was almost more than he could bear. It was tempting to greet the Boers with fire and with wrath. He could fight, and he could kill, ending his days in a bloody rampage of death. There would be joy in that moment, he knew that, a wonderful release of the emotions that were coming to the boil deep in his gut. There was no thought of victory, of finding a violent solution to the mess his life had become. There was just the need to release the killer inside and so end the screaming in his mind. He had done it before. He had gone into battle fuelled by fury, bloodlust filling every fibre of his being so that he no longer saw men and other living creatures, just targets and enemies. In those moments, he lost all sense of self. That was the idea that tempted him most of all, its allure almost irresistible.

But a single thought held him back.

If he died, Anna would be alone. She would have nothing and no one to protect her. And he could not let that happen. While there was still breath in her body, he would hold himself together, doing whatever it took to keep his demons at bay for a while longer.

But if she died . . .

He left the thought unfinished. A number of shadowy figures were walking towards his claim. With the sunrise starting to lighten the sky behind them, he could pick them out clearly enough, each one silhouetted against the warm oranges and ochres filling the far horizon. There were three men in total. Good odds.

'Stay there!' he shouted as he rose out of the shadows. They would not have seen him until that moment and he was determined to seize the initiative so that this meeting would be on his terms, not theirs.

The small group came to an abrupt halt, a low murmur greeting his sudden appearance.

Jack held his ground, hand resting on the handle of his revolver without him realising it, his fingers curling over the grip. 'Don't come any closer.'

'I'm glad you did as you were told, *brü*.'

Jack recognised de Klerk's voice. 'I said I would,' he called, tone firm. The moment was his to control. 'So, are we doing this?'

'Did you bring the diamond?'

'That depends.' De Klerk was on the left of the three, the other two shapes silent thus far. But Jack reckoned they would be the older men he had seen the day of the fight. Oom Joost would be one of them, but he did not know which.

'On what?' de Klerk demanded.

'On whether those old boys standing next to you agreed to what you suggested.'

De Klerk paused, then muttered something in Afrikaans, the words carrying clearly to where Jack stood watching.

'Well?' He was trying to keep hold of the initiative, interrupting the one-sided discussion before it could develop.

He was greeted by silence.

Then one of the men waved a hand at de Klerk, the gesture easy to see against the golden glow behind them, and stepped forward.

As he emerged out of the gloom, Jack recognised Oom Joost easily enough, though the Boer looked older somehow, as if the few days since the killing had aged him. He appeared to be bound tight with emotion, tension in his clenched jaw, his lips pursed.

Jack stayed silent even as the Boer approached to within arm's reach.

The two men stood there then, each meeting the other's gaze. There was no sense of searching for understanding. The silent exchange spoke more of hate and anger. And grief.

Suddenly the old Boer moved. His right hand balled into a fist and he punched hard, the blow delivered with the full force of his swinging arm.

It connected with the side of Jack's jaw with a loud smack, the force of the punch snapping his head to the right. Pain flared, reverberating through his head and flashing a bright white light across his vision. Yet he managed to keep his footing, taking the punch as well as he could. He had seen it coming, something in the Boer's eyes telling him what was about to happen. Yet he had not tried to duck away or pre-empt the strike with one of this own. Instead, he had chosen to stand still, letting the blow come.

'Your woman killed my son.' Spit was flung from the Boer's lips as he spat the words, his loathing on full display.

Jack understood what it was to hate; he had felt it himself more times than he could recall. Yet he was not there to be a punchbag for the man's grief.

'Hit me again and I'll kill you,' he hissed.

For a heartbeat, he thought the Boer would ignore the warn-ing, such was the spasm of fury that flashed across his features. But somehow the man controlled his rage, even though it left him shaking.

'Give me the diamond.' The words were spoken in a heavy, guttural accent. They clearly cost the Boer dearly, his expression twisting as if Jack was force-feeding him a turd.

Jack did not move. He could feel the diamond in the chest pocket of his shirt. It hung heavy over his heart, its weight speaking of its value.

His fingers twitched. He could feel the hilt of the Lefaucheux under his fingertips, the metal cool to the touch. It would be so easy to draw the weapon, the holster's flap left unbuttoned for just that reason.

And then he would start to kill.

He would begin with the old Boer in front of him, his first shot delivered at such close range that he could not miss. The second shot would be harder, but he could still see it clearly in his mind's eye, feeling the movements he would have to make as he levelled the revolver at de Klerk. When de Klerk fell – and Jack knew he would not miss, no matter the distance and despite the shadows that still stalked the land – he would fire on the third man. That man would have had time to react, perhaps long enough to draw a handgun of his own. That thought did not faze him, the idea that he could be struck down even as he changed his aim barely even registering in his mind. Instead, he thought only of the moment when he would fire that third bullet, plotting its path as it seared through the chill morning air on its way to its deadly collision with the Boer's body.

Three bullets and he would be free.

And the diamond would still be his.

'Give me the diamond and you can walk away. Otherwise, you die here and now. Then we will find your woman and hang her from the nearest tree. No one will stop us. Not here.'

The words brought Jack up short.

He was not alone. At least not yet. And so he would have to control the urge to fight, just as the Boer standing a yard away was forcing down his own need to kill.

Moving slowly, he raised his right hand, his fingers lingering on the hilt of the revolver for one last moment before they reached up to take the diamond from his pocket. He watched the old Boer the entire time, eyes boring into the Dutchman's. He saw another emotion on the man's face in that moment, replacing the hatred and grief that had been filling them up to that point.

He saw greed.

It made the next action easier somehow. He handed over the diamond, placing it carefully into the Boer's outstretched hand. But he did not let it go.

'You take this and it's over. You hear me? No more threats. No more talk of a hanging. You take it from me now and that's the end of this, you hear me?'

The Boer's fingers closed around the diamond, his skin cool and dry as it brushed against Jack's. Still Jack did not release his grip on the stone.

'Give me your word.'

For a moment he thought the Boer would pull his hand away and lash out for a second time as a dreadful flare of fury flashed through the man's eyes. It was gone a moment later, disappearing as quickly as it had arrived.

'You have my word.'

'Then it's done. Here and now. It's over.' Jack spoke slowly, clearly, making sure all three Boers understood. Only then did he let go of the stone he had broken himself to find.

The Boer withdrew his hand sharply, as if worried Jack would try to snatch the diamond back, stepping away as he did so, opening up a gap between them.

'*Ja*. It's over.' He turned away, showing Jack his back.

Jack stood still. He stayed like that for a long time as the old Boer rejoined his countrymen and the three of them walked away. He did not move even as the sun's first rays spread into the sky above the far horizon to send a shock of warmth and colour into the world.

For he did not believe it.

It could not be over. Not so easily.

But he did not know why.

Chapter Twenty-three

Anna lay as if a corpse, her breathing shallow. Jack sat beside her meagre bed and stared at her, horrified at the change wrought in such a short space of time. It was as if the illness were sucking the life out of her. Her cheeks were sunken, her face the colour of year-old ashes.

Then there was the smell.

She smelled of death, or at least of dying. He had stood on a hundred battlefields, breathing in the hateful miasma, the sweet, cloying stink of rotting flesh and torn guts that once experienced was never forgotten. And here it was again, the ripe aroma rising from Anna's emaciated body pungent and growing in power by the day. He could smell it even from outside the tent, and it terrified him.

It was four days since he had handed over the diamond to the Boers. Thus far, they had been true to their word and left him alone. Each day he had left the tent to purchase the bare necessities he needed to keep them both alive and any medicines he could find that might help Anna get better.

Yet nothing worked. Her sickness was getting worse and he was powerless to help.

He knew she was going to die.

The thought set off the screams in his head. They were almost ever present now, a silent cacophony that drowned out all other thoughts so that he heard only the sound of his soul being torn in two. They reverberated through him, constant, chilling, cold. It was taking all he had not to release them into the world and shriek his fear into the sky. Yet somehow he was holding on, letting his terror bubble away just under the surface. No one would know the screams existed. No one could see the turmoil in his mind. No one would be able to understand why he could barely speak, or move, or eat, while the terrible sound shrilled in his mind.

'Jack?'

His name was uttered so quietly that at first, he thought it was only an echo in his mind.

'Jack?'

It came again, no louder, but it was enough for him to know it was not just his senses playing him false.

'I'm here, love.' Once he would have reached out to touch her, offering a moment's reassurance. Yet her pain had become too severe, and he could not bear to see her recoil the moment his fingers brushed against her skin.

She said nothing more. But he sensed that for once, she was awake. Her periods of lucidity were becoming rarer by the day.

'What can I do for you?' The words were pulled from him, each one etched in grief and panic.

No reply came.

'Anna, what do I do?'

Again he was greeted by silence.

'I don't know what I'm doing, Anna, do you hear me?' He began to sob, the screams in his head intensifying, the

incoherent babble roaring in his ears. 'I don't know what to
do!' He hissed the words for a second time, desperate to hear
something, anything, by way of reply.

There was nothing but silence.

Never before had he felt so impotent.

Helpless.

And afraid.

Jack strode towards the tin shack that formed the office of the
diggers' committee. He had been there before just the once,
when he had purchased his claim. This time he had been
summoned, the message delivered by a young lad early that
morning, well before the digging day had begun. He had no
choice but to go, and he had left Anna alone, hoping that the
meeting would be brief. He did not want her to be by herself
for a minute longer than necessary.

His eyes took a moment to adjust as he walked into the
shack, the inside of the building so much darker than the bright
morning outside. There was little to look at once his eyes had
accustomed themselves to the gloom, and nothing much had
changed since he had last been there. The rudimentary desk
was just as messy, a bewildering array of claim registration
forms scattered across the top.

'Can I help you?'

He recognised the fat clerk who spoke; the same man who
had registered his claim all those weeks before.

'I was told to come here.' His reply was gruff. He had not
spoken to anyone but Anna for several days now. It took nearly
everything he had to form the words, to speak as a normal
person would. It felt as if his body was vibrating.

'What's your name?'

For a moment he could not find a way to reply, causing the clerk to look up and stare at him as if he were a fool. Eventually he managed to offer the bare minimum. 'Lark.'

'Ah, Lark.' The clerk seemed absurdly pleased to hear the name, a wide smile breaking out on his face. 'I was expecting your arrival.'

He held Jack's gaze, his eyes sparkling with devilment, then reached across his desk to rifle through one of his stacks of paper. He found what he was looking for easily enough.

'Here we are, the deed of sale for your claim. I am pleased to tell you that the sale has now been completed and fully registered in our accounts. This is yours to keep for your own records.' He held out the single sheet of thin paper.

Jack glanced at it, his hackles rising. The spidery writing on the paperwork was neat enough. But it was not his. The document was a forgery. 'What the fuck is this?' he snarled.

'Your deed of sale.' The clerk spoke slowly, as if to a halfwit. 'For your claim. Everything has gone through, and I will lodge the transaction in the accounts later today. You can return tomorrow to receive your payment,' he squinted at the document as if he was having trouble discerning the amount, 'of five pounds.' He looked up, a faint smile of satisfaction creeping onto his lips. 'You seem surprised, Mr Lark.'

Jack knew he was being set up. He did not yet know who had gulled him so neatly, but he understood what had happened. 'I did not complete that document.' He spoke the words knowing they would have no effect, but unable to hold them back nonetheless.

'Do you recognise this signature?' The clerk held the form out towards him again.

'No.' The signature was not his. He did not know who had

scrawled his name, but it was not him, even if they had done a fair job of it, likely copying it from the original registration form.

'Well, I must say, it looks good enough to me.' The clerk placed the paper carefully back into his pile before looking at Jack once more. 'I'm afraid that's that, Mr Lark. The sale is complete. I would say you are fortunate the claim was not jumped. From what I hear, it has not been worked for several days now, and it would be quite lawful for someone to take ownership.' He raised his eyebrows. 'Is there anything else I can do to assist you?' From his tone, it was apparent that helping Jack was the last thing on earth he wanted to do.

'Will you tell me who signed that?' Jack knew the question was futile. He was tempted to snatch up the form and force-feed it to the gloating little shit in front of him. But no matter how satisfying it might be to show the fat fool just what manner of man he was dealing with, it would achieve nothing and would more likely prevent him from finding out who his enemy was. And he would find them. Then they would discover the true Jack Lark, the man who had stormed the Hornets' Nest and been the first into the breach at Delhi. The man who would kill without a qualm.

'Come now, Mr Lark. Are you alleging that someone other than yourself signed this form?'

'You know that is the case. Who paid you off?'

The clerk pulled a face that suggested he had never been so affronted in his life. 'Mr Lark, please, there is no need for such wild accusations.' He rocked back in his chair, his ample gut spreading over his lap. 'Now I would say the matter is closed. We are done here.' The words were spoken in a harsher tone, meant to remind the listener of the man's power and influence.

Jack laughed. The humourless sound came from deep in his belly, and he let it out, loud and raucous. He had spent half his life pretending to be someone else. It appeared that now someone had done the same to him. There was something rather fitting in the way he was being cheated.

For the first time, the clerk looked flustered. 'I do not know what you can possibly find amusing in this situation. Now, as I told you, you are to return tomorrow to receive the proceeds of the sale. After that, you are to leave the diggings immediately. Your business here will be done.'

The laughter stopped. 'No.'

'No?'

'No.' Jack took a step towards the desk. 'I will stay and find whichever bastard has done this, and then I will kill him.' He glared at the clerk, but otherwise spoke deadpan, his emotions held in check. The anger was helping. It gave him power.

'Then the committee will have no option but to detain you until such a time as the authorities are next here.'

Jack snorted with disdain. By the authorities, he knew the clerk meant the British. Both Clarke and the wagon master, JW, had told him that the diggings had long been a source of political conflict, the land claimed by the British-supported Griqua people as well as the Orange Free State and the Transvaal Republic. The previous year, the Transvaal president, Marthinus Wessel Pretorius, had declared the diamond fields to be Boer property and had installed a temporary government. The diggers had rejected all these claims, and a former British sailor called Stafford Parker had organised a group of them into a Mutual Protection Association and declared a Diggers' Republic. That had not lasted long, and earlier that year, the British had arrived to take charge, throwing out both the diggers and the Boers. A committee had been set up to hear the evidence of all claimants to the land, but Jack was sure the British would not let go of it now they had it, and that meant he would be facing British justice if he was incarcerated at the pleasure of the diggers' committee. That did not bother him. He had run rings around the British authorities for most of his life. He could do so again.

But he was not done. Not yet. 'What if I don't recognise the committee's authority?'

The clerk chortled, setting off a wave of movement across his many chins. 'I hardly think you are in a position to do anything of the sort.'

For a moment, Jack was tempted to draw the Lefaucheux from its holster and show the overweight clerk just what sort of position he was in, but he resisted the lure. 'Who signed that form?' He stood stock still, holding himself tight.

'Now that's enough. This form was signed and logged quite legitimately. There is nothing wrong with it whatsoever.'

'Bullshit.' Jack snapped the word with a flash of barely contained rage.

The clerk's eyes widened as he belatedly realised quite how much danger he was in.

But Jack had no intention of wasting any more time on the fat little man now gripping his makeshift desk so tightly his knuckles showed white. Instead, he turned sharply on his heel and stalked from the tent.

He would find out for himself who had cheated him.

And then he would do what had to be done.

Chapter Twenty-four

Jack spotted someone half hidden in the five-foot-deep hole he himself had dug near one corner of his claim. It was the last shaft he had sunk before they had found the diamond, and the one closest to the spoil heap that filled a good tenth of the claim now, the mound of earth quadruple the size it had been when he had taken on the parcel of land, the broken soil a legacy to the hours he had spent pouring blood, sweat and tears into the remorseless ground.

The morning light was casting long shadows, the sun low on the horizon as it committed another night of darkness to memory. Another day was beginning. For many, that would mean another day of wasted labour, the daylight hours spent shovelling and sifting in the hope that something other than fragments of diamonds would be found.

But for one man the day would be different.

He would see to that.

There was no need to be circumspect in his approach, and he walked directly towards his claim, the dusty path that wound its way past the nearby plots as familiar as the back alleys around the gin palace where he had been brought up.

There were other diggers abroad, despite the early hour, many of those working the nearby claims, already starting another exhausting and frustrating day. He knew them all, or at least he knew their faces. He knew which of them would cuss and holler, and which would work in silence. He knew that the man from the Cape in the claim adjoining his own would beat his black workers with a long whip if they slacked, and he knew that the Italian two claims over would sing throughout the day, his voice underscoring the ever-present sounds of shovels, picks and sieves at work.

That morning, he did not look at a single one of them. He had eyes only for the man working the claim that had been stolen from him. A man who was just minutes away from being taught a forthright and painful lesson.

The man's head disappeared from sight as Jack stalked closer. It reappeared a moment later, as did his hands, which were now holding a tin bucket full of soil. Slowly, gingerly, the man placed the bucket on the lip of the shaft above his head, then paused as he gathered his strength to haul himself out of the ground.

It was then that he spotted Jack.

His eyes widened as he realised who was walking directly towards him. There was fear in those eyes, real fear, the type Jack had seen before when he had thrust a revolver into an unarmed man's ribs, or when a man had fallen to his sword and suffered the awful realisation that death was on its way.

This time the face those eyes belonged to was familiar to him, the man who had stolen his claim easy to recognise after so many hours spent together on the trail from Port Elizabeth.

'Clarke!' He shouted the name partly in anger, partly out of surprise at seeing the Australian where he had been almost certain he would find one or more Boers, the claim taken as further recompense for the man Anna had shot dead.

Arms working furiously, Clarke tried to scramble up and out of the pit. He got his belly onto the ground, his feet kicking hard at the air as he attempted to wriggle forward so he could stand.

But there was not enough time.

He was still wriggling on his belly when Jack came to stand in front of him. The Australian went stock still as he saw Jack's heavy army boots appear no more than an inch in front of his face. He was still lying there when Jack reached down to grab hold of the back of his shirt, and he was powerless to resist as he was hauled to his knees and then to his feet.

'Jack!' He managed to gasp the name, face flushed with the exertion of digging and the aborted attempt to flee.

Jack said nothing. Instead, he grabbed the front of Clarke's shirt, holding the thin, grimy fabric in his left hand while his right balled into a fist that he lifted to make sure it was seen.

'I can explain, mate, really I can,' Clarke blurted, trying desperately to move away from the threat of the knuckles aimed squarely at his face.

'Oh, I know you can.' Jack spoke in an iron-hard tone, his fist twitching slightly so that Clarke stared at it and nothing else.

'Look, it's honest work, Jack. I know the claim used to be yours, but you can't blame a man for doing what he's told, now can you?'

'Who told you to work here?' Clarke could wriggle as much as he liked. He was an eel caught in a trap. And knifing even the largest eel was easy once it was in the barrel.

'Those bloody Boers.'

Jack's grip still did not falter. 'Why the fuck are you work-ing for them? You were doing all right on your own, weren't you?'

'Fair dinkum, Jack, I was doing bloody well. Then I got into a game of cards with some stinking old Boer and I lost the lot.'

'You bloody fool.' Jack could not believe the Australian had been so stupid.

'I know, Jack, I know.' Clarke's face fell as he told his sorry tale. 'I'm a bloody idiot.'

'So they took your claim?'

'Yep.'

'And now you work for them.'

'Only until I've paid them what I owe, then I'm my own man again.'

'And how long will that take?'

'Until I find them something decent. Then we're even. I've done it before. It always turns out all right. I just need time to find my feet again.'

Jack absorbed the story, wondering how much of it was bullshit. 'And you never stopped to ask why you were working my claim?'

'They told me you'd sold it to them.' Clarke sagged. 'I took them at their word, Jack.' He paused. 'They took it from you?'

'They stole it.'

He shook his head as if in disbelief. 'Those bloody bastards.'

Jack was not taken in. 'I bet you never even stopped to ask.'

'I didn't have much of a choice, mate.' Clarke hung his head. 'They wanted someone to work the claim. So they told me to do it.'

Jack sucked down a breath. He had known the Australian was a sorry sack of shite from the moment he first clapped eyes on him. 'And they trust you?' He could not help the derisive tone as he fired off another question.

'What do you mean?'

'They're certain you won't just pocket the good stuff if you find it?'

Clarke looked up at the accusation, a flash of devilment flickering across his face just for a second. Then his head dropped and he went back to looking at the dirt in front of his boots. 'They send someone to keep an eye on me.'

'Who?'

'Some old woman. She watches me like a bloody hawk.'

Jack absorbed the information. It made sense. The Boers would not trust Clarke as far as they could throw him, but they would not spare someone with the strength to work on their own claims, so giving the role of supervisor to one of their older women made sense. It also clarified something else.

'So that's why you're here so damn early.' He made sure to squeeze tight as he spoke, jerking Clarke back and forth for emphasis. 'Having a little look-see before she turns up to watch over you.'

Clarke said nothing.

But he was to be spared any more questions.

'Hey!'

Jack glanced over his shoulder as he heard someone shout nearby. He saw de Klerk walking with a stout woman. She could be any age from thirty to sixty; it was hard to tell under the enormous dark orange shawl wrapped over her head and shoulders. It did not take a genius to realise this was the woman Clarke had mentioned, and it made sense that de Klerk would escort her to the claim, a reminder to the Australian, if one were needed, of who was really watching over him.

'What the *fok* are you doing here?' the Boer snapped as he approached, his face already bearing the first flush of anger.

Jack kept hold of Clarke as he turned to face the new arrivals, not caring that the Australian stumbled and almost fell as he was hauled around. 'You want to tell me what this thieving bastard is doing working my bloody claim?'

De Klerk's jaw clenched. He gestured sharply to the woman at his side, directing her away, a curt command given under his breath in Afrikaans. He was obeyed immediately.

'It's not your claim any more,' he said, turning back to Jack. 'That *poephol* is just doing whatever the *fok* we tell him.'

'You forged the sale, you bastard.' Jack felt an odd fluttering in his bowels. It wasn't fear; he had faced that enough times to know what it felt like, the icy wash of terror nothing like this uneasy stirring deep inside.

'*Ja*, what of it?' De Klerk shook his head, unimpressed by Jack's discovery.

Jack opened his mouth to answer. But no words emerged. The odd sensation came again. It picked away, gnawing at the sinews that kept him from falling apart. And it left him quite unable to speak. For the first time in his life, he did not know what to say, or what to do.

'Why?' He managed to utter the single word.

'Why?' De Klerk barked a short, scornful laugh. 'Because we could.'

Before Jack could reply, Clarke twisted in his grip, both arms rising at the same time to force him to let go. There was little strength in the attempt, but something deep inside Jack was tearing apart, and his fist fell away. Clarke staggered free, leaving Jack standing alone.

'This is my land.' He delivered the words without force.

The weakness in his voice shamed him. But he could not summon the strength to fight. The fire in his belly had gone out. It had been replaced by nothingness.

He felt empty.

Broken.

'Not any more.' De Klerk stepped forward, closing the gap. Clarke had moved to his master's side. It was clear from the look on the Boer's face that he was ready to fight. Once Jack would have met the challenge head on, refusing to be cowed, battling for what was rightfully his with every scrap of strength he could summon.

But no longer.

'Now why don't you *fok* the hell off. We own this land now and there is nothing you can do about it.' Triumph flashed across de Klerk's face as he read Jack's expression easily enough, the absence of any resistance emboldening. 'Go back to that *vrouw* of yours while you still can. From what I hear, she'll be in the ground before long.'

Jack took a step backwards, then another. His boot scuffed against the edge of the pit he had dug, then it slipped backwards, throwing him off balance. For one drawn-out moment, he stood there teetering, feeling the force of gravity pulling at him, his eyes locked on to de Klerk.

Then he fell.

His head hit the far side of the pit as he tumbled down into its depths. The blow stung, a momentary flash of pain before the much harder impact with the compacted dirt at the bottom. The collision crunched through his bones, setting every nerve on edge and filling his mind with a remorseless, all-consuming agony so that he could do nothing but lie there gasping for air.

The fiercest pain subsided, but he was left in a sorry state, his back on fire and his body feeling bruised from head to toe. It was enough to make him groan as he started to ease himself up, moving with all the agility of an old codger.

Then he heard laughter. Peals of it. Loud. Raucous and mocking. The sound made his cheeks burn with shame.

Slowly, gingerly, he eased first to a sitting position then up onto his feet. The pain was fierce, but it could be managed.

De Klerk's face appeared. It was streaked with tears of laughter. 'Get out of that *blerrie* hole, then *fok* off.' The words came laced with scorn and in a tone only used by the young addressing the very old.

His face disappeared. More laughter followed, then a flurry of instructions that faded as the two men at the top of the pit moved away.

Jack was left in the hole. He was no longer seen as a threat, or even something worthy of the Boer's time.

He smeared a hand across his face, as if he could somehow wipe his shame away. But he knew it would linger, as would the dreadful feeling of emptiness that now filled his belly.

But no matter how he felt, he knew he would obey the Boer. He would haul himself out of the pit and scurry back to Anna.

While he still could.

Chapter Twenty-five

'Jack, is that you?'

'Yes, it's me.' Jack grimaced as he crept back into the tent. He had tried to be quiet, so as not to disturb her, but had failed. It was becoming a habit.

He had stood outside the tent for nearly half an hour before he had finally slipped inside. Entering the realm of the sick was becoming harder with each visit. Not that he didn't care about Anna; far from it. But there was something so dreadful about being inside that tent, something truly awful in the miasma that filled the air. Unsettling. Uncomfortable. Wretched. The emotions it stirred were almost more than he could bear. And there was fear. Fear that Anna would pass away when he was absent. Fear that he could return to nothing more than a cold corpse and a memory of what could have been.

There was something else too. Something evil.

For a part of him just wanted it to end, one way or another. He could barely acknowledge the thought, but it was there nonetheless, and it picked at his mind day and night, like the devil himself was murmuring in his ear.

For if Anna died, then at least he would be free.

He eased himself to the ground so that he sat beside her in his now familiar position. He did not know how many hours he had spent in that one spot, his hand resting gently on her shoulder, his mind wandering through the past.

'Where were you?'

The question came at him as he squirmed slowly from side to side, trying to ease the dull ache in his bones after the tumble into the pit. The pain was buried deep inside, but it was as nothing against the burn of shame. The man who had held the cantonment at Bhundapur had fallen into a hole in the ground like a drunk slumping into the gutter.

'I went to the claim.'

'Why?'

'Someone sold it,' he answered. He would not lie or dissemble. He would not allow what might be his last hours with her to be filled with falsehood. 'They forged a bill of sale. Paid the clerk to accept it, I'll wager.'

'No matter. We were going to sell it anyway.'

'Yes.' He grunted as he acknowledged the truth.

'So why go there?'

'To see who has it now.'

'Did you find them?'

'Yes.'

'Did you fight?' Anna knew Jack.

'No.'

'But you're hurt.' Even in her debilitated state, she could see the way he sat awkwardly, the way he held himself to ease the pain.

'I fell into a shaft. The last one I dug. You remember that one?'

'Yes.'

'I landed on my arse. It hurts. And my spine feels like someone is trying their damnedest to remove it with a spoon.'

Something flickered across Anna's face, the hint of a smile or a fleeting moment of pain at the effort of speaking, he could not tell. But she was alive and she was awake, and for now that was enough. She was still with him. The fear that she would soon never be any of those things again felt very real now, the hours she spent lost in the darkness pointing towards a fate he could not bear to face.

He gazed down into her sunken eyes. The spark that had once lit them was dulled by suffering. The illness was stealing her away as effectively as the land they had purchased had been taken from them.

But his Anna was still in there. Somewhere. Hidden, perhaps, sheltering away as she fought the sickness ravaging her body. But still there.

'We can go someplace new when you are feeling better.' He spoke slowly, letting each word settle. He was not one to chatter, but he wanted to keep her with him. He was terrified that should he pause and fall silent for even just one moment, she would slip away from him and return to oblivion, perhaps for ever. He deliberately spoke of the future, one far removed from the place where she had killed a man. 'We can go wherever we please.' He reached out then, stroking her forehead, pushing away the strands of hair that had stuck to her skin.

'So there is nothing keeping you here now?'

Jack's hand stopped its gentle movement. She had not listened to his plan, fixing instead on a fact he would not have wanted her to dwell on. 'Of course there is, you daft bint.' He tried to sound light-hearted. '*You're* here.'

'We will need money.'

'I'll find it.'

'How?'

'There's always a way.'

'You'll steal it?'

'If I have to. I'll pinch if from those bloody Boers. Pay them back for nicking our bloody claim.' As soon as the answer left his lips, he cursed his own stupidity. There was only one reason for the Boers to steal the claim. It was the same reason they had taken the diamond, and he was sure it was why Anna was lying in a pool of her own stale sweat. One man's death had changed his world.

'I see his face.' It was as if she had read his mind. 'I see it all the time.'

'Then don't.' Jack leaned forward, the words spoken softly but firmly. He knew which face she could see in her mind, the image likely haunting every lucid moment she had. 'Let it go and it will fade, I promise.'

'Do you remember the first man you killed? Can you picture him?'

He sighed. He did not know how to find the words that would help her come to terms with what had happened. With what she had done.

'I see them all,' he said at last. They came for him at odd times when he was awake, and they haunted his dreams. Some of them he had seen in life for no more than a fleeting second. They had fallen at his hand or another's, the moment of their death forgotten in that instant, only to return when the fighting was done. Others had been up close and personal, his sword slicing through their flesh, or his knife punching deep into their body. He had been able to look deep into their soul as they died. Seeing their anger. Their fear. Then seeing it all fade into nothing as the light was snuffed out.

Some faces came to mind regularly. Others less frequently, so that there was a moment of surprise when he saw them again. A few lingered constantly. A Mexican bandolero he had killed with his bare hands, fingers gouging out the man's eyes without thought of mercy. A Russian artilleryman cut down with the first sword Jack had stolen. A man stabbed to death for the right to own a repeating rifle. No matter the manner of their death, they came back with the utmost clarity, the moment relived so vividly that often he was back on the field of battle, the smell of powder, blood and shit filling his nostrils, the taste of fear on his tongue.

And with the faces of those he had killed came the faces of the ones he had lost.

These were the worst of all, the memories that not only tormented him, but twisted his soul so that he could no longer think. The faces would not let him go, no matter how much time passed, no matter how hard he tried to forget or to lock them away. There was the first woman he had loved. In his mind's eye, she still lay on the floor where she had died, body contorted like a discarded doll, a pool of blood forming around her shattered skull like some grotesque halo. Then there was the former slave who had given so much to get to the northern states of America, only to be stolen away from him by the men in grey who had caught them running together. With the image of the two women came the faces of those he had lost on the battlefield. The young officer who had died in his arms. The shattered body of the general who had been shot down leading his men into the breach. The men who had died at his side along with those who had been slain doing what he had ordered them to do, condemning them to death as surely as any judge sending a criminal to the gallows.

'I will never forget that man,' Anna whispered. 'I stole the life he should have led.'

Jack had no words of comfort. No kindness to soften the pain. No magic to remove it.

'I killed him.' She wept now, tears running freely down her face.

Still Jack said nothing. There was nothing he could do. Not really. He could keep her warm. Feed her. Clean her. Hold her. But he could not fix her. She would have to do that for herself, so that she could rise out of her sickbed and try to function as an approximation of a human being. For that was the greatest charade he had ever undertaken. One infinitely harder than merely masquerading as an officer.

Just pretending to be Jack Lark was the most difficult thing he had ever had to do.

'I killed him,' Anna repeated between sobs. She was gasping for air now, her face contorting into something ugly. 'I killed him.'

'Yes. You did.' Jack moved slowly, ignoring the pain and forcing himself to his knees. He reached out to her then, a worshipper before an effigy of his god. 'Thank you.'

'What?' Anna looked confused.

'Thank you for saving me.' He held her gaze, her bloodshot eyes locking on to his. There was snot under her nose, her pale skin blotchy around lips lined with crusty scabs.

She shook her head. She was looking directly at him, but she did not see him. She was staring at something a thousand yards away, his words barely registering. They could not penetrate the horror of the scene that was surely replaying over and over in her mind's eye, an endless repeat of the moment when she had pulled the trigger and a single bullet had sent a young man's soul into oblivion.

Jack awoke with a start. He did not know when he had drifted off to sleep. He had held Anna for a long time, waiting for her sobs to subside. Eventually, when she was spent, he had once again sat at her side, letting the moment settle and holding tight to the barriers that kept his nightmares at bay. At some point, he had closed his eyes. And he had slept.

Now he was awake.

And he awoke to noise and confusion.

Outside, the air was filled with a roar like an express train thundering through a station. The tent was being battered from all directions, the canvas bulging and billowing as it was pushed and pulled by a wild wind that had risen up out of nowhere. Underscoring the rush of the wind and the thwack of canvas was the sound of something hitting the sides of the tent. It sounded almost like rain, but it was harder and came faster than even the heaviest storm.

'Shit.' Jack blinked hard, forcing his mind to come alive.

The tent shook as if it were about to be ripped from the ground.

He moved quickly, bounding to his feet, then running for the tent's flaps, which were bucking in and out as if a demon was trying to force its way inside. Working hastily, he untied the knots that held them fast, fingers working quickly and efficiently.

Snatching back the flaps, he got his first look outside.

The world was shrouded in dust. It whipped through the air, driven by a ferocious wind, flaying the nearest tents and scouring across the ground. The light had changed from the clear blue of morning to a dirty, piss-coloured yellow.

All around him was chaos. Men were shouting, desperate cries that were barely audible over the roar of the storm. A nearby tent collapsed, the canvas twisting around itself before it was driven across the ground, guide ropes whipping about as though the canvas was being flogged for desertion.

For one long-drawn-out moment, Jack could not make himself move. To re-enter the world would be to endure more pain, and so he hesitated, the urge to stay in the tent almost more than he could bear.

Another tent was torn from the ground no more than a dozen yards away from where he cowered, the storm plucking it up like it weighed no more than a single sheet of paper.

'Fuck it.' He hissed the words under his breath, then pushed himself outside. The wind hit him immediately, thumping into him with enough force to knock him sideways. With the wind came the dust. It lashed against him, striking his clothing and raking over the exposed skin on his face like the nails of an angry lover, stinging and sharp.

It was all he could do to stand. He could see no more than a couple of yards and hear nothing over the roar of the wind and the sound of flapping canvas. Already the dust was filling his eyes, making them gritty and sore, and it had found its way into his mouth too, coating his tongue and stealing every drop of moisture.

He pulled up the bandana he wore wrapped around his neck, covering his nose and mouth as best he could. Then he turned and ducked low as he refastened the ties to hold the tent flaps closed. Inside, the simple task had taken a few seconds; now it took ten times as long, his eyes screwed shut as his whole body was pummelled by the raging storm.

When the flaps were finally secure, he moved to his left, fingers reaching out to the nearest guy rope. He traced along its length, feeling his way, moving like a crone, back bent and hunched over as he forced his way into the teeth of the gale.

Reaching the end of the rope, he pushed down on the peg that held it fast, using every scrap of strength to drive it further into the earth. He felt it move, the peg sinking a good few inches lower into the dry ground. It was a reminder why he was there, bearing the brunt of the elements. If he had not ventured out, it would not have been long before the tent would have been torn free, exposing them both to the full force of the dust storm. If that had happened, he did not think Anna would have survived for long.

He moved on, keeping low, hand lifting to shield his face as much as possible. It was a struggle just to move. With every step, the wind and dust buffeted against him, forcing him to stagger forward, eyes screwed tight as he sucked down hot air through his bandana. It took everything he had to reach the next rope and force the peg into the ground.

It was as if the world was ending, the storm Fate's way of reminding him he was powerless against the forces at her disposal.

At last he hammered home the final peg, knocking it in with the heel of his boot. Then he stood there, a man alone in the storm. It buffeted against him, dust stinging his skin, the wind striking him with such force that he had to lean forward to stay on his feet.

Yet there was something wonderful in that moment. Something primeval. It was as if the storm was alive, there for him and him alone, a natural force so strong that not even the most powerful human could stand against it.

Chapter Twenty-six

J ack stood still, hands thrust deep into his pockets, keeping out of sight.

It was the morning after the dust storm. He had kept their tent standing, unlike many of his neighbours. The effort had left him utterly spent, but he had not slept a wink when he had finally crawled back inside. Instead, he had lain next to Anna, listening to breathing that was getting shallower and shallower with every passing hour. He had left her at dawn, unable to stay a moment longer. For he knew he was waiting for her to die. And that thought lent strength to his exhausted body, even if it did nothing to quell the screams in his mind.

He had chosen his spot with care. He was screened by a wagon parked adjacent to a claim five down from the one he still believed was his. From there, he could watch over his claim and see anyone coming and going. He had arrived at his chosen station when the sun was just rising, and he was still there as it crept slowly above the eastern horizon, its blazing morning glory promising a beautiful day to follow the misery of the one before. It was as if the storm had never been, the fine covering of dust that shrouded every object its only legacy.

Clarke walked onto the far edge of the claim. He moved calmly, comfortably even.

Jack held his position. It was not time. Not yet.

Clarke shrugged his jacket from his shoulders, placing it carefully over a shovel that had been left with its blade buried deep in the soil. Then he stretched, arms spreading wide as he prepared aching muscles for the hours of toil that lay ahead, before calling to someone over his shoulder, the words just about carrying to Jack's ears.

A second figure came into view. She was moving slowly, arms stretched straight down at her sides as she carried two heavy iron pails, their weight reducing her gait to little more than a slow, awkward waddle. As she approached, Clarke called out once again, chivvying her along. She did her best, her pace increasing a fraction. From what Jack could see, she was a well-built, sturdy lass, a different woman to the day before, thick at the hips and broad of beam. He watched as she placed her buckets on the ground near the sieves that awaited her.

Clarke walked slowly to the same pit Jack had seen him in the previous day. When he reached the edge, he paused, his reluctance to start another day showing in his posture. Jack could almost hear the sigh as the Australian sucked down a breath then sat on the edge of the hole, the seat of his trousers smearing across the soil as his feet searched for the footholds Jack himself had hacked into the wall of the pit.

He kept watching as Clarke lowered himself down. The pit was a good six feet deep now, and the Australian was tall enough for Jack to see the crown of his head bobbing around as he found his footing.

He could picture the scene that faced Clarke that morning. He had left one side of the shaft flat, the toe- and handholds in the face cut deep and wide enough for a heavy, muddy boot to find purchase. The opposite side was the working face. Jack had liked to hack at the soil with a pickaxe before shovelling the spoil into a bucket that he would have to heave up onto his shoulder, then up and over the lip of the pit and onto the ground beyond. He had learned never to fill it to the brim, a full load too heavy for Anna to drag away. At two-thirds full, it was still heavy, but she could cope well enough. There had been no need for him to work fast, and he could remember the easy pace that would last all day long, the rhythm hypnotic. He could continue for hours with barely a pause, his body immune to the jarring contact of axe with ground.

From what he was seeing now, it was clear the pair working the claim today had yet to set a pace they could both work at. The first bucket of broken soil appeared over the edge of the pit before the woman had even set herself at the sieves. Terse words followed the bucket's arrival, shouts coming out of the ground as Clarke summoned the Boer woman to collect it.

Jack stood still for one more moment, eyes fixed on the scene playing out in front of him. Then somewhere deep and hidden in his belly, something snapped.

He slipped from behind the wagon as the woman came towards the offending bucket. He walked fast, boot heels digging deep divots in the ground. He did not bother to look around to see who might spot him coming back to his claim. The rage in his belly had ignited the moment he had seen Clarke disappear below ground. It was *his* pit. It did not belong to the Australian. It did not belong to the bloody Boers. It was Jack's. He had dug it out, paying for its existence in sweat and callused hands. Seeing another man take it as his own was more than he could bear.

He covered the ground in great loping strides. There were no thoughts in his mind. No plans. No strategy. He was propelled only by the fire that was burning in his belly. A fire fuelled by everything he had endured since he had arrived at the diggings, and which had ignited as he stood in the eye of the dust storm.

The Boer woman saw him coming. She looked up just as she levered the heavy bucket from the ground, her face showing the strain of moving the pail that had been filled to the brim.

The two looked at one another, one still, back bent, hands full, the other striding forward, hands balled into fists, face set like thunder.

The woman dropped the bucket. Soil cascaded out as it hit the ground, some spreading around the fallen pail, some tumbling over the edge of the pit and down onto the digger below.

Jack heard the bellow of sudden anger as Clarke was hit by the debris. He could see the top of the man's head move as he looked up, invective spewing forth as he bawled out the woman for her clumsiness.

The woman hesitated, confusion mixing with fear, eyes locked on to Jack's own.

'Go! Now!' Jack commanded, the words coming out strong and clear. He waved her away, the short, sharp gesture understandable the world over.

The woman obeyed. She turned and jogged away, her hefty haunches rolling from side to side as she tried to find speed on the uneven ground. Jack paid her no heed. He would not fight a woman.

But he would fight a man, especially one who had stolen from him.

Clarke bellowed with anger as the woman disappeared from

sight. Then he started to clamber out of the pit, his head appearing over the lip.

It would get no further.

Jack did not hesitate. He came on at speed and kept going until he reached the edge of the hole. Clarke turned around as he heard the onrushing footsteps, the action made awkward by the fact that he was still clinging to the foot- and handholds on the opposite side of the shaft.

Jack jumped into the pit without even breaking stride.

He hit the bottom, knees bent ready for the impact. Still the contact with the rock-hard ground jarred up his spine, a moment's pain flashing through him. Yet he did not stumble, his knees up to the task of holding him upright.

He had dug the pit wide enough that there was enough room to swing a pickaxe with ease, and so there was more than enough room for the two men to stand side by side.

Now he reached forward, ignoring the protest in his joints, grabbing hold of the waistband of Clarke's trousers.

It was easy then. He pulled back sharply, tugging the taller man backwards, then spinning him around so that they faced one another.

There was time for him to see a flash of recognition register on Clarke's face before he hit him.

The first blow caught Clarke in the gut with enough force to bend him forward. Jack followed it with a second, a sharp jab into the Australian's chest, right where his heart would be beating fast. Clarke let out a grunt of pain before Jack lashed out again and then again, with every ounce of force he could muster, hitting the Australian on either side of his chest, driving the breath out of his lungs so that Jack felt the rush of air on his face as he swayed with the rhythm of the punches, his body reacting to the irrepressible urge to fight.

Clarke never stood a chance. Winded and surprised as he was, his fists barely managed to leave his sides.

Jack felt the first pain in his hands as they bounced off Clarke's ribs, but it didn't slow him. The rage was bright now, and getting hotter. He lashed out again and again, lips pulling back from his teeth in a snarl as he unleashed his fury. The punches were coming almost faster than he could track, battering Clarke backwards into the side of the pit.

He pressed forward, his fists never still. Clarke's knees started to buckle. The movement brought his face down. Jack needed no more of an invitation than that. He swayed back for one moment, summoning his full force, then punched his right fist forward into the Australian's nose.

'Come on!' He roared in delight as he saw the first blood fly through the air, droplets of the warm liquid splattering across his own face.

'Fuck you!' He was bellowing, incoherent with rage now, his left fist crunching into Clarke's unprotected mouth. 'Do you fear me now, you fucking bastard!' Rage sustained him. Days of impotence and fear were adding fuel to the burning fury in his belly, filling his head with madness as he beat Clark without mercy. 'You hear me. Fear me, not the fucking Boers. Fear me!' He drove his fist home once more as he shouted the words into Clarke's face.

The Australian's eyes glazed over and he started to slide down the pit wall, his back pressing against the earthen face behind him. But Jack would not let him go. He reached out with his left hand, taking firm hold of Clarke's shirt front and forcing him to stay where he could be hit. Then he punched him again and again, every blow delivered straight and sure, his fist coming away slathered in blood.

The grip of his left hand faltered, his fingers finally losing their hold on Clarke's shirt, and the Australian slumped downwards, his senses long departed.

Jack stepped back, chest heaving, blood dripping from his bruised and puffy knuckles. He stood like that for a long time, his breath slowly coming back under control, the fury that had pushed him far past the point of reason receding into the darkness deep in his mind.

Clarke stirred. Then he groaned. The Australian was still alive.

Jack did not let him lie.

Bending forward, he took a firm hold of the front of Clarke's shirt again, then hauled him upwards, lifting his head and shoulders from the ground. Thrusting his own head downward, he paused, waiting for some sign of life to flicker back into the Australian's gaze. It took a while, but eventually the lights went on, Clarke's eyes widening as he saw the face looming large in front of his own.

'I want you to leave this place, you hear me.' Jack spoke slowly, his words coming out as sharp as flint. 'Leave this place and don't come back. If I see you here again, I'll kill you.'

Clarke nodded, fear filling his bloodshot eyes.

And it was enough.

Jack held the Australian's gaze for one more moment, letting the words settle. Then he let go of him sharply, not caring that Clarke's head fell back to thump onto the ground. He knew he would be heeded. Clarke was no fighter. He would leave the diggings, just as he had been instructed.

Jack stepped back, then turned to pull himself out of the pit. Not once did he look down at the slumped body he had beaten to a pulp, not even as he clambered back onto level ground.

He had delivered his message and now he tasted the first delicious morsel of revenge. He was not yet done, not by a long way, but he had made a start.

The rest would follow.

He became aware of the sound of a crowd gathering. There was no mistaking it. Voices were blending together, some shouting, others crying out in excitement or alarm; he could not tell which it might be.

He heard Clarke moan, then whimper from the bottom of the pit. It was a pitiful sound, one laced with pain. Jack ignored it. The Australian was lucky. He was alive.

Now he saw the crowd. It was congregating about five hundred yards away, near one of the biggest claims in the dry diggings. The owners had linked a dozen claims together and brought in both manpower and scaffolding in an attempt to at least partly industrialise the process of extracting diamonds from the ground. It was an impressive enterprise, with two assemblies of poles and rope standing tall on either side of the claim, the simple machinery used to bring the buckets of soil out of the ground quickly and efficiently. Yet for all the industry and purpose, the diggings' rumour mill had it that the men being paid to work the claim were taking more of the valuable stones than the owners ever saw. For the other diggers, the two towers were more of a navigational beacon than something that pointed to a successful modernisation.

Yet that day one of the towers, the one further to the east, was drawing a crowd for a very different reason.

Jack walked towards it, stuffing his bloodied hands deep into his pockets lest anyone see them. Both hands throbbed, his knuckles already hurting badly after the mauling they had administered.

The noise of the crowd grew steadily louder as he got closer. Most of those present were diggers, drawn to the spectacle even though it would delay the start of another day's labour. A few women were there, wives and daughters just happy to be diverted from their sieves for a moment or two.

It was only as he came closer that he saw many of the women were crying. Their wails of anguish were only adding to what was quickly becoming a growing clamour. A few of the men were shouting and becoming more vocal, and Jack heard the first cries for justice and revenge being shouted out amidst the sound of sobbing.

In that moment, he was confused. It made no sense. Not here in the heart of the diggings. The diggers were many things, but they were not an emotional bunch.

Then he saw the body. And he understood at once.

It was swinging back and forth in the breeze. Its boots were no more than a foot off the ground, but that foot was as good as a dozen yards, and it had sealed the man's fate as surely as if he had been dropped through the floor at Tyburn. A hanging was a hanging, and a noose could kill just as surely no matter the distance from the ground. And kill it had, the coarse hemp throttling the life out of the young Englishman who had once been so foolish as to steal a few pails of water.

Flanagan was hanging by the neck from the easternmost tower. He was quite dead, his tongue lolling from between purple lips, while bulging eyes looked sightlessly down at the growing crowd.

The Boers had got their man in the end.

Chapter Twenty-seven

'And I say someone must do something about it.'

'That's damn right. Them bloody Dutchies have been taking liberties for too long. This is English land, yet them damn Boers think they can do whatever the fuck they want.'

'You speak the truth, brother. Amen to that.'

Jack had said nothing as he listened to the two men. They were way towards the rear of the group that had gathered to see Flanagan's body cut down, and had made no move to help with the removal of the corpse. Instead, they had stood by demanding action while offering nothing.

'You want to do something?' Jack spoke just loudly enough for the two to hear him.

They turned as one.

'What's that you say?'

Jack nodded as he recognised the pair. The Thompson brothers, who had shared the wagon with him and Anna on the way up from Port Elizabeth. He had not clapped eyes on either Thomas or Arnold in the weeks that had followed.

'I say I agree with you.' He looked from one man to the

other. He knew they were brawlers; the journey had proven that. And he knew they had no love for the Boers. That suited him nicely. 'Something needs to be done about those murdering Dutch whoresons. They need to know who's in charge here.'

'What are you thinking?' Thomas asked warily.

'They committed murder.' Jack held the man's gaze. 'What's the penalty for that?'

'Death.' Thomas's pugnacious face creased into a smile. It was not a pleasant expression. He looked across to his brother. 'What say you, Arnie-boy?'

'I say that's about right.' The younger of the two men was watching Jack closely. 'You weren't all that keen on fighting them Dutchies before. What's changed your mind?'

'That.' Jack nodded towards the body of Flanagan. The young Englishman was now being carried away.

'Is he your friend now?'

'No.'

'Then what's it to you?'

Jack did not answer immediately. He had no intention of revealing the turn of events that had led him to this point. But he wanted these men with him. Needed them, even. As tempting as it was to take the Boers on by himself, the truth of it was that he needed allies. Men who could fight and who would be happy to do so. He needed soldiers.

'You said it. Something needs to be done. The way I see it, no one else round these parts will do anything. So it's down to some true-hearted men. Good men who know what's right.'

Thomas grunted. 'That's as maybe. But why us?'

'Because there isn't anyone else.' Jack kept his tone even and his voice pitched low so they would not be overheard.

The brothers looked at one another. Jack could see in their

eyes that they were not convinced. Like many men of their age, they held firm opinions on the world and everything in it, and they would happily call for someone to do something just so long as that someone was not them and that something did not involve them getting their hands dirty. It was time to change tack.

'You know those bastards have found a couple of big ones? It's typical, isn't it? That it's them that found them, not decent men like us.' Jack watched closely as he laid out his lure.

Thomas looked at him, eyes narrowing. 'They still got 'em?'

'Far as I heard, they've kept them all. They don't trust the buyers here. They won't sell till they get back to the Transvaal.' Jack had been lying for decades. He had convinced men born into the upper echelons of British society that he belonged amongst them. Lying to these two was as easy as picking the pocket of a drunk.

The two brothers turned away. A whispered conversation followed. Whatever was said was said softly and quietly. Jack heard nothing. But he didn't need to. He understood what had passed between them as soon as the pair turned back to face him.

'We should talk about this.' A flicker of a smile wandered across Thomas's face. 'Come see us tonight.'

'Where?'

'Meet us behind the diggers' office at sundown. No one will be there at that time of day. You know it?'

'I know it.' Jack felt no need to show his gratitude. He was going to do what he was going to do with or without them.

Thomas nodded once. The conversation was over.

'You think they will agree to help?' Goodfellow asked as he

and Jack waited at the designated spot. The sun was setting, creating a spectacle, as if reluctant to yield the day to the night. It was casting a warm pink glow into the sky, which bounced off the few clouds to fill the world with a beguiling pale light.

'Pink sky at night, shepherd's delight.' Jack muttered the words to himself as he scanned the horizon. There was beauty on display that evening that should have reminded him of the warmth of life. Instead, he felt cold, even as the last heat of the sun's rays bathed his face.

'What's that?' Goodfellow plucked at his sleeve. 'Are you even listening to me?'

'No.' Jack was blunt. 'Look. Either they will agree to fight or they won't. That's it.'

Goodfellow shook his head, clearly disappointed by the pragmatic answer. 'I was passing the time of day, Jack. That is what civilised folk do at a time such as this.'

'Then don't.' Jack had no space in his mind for anything but the task at hand. The thought of hitting the Boers hard was all he cared to think about. As soon as his mind left that task, it returned to Anna. She was no better for another day of rest. In fact, she was getting worse. Just like the sun, she was fading fast. And so he thought of the one thing he was good at. He conjured pictures of fighting and killing, of wreaking havoc on the Boer encampment and reclaiming all that had been taken from him. The images sustained him. He did not like to wonder what would happen if he let them go.

'You are not an easy man to be with, Jack.' Goodfellow scuffed the toe of his boot in the dust.

'You don't have to be here.'

He flinched from the lash in Jack's tongue. 'I know that. Yet still I choose to be. Even with you insisting on acting like a boor.' He smiled at his own deliberate choice of words. That smile faded as Jack showed no sign of having heard his pun. Instead, he was staring into the middle distance as if transfixed by an object only he could see.

The two men stood in silence for another ten minutes. It was only as Jack was contemplating leaving that the Thompson brothers approached.

'You're here.' Thomas spoke first, as he usually did.

Jack noticed there was no apology for their tardiness. 'I said I would be. You will find I am a man who does what he says.'

'What's he doing here?' Arnold gestured towards Goodfellow with his head.

'He's with us,' Jack answered quickly.

Thomas pulled a face.

'I know what I'm doing.' Goodfellow was waspish. He understood the man's expression well enough.

Thomas gave a grunt by way of a reply, then directed his attention towards Jack. 'We're in.'

'Good.'

'But we want you to understand what we are about.' Thomas looked around him, checking no one else had wandered into earshot. No one had. The four of them were quite alone. The diggers would still be out at their claims for a while yet. They would work until night had fallen and they could no longer see what they were doing. Only then would they down tools and head back to their wagons and tents to prepare some sort of dinner. But the clerks in the office stopped work much earlier. They did not have the same motivation as the diggers, the men who controlled the documentation earning a wage, nothing more.

'Go on,' said Jack.

'Those Boers need to be taught a lesson. We all know that.'
Thomas's eyes narrowed as he got down to brass tacks. 'But
that's not what this about. You get me?'

'Then what is it about?'

'We want them stones.' Thomas licked his lips, his tongue
darting back and forth quickly.

'What about Flanagan?'

He turned his head and spat before he replied. 'I don't give a
rat's arse about him. If he was dumb-fool enough to get caught,
then I don't reckon any of us give much of a shite. No, son, this
is about them stones those bastards have in those wagons of
theirs. We don't think they should be allowed to cling on to
them.'

'So this is to be a robbery?' Goodfellow huffed at the notion.
'I thought it was about justice!'

'Justice be damned.' Thomas sneered at the Englishman's
naivety.

'Good grief.' Goodfellow turned to take Jack's elbow in a
firm grip. 'Let's leave these fellows to their thievery.'

'No.' Jack shook him off. 'You want the stones. Fine. You
can have them. Apart from one. The one I hacked from the
bloody ground. That's mine.'

The brothers looked at one another. 'You think you'll know
which one it is?'

'I'll know.'

'And what about him?' Thomas nodded at Goodfellow.

Jack turned towards his fellow countryman. 'Well, what do
you want?'

Goodfellow pulled a face at the direct question. 'I thought
this was about justice for that poor lad.'

'It is.' Jack's reply was quick and seasoned with a touch of pepper. 'Is that it? That all you want?'

'I suppose I should be due a share of any diamonds we happen to take.'

'Fine. You get a third each.' He gestured to include the three men standing with him. 'You all good with that?'

'Done.' Thomas was quick to agree. But he did not offer his hand as the deal was struck. 'When do we do this?'

'Tomorrow.' There was no need to wait.

'Fair enough.' Thomas answered for the brothers.

'Very well.' Goodfellow puffed out his chest as he gave his own agreement.

'Have you got weapons?' Jack fired the question at the two brothers.

'Don't worry about us. We'll be ready. You just worry about Fatty there.' Thomas jerked his head at Goodfellow.

'Now look here—'

Jack cut Goodfellow off. He took a deliberate pace forward so that he was closer to the two brothers. 'We meet here, same time tomorrow. Be ready.'

He had found his soldiers. There might be only three of them, but they would do.

They had to.

For tomorrow he would release his rage and his fury.

Tomorrow he would take back what was his.

Tomorrow.

Chapter Twenty-eight

Jack tiptoed across the dark tent. He had removed his boots and left them outside, in an attempt not to wake Anna, who gave every appearance of being nothing more than sound asleep. He moved with stealth learned in the rookeries of his youth, the ability to tread soft and slow a prerequisite for survival in the dark back streets of the metropolis. And he had been good at surviving. Expert even.

He placed the carpet bag he was carrying down carefully. He had retrieved it from the storage hut outside Goodfellow's tent after their short meeting with the Thompson brothers. It had seen better days, but it did its job, and it had been with him for many years now. He reached for the clasp, the touch of the metal igniting memories of the many times he had opened it prior to battle. The simple latch was scratched, and his fingertips played over the surface, tracing the fissures. The carpet bag held more than just his weapons.

He unfastened the clasp, moving the mechanism slowly so as not to make a noise. As he opened the bag, the smell of gun oil and spent powder was released. It was a familiar aroma, one that stirred more memories. There was something homely in the taint of metal, something that spoke of who he was. No matter that he had lived in more locations than he could even try to recall, this scent had always been with him, as constant as the smell of his own sweat. It defined him more than any words could ever convey.

He reached inside, hands moving with care until his fingers closed around the familiar shape of a knife. The blade was around eight inches long and was encased in a thick brown leather sheath. He had bought it from a back-street smith in Cairo and the edge had once been sharp enough to shave with. It might have lost some of its sharpness now, but it was still a deadly weapon. He had killed with it before, sawing through a man's neck with ease.

He pulled it from the bag, laying it gently on the ground beside him. He would spend the next day getting it ready for the fight that was to come, a nearly new whetstone stored with the blade for the sole purpose of putting a new edge on the weapon.

He continued his search, working his fingers through cardboard boxes of cartridges until he found what he was looking for: the holstered Lefaucheux revolver. It was a brute of a handgun, heavy to the point of being almost unwieldy, and it fired six pinfire cartridges. He had not purchased the weapon. It had been taken from the hands of a dying ivory trader, a Frenchman, a man Jack had once thought of as a friend. As his hand closed over the holster and its heavy contents, he was transported to a gory battlefield not far from the Nile river. The ground around him was carpeted with the bodies of the dead and the soon-to-be-dead. Some wore the workmanlike clothes of those who had ventured into the wild lands far from civilisation. Others wore a scarlet shirt over simple white army-issue trousers. Some Jack had killed, others he had ordered to their deaths. All were there at his command, his need to fight the Frenchman casting dozens of souls into the nothingness of eternity.

'Jack?'

He started as Anna called his name. The memory fled. 'Yes, it's me. I was trying not to disturb you.'

'What are you doing?' The question took several long moments to form.

'Nothing important.' Jack placed the Lefaucheux back inside the bag. He had time. He would not be meeting the Thompson brothers and Goodfellow until the following evening. Like the knife, the revolver needed work, and as soon as it was daylight, he would clean it with meticulous care before loading it with fresh cartridges that he would check over and polish beforehand. He would leave nothing to chance.

But all that was in the future. Now he came closer to Anna's simple cot, kneeling beside her, concentrating on her rather than the tools of his bitter trade. 'It is good to see you awake.'

'I am not sure I am ever awake. Not any more. It is all a blur.'

Jack breathed slowly, trying to make as little noise as he could. 'Rest now, love.' He reached out, smoothing his fingers across her forehead, his touch as gossamer light as he could make it.

'Tell me what has been going on. I feel like I have been here for ever.'

'You should rest.'

'There will be time for rest when I am dead.'

The gallows humour did not sit well, and for a moment Jack could not form a reply.

'Flanagan is dead. The Boers hanged him.'

Anna gasped. 'When?'

'Early this morning.'

'So it was all for nothing.'

'No.' Jack shook his head. 'I'm going to make them pay for what they did. And I'm going to take back everything they took. You hear me, Anna, I'm going to make this right.'

Anna fell silent. Yet he knew she was still awake.

'There is something you need to hear.' She spoke suddenly, the words firmer and louder than she had managed for days.

Jack eased away from her. A lump of ice-cold dread landed heavily in his stomach.

'I do not know if there will be another time when I can say this.' She reached out, fingers like claws taking firm hold of his arm to stop him getting away.

Jack rocked back on his knees. 'Don't say that.'

'No.' Anna shook her head, eyes closing in pain. 'You must listen.'

He waited for her to say more, but she fell silent, swallowing with difficulty. Talking was clearly costing her dearly, but he knew she would not stop until she had said whatever it was she wanted to say.

'You need to go.'

The words came out with finality. Not for discussion. And they were spoken with a force summoned from he knew not where.

'Go where?' he asked. 'What do you need?'

'No.' She shook her head again, face screwed up with pain. 'You must leave me. Leave this place while you still can.' He could see beads of sweat at her temples as she somehow found the strength to talk.

'Don't be daft. I'm not leaving you.'

'You must.' She coughed, the sound of phlegm shifting loud in the quiet of the tent. 'They killed that boy for what he did. They will do the same to you if you confront them.'

'No.' Jack reached out and took her hand. Her skin was cold, clammy.

'They will. You know it.' She pulled away from him. 'Leave now, while you still can.'

'No.' Jack eased away from the cot. He did want to hear any more. But Anna was not done.

'So you will fight them? No matter what I say.'

'Yes. I have to.'

'Then you are a fool.' She rose up out of her bed, pushing down with her elbows then using them to hold herself up. 'And you will die.' She glared at him then, eyes red raw and blood-shot, skin pale and blotchy and sheeted in sweat. 'You will die to get revenge. To prove you are the man you think you are. The man you want to be.'

Jack could say nothing. Anna's eyes were wild, anger and pain combined.

'You want to prove yourself. Over and over again. And you won't stop until you are dead, even though you have done this a hundred times.'

'What would you have me do?' Jack snapped back at her. Her words were cutting deep. And he knew they were true.

'I would have you leave.'

'I won't leave you.' He hissed the words, filling them with passion.

'You must. I am dying.'

'No.' The word was wrenched from him.

'You know it's true.' She could hold herself up no longer,

and she fell back into her sweaty sheets. 'Go. I release you.'

'I am not yours to command, Anna.' Jack forced the anger away as he saw the state she was in after the effort of speaking, her breath coming in laboured gasps so that her chest rose and fell as if she had just run a race. 'And I am not leaving you.'

'You must. You must leave me now. Be your own man like you always wanted. Be free.' She shuddered as the words left her, then gulped a breath and lay still.

'Anna?' Jack reached out, desperate hands moving to her neck. The blood was still pumping, and so he laid a hand gently across her lips. He felt the slow movement of breath on his skin and let out a long sigh of relief. She was still alive. For now.

He moved away with care, watching her face the whole time. For a moment, he was tempted to do as she said, the notion matching the dark seam of evil that existed deep in his heart. It would be so easy. It would take but a moment to gather his few possessions, and then he could be away. He had left people behind before. He could do it again.

He would be alone again.

But he would be free. Beholden to no one but himself.

'No.' He muttered the word under his breath, then moved stealthily to his carpet bag. He would take what he needed, but he would not abandon her.

Not now.

Not ever.

Not whilst she still lived.

Chapter Twenty-nine

'You want to tell me what the hell that is?' Jack could not keep the derision from his tone as he stared at the object clutched in Goodfellow's hand. The two men were at the rendezvous near the digger committee's office. As before, they were the first there.

Goodfellow pulled a face at Jack's tone. 'It is a fowling piece. My father's, as it happens.'

Jack looked the weapon up and down. It resembled an ancient musket, but one where the end of the barrel had been replaced with a funnel. 'You think that can kill a man?'

'Kill?' Goodfellow paled.

'You're not going on a duck hunt.' Jack spoke dourly. He himself was ready to fight. The Lefaucheux had been cleaned and now sat on his hip, snug in its holster, while his freshly sharpened knife hung on his left buttock. 'Have you loaded that thing?'

'Good God, no.' Goodfellow puffed up with surprise. 'Why, that would be dangerous. My father taught me never to load until we were close to the target.'

Jack looked away before he snapped something he would

regret. The other two men who would make up his small army were approaching. The Thompson brothers seemed better prepared for the fight, both carrying double-barrelled hunting rifles. From what Jack could see, they were heavy bore, suitable for hunting large game. Unlike Goodfellow's duck gun, both would kill a man with ease.

It was nearly dark, the last of the day's light fading fast. Around them, the diggers were returning to their tents, another day of toil coming to an end as the light slipped away. Not many had the energy to glance at the four men standing together. Those who did would have seen the array of weaponry on show, yet the sight of rifles was not uncommon here, with many of the diggers feeding themselves on the game they could hunt in the veldt nearby. Had their true purpose somehow been divined, Jack doubted few would try to hold them back. The Boers were universally disliked, at least on this side of the encampment.

He sniffed as he caught the smell of woodsmoke in the air, the warm aroma beginning to overpower the taint of dirt and dust as the men and women of Du Toit's Pan turned their attention to that evening's dinner. It was a reminder that they had a while to wait until they could put his plan into action.

'Take that fucking thing back to your tent,' he snapped at Goodfellow. 'Don't you have a revolver?'

'I do not.' Goodfellow bristled.

'Then get one. Borrow or steal it if you have to. But you are not bringing that piece of shit with us.'

Goodfellow came closer. 'I did not think we were at war, Jack.'

'Then you were wrong.' The man needed to wake up. There was no point going to a fight with a gun that would do nothing but make a noise. It was time to be armed and dangerous.

Goodfellow nodded, then swallowed with difficulty. 'I do not think I have it in me to kill, Jack.'

'Then stay behind.' Jack did not care that he was being cruel. Goodfellow might look like a buffoon, but there was more to him than his appearance suggested. Yet this day, he was doing little to come across as anything but a dolt.

'Perhaps I will.' The portly Englishman took a step away. 'I hope you understand, Jack, I really do.'

'I do.' It was an honest answer. He did understand. Some men were not cut out for killing. That did not make them weak or somehow inadequate, at least not in his eyes. But he did not need a man like that at his side this night. 'Go. Walk your chalk.' He jerked his head to indicate that Goodfellow should leave. 'But will you do one thing for me?'

'Certainly.' Goodfellow replied swiftly, eager to please now he had been dismissed.

'Check on Anna. Sit with her for me.'

'Of course, Jack.'

'And if I don't come back, see her right.' Jack did not look at Goodfellow as he gave the request.

There was a pause. The silence heavy.

'Yes. I will.' Goodfellow's rely when it came was earnest.

'Good. Thank you. Now go.' Jack spoke brusquely. He did not wait to see if his fellow countryman would do what he was told, instead turning to face the Thompson brothers.

'We wait here until the early hours. That good with you?'

'Yes.' Thomas nodded.

'And you know where we are going?'

'We've been there before.'

'When?' Jack pressed for more.

'A couple of days ago.' The brothers looked at one another.

Jack saw the silent exchange, noting the guarded looks on the two men's faces. 'What for?' he asked.

Thomas shrugged. 'We were just sniffing around.'

Jack understood. They had likely been looking for something to steal. Theft was rife in the diggings, a man's possessions viewed as fair game for anyone light-fingered enough to take them. The rule was simple. Look after your shit. If you didn't and it went walkabout, you had no one to blame but yourself.

'Tell me what you saw.'

'Well, there's loads of them damn wagons of theirs, scattered all over the damn place, they are.' Thomas looked at his brother for confirmation and was rewarded with a quick nod. 'Maybe a dozen smaller ones. Of course, there's loads of gear lying about the place. Nothing much of value in it, not that we saw. Just the usual shovels, picks, that sort of thing. Them Dutchies are canny enough to keep their valuables locked up nice and tight in those bloody wagons of theirs.'

'Go on,' Jack urged when Thomas paused.

'Well, there's plenty of room between the wagons. Enough space to get around, if you're quiet like. They sleep inside them, of course. There are a couple of tents, but not many, not like on our side. But when we was there, there was a few Dutchies sleeping by the fires. Full of grog, they were. You could smell it on 'em. Smelled like a fucking gin palace.'

Jack grunted at the reference. He had been brought up in a gin palace. It had smelled of many things, few of them pleasant. But it had rarely smelled of alcohol; his mother had watered down the gin too much for that to happen.

'Then there's their boss's wagon.'

'Their boss?'

'Old Um or whatever shite they call him. The fella with the big grey beard. His wagon is up on a little lip, so he can look down over them all, I reckon. It's pretty much right in the middle, with the others all scattered around it.' Again Thomas glanced at his brother. 'That's where the real good stuff will be, we reckon. In that old man's wagon, under his bloody bed I shouldn't wonder, with his big old arse sleeping right on top of it. We tried to get close,' he winced at the memory, 'but there was this fat fucker sleeping right where we wanted to go. We ain't had the chance to go back since.'

Jack noted the furtive glances and the uncomfortable set of both men's faces as they admitted their failure. It did not bode well. He was sure that if he himself had wanted to walk right into the old Boer's wagon, he would have done so and not been deterred even if the devil himself was sleeping outside. It seemed Thomas and Arnold were cut from a different cloth.

'We should work out what we are about.' Thomas eased himself forward to catch Jack's attention.

'What do you mean?'

'I mean, what we are going to do when we get there.' He looked at his brother once more. 'The rules of engagement, as it were. It's best to be clear about it.'

Jack nodded. He understood the question. 'We are going to find that old man of theirs. He's the one who will have strung Flanagan up. Or at least ordered the others to do it. We find him and we take him with us.'

'And then what?'

Jack smiled wolfishly as he felt a rush of fire in his veins. He had been impotent for too long. The Boers had bested him more than once now, beating him black and blue, stealing his claim and taking his diamond. Not once had he stopped them.

Now they would see the manner of man they had made their enemy. 'We string him up. Same as he did to Flanagan.' He did not shirk from making the statement. The Boer leader had ordered Flanagan's death, just as he had ordered the taking of Jack's claim. Now he would have to pay the price.

Brother looked to brother. 'You mean to kill him?'

'Have you got a problem with that?' Jack's eyes narrowed. 'They killed young Flanagan. Left him kicking his heels while they wrung his scrawny little neck.'

'That lad was a damned fool,' Thomas sneered, his scorn for the dead thief obvious.

'He was.' Jack made no attempt to defend the young man. 'But they still need to be taught a lesson.'

'And that old Dutchie, he should pay for what he did. He controls all those bloody Boers.' Thomas gurned at the notion. 'So long as we get them stones, all of them now that fat chum of yours has fucked off, we don't mind if the old bastard is hung, drawn and quartered. So long as you do it.'

Jack did not miss a beat. 'Fine. But we need to keep it quiet. We go in, take the old man and his diamonds, then get out of there before they know what's what. You hear me?'

'We do.' Arnold grinned. 'Keep it simple.'

'Yes.' Jack could not have agreed more.

He was about to continue when to his surprise he spied Goodfellow approaching. The fowling piece was gone.

'Jack!' Goodfellow called to him even though he was still a good ten yards away.

'I thought you were going to sit with Anna for me?'

'I need you to come with me.' He ignored Jack's question. 'Now.' He spoke softly but urgently.

Jack's brow furrowed. 'What is it?' The joy of the fight to

come had been fizzing through his veins, the feeling awakening parts of him that had been slumbering for far too long. But something in Goodfellow's tone quenched that fire. It was replaced by a rush of ice.

'It's Anna.' Goodfellow's expression was solemn. Grave, even.

'What's wrong?' Jack stepped towards his countryman, both the Boers and the Thompson brothers forgotten in an instant.

'You need to come with me.' Goodfellow repeated the words, reaching out to take hold of Jack's sleeve. 'Now.'

'What is it?'

His mouth opened to reply. It closed before any sound could emerge. Instead, he looked at the dirt, his eyes closing as if he were in sudden pain.

'Tell me.' The words came from Jack shackled in a shroud. He knew what was coming.

Goodfellow looked up, moist eyes opening. For a moment, he did nothing but stare at Jack, lips quivering as he tried to form the words that had to be said. Words that would change Jack's world.

'She's dead.' He sucked down a deep breath. 'Anna has gone.'

Jack trailed Goodfellow through the encampment. The sun was setting and it filled the cramped confines of the tent lines with long shadows. The sky glowed with a rich golden hue. On a different day, he would have looked up and enjoyed the sight, the beautiful end to the day a picturesque conclusion to hours of hard work.

But not that day.

For that evening, Jack saw only the encroaching darkness, a world of shadow and sorrow.

They reached the tent. He found he could not take another step. He had nothing left. No strength. No energy. It was as if the life had been sucked out of him to leave an empty husk.

'She is inside.' Goodfellow came to stand at his side, then bent forward to undo the ties that kept the flaps closed. 'If you wish to see her.'

Jack did not move an inch. He simply stared at Goodfellow, the weight of his own soul crushing him.

Goodfellow looked back at him, then pulled the flap aside. He said nothing.

Jack looked inside the tent where he had passed so many hours. The smell that crept out was a putrid mix of sun-warmed canvas and sickness. But he paid it no heed, its noxious miasma no longer holding the power to offend. Instead, he glanced across to Anna's cot. He saw her body lying there. She was utterly still. Silent.

Goodfellow had covered her face with a blanket so that Jack was spared seeing the dreadful pallor of death on her features.

'You can go in if you wish.' The other man spoke quietly. 'Sit with her for a while if you would like.'

'No.' For a moment, Jack thought his limbs would fail him. Never before had he felt like this. Never before had he felt as utterly exhausted. Or as empty.

Coldness crept through him. He could sense it filling him with the bleak hopelessness of oblivion. He relished its arrival, welcoming it as it crept through every fibre of his being.

'Jack?' Goodfellow reached out to lay a hand on his forearm. 'I am so very sorry.'

'No.' Jack snapped the single word. 'Do not pity me.' He fixed his eyes on Goodfellow. 'Bury her for me.'

'I will. I promise.'

'I am in your debt.' He spoke briskly. He meant it. Goodfellow had proven himself to be a good friend. In other circumstances. Jack might have been able to enjoy that friendship.

But not now.

He said nothing more as he stalked into the encroaching darkness.

He felt nothing. Nothing at all. Spent.

Anna had been taken from him. He did not need to see her corpse to know she was gone. Her body was not her, not any more.

She had left him.

And so it was time for revenge.

Time to forget.

Time to kill.

Chapter Thirty

Jack crept towards the Boers' wagons, moving slowly and carefully, the two Thompson brothers following in his wake. He stuck to the darkest shadows, avoiding any patch of light thrown by the few fires left to burn through the night. He had planned the route with care, holding the three of them far back from the Boers' section of the encampment as he plotted a path through the widely dispersed wagons. Only when he was certain he had memorised the route did he let them move.

It had been a long vigil, time dragging with excruciating slowness. Jack had wanted to wait for the dog hours past midnight when no one sane or sober would be abroad. It was the time of night when men slept and dawn was still far away. In the rookeries of his youth, it was the hour for mischief or worse.

Now it would be the time for revenge.

Oom Joost's wagon sat close to the very centre of the Boers' encampment on a patch of raised ground, just as the brothers had described. His status would work in their favour that night, the rest of the Boers keeping at a distance out of respect for their leader and to give him more space, something infinitely precious in the cramped confines of the diggings. It gave Jack and his two accomplices the opportunity to get to the wagon unseen and put their plan into action, stealing both the old Boer and his precious stones away into the night before any of those slumbering nearby even knew anything had happened.

As he got closer to the first of the wagons on his chosen path, he sniffed the air, smelling the meaty, sweaty odour of men who had sat around a campfire long into the evening drinking and eating. The taint of those same fires lingered in the air along with the aroma of cooked meat. The smell was familiar, calming even. It spoke of contentment. Of a home that had been found even here in dusty diggings half buried in the veldt. It should have evoked memories of the hours he himself had spent by similar fires with men he had thought of as friends. Comradeship. Security. Happiness even. He had relished those times when he had not been alone, when he had enjoyed the company of others at the end of the day.

But like so many things, such sentiments were from way back in the past. Now he smelled the campfires and thought only of what was ahead, and the mayhem that he would spread in the night.

He paused, holding up a hand to halt the two men following him, straining to hear the sounds of anyone moving close by. His mind was still. Empty. Calm. All that mattered was this moment he was in, the threat and the sense of danger enough to dull the screams in his mind, at least in part. For even here, in the heart of the enemy's domain, they echoed deep in his soul. But he held them tight, forcing himself to concentrate on what he could see, what he could hear, smell, feel, letting his senses probe the darkness that surrounded him, or at least the darkness that was outside. The darkness inside would have to wait.

'You see him?' He whispered the words over his shoulder, his left arm pointing towards the slumbering figure lying beside a fire near a wagon they would have to pass, and no more than fifteen yards to the east of where the three men now crouched.

'Yes.'

The reply came instantly. Jack did not know which of the brothers had spoken and he did not care. The two men at his side meant nothing to him. They were tools, nothing more. He cared more for his revolver than he did for them.

'We'll go around.'

There was no good reason to stay on their current path, and he led them off at an angle to the route he had settled upon. He moved forward with care, every movement planned then carried out with painstaking attention. Stealth was all now. There would be a time for noise. A place for chaos.

But not now. Not yet.

They reached another wagon on the periphery of the area the Boers had claimed as their own. He slid along its side, then paused. He could hear someone snoring inside, the sound rhythmic and regular. It was a good sound, just what he wanted to hear. These Boers were his enemy now, but they did not know that yet, and they would not have contemplated the need to place sentries, to have men on guard through the small hours of the night. They would regret that soon enough.

He eased forward, feeling his way along the flank of the wagon until he reached the rear. From there, he could look ahead. He took his time, letting his breathing settle as he surveyed the scene in front of him.

The Thompson brothers' description of the Boers'

encampment and his own reconnaissance had done a decent
job of preparing him for what he would find. There were
dozens of the heavy wagons the Boers favoured, and they
were arranged haphazardly, some close together, others more
isolated. All were surrounded by the familiar detritus of the
diggings. Shovels and picks lay here and there, or else had been
piled together on the ground, while dozens of tin buckets were
scattered around. Wooden packing crates and boxes were
stacked neatly, along with at least a dozen wooden barrels of
varying sizes. Tarpaulins stretched between some of the wagons
were being used to shelter piles of supplies, and one or two had
a small corrugated-iron store nearby. The structures added a
sense of permanence to the encampment. In front of every
wagon was a campfire, some still burning, others smouldering
or even completely extinguished. Each one was surrounded by
pots, griddles and every manner of cooking utensil, with sacks
and crates of vittles left nearby ready for use. To Jack's eye it
looked little different to the encampment he had left. But that
familiarity meant nothing. For this was the home of his enemy,
and nothing would stay his hand.

He could see the wagon he wanted up ahead. It stood
slightly apart from the rest on a low rise. It was a place that
demonstrated privilege and command. The spot he would have
chosen for himself if he'd had the option. He knew that was
where the old Boer would be sleeping. It gave him a target. A
destination. An objective.

He stepped into the open and started towards it.

The three of them came forward in a tight line, barely a foot
between them. All were crouching, so that they would not be
silhouetted against a night-time sky that was filled with stars.
The Thompson brothers were breathing heavily and loudly

enough for him to hear them. But he paid it no heed, concentrating on his route towards their target.

As they left the closest wagons behind, he picked up the pace. This was the moment of greatest danger. It was unlikely anyone would have spotted them lurking in the shadows on the periphery of the encampment. Now they were well inside the Boers' domain and they could easily be seen.

He did his best to pick a path furthest from those fires still alight, darting left and right like a skirmisher advancing on an enemy, determined to use every scrap of cover he could. There was plenty available, the wagons themselves and the arrangement of tents and digging equipment providing dozens of places they could use. Jack had chosen the hour with care, and his patience now paid dividends. In the small hours of the night, no one spied the three figures cutting through the encampment.

They made it to their objective without an alarm being raised, huddling close to the side of Oom Joost's wagon. All were breathing hard, chests heaving. Jack saw beads of sweat on the brothers' faces as they squatted down in front of him, bracing themselves for what was to come.

'You two ready for this?' he whispered, settling his own breathing as he did so.

'Let's do it.' The reply was quiet but firm.

'Then follow me.' He whispered the instruction, then froze. The words resonated. They were the words of a commander. Leading men meant just that. Leading. Too few officers understood that, but he had learned that an officer served his men, not the other way round. That meant setting an example and being the first to advance, no matter the danger, showing the men what had to be done. He had spoken those simple words many times, drawing men to follow him into the cauldron of fire on more battlefields than he could recall. Now he whispered the same words to a pair of thieves as they stole into a sleeping encampment. That cheapened them, demeaning what he had done before and those who had once followed him.

He had fallen far over the years.

'Get on then, man.'

One of the brothers hissed the words as Jack hesitated, his meaty hand thumping into his back. It was enough to annoy. To spark the fire.

He pushed his emotions away.

He was no longer an officer, or even a soldier.

He was a man alone. A wanderer fending for himself and doing as he saw fit.

He was an avenger seeking retribution.

He was a thief, come in the darkness to steal.

He stepped forward, drawing the heavy Lefaucheux from his holster as he moved beyond the shadows.

It was time to stop creeping around like a coward.

It was time to start fighting.

There was time for a last deep breath, then he was darting around the side of the wagon, foot lifting onto the step at the rear. Pushing down firmly with his boot, he boosted himself up, his head coming level with the open awning, his right hand raising his revolver so that it would be aiming at the open space, ready to fire.

Time slowed, even as his heart beat ever faster. His eyes were roving over the inside of the wagon, picking out two bodies lying on the floor swaddled in blankets, the shapes immediately identifiable as a man and a woman sleeping close together. There was a moment of joy as his plans came to fruition and the enemy was located.

Then a child's face loomed up right in front of him.

For one long-drawn-out moment, Jack stared into the pale blue eyes of a blonde girl no more than five or six years old.

Then she screamed.

The scream went on and on, the girl shrieking as only a frightened child could shriek, the sound reverberating around the slumbering encampment, shattering the quiet and throwing peace into chaos.

Jack froze. For what seemed like for ever, he stared at the little girl. He was close enough to see every detail of her open mouth, the strands of saliva and the missing teeth. He knew he had to act, and act fast, but everything was locked tight and he could do nothing but stare back at her, even as he saw the sleeping shapes behind her throwing back blankets and leaping up to see what had caused the dreadful sound.

The Lefaucheux seemed to be moving of its own accord. Even as his mind stayed in paralysis, the gaping maw of the huge barrel covered the face of the child. It was now no more than six inches from the open mouth that was emitting the scream.

His finger tightened, curling around the thick trigger just as it had done a thousand times before. Faces flashed past his eyes. Images of the dead and the lost, the girl's young face disappearing behind the memories of those he had slain. He no longer saw a child.

He saw his nightmares.

He was surrounded by commotion. A dog was barking and he heard the first warning shouts of alarm. The two men who had followed him were turning to run, the sound of their heavy bodies lumbering into motion reaching him a moment before the first roar of anger and alarm as one of the wagon's occupants became aware of the interloper.

His finger took up the tension on the trigger.

It was time to fight. To shoot. To kill. The urge overwhelmed him, just as the memories of past battles filled his mind so that he no longer knew where or who he was.

There was just the need to fight.

The trigger moved the first fraction of an inch.

And there it stayed.

His mind awoke. The faces of the dead fled. They were replaced by the face of a terrified child and the chaos of an encampment reacting to a sudden alarm.

'Shit.' He hissed the word as his body and mind came back under his control.

The girl in front of him was snatched out of the way. Her bright blue eyes were replaced by the glowering face of the grey-bearded Boer he had come to find. He read the man's emotions in a fraction of a second. Fury. Anger. Fear. All were present before they were replaced with something else. Something more purposeful.

Joost twisted around. When he turned back, he was holding a revolver of a make Jack did not recognise. The old Boer must have slept with it at his side for just such an eventuality as this, and now it rose just as the Lefaucheux had done, although this time, Jack was sure there would be no hesitation when it came to shooting.

Acting fast, he turned, jumping down from the wagon, his body reacting instantly to the threat to his life. He hit the ground hard, the impact jarring up his legs and into knees that half buckled under the strain. Staggering away, he heard the brutal roar of a revolver firing. There was a cracking sound in the air an inch from his head, and the thud of a bullet hitting something solid.

Then he ran as fast as his painful legs would carry him.

The encampment had been thrown into pandemonium. Dogs were barking in righteous fury, while men were shouting orders and questions as they tried to make sense of the commotion that had stolen away the quiet of the night.

Ducking under an awning stretched between two wagons, Jack came close to decapitating himself on one of the guide ropes holding it aloft, the vicious impact avoided at the very last second by a frantic swerve. The wild movement left him unbalanced, and he fell, hitting the ground hard, the reverberations awaking the pain in his spine. But he could not stop. Not now. And so he rolled over and stumbled to his feet, his body swaying momentarily before he found his balance and could run again.

As he sped around another wagon, he saw the Thompson brothers. Both had fled before him, but neither was in prime physical health, and they hadn't got far, both men just a few yards ahead of him. Their size slowed their escape, and it also provided a large target for the Boers, who were reacting fast to the sudden and unexpected danger.

A single rifle shot snapped through the air, the retort echoing. Jack had no idea where the bullet went, or even if he was the one being shot at. There was nothing to do save run on, skipping from side to side, ducking and weaving through the encampment, leaping guide ropes then dipping low behind a pile of crates that would screen him for a second but no more.

Another shot came. Then another. The first stung the air near his head, the whip-crack sharp in his ear. The second was followed by the meaty thwack of a fast-moving projectile striking flesh.

Arnold Thompson cried out, his body arching as the bullet caught him in the back. Jack did not linger to see him go down, his attention focused on his own path. But he heard the cries that followed, the first coming from Arnold himself as the pain swamped him, then a roar of disbelief as his brother reacted.

Thomas called for Jack then, voice loud and desperate.

'Jack, help us!'

But Jack paid him no heed and ran on. He was close to the wagons on the edge of the Boers' encampment. He would not turn. Not now. Not for a pair of thieves.

Another shot followed, then another. The darkness should have provided as much cover as the wagons and the tents, but to Jack's astonishment, he heard another yell, the odd, gulping mewing made by a man when a bullet buried itself deep in his flesh.

He turned, pace slowing just a fraction as he looked across to see that Thomas was down too, his weighty body now lying next to that of his brother. There was time to marvel at the accuracy of the Boers' shooting before what felt like an express train thumped into the flesh of his upper chest an inch above and to the right of his nipple. The pain came a split second later, a flash of agony tearing a gasp from his mouth as the force of the blow spun him around.

He hit the side of a wagon, his left arm just about bracing in time to lessen the impact. But still he fell, legs buckling underneath him so that he slumped rather than tumbled, his back sliding down the side of the wagon.

He landed on his arse.

For a moment, all he could do was sit there. He could feel

blood pumping from his body, warm and wet on his shirt. But the pain was gone, or at least it had somehow disappeared into the distance. He saw the first Boers reach the two brothers, who still lay where they had fallen. He saw boots fly as angry men lashed out at the interlopers in their camp, and he heard the thump as bare feet, boots and rifle butts smashed into unprotected bodies and heads. The brothers were defenceless, their wounds leaving them unable to fight back, and the Boers showed no mercy. Kicks came without pause, the men taking turns to pummel the two bodies, until a latecomer pushed through the circle, a heavy hemp rope held in each hand.

There was laughter then. Short, sharp guffaws as the Boers hauled the two bodies to their feet. Neither could stand – from what Jack could see, both had long been beaten insensible – and so they were dragged away, feet trailing in the dirt, nooses tied around their necks even as they were marched to their deaths.

The sight spurred Jack into action. To sit there was to die himself.

But even as the decision to move was made, another Boer shouted in anger, meaty finger pointing directly at him.

'There!'

It was Oom Joost, the man they had come to bring to justice. Now he called for justice of his own, shouting the orders that saw rifles lift towards the third stranger who had brought chaos to a slumbering camp.

Time slowed. Jack could see at least three Boers taking aim, their rifles suddenly going still as they settled ready to shoot.

Three rifles aimed at him and him alone.

Three rifles that fired as one.

Chapter Thirty-one

Three bullets tore through the air.

Three bullets missed.

They hit the wagon Jack sat against before he even heard the crack of their firing, splinters of wood cascading over him and catching him on the hands and face.

The Boers had missed with their first shots. He knew they would be unlikely to miss with their second, especially if he sat there on his arse waiting for the bullets to strike him.

There was temptation in that notion. He could stay still and let Fate decide if he should live or die. She could spare him the pain of fighting for a life he no longer knew if he wanted.

The idea of giving up died quickly. He would decide if he would end it. Not Fate.

The thought stirred him into life, igniting something in his gut. A new rush of energy pulsed through him. He did not know where it came from, but he felt it in the fire in his belly and the strength that filled his battered muscles. Pushing down with his left arm, he levered himself to his feet. Pain flared. Then he was up running, arms pumping, boots scrabbling for purchase, his right hand just about managing to holster his revolver lest he drop it as he committed everything he had left to flight.

Yet he was slow. Horribly slow. And time seemed to stand still, so that he felt as if he were somehow suddenly paralysed, limbs powerless, his body unable to progress no matter how hard he tried to force it to move.

Bullets chased after him, the air around him buzzing as if he were under attack by a swarm of insects, except these insects would kill if they struck. None of the bullets found a mark, his sudden movement saving him for a moment longer.

Time sped back up, the horrible feeling of being unable to move replaced with power that propelled him forward, and he darted around the wagon he had sat against, feet dancing across the ground. Ducking under a rope that held up an awning then jumping a single wooden crate, he fled into the darkness, his body moving freely, arms and legs strong, heart pumping.

No more shots followed him as he dashed out of sight, not even the Boer riflemen able to hit a target they could not see.

As he ran, he heard shouts of frustration from men denied their target. Somewhere a child was screaming, while dogs barked in impotence. He rushed on into the night, giving no thought to direction, his only aim to get away. Yet as he ran, he felt his vision start to grey, the rush of energy that had propelled him to his feet fading fast. What had been a run turned into an awkward, stumbling gait, and he gasped as a flood of pain seared through him.

He took another pace, then another, trying to force his body to respond. But he was roundly ignored and he felt his knees begin to give way under the strain of keeping him upright.

Voices followed him, cries filling the air as the Boers rushed from their encampment to find the last of the three intruders. He heard orders shouted, groups dispatched to every point of the compass as the grey-bearded Oom Joost sent his men to give chase into the darkness.

Jack could barely breathe now. He was doubling over even as he tried to keep moving, his body twisting around the thumping pain that was threatening to overwhelm him. He staggered forward, panting hard, sucking at the air as his head started to spin. Around him the world was turning black, his vision narrowing to two small circles so that he saw only what was to his front.

He tried to keep moving, straining his muscles, forcing his legs to hold him up and take him on. He took another step, then another, lurching from side to side like a drunkard, then he was falling forward, the ground rushing up to meet him before he was able to register that his desperate attempt to flee was coming to an end.

He hit the ground face first.

The pain was almost more than he could bear. It cut through him like a dagger to the throat, the wash of agony filling his mind before it was cut off in an instant and the darkness claimed him.

Jack came to, his eyes opening suddenly as if mounted on springs. There was a moment of confusion, of not knowing where he was or what had happened, before a sudden rush of noise filled his ears, cutting off the sounds of the world around him. It went on and on, the odd roar slow to fade. Yet his mind was starting to make sense of where he was, even if he could not yet recall why he was lying in the dirt, warm blood flowing freely, his body throbbing with a constant pulse of agony.

Slowly the rushing sound faded away. It was replaced by the shouts of men and dogs giving chase.

He lay still, blinking hard, forcing himself to think. He could see men all around him, the Boers spreading out, taking their time, moving slowly and deliberately. Most carried torches lit from those campfires still burning, while a few had oil lanterns. The lights bobbed up and down as their carriers explored the shadows, leaving no space unsearched.

An urge to run was filling Jack's mind. It was almost overpowering, the impulse surging and building to a climax, so that he found himself bringing his knees up into his chest, readying himself to get back to his feet and flee into the night.

Yet he refused to give in to the notion, no matter how much it tempted him. It would be a foolish thing to stand now and reveal himself to any of the hunter groups nearby. In his battered state, he knew he would not be able to outrun the Boers. Not now, hurting as he was.

To stand was to die.

But that did not mean he would lie in the dirt and wait for his fate. That idea was banished from his mind as soon as it was fully born, as was all thought of what had happened just hours before. All that mattered was the present.

And now there was a different urge swirling around deep in his belly. One that was dark. Evil. Deadly. A desire that was meaner and more dangerous than mere flight. It was the same desire that had brought him to this place and to this moment where his life hung by a thread.

It was an irresistible urge to fight and to maim and to kill.

He began crawling, keeping his face an inch from the ground. The pain coursing through him meant nothing, and he ignored it, just as he ignored the sharp stabs as stones and rocks cut into his hands. Keeping his movements slow, he wormed along, sliding through the dirt like a slug trawling through freshly turned earth. All the while, his face was kept low, pressing down into the ground so that he could smell its warm, dry, dusty tang. Keeping out of sight was everything now; his pale skin was sure to catch the light should any of the hunters turn a lantern into the shadows around him.

Every now and again, he risked looking up, searching for a route away from the chaos. At last he saw a way out, a path that would take him through the darkest shadows and away into the night.

But there was a problem.

A Boer was standing smack in the middle of that path.

Jack's escape route was blocked.

The Boer was holding a torch aloft, flames flickering and spluttering. The light bathed his face in a warm orange glow, while the rest of him was hidden in the darkness. It let Jack see the details of his face: the hooked nose that must have been broken in a fight at least once, the heavy beard that smothered him from well below the neck to high on his cheeks. The hair on his head was thick and tousled, with sharp angles that spoke of crude shears butchering it when it grew too long.

Despite the man standing directly in his way, Jack continued to squirm along, increasing his pace, elbows working hard while the toecaps of his heavy boots dug crescents in the soil as he forced them into the crust to find purchase before pushing them down and backwards to propel him forward. Every few seconds he made sure to glance up, holding the Boer's position in his mind and looking for the deepest shadows to screen him from sight from the men searching nearby. For there was only one thing he could do if he wanted to get away, and that was to fight his way free.

If Jack were to escape, the Boer would have to die.

The man was twenty feet away now. He was facing away from Jack, one hand thrust deep into a pocket while his boots scuffed at the ground.

Twenty feet became fifteen.

The Boer turned a slow circle. Jack saw him yawn then scratch at his groin. For the first time, he saw the man's heavy gut hanging over his belt, tufts of belly hair poking through his tan-coloured shirt. He smiled then. The Boer had clearly thrown his shirt on in a hurry, the buttons pushed through the wrong holes to leave a wide stretch of stomach revealed to the night. It gave him hope that his enemy was not fully awake. That he was vulnerable.

Fifteen feet became ten.

The Boer farted.

Jack snuffled as the smell reached him. Rotten eggs and latrines, foul and cloying. But he was almost there now, so he deliberately slowed his pace, easing himself along the ground an inch at a time then lifting himself up on his elbows as he prepared to strike.

Either the Boer would die or he would. It was that simple.

Ten feet became five.

Jack stopped. He barely dared breathe. The Boer lifted a hand, scratching it vigorously through his mop of hair, turning as he did so, the angle changing so that he faced directly towards Jack.

Then he shouted.

Jack froze, heart hammering in his chest. Every muscle tensed, his body preparing to explode up and away as he was spotted.

An answering shout came almost instantly.

He held himself still, his muscles quivering with anticipation. Yet he did not move. Not so much as an inch.

Instead of a triumphant roar of discovery, the Boer standing just five feet away had shouted in frustration and tired boredom. He was answered with a snap of command, the tone clear even if the words were not. It was an instruction to get his lazy arse into motion, a moment of anger colouring the order.

The Boer shook his head. Then he spat, a thick wad of phlegm shooting into the darkness ahead of him. It landed on Jack's forehead, heavy and wet, then slowly dribbled lower, worming across his skin just as he had wormed across the ground.

It was to be the final act of the Boer's life.

Even as the gooey gobbet reached his lips, Jack braced his weight onto his knees while he slipped his left hand down to the knife on his belt. Moving it no more than a quarter-inch at a time, he eased it out of its sheath, holding it low, hiding as much of the blade under his palm as he could lest it catch the light from the Boer's torch. It would be awkward to strike with his left hand rather than his right, but he would have to manage, his right shoulder and arm almost completely numb from the bullet strike.

It was time.

He took one last, slow breath, holding it in his lungs, filling his chest, feeling the muscles stretch tight.

Then he launched himself upwards.

He came up fast, exploding away from the ground and out of the darkness, knife held away from his side. The Boer's eyes widened in a moment's horrified surprise as a shadow burst into life.

Jack struck him for the first time, punching the blade sharply into the side of his neck, then pulling it back for no more than an instant before striking again, driving it back into the Boer's neck on the same side, thrusting it deep and tearing through gristle and sinew, filling his target's throat and gullet with blood.

A third strike followed, then a fourth, the knife moving fast. In the span of little more than a heartbeat, the Boer's neck had been torn into so much offal.

The blade stuck fast as Jack rammed it home for a fifth time. He left it there, his good hand now grabbing for the Boer's heavy beard and pulling, dragging the Boer down with him.

He hit the ground on his back, the Boer landing on top of him with enough force to drive the air from his lungs. But he had been ready for the impact, bracing his muscles so they absorbed both the bone-jarring contact with the sun-baked earth and the crushing weight on his chest. He gasped as the air exploded out of his mouth, but he was already turning, heaving the Boer over so that their positions were reversed, the bearded man lying beneath him.

There was no thought of mercy, or of delivering a clean death. There was just an all-consuming rage that had him hissing with fury as he reached down, yanking his knife from where it was still stuck fast in the Boer's neck. As it came free, blood spurted around it. Then he was thrusting it down, driving it up to the hilt into the Boer's chest.

The man tried to cry out, his mouth working furiously as the blade tore into his heart. Yet nothing emerged save a torrent of blood that frothed and foamed over his lips, soaking into his beard.

Even now, Jack was not done. His blade punched down time and time again, moving fast and cutting deep, tearing great gashes in the Boer's chest and stomach. His mind was aflame as the joy of the moment filled his head.

Then, suddenly, he stopped. He was not sure why, but the fury was done. He was lying on top of the Boer, covered in the blood rushing from the man's body, his breath coming in ragged gasps. He felt his own pain then, the wound to his shoulder making itself known with enough power to almost steal his senses away. Yet he was alive to the sounds around him, expecting to hear shouts of anger as he was discovered. He heard nothing save his own breathing and the thumping of his heart in his ears.

A shudder ran through him. Feelings of both revulsion and joy intertwined to create something that could only come from the depths of hell itself. The force of the emotion left him shaking, and for a moment he could not breathe, every muscle trembling, his mouth opening and closing as if trying to scream.

The feeling passed. It was replaced with an exhaustion so intense he did not know if he could find the strength to move. He let his body slide to the right, the motion greased by blood, and flopped onto his back, lying next to the man he had shredded.

The Boer was still alive. Jack did not know how, but he could hear the man's breath rasping in the ruin of his throat, his blood-soaked chest still rising and falling. He turned his head and saw the Boer's right hand lift, then drop onto the remains of his chest. It lay there unmoving.

He forced himself up onto his elbow and looked down into his victim's blood-splattered face. The Boer's lips moved, as if he were trying to say something to the man who had taken his life. But no sound came out.

Jack gazed deep into his eyes, seeing the emotions that were filling the Boer's soul as he took his last few breaths. Agony. Shock. Surprise. Fear. He recognised them all. Yet he himself felt nothing at all. He felt calm, tranquil even, the fury that had sustained him quenched. For the moment at least. He could still feel it squirming deep in his gut, like a fire smouldering through the last hours of the night. And just like that fire, he knew he could stoke it back into life.

For it was not spent.

Not at all.

The Boer gasped, an odd little sound that was quickly smothered by the gurgle of blood moving deep in his throat. Jack watched as the light faded in his eyes, the torrent of emotions he had seen replaced with the complete nothingness of death.

It was time to go.

He did not want to. He wanted nothing more than to lie there, flat on his back, staring up at the sky, his exhausted body given the rest it so desperately craved. But to lie there was to invite discovery, and he had too much left to do to let himself be taken. And so he rolled onto his front and began to crawl awkwardly away, the pain from his wound forcing him to stop using his right arm completely.

Time had no meaning then. All that mattered was the dirt underneath his belly and the excruciating effort of moving. Somehow he kept going, inches slowly turning into feet, feet grinding into yards.

He had been crawling for no more than ten minutes when he heard shouts behind him. He did not have to speak Afrikaans to understand the oaths of fury as the Boers saw what the fugitive had done to one of their own. Then he heard a woman shriek in horrified grief. He did not know if the cry belonged to a mother, a wife or a daughter, but he recognised the dreadful wail of emotion as someone saw what had happened to a loved one.

A flash of hatred scoured through his mind. But it was not directed at the Boers. Never before had he felt such self-loathing, no matter what he had done, no matter how many times he had killed. It was raw, this new feeling. And it cut deep.

Then he saw Anna in his mind's eye and the emotion was banished. As he slithered through the dirt, her face was in front of him. It was the face he remembered, the one full of life and animation, the one that had first captivated him all those months ago when they had first met on the quayside in Khartoum. Yet now her eyes were dulled. Lifeless. It was Anna's face as he remembered her, but with the eyes of the dead.

It was all he saw as he crawled away.

And he knew he would see it always. In his mind when awake, and in his nightmares.

For Anna was gone, and nothing would ever be the same again.

Chapter Thirty-two

The moon was low in the sky when Jack could go on no longer. At some point he had forced himself to his feet and tottered on through the darkness for what had seemed like hours. But now he went down onto his knees, half falling, half lowering himself to the ground. His first thought was to sit, but his body moved of its own accord and he flopped onto his back, knees bent so they pointed up to the sky, arms laid out at right angles to his torso.

He didn't move again.

The sun was just starting to rise above the eastern horizon when he opened his eyes. Looking up, he could just about make out a few dozen stars, the pinpricks of light fading fast as the sky turned from black to dark blue to navy. Normally he found their presence a comfort. They had long been one of the only constants in his life, the bright spots of light looking the same to him no matter the continent he found himself on. Yet not that day. There was no comfort to be found in their presence when his mind was in turmoil and his body was racked with pain.

Moving his left hand gingerly, he tried to probe the hot bed of agony that was his right shoulder. Hissing with pain, he let his fingers slide over the wound, searching to see how badly he'd been hit and to discover whether the bullet that had struck him was still lodged in his flesh. He was lucky. It had been fired from a high-powered rifle and had gone straight through the soft flesh underneath his armpit. The wound hurt, but it would not kill him. At least not immediately. He knew it could easily fester; he had seen enough wounds over the years to know that even the most innocuous could still put a man on his deathbed within a few days. But it would not kill him that day, and for now that was enough.

With that knowledge discovered, he let his arms fall back to the ground. The wound needed to be cleaned, and he would have to find something to bind it tight, but that level of will-power was beyond him. Not that he really knew what he was doing. He had always been the one to inflict wounds rather than heal them. Anna would know, though. She would know how to treat the wound and make sure that it healed so that it would be nothing more than another scar amidst the many that decorated his body. For a moment, he planned what he would ask her to do when she came to him, as he knew she would. He could picture the expression on her face as she berated him for getting hurt yet again, for the foolishness of his pride that would see him fight when a sane man would beat a retreat. A smile played on his lips as he imagined what it would take for her to forgive him.

Then he remembered that she was dead, and the darkness returned.

He closed his eyes. Banishing the feelings that surged inside. Searching for the coldness he would need to go on living.

* * *

Jack awoke when the sun was high in the sky. He did not recall falling asleep. Now he prised open his eyelids, blinking as the bright light stung. It was a long time before he could bear to keep them open. When he finally managed it, he glanced around at his surroundings.

There was not much to look at. He was lying on the edge of a long, shallow depression in the ground. A few stunted thorny bushes lined the lips of the gully, the sparse shrubs dry and desiccated, with not an inch of green on their bare stems. As a picturesque resting place, it left a lot to be desired, but as a place to hide out, it offered something.

Still lying on his back, he turned his head, twisting his neck this way and that while doing his best to keep his shoulder still. From what he could see, he was in the middle of nowhere. He had no idea how far he had come from the diggings, or even which direction he had taken. With the sun overhead, there was no way of knowing, but for now he did not care. That knowledge could wait.

As he finished his inspection of his surroundings, he spied a deep trough in the ground perhaps a dozen yards from where he lay. It shelved off from the gully next to him, forming a small bowl about the size of a bell tent. The bottom was covered with rocks, and the soil was darker than that surrounding it. It was not much, but he saw its potential as a hideout, at least temporarily.

With a groan, he pushed himself up with his left arm until he sat upright. He stayed like that for some time, letting his mind accept the pain that was coursing through him. Everything hurt, his shoulder and his back most of all, and his mouth tasted like a vagrant had established a camp inside. But he knew the aches and pains would pass, just as they had passed before. Accepting that fact helped, and it was all the respite he was going to get.

As he sat there, he contemplated what to do next. He had nothing with him save the blood-soaked clothes he was wearing and his revolver, the Lefaucheux snug in its holster. He had lost his knife at some point, and he had no food. No water. No shelter.

Yet the lack of possessions did not faze him. He could find what he needed, taking whatever he required to stay alive, the notion of theft of no consequence. He just had to decide if he would stay or go. He might not know where he was, but he knew he could not be far from the diggings, his battered, exhausted body unlikely to have stayed upright long enough for him to have covered much more than a mile. It would be easy enough to retrace his steps to the encampment, and once there, he could snaffle the food, water and gear he would need to stay alive. He had stolen from harder places.

But he did not have to go in that direction. Not if he did not want to. He could stand up and walk away. There would be enough farmsteads and travellers in the immediate area for him to keep himself fed and watered. If he so chose, he could leave the diggings behind and find a new life. He had done it more times than he could recall, and there was something in the idea of starting afresh that appealed. He knew the memories would fade with time, just as his body would heal. Thoughts of what might have been and the image of the lifeless Anna would haunt him for the rest of his days, but it would lose the power to consume him, and he would be able to function, perhaps even thrive, despite the memories that would arrive unbidden in his mind and fill his night with horror.

He would be able to start again.

He could go anywhere.

Sucking down a breath through gritted teeth, he clambered to his feet, then turned and began to trudge towards the depression in the ground he had spied earlier.

He had made his decision.

He was not leaving the diggings and heading to a new future.

He would not deviate from the path he had chosen.

For he might be near broken. But he was not done.

Jack moved out of the gully once darkness had enveloped the land. It was not the first time he had left his shelter. Late in the afternoon, he had ventured out, keeping low and circling around until he had a sense of where he was. The diggings were far off to the west at a distance that he estimated to be just under two miles. That was impressive, his bloodied, exhausted body getting further away from the encampment than he could have imagined. But it was not far enough to deter him from making plans to return. Plans that now saw him up on his feet and walking back towards the place where he had killed and nearly been killed.

He had done his best to repair his body. While on his reconnaissance mission, he had found a small amount of water deep in a hole further down the gully. It had tasted foul, but it had quenched his thirst, and he had torn a wide strip from the back of his shirt that he had used to first clean and then bind the wound to his right shoulder. The pain was still bad, but no worse than he had suffered before, and downright better than some he had endured. Yet it was still enough to leave his right arm stiff and sore, and so he had switched the position of his holster on his belt, turning it around so that he could draw the revolver with his left hand. The idea did not concern him. He had fought with a revolver in his left hand and a sword in his right on so many occasions that he was a passable shot even when not using his dominant hand. And anyway, he did not intend to engage in a firefight. What he had planned would be up close and personal.

Jack came into the outskirts of the encampment quickly and quietly.

He advanced at a crouch, left hand held ready to draw the Lefaucheux.

He skirted the more heavily occupied parts of the camp, keeping away from every tent and wagon. Taking his time. Choosing his place.

It was easy enough to pick a path, the moon close to full and a legion of stars lighting up the heavens. The pale moonlight also lit the ground enough for him to find a rock of the size and weight he was looking for.

The Boers were ready for any more intruders. They had circled their wagons, forming the laager that was so typical of the way they made camp in the veldt. The heavy vehicles were packed nose to tail, the gaps that had been deliberately left every fifty yards or so filled with roaring fires and at least two Boers on guard. These sentries stood outside the fires, eyes looking into the darkness so that the light of the flames would not ruin their night vision. All were watchful, even now, in the small hours. All were armed, long rifles either held ready in their hands or else resting butt first on the ground. Each man sported a bandolier of ammunition across his chest, and all had a canteen slung over their shoulder. They were clearly prepared to face anyone foolish enough to try to repeat the events of the previous night.

But Jack had no intention of attempting to sneak inside the laager. No intention at all.

He found what he wanted after he had circled the Boers' encampment for a solid hour. The sentries were all doing their job well enough. Yet they were still men.

And men had to relieve themselves.

He stopped where he was and became motionless.

The lone Boer stepped away from the gap in the wagons, his rifle shouldered on a sling. He was moving into the darkness so that he would not piss in front of his mates. He did not go far, no more than a dozen yards. But it was far enough to condemn him to death.

Jack started to move, slowly at first, eyes fixed on the man he would take down. There was something familiar about him, but he only realised what it was as he increased his speed. It was the Boer who had brought the two ropes when the Thompson brothers had been taken, the man who had looped the nooses around their necks as they were dragged to their deaths.

Fate was rewarding Jack and giving her blessing to what he was about to do.

He moved faster still, judging distances and closing the gap between him and the Boer with the full bladder. He was no more than ten yards away from the man as he unbuttoned his fly. Close enough to see his cock as it was pulled out and to hear the stream of water as it surged then splattered noisily on the dry soil below.

There was time for Jack to glance one last time at the other Boers near the watch fire. The pair were talking, but both stood looking outwards. Their mate would be easy to see, his silhouette clearly visible against the starlit sky.

But Jack was prepared.

He crouched a little higher, the rock he had selected held ready. It would be an awkward throw with his left hand. But he was not looking for any great accuracy.

The pissing Boer's stream started to falter. The man grunted as he strained to force out the last of the contents of his bladder.

It was time.

Jack hurled the rock. He could just about make it out as it arced over the heads of the sentries and into the encampment beyond. Fate was with him that night. It came down fast, striking a metal pail left near a pile of cooking utensils.

The clatter was loud against the quiet of the night, the sound carrying clearly. It was enough to turn the two sentries around, a sudden cry of alarm stolen from one of the pair as they tried to peer past the roaring campfire and discover what had made the sudden noise behind them.

The Boer pissing into the darkness whirled around as he heard first the clatter then the shout, his faltering stream splashing noisily across the ground as he pissed out the last of his urine. His limp cock was still in his hand when Jack came for him.

His eyes widened, a moment's shock registering before Jack struck him down with the butt of his revolver. It was a brutal blow, the heavy weapon connecting with the Boer's temple with enough force for Jack to hear the crack of breaking bones.

The Boer fell like a sack of shite, all senses gone. But Jack did not let him lie.

As soon as the man hit the ground, he struck again and again, hammering the butt of the revolver directly into his face. His nose broke instantly, blood flowing black in the darkness. Still Jack was not done. Bones broke as he thrashed the revolver down, pulping the Boer's face. There was no thought of mercy, not for the man who had slipped the noose around the necks of two defenceless men and who was part of the gang that had ruined Jack's life. So he carried on, even as his arm tired and the sound of the impacts changed from the crunch of metal on bone to an obscene squelch. He did not know when the man died and he did not care. It did not matter. For this was about more than a simple killing. It was about setting the scene and creating something grotesque and shocking.

Something that would inspire a response.

His breathing was laboured when he finally stopped. The beating had taken less than a minute, but it still left his arm aching and his heart beating fast.

He looked across to the fire. The two Boers were still staring inwards, watching the other sentries who had gone to investigate the noise that had taken their attention. Neither had seen their countryman fall.

Jack worked fast. It did not take long to pull the long rifle off the dead Boer's shoulder or to unbuckle the heavy bandolier of ammunition. He threw the bandolier over his own shoulder, then grabbed the man's canteen, shaking it quickly to hear the slosh of water inside. It was full, or nearly so. Certainly enough to see him through to the next day.

Hefting his revolver in his left hand, he scurried into the night, making sure to tread as heavily as he could. He kept moving away from the laager, scuffing his boots every few paces, marking the path he was taking and leaving a trail that would be easy to follow in the morning.

For he had no desire to hide. Not any more.

He was inviting the Boers to follow him.

And he would be waiting for them.

Chapter Thirty-three

——◆—◆◆—◆——

Jack stared to the west as the sun rose behind him.

He had chosen his spot with care, using the grey light of the pre-dawn to find the raised kopje just over what he estimated to be a mile from the diggings. It was a sparse, dry place, the desiccated ground a pale orange colour, the soil giving way under every step as he hauled his aching bones to the top. It was no mountain that he had chosen to climb, not even a hill. But it would do, the kopje the only high ground he had been able to find. The vantage point it gave him would be enough for what he planned.

Yet it was not ideal. The kopje was little more than a craggy mound with sharp-faced rocks scattered across the uppermost reaches. There was no place for a man to lie down, let alone hide. And so he was forced to go to work.

It was torture, his wounded shoulder forcing him to use just his left hand as he clawed away enough soil to create a shallow pit in which he could lie if he curled his legs to one side and twisted his body so that his weight was on his right hip. He could not dig lower, the rocks just underneath the surface buried too deep for him to shift one-handed. And so he stopped, saving his energy for what was to come.

It was only as he finished his toil that he realised what he had dug. It was a grave, one just about big enough for a single body. The notion sat well in his mind, a reminder of what the cost of his foolish endeavour was likely to be. He wondered if the Boers would see what he had done. If he closed his eyes, he could picture his body lying there, the image sharp in his mind's eye. He wondered if the grave would bring him peace. If nothing else, he imagined it would put an end to the screams in his head and steal away the visions of the dead that plagued his thoughts. He could think of worse places to end his days.

The thought of his own death was enough to make him sit back and survey what might be his view for the rest of eternity. In the pale early light, it was beautiful. The horizon stretched away in every direction so that it felt as though he was sitting under a great bowl of sky. There was nothing to break up the wide expanse of veldt; just mile upon mile of unspoiled open ground, the only blemish a yellow stain in the air – the dust hanging over the diggings. It was the only evidence of the presence of man in the untamed wilderness, the diggings a blot on the landscape that spoke of human intrusion into the beauty of the veldt. In the meagre light, the wide-open spaces made him feel tiny, insignificant. And that was a good thing, a reminder of the futility of man and his place in the world.

It was a good place to be buried. At least as good as any.

As the sky brightened, he tried out the position he had dug, settling down with his stolen rifle aimed back the way he had come. The pain from the awkward stance started within five minutes, and after twenty it became unbearable. Just lining up the rifle with its butt against his wounded shoulder brought on a flash of agony that almost unmanned him. But it would have to do. He would have to endure the pain and the discomfort if he were to put his plan into action.

After all, he would be more comfortable when he was dead.

As the sun came up, he sat checking over the rifle and the ammunition he had taken from the Boer. The weapon was the twin to the one he had inspected on the route up from Port Elizabeth, with the now familiar monkey-tail shape to the receiver. He had seen more examples of it in and around the diggings, the shortened rifle clearly a favourite amongst the Boers.

He worked the breech, opening and closing the chamber so that he could get a feel for the weapon that he would soon be using for real. Now that he was holding it, it felt more like a carbine than a rifle, the barrel just under two feet long. It made it lighter, and he held it up in his left hand, hefting it up and down as he tried to make sure he could move it with ease using just the one arm. Setting it back down on the ground, he turned his attention to the breech. Unlike the Snider he had used in the Sudan, it was operated by a lever. This was mounted on the top of the rifle and hinged forward, opening the chamber for the insertion of the cartridge. That cartridge was fired by a percussion cap mounted on a nipple rather than a device contained in the cartridge itself. It made for a rather simple weapon and he could understand its appeal to the Boers, who would quite possibly struggle to obtain more modern cartridges when they journeyed far from the major port towns of the Cape.

Laying the rifle down, he turned his attention to the bandolier. It did not take long to discover that it was packed full of what looked to be home-made paper cartridges and four small cardboard packets of percussion caps. Clearly the Boer he had taken it from had wanted to make sure he didn't run out of ammunition, and Jack was grateful for that forethought. He had more than enough for what he had in mind.

He took his time with the cartridges, laying them out so that they would be readily to hand once he settled down into his shallow grave. But even as he did his best to prepare, there was still a nagging doubt in his mind. No matter how much he tried to get the feel of the rifle, he knew it would still feel horribly unfamiliar in his hands when he came to use it in anger. Every firearm was different, and he would need to shoot with this one to really get to understand it. But he did not have that luxury. As soon as it was light enough to see, he expected to be firing the weapon to kill.

He would just have to learn fast.

The sun rose quickly that morning, the shadows chased from the land. The warm glow heralded a fine day, the sky directly above the kopje turning to a pale watery blue with a thin smear of whitish cloud. It would be a hard day in the diggings, the men who would soon pass the daylight hours hacking away at the soil paying for every inch of earth they extracted with buckets of their own sweat. The idea made Jack almost smile. It was nice to think of others toiling away, breaking their backs to extract little more than rock and the odd nugget of carbon from the unyielding soil. He knew he would never dig again. Not after he had put his plan into action.

It was not much of a plan, and he accepted it for what it was. It had been conjured in a mind filled with pain and grief, and he knew it had little chance of bringing about anything save his own demise. A sane man would surely turn and walk away. That man would scramble down the rear of the kopje and take the first steps on a journey that could take him anywhere in the world. A new life could be found, far removed from the dust and misery of the diggings. All it would take was the placing of one foot in front of the other.

But Jack was not that sane man. For he knew there could be no new life for him. Not until this was finished. Not until the Boers were held to account for all they had done. If he left before the score was settled, he knew it would haunt him for the rest of his days, no matter how many, or how few, they might be.

To leave now was to retreat.

And to accept he had been beaten.

And he could not do that. Not now. Not ever. No matter the price.

So he would stay. He would balance the ledger by adding justice to counter the tally of his losses.

But it was not for the lynching of three men that he wanted justice. It was for himself. For the Boers had stolen everything from him, and now he would exact retribution. He could not leave without it. To turn away now, with Anna's body fresh in the ground, would be to deny the man he had become and to cheapen all that he had lost.

He would fight for justice.

He would fight for Anna and for vengeance.

But most of all, he would fight for himself.

The Boers came an hour after dawn.

He had expected them to be earlier, and he had lain in his shallow grave for as long as he could bear, certain he would see them arriving with the first light of day. He had given up when the cramp had become unbearable, and so he was sitting at the front of the kopje when he spotted them for the first time.

A dozen Boers were following the trail he had laid across the veldt. He had heard of Boer trackers able to follow the spoor of a herd of elephants across dozens of miles, or the subtle path taken by a lone lion even when there was nothing to be seen to the untrained eye. Still, he had left nothing to chance and had made sure to mark his retreat from their encampment so that even the most incompetent tracker could spot it.

The Boers came on any old how. De Klerk led them, taking point with another man of his own age. The pair were a good fifty feet in front of the larger group that followed.

All were armed, every man carrying a rifle like the one Jack now held in his own hands. The odds stacked against him were not good. It would be twelve against one, or perhaps he should call himself a half, his right arm near useless. If he were a gambling man, he knew where he would place his wager, and it would not be on the battered and bloodied Englishman holding a strange rifle while lying in his own grave. But he had never been much of a gambler. Other men might trust to luck and throw a week's wages on a good ratter or a prime bitch, but it had not been for him, even though he had been to dozens of dog fights and rattings, standing against the wall of the wooden ring as a terrier tore rats apart by the dozen, or fought another dog until one of the two was either maimed or killed. Not that he was frugal. He would spend money without a qualm, seeing it as a tool, nothing more.

The thought of money made him snort, a moment's wry humour found even as he sat and waited for what was almost certain death. For he would die penniless, and he could not help but think that there was something fitting in that. He had been born poor, had found wealth then lost it, found it again before losing everything.

Now he would likely end his days without a brass razoo to his name.

The Boers kept moving, following the trail at a measured pace that could be kept up for hour upon hour.

They were headed straight for the kopje.

Exactly as he had planned.

He took his time settling into position, doing his best not to jar his damaged shoulder any more than he had to. He made sure to place his loaded Lefaucheux on the ground near his left hand, just in case it should be needed. Only when he was as comfortable as he could make himself did he look back at the Boers once more.

They were close now, no more than four hundred yards from the kopje.

He slid the rifle forward with his left hand, then settled down behind it. Supporting the weapon's weight with his left hand, he brought it into position, resting the butt as gently as he could against his wounded shoulder. He dared not think about the pain that would follow the moment he pulled the trigger for the first time. Not having fired the rifle before meant that he did not know how much it would kick, but he was certain the recoil would be brutal. It might transpire that he could manage just a single shot, the pain more than he could bear, but that did not sway him as he looked down the barrel, aiming the simple iron sights at the group of Boers. He would take the pain. Or he wouldn't. Either way, he knew he had at least that first shot, and he would make it count.

He knew who he would be firing at.

The Boers kept coming. The pair leading them were working

hard, heads bobbing this way and that as they studied the trail while also keeping a weather eye on the path ahead. They were talking as they advanced, and he could just about make out the words being spoken, even if he did not understand them.

The distance was closing fast now, so he started to slow his breathing, settling down behind the rifle, preparing for the shot that would have to count more than any of the others.

To miss was to die. Only by hitting with the first round did he stand any sort of a chance. If he failed, all he would have done would be to reveal his position. But if his aim was good, and that first round found its target, he would have a chance, the confusion and chaos that would follow a sudden and unexpected killing giving him time to reload and fire again. And if he hit enough times, the Boers might run.

He inched the rifle to the left, eyes tracking the group coming towards him. Some of them were vaguely familiar. He had recognised de Klerk instantly, and at least half the faces belonged to men he had seen surrounding the Thompson brothers. But he was looking for one in particular, and he found it easily enough, the grey-bearded man walking in the midst of the main group.

He did not know how much of his downfall had been ordered by the man now in the sights of his rifle. But it did not matter. Oom Joost was the leader of these Boers, and so that made him responsible, whether or not he had given the orders that had seen Flanagan and the Thompson brothers hanged and Jack and Anna's lives thrown into turmoil. And so now he would pay the price for starting the chain of events that had culminated with Anna's death and Jack lying ready to be buried in his own grave.

The Boers came to a sudden halt.

He did not know why they stopped or how they had sensed danger, but there was a single shout from de Klerk, followed by an urgent gesture to spread out. The main group obeyed instantly. What had been a gaggle of ten men grouped closed together broke up as they fanned out, forming a widely spaced line that straddled Jack's trail, half the group on one side and half on the other. Every one of the twelve Boers was facing his little kopje. Only Oom Joost stayed where he was as he directed the others into place, his right hand gesturing sharply to his men.

Jack sipped one last breath, holding it deep in his lungs. He was ready. Calm.

His target was in his sights.

It was time.

His finger curled around the trigger. The rifle barrel was wavering ever so slightly from side to side, the sights filling with the bearded face of the Boer leader, then losing him again.

He paused, then let out half of the breath he had been holding.

The barrel steadied as he took up the last ounces of pressure on the trigger.

He dropped it a fraction of an inch, aiming it squarely at the broad chest of the man he blamed for everything.

Time stood still.

Then he fired.

Chapter Thirty-four

The rifle kicked like a bastard.

The pain came in one great wave, a lance of agony that shocked through every inch of his being as the butt slammed back into his wounded shoulder. Daylight disappeared, his vision clouding with grey. In that moment, there was nothing in the world but the pain, the sensation somehow worse than anything he had ever felt before.

Blinking hard, he tried desperately to see if he had hit his target, but his eyes were watering too much for him to be able to make anything out, and he could do little but screw them tight. He could hear shouting, but the sound was muffled, as if it came from far away and not from just a couple of hundred yards distant.

A shot rang out, followed by another. He heard the distinct crack of rifles firing, then the sharper retorts of bullets striking rock. He had no notion of where they were hitting, or if they were even directed at him.

Gritting his teeth, he forced his eyes to open. Through the tears, he could just about discern that the line of Boers had not moved. Every man had hit the dirt the moment they realised they were under attack, taking up firing positions and scanning the ground ahead. He saw that at least two had fired, the men now rolling onto their sides as they reloaded. The rest were waiting, squinting down barrels that moved to and fro as they searched for a target.

Only one man was still.

Oom Joost was lying on his back, his rifle dropped at his side. As Jack watched, the Boer curled his legs up, and both hands scrabbled at his belly.

They came away covered in blood.

Jack had aimed at the Boer's chest. He had missed, his stolen bullet striking the older man lower down. It was a cruel wound, one that would kill as surely as a bullet to the brain, but that might take days to bring about that death. By the time it belatedly arrived, it would be welcomed, a man shot in the gut almost sure to be pleading for a second bullet to end his misery long before oblivion came to bring eternal peace.

Jack smiled.

Another Boer fired, and then another. Both bullets snapped through the air before striking the kopje. They hit far to the left of his hiding place.

The Boers were firing blind. They had not spotted him. At least not yet.

He felt a surge of energy rushing through him. It lent him strength, and he slid the rifle down and began to reload, left hand opening the breech, tumbling out the spent cartridge then forcing a fresh one inside. Snapping the breech shut, he fumbled for a percussion cap, dropping the first he picked up but holding on to the second and pushing it home onto the nipple.

With the rifle loaded, he took aim for a second time. He could see the nine men lying where he had last seen them, every one of them still searching for the source of the bullet that had struck their leader down. There was no sign of the pair who had been leading the group forward.

Jack aimed to the right of the body of Oom Joost, choosing the man he judged to be closest to his eyrie. Once again he slowed his breathing, steadying the rifle so that he had his target firmly in its sights. Then the rifle's butt touched his damaged shoulder.

He cried out, the sound torn from his lips as the pain came on fierce and strong. The idea of pulling the trigger and sending the butt slamming back into his shoulder for a second time was more than he could bear, and he lowered the weapon.

Another of the Boers fired. The bullet struck a rock a good twenty yards away from where Jack was hiding.

As the sound of the impact died away, an odd whimpering noise followed. It took him a moment to realise he was making it himself, his body trembling now, his mind fogging with pain.

The sound was shaming. This was not who he was. He forced himself to be quiet, feeling the first stirrings of an old anger. Up to that point he had been calm, icy even. Now the flames of fury flickered into life deep in his belly. Almost immediately, they started to grow, the fire beginning to rage, warming his soul and setting it ablaze.

He pulled the rifle hard into his shoulder, refusing to listen to the scream of agony that left his mouth. Lining up the shot, he sucked down the breath he needed, nostrils flaring as he wrestled with his own flesh, forcing it to obey.

The nearest Boer came into his sights. A moment's pause.

Then he took the shot.

He was ready for the pain, and he held himself still even as the brutal shock of the butt's impact seared through him. This time he saw the bullet strike, a momentary puff of bloody mist filling the air around the man's head as the heavy bullet obliterated his skull.

'Come on!' Jack found himself shouting. The pain was burning hot, but the flames in his soul were fiercer, and he rolled onto his side, staying low as he began to reload the rifle once more.

More shots rang out, the sounds blurring together. None even came close to where Jack was raising the freshly loaded rifle.

It took no more than a heartbeat to sight the rifle for a third time. This time he chose a Boer on the far left of the line, the barrel seeming to move of its own accord. He fired fast, rushing to get the shot away as soon as he'd lined up his target. The rifle butt slammed into his shoulder. Once again, the pain followed immediately, blinding in its intensity, another howl rising from deep inside as his body reacted to the awful abuse he was putting it through. He was shaking now, tremors running up and down his spine, the pain all-consuming. But the fire in his belly was an inferno, and he cared nothing for the agony, the need to keep fighting overwhelming even the heat of the pain.

He looked for his target. The Boer was lying still, but he was not dead, not even wounded, and he was aiming his own rifle towards the kopje.

Jack had rushed his third shot. And he had missed.

Reloading as fast as he could with just one hand, he lifted the rifle once more. This time he rose as he readied himself, his knee bracing underneath him to help steady the shot. He aimed and fired in one smooth movement, his body working without conscious input from his mind. The Boer he was aiming at slumped to the ground as if the stuffing had been pulled out of him.

Three Boers were down. Two had disappeared from his sight.

That left seven.

Seven men who were up and running.

It was no easy thing to lie in open ground as a hidden rifleman picked off your comrades one by one. With three men bleeding into the dusty soil, the others had jumped up and turned tail.

Jack saw that those running were older men. Men in whom the fire of youth had long been extinguished. None were keen to risk a slow, lingering death with a bullet buried in their guts. He lowered the rifle as he watched them break away. Had he been asked, he would not have been able to describe the emotions that surged through him in that moment. The fire was there, and part of him howled in frustration as he was denied more targets for his fury. Another part of him felt something akin to relief, the need to fight on tempered with the joy of having survived. And then there was a touch of guilt. He had lain hidden and killed without a qualm. Three men had been shot down like dogs and he had felt nothing more than a momentary flash of joy at hitting the target he had chosen. He had not faced them as a man should, or as a warrior would. He had shot them down so that they never even saw who had delivered their demise.

And then there was the pain. He could feel blood flowing freely from his shoulder. A quick glance showed him a shirt soaked black, the bullet wound torn open so that it was now the size of a man's fist. It burned as though a red-hot poker was being twisted in his flesh by the devil himself.

He dropped the rifle, his left hand instinctively clamping over the wound in an attempt to stem the flow of blood. Twisting around, he lowered himself down onto his backside, a feeling of utter exhaustion spreading through his muscles so that everything felt extraordinarily heavy.

It was all he could do to hold himself up and keep his eyes open.

But the fight was not over. Not by a long shot.

It had barely even begun.

Two faces loomed into view at the edge of the kopje's meagre summit.

Jack had shot at the main group of Boers, knocking three down and sending the others fleeing. In the midst of the combat, with pain and rage fogging his mind, he had not spared enough of a thought for the two men who had led the Boers towards his ambush.

But they had not forgotten about him.

Now they surged over the edge of the kopje, boots scrabbling for purchase on the friable soil.

Two young men, faces flushed with exertion, rifles held ready to fire.

The odds had shortened to two to one.

And Jack was doomed.

Chapter Thirty-five

The two Boers looked at Jack, a moment's surprise at finding the hidden shooter right there in front of them reflecting on their faces.

Then they came for him.

Both carried rifles, but neither raised them to fire; instead they charged forward, roaring a challenge as they faced the man they had hunted down across the veldt.

Jack was close enough to see the way their lips pulled back from their teeth as they snarled in anger. He had seen such expressions before. In the Crimea. In Delhi. In Persia. In America. In Mexico. In Italy. In the Sudan. It did not matter the colour of a man's skin, his nationality or what uniform he was wearing. This was the moment when men braced themselves to kill or be killed. It was the true face of the warrior. It was not noble. It was not heroic. It was an expression born of fear and horror, anger and rage intertwined with terror. It was the face of a man screwing his courage tight as he faced his foe knowing that death could come at any moment.

It was the face of war.

Jack reacted as fast as his dulled reactions would allow. The unloaded rifle was lying at his feet, so he snatched up the Lefaucheux with his left hand.

But he was hurting and he was slow, and the two Boers were already right on top of him.

With desperate haste, he threw the revolver up, pulling the trigger without aiming, his only thought to shoot before they reached him.

The handgun coughed, smoke and fire flashing for the briefest moment as a bullet exploded out of the barrel. The distance between Jack and the two men was no more than a couple of feet. At such close range, there was little chance of missing, and the heavy bullet smacked into the very centre of the left-hand Boer's chest before tearing out through his spine, blood spraying bright in the early-morning sun. The man seemed to crumple, his body collapsing around itself as he went down, disappearing from sight as if snatched out of existence.

One Boer died without ever hearing the sound of the shot that killed him.

But the other was still very much alive.

The surviving man threw himself at Jack, his pace unaltered even as his comrade was shot down.

Jack saw the man's face a moment before he struck.

It was de Klerk.

The impact was terrible. Jack was off balance from making the desperate shot, and de Klerk hit him hard, leading with his shoulder.

Jack fell backwards, the air leaving his lungs in a great whoosh before he hit the ground. His head was thrown back, connecting with a rock, the brutal contact sending a shock wave running through his entire body.

De Klerk seemed to bounce away from the collision. He

went sprawling, rifle knocked from his grip, arms and legs thrown wide as he hit the ground face first then rolled on, all control of his limbs lost as he tumbled down the far side of the kopje.

Jack tried to get to his feet, but his body would not respond. He was desperate to see where de Klerk had landed, and he managed to twist around, his back scraping painfully across the ground.

He saw the Boer at once. De Klerk was lying in a heap a good ten feet down the slope, his head lifting then shaking as he tried to shrug off his own clash with the unforgiving ground.

It gave Jack a few precious seconds, something he desperately needed. Finding some strength from he knew not where, he managed to scrabble onto his knees, left arm bracing against the ground, right hanging useless at his side.

Below him, de Klerk was clambering slowly to his feet.

Jack looked for his revolver. The Lefaucheux was lying two feet away, and he moved as fast as he could, going for the weapon with a desperate shuffling motion that left him floundering for balance.

De Klerk turned just as Jack grabbed the revolver. There was no time for him to do anything other than stare at the stubby barrel aimed directly at him.

'Fuck you.' Jack spat out the words as he took up the pressure on the trigger.

A moment later, he fired.

Or at least he applied enough pressure to the trigger to fire.

But nothing happened.

'Shit.' He stared at the weapon in his hand, unable to quite comprehend what had happened. Or what had not happened.

And in that moment, de Klerk charged.

He came up the slope, feet slipping and sliding as the soil gave way beneath him, so that he could only move slowly, his arms pumping hard as he drove himself towards Jack. He was unarmed, but he came on with hands balled into fists, eyes burning with rage.

For one long-drawn-out moment, Jack could do nothing as the Boer rushed towards him. Then he managed to aim the revolver and pulled the trigger for a second time, even as his mind screamed at him that to do so was pointless.

Again nothing happened.

De Klerk was yelling now, a wild, searing war cry, as he came forward, fists rising. He led with a right hook aimed squarely at Jack's chin.

Jack saw the punch coming and ducked away, just about getting underneath the swinging blow. The sudden motion stole what little balance he had, the world spinning around him as he tried to straighten up. A great wave of nausea rose from his gut, a surge of vomit rushing up to burn his throat. His mouth opened to spew it out, and it was still open when de Klerk's left fist crunched into the centre of his face.

For a second time, he fell, vomit spraying from his mouth as he tumbled away down the slope. He lost hold of the Lefaucheux, the revolver thrown from his hand, and only came to a halt when his ribs connected with a flat-faced rock sticking up from the ground.

Bright morning daylight turned ashen. Even as he tried to breathe, he felt himself slipping away. All had gone still, time stopping as he tried to hold on to something, anything, that would stop him sliding into oblivion. But the pain was just too much, too overwhelming, and he felt the darkness rushing up to drag him down.

He clung on, even as his ears filled with a rushing sound and he could make no sense of the light or the shapes around him. Every inch of his body was on fire, the pain simply shattering. But he was aware of being held, then being shaken hard enough for his brain to be battered back and forth in his skull.

He managed to focus on de Klerk's face. It was no more than two inches from his own. The Boer was shouting, screaming even, his features contorted with rage, but Jack heard nothing save the roar of the blood in his own ears. Details rushed at him faster than he could track. Spittle flying from de Klerk's lips. A thin stream of blood snaking down from one nostril. Dust clotted in his beard and hair, more streaked across his face. Sweat running from his brow, carving thin rivers in the layer of dust. Teeth smeared red from lips crushed and bruised. He saw it all, even as he was shaken back and forth. But he could do nothing to resist, control of his own body lost.

De Klerk roared in anger, his voice reaching a pitch loud enough to penetrate the thunder in Jack's ears. Then he threw Jack to the ground, tossing him away as if he weighed no more than a rag doll.

Jack hit hard. But there was no room for more pain, his body and mind already filled to capacity. So he lay there, eyes tracking de Klerk's movements as the Boer searched across the ground.

Suddenly he stopped, bending down as he found what he was looking for.

He came up holding the Lefaucheux.

Jack could do nothing but watch as de Klerk broke open the revolver, fingers prying into the chambers, brushing away dust and debris, his head dipping down towards the open weapon so he could blow away anything too small for his fingers to reach. Satisfied with his work, he straightened up, snapping the revolver shut then lifting his arm as he drew a bead on something in front of him. A moment later, he pulled the trigger. The crash of the weapon firing echoed around the kopje, the revolver now working as it should.

De Klerk whooped as he brought the Lefaucheux back to life, and he was smiling as he turned to face Jack one last time.

'Time to die.' He muttered the words in English as he began to walk slowly forwards. He took his time, placing each foot carefully so that he would not trip and fall.

Jack saw what was to come, and he tried to move, pushing down with his good arm as he made one last attempt to get to his feet. Yet no matter how hard he tried, his body would not respond, his left arm buckling under the strain of trying to lift his hefty frame. He could do nothing but sit there, only his head moving as he followed the Boer's careful progress towards him.

'Was this all worth it?' De Klerk paused to spit out the question.

'Yes,' Jack croaked. Just the simple act of speaking hurt him badly.

De Klerk looked down at him, holding his gaze for several long moments. Then he shook his head, face cast down, as if saddened by the simple answer.

'It's all your fault.' Jack tried to swallow as he spoke, but he failed, his parched throat almost closed. Yet he would not be silent. Not now. Not at the end of his days. 'You killed her.'

De Klerk frowned. 'Who did I kill?'

'Anna.'

'She's dead?' He seemed genuinely surprised.

'She's dead.' Jack felt tears well. The words hurt more even than the pain of the battering his body had taken.

'I'm sorry.' De Klerk spoke softly. Then he sucked down a deep breath and began to move forward again.

'No.' Jack spat the word out. 'Don't you dare be sorry, you fucking bastard. You and your lot killed her as surely as if you had stuck a knife in her heart.'

'You are a fool if you believe that.' The Boer's rage seemed to have disappeared. He sounded saddened more than anything, yet still he made his way towards Jack.

Jack knew what was coming. At last he knew the future Fate held in store for him, one that would arrive in the time it took de Klerk to come close enough to be sure he would not miss.

'I've been called that before.' He spoke the words for himself alone. They resonated deep inside. He was truly a fool. But he was also Jack Lark. And he would go down fighting.

De Klerk was lifting the revolver as he approached, pointing it towards Jack's skull. There was no doubt in Jack's mind that the Boer intended to place the muzzle against his head then pull the trigger. He would be thorough, and Jack's life would be snuffed out in an instant.

'It's over, Jack.' De Klerk was speaking quietly. 'Your time on this earth is done.'

Jack barely heard the words. His left hand was feeling in the dirt at his side, fingers digging into the earth until they found what they were searching for. Then he went still. Waiting.

De Klerk was still moving forward. He stepped over a dip in the ground, then took a smaller stride as he covered the last yard, careful to the end. As he reached Jack, he squatted down, his knees cracking as they bent.

'I'm getting old, Jack,' he said wryly. 'At least *you* won't have to worry about that.'

The revolver came up. Just as Jack had predicted, de Klerk placed it carefully against the side of his head. He could smell it now, the taint of gun oil and spent powder.

The end was near.

But not for Jack.

The moment he felt the cold touch of metal against his temple, he came up, roaring like a banshee. Every last scrap of strength went into the action, his body pushing through the pain, his left hand swinging, smashing the rock he had pulled from the ground against the side of de Klerk's head. It was a vicious strike, and there was a grim crunch as it caved in the side of the Boer's skull.

The revolver fired, and Jack felt something lacerate the side of his head, the bullet scoring through his skin. But it did not stop him, not even for a second, and he lashed out again, punching the rock into the Boer's head for a second time, and then a third.

But then he could do no more.

The rock fell from his hand.

Breathless and hurting, he slumped to the ground, landing on his backside then falling onto his side.

Then the blackness came.

The world and everything in it disappeared into the dark.

Chapter Thirty-six

---

ack did not know how long he had been unconscious, but the sun had yet to move far in its travels and so he knew it could not have been long.

He awoke to the silence of the veldt.

As he opened his eyes he saw a black and white marabou stork. It was not a handsome bird, its naked head bobbing up and down above a grotesque neck the colour of raw pork, and it was sitting on a rock, looking down at him, patient and stoic, its beady eyes fixed on his body like a starving man would look upon a great hunk of steak.

The bird had come for carrion.

It would not be disappointed.

The sight of it stirred him to action. He did not want to move, the very thought repugnant to him. But something inside him was still functioning, and he knew he had to find the strength to get away from the bloodbath he had created.

He took his time, moving at a speed that would have put a one-legged octogenarian to shame. But slowly and carefully he got up, going first to his knees, then to a low crouch, then finally to his feet, until he was standing on top of the kopje, a brisk breeze scouring across his face.

Only when he was sure he would not tumble back onto his arse did he look down. De Klerk was lying at his feet. The Boer's body was twisted around itself in a pose that told Jack he was quite dead. He could barely remember striking the blows that had killed the Boer, the fog of those last moments shrouding his memory of how he came to still be alive while the younger and stronger man lay dead. There was little blood, just a small puddle around the side of de Klerk's head, which was now concave. But a thin smear of something gooey and grey was oozing out of the Boer's ear, revealing the damage that had been done inside.

Jack stood still, swaying on his feet as he took in his surroundings. Other than the fresh corpse, little had changed. The view was the same, the untamed expanse of veldt stretching away in every direction as far as the eye could see. It was a reminder that the world was still turning around them, and that the acts of a few men, no matter how devastating to those involved, meant nothing to the wider world.

It was time to move.

He bent down, wincing at the pain the movement set off, picking up the Lefaucheux, which had come so close to taking his life. He thrust it into the holster still on his belt, resolving as he did so to sell the revolver at the earliest opportunity and replace it with a Navy Colt or a Beaumont–Adams. He would not trust it again.

With the handgun holstered, he took a moment to retrieve the rifle that had claimed three men's lives, then picked a slow path down from the kopje. He took his time, just as de Klerk had taken his time as he came to deliver Jack's death. That moment was replaying itself in his mind: the Boer's slow, measured progress up the slope, the feel of metal on his temple. He knew the memories would linger, as would the sight of the dead Boer with the broken skull. But these new memories would have company at least. And he had seen worse.

It took him a fair while to make his way down off the kopje. He would have liked to have moved faster, the knowledge that the Boers who had fled the scene would surely be raising the alarm at that very moment a good incentive to get away as rapidly as he could. But despite that risk, there was one thing he had to do before he disappeared, one question that was itching away deep in his brain and that he refused to leave unanswered.

Oom Joost was still lying where he had fallen. The hands that had been scrabbling at his wound now lay still, both forearms caked with blood to the elbow. But his chest was moving up and down above the raw, red, ruined remains of his belly.

Jack came to a halt, looking down at the man he blamed for Anna's death. Oom Joost stared back at him, his pale blue eyes darting back and forth as he searched Jack's expression for something, Jack did not know what. But the old Boer said nothing, his lips, dry and cracked by the sun, clenched tight.

Without speaking, Jack looked at the Boer's belly. Something blue pulsed deep in the wound, and the ground around Oom Joost's body was caked with blood that was already blackening in the midday sun. It was as he'd expected, the dreadful wound sure to kill, no matter if the Boer was found quickly or not. He nodded as he confirmed his verdict.

'It's over,' he muttered, repeating the words de Klerk had used just before he died. Then he bent down, wincing as he did so, his left hand beginning a long, slow search of the Boer's pockets.

He found what he was looking for in an inside pocket nestled against Joost's chest. The brown pouch was small and well worn, the leather scuffed and cracked with age. And it was heavy, just as he had hoped it would be.

He didn't bother to look inside. He had held the diamond before, its feel imprinted on his memory. Instead, he simply slipped the pouch into his own chest pocket, taking back the stone he had found, and which he had given in payment for a man's death, a trade that had proven as worthless as the stone now was to the Boer who had taken it.

It was as he straightened up that Oom Joost spoke for the first time.

At first, Jack didn't understand, the sound too faint. Then the words were repeated, louder this time. Firmer. More certain.

'Kill me.'

Jack did not reply. He stood over the grey-bearded Boer. It would be easy to do as the man requested. Kind even.

And that was the problem.

He searched in his heart and found he did not have such kindness left.

'No.' He spoke the single word, then turned away. He would leave Joost to find his path to the devil for himself. Sometimes life was worse than death. The Boer would learn that soon, if he hadn't already.

Jack took his time as he walked away from the three bodies stretched out on the veldt near the kopje. He could not hurry even if he had wanted to, his strength already running out, so that he did not know how far he could go before he fell.

But he plodded on nonetheless, placing one dusty boot down after the other. Every step took him further away, and that was good enough for the moment.

Time passed. He did not know how long. But he was not alone. And for that he was grateful.

Anna walked at his side. She was dressed just as she had been the first time he had met her, her khaki-coloured cotton trousers and long-sleeved shirt unspoiled and clean. Her dark hair was braided, the thick plaits laid neatly across her scalp and held in place with simple golden pins that glinted in the sunlight. She was wearing her wideawake hat, and she was craning her head back so she could look up at him, her face fixed into a warm smile. At times she laughed, the sound gentle and kind, and he could feel her hand on his right arm, the heat of her skin pressing down on his, which he knew was odd, as the rest of the arm felt dead and lifeless. But he dared not look at her directly. He had risked doing so once, and the sight of her lifeless eyes in her vivacious, beautiful face was almost more than he could bear. Still, he was glad to have her with him, her company at his side comforting, even though he knew she was quite dead.

They walked on together. Step by step. Pace by pace.

He did not know when the tears started. They were flowing freely through the grime on his face when he noticed them for the first time. It was only as he became aware of their warm dampness on his skin that he felt the dam break inside him.

He sank to his knees, the rifle he had been carrying falling into the dust at his side.

And he wept.

For Anna was dead and he did not know where he was going.

He was quite alone in the world.

Chapter Thirty-seven

———◆———

*J*ack sat in the back of a digger's cart, rocking to the motion as the pony hauled it across the veldt. He was as comfortable as he could be, his good left arm bracing him in position while his right was immobile, his wounds bound tight with clean bandages brought in the cart just for that purpose.

It was the evening of the day after his single-handed fight with the Boers. He recalled nothing of the hours that had followed his walking away from the kopje, that time passing in a blur of pain and suffering.

And then Goodfellow had found him.

He did not recall his countryman's arrival. One minute he was alone. The next Goodfellow was there. He had come by himself, spurred on, he had said, by rumours of the battle – his choice of words – that had taken place in the veldt surrounding the diggings. He had set off as soon as he had heard the tale, borrowing a pony and cart, with the sole intention of finding Jack, or at least of retrieving his body.

'Are you still with me back there, Jack?' he sang out from the bench at the front of the cart. He was not a great driver, and the pony began wandering to the left as he turned to look back at Jack.

'Yes,' Jack answered simply. Once he would likely have either chided or mocked Goodfellow for his lack of skill. But such things were beyond him now, his mind and body unable to do anything much at all.

The cart jerked sharply to the right as Goodfellow over-corrected their course, then veered back to the left as he brought it under full control. Jack gasped, the jolting reverberating through his wounded shoulder. For several moments he could do nothing but endure, breathing his way through the pain. Only when it had faded to a bearable level did he sit back, staring up at the darkening evening sky as the cart made slow progress towards the diggings, wondering if he was grateful to Goodfellow for his rescue or if he should damn the man for averting the fate that would have seen his pain come to an end once and for all. For he did not know if he wished to carry on with the life that was now in front of him.

'We'll make a nice cup of tea when we get back. Some toast, too. I imagine you're famished.' This time Goodfellow kept his attention facing forward, raising his voice to com-pensate. 'It should not take long; it is not far. Of course, it took me all day to find you. I had no idea where you might be, you see, no idea at all. The story of your escapade was light on details. I dare say I was lucky to find you at all. Very lucky indeed.'

Jack let the man prattle away, allowing the words to wash over him. He felt no fear at returning to the diggings. The Boers could come for him if they so wished. He would not fight them, those that were left. He had done all he wanted.

Goodfellow fell silent as the pony plodded its way towards

home. He only spoke again as they drove through the fringes of the encampment.

'Perhaps it would be wise for you to lie a little lower, Jack. No sense drawing attention to ourselves,' he advised as he spied faces turning their way.

Jack obeyed, slinking down so that his head was below the side of the cart. He stayed there until it came to a stop.

'Here we are then, home at last.' Goodfellow began lowering his bulky frame down to the ground. 'Stay still for a moment longer, Jack, while I release this poor exhausted creature from his toil. He has served us well, I should say.' His praise of the animal was brought to an abrupt end as the tired pony tried to bite his face.

Jack did as he was told. Everything hurt. Badly.

He lay there for some time. He could hear the familiar sounds of the encampment all around him, weary voices talking to one another as exhausted men and woman settled down after another day of work in the diggings. It was twilight, and he could smell the first aromas of cooking, the warm, distinctive smell of bacon frying filling his nostrils. Yet he felt no hunger or desire to fill his empty belly. It was enough to just lie there and endure.

'Up you get, Jack, there's a good fellow.' Goodfellow chortled at his own choice of words. 'Jack?' A trace of concern entered his tone as he was ignored.

Jack stayed where he was a moment longer. But he knew he had to move, and so eventually he started easing himself up. Crawling to the rear of the cart, he reached out with his good arm, taking a firm grip on the hand that Goodfellow offered. Getting down was difficult with his right arm clamped tight against his chest, but he managed it with Goodfellow's assistance. He even managed to stay upright when his boots hit the ground, even though his knees half buckled under the strain.

He saw he was near Goodfellow's tent. The usual accoutrements of the diggers' camp surrounded him: cooking gear, shovels, buckets and a single hemp food sack. It felt familiar. Safe. Even comfortable. Yet he had eyes only for the ground in front of his dusty boots. It was taking all he had just to stay upright.

'Come on now, let's fix you a bite to eat. But first there is something you must see.' Goodfellow kept a firm grip on Jack's left arm as he spoke, lest his charge fall flat on his face. 'Or should I say someone.'

Jack paid no attention. He tried to shuffle forward, his only thought to crawl into Goodfellow's tent. There he would be able to rest, and for now, that was what he craved more than anything. Just to lay his head down and close his eyes would suffice.

'Did you hear me, Jack?' Goodfellow held him fast, even as he tried to step away.

'What's that?' Jack kept his gaze on the ground as he snapped the crabby reply. He did not care for the delay.

'Jack, there is someone you must see.'

'Who?'

Goodfellow did not reply. He just stood there holding Jack by the elbow.

Jack became aware of footsteps. They came from the direction of the tent, the soft sounds just about registering in his pain-addled brain.

'Hello, Jack.'

The words pierced deep. He looked up, vision swimming as

he moved his head too quickly. At first he thought he was
dreaming, his mind playing tricks on him as it struggled to cope
with the pain. He had been deceived before. He had lost count
of the times he had seen her face in the last dozen hours. But
this image was different. For she no longer possessed the flat,
dead stare of a corpse. Her eyes were alive with life, and she
was standing just in front of the tent, one flap still held in her
left hand. She looked thin, emaciated even, her body reduced to
little more than skin and bone, and her skin was the colour of
old whey.

But she was most definitely standing there.

And she was most definitely alive.

Anna was alive.

Chapter Thirty-eight

———◆———

Jack stood on the kopje where he had fought just over a fortnight before. There was no sign of the battle, no evidence that the ground had recently been fed with the blood of five men. The Boers' bodies had been taken away, and the kopje, and the veldt that surrounded it, was quite unchanged, the deaths of those five men making no impact on the ageless, timeless land.

Something on the ground caught his eye. It was hard to break the habit of scanning the soil, his digger's instinct still prompting him to search for the glint of a precious stone. But this time, he spotted nothing of value, just an empty cartridge case lying half buried in the dust. Bending over, he picked it up with his left hand, his fingers rubbing the brass free of dust. He recognised the casing easily enough. It was a pinfire cartridge, and he knew it had come from his Lefaucheux, the bullet it had once contained now buried somewhere in the landscape after it had passed through a man's body.

He sighed and stood up, the memories of the fight replaying themselves in his mind's eye. For a moment, he thought he caught the faintest whiff of spent powder on the air, and as he looked around him, he saw again de Klerk's body stretched out on the ground, his skull caved in by the rock Jack had wielded in desperation. Not far from the place where the Boer had died was the shallow firing pit Jack had clawed into the ground. He had believed he had been digging his grave, but now the low depression was already half filled with fallen stones, the land reclaiming the ground so that his efforts were lost for ever.

As quickly as they had arrived, the memories fled, and he saw once again the open veldt. The breeze was brisk that morning, and he felt it on his cheeks, making his skin tingle. It was a reminder that he was alive, that he had found a way to survive despite facing a lonely death here in the arse end of nowhere.

He stood still, letting the breeze play across his face as he stared towards the distant horizon. He was carrying all that he owned, the knapsack on his back containing the few clothes and necessities that Goodfellow had provided, his Lefaucheux snug in its holster on his right hip, the monkey-tail rifle he had taken from the Boer slung over his left shoulder. He did not own much, but he had all he needed.

He turned, reaching out with his left hand to help Anna take the last few paces that would bring her to his side. She still looked awfully thin, and her eyes were surrounded by dark grey sacks that spoke of a long illness only just defeated. But the eyes themselves were alive and filled with the spark of her life essence.

'Still with me, love?' he asked as she came to stand next to him. Like him, she stared out at the wide expanse of veldt, eyes drinking in the sight of such an enormous world.

'Always. You'll have to try a hell of a lot harder to get rid of me.' She laughed at her own words, then rested her head against his arm, her hands entwined around his. It was a good sound. Warm and full of life, and the sound of it made him smile.

It had all been Anna's own idea. Believing she was dying, she had begged Goodfellow to fake her death. He had gone along with the plan, accepting that it was the only way to force Jack to leave her and make a new life for himself. Neither of them had expected him to react as he had done.

He had told her his own sorry tale, leaving nothing out, no matter how brutal or cruel. She had listened to it all without saying a word. When he was done, there was no recrimination. No judgement. There was just acceptance, and she had held him close when he was spent.

Now, out of nowhere, they had found a new future, and Jack stared at the distant horizon and wondered where Fate would take him next.

But for once, he was not alone.

He and Anna would face the future together.

Epilogue

Port Elizabeth, Algoa Bay, Cape Colony, 2 September 1871

The Englishman knew where he was going. He had scouted the row of merchants the day before, conducting a reconnaissance as thoroughly as any general planning an attack on a well-fortified encampment. He had selected the one he would visit, picking the man who to his eye appeared the wealthiest and the smartest. For he wanted the best price and he had learned long ago that it would most likely come from those able to waste precious cash on appearances.

He had returned to join his companion and they had left their hotel shortly after nine. They had breakfasted in the small dining salon, both tucking into thick slices of bacon washed down with tea. Now they approached their chosen establishment, walking hand in hand, not caring that their rough clothes and weathered appearance drew disapproving glances from the few denizens of the better side of Port Elizabeth abroad that early in the morning.

The door jangled as the Englishman pushed it open, a short

bar on the top of the frame hitting a bell mounted just above the entrance.

He walked inside, then paused to hold the door for his companion, his eyes scanning the room as he did so. Three desks were arranged in a horseshoe shape. Under his dusty army boots was a fine Indian rug made from a dozen shades of red, cream and yellow thread, arranged in an intricate and pleasing pattern. The walls were painted a simple cream, but all bore sporting prints of the type he would expect to find in any of the better gentlemen's clubs in Piccadilly. The decor spoke of wealth and refinement, two things not often found in the rough and ready town of Port Elizabeth, and the Englishman smiled with pleasure at his choice of venue for the transaction he planned to make that morning.

'May I be of any assistance?'

One of the three occupants of the room addressed the Englishman in a delightfully supercilious tone that would have been at home in those same gentlemen's clubs. Each man had his own desk, and all were dressed in formal dark suits, paired with matching waistcoats decorated with thick gold watch chains. None of the men could be called either young or handsome, and all sported wide bellies that spoke of good eating and too much claret. To the Englishman's eye, it looked as if the three had all been purchased from the same supplier, their identical appearance enhanced by matching moustaches and sideburns that were neatly brushed and gleaming with oil.

He smiled. It was just as he had expected, and that pleased him. He liked to know what he was facing, and he was on familiar ground here. He had dealt with a number of supercilious clots over the years, and he knew how to conduct himself to garner their attention.

Turning to his companion, he smiled, relishing the chance to speak in a haughty tone that matched the upper-class drawl with which he had been greeted. 'What say you, my dear? Shall we ask this gentleman for his assistance?' He paused. 'Or shall I rip his fucking head off and shit down the hole?' He deftly replaced the polite, well-to-do accent with one that came straight from the rough end of Whitechapel.

His companion laughed, just as he had known she would.

'Now, now, my dear. There is no need for such talk. At least, not yet.' She smiled up at him, her neck craning back so she could look into his hard grey eyes, then reached out to brush one of a million specks of dust from his lapel.

Still smiling, she turned to face the man who had greeted them. 'We have a transaction we think would interest you, if you have the time to assist us, of course.'

The man behind the desk smiled, or at least his lips twisted into a different shape. It was not a friendly expression. 'I think perhaps my colleague will be able to help. He deals with our . . . smaller transactions.' He gestured towards the man at the desk to his left, half bowing as he did so, then sat back down and returned his attention to a thick ledger that took up nearly all of the desk's red leather top.

The Englishman cocked his head to one side as they were dismissed, then glanced at his companion. She was still smiling, but this time she added a slight nod.

Permission was given.

The Englishman stalked forward, covering the distance to the man's desk in two long strides. 'Now listen to me, chum,' he growled. 'I rather think you will want to help us out, you hear me?'

'Now, really.' The man remained seated, his expression

betraying nothing but disgust. He even went so far as to sniff the air, as if the Englishman smelled as ripe as year-old cheese. 'I am sure Mr Bertram can arrange this transaction of yours, although I would suggest you may wish to take your trade to De Witt. He is more used to dealing with your sort.'

'My sort?'

The man looked down at his ledger. 'De Witt is more familiar with dealing with those from the . . . Dutch territories.'

'You think I'm a Boer?'

The ledger was clearly fascinating. 'Hmm?' It was all the answer the man deigned to give, the snub deliberate.

'What's your name, chum?' The Englishman felt the first spark of anger, and he reached forward to place his hand on the very centre of the ledger. The hand was clean enough, but the nails were short and torn, and the fingers thick and callused. It was the hand of a working man and it stayed on the ledger, the heel of the palm smudging the carefully pencilled numbers.

The man whose precious ledger was being ruined half rose to his feet, his pale cheeks colouring crimson.

'Now look here. I really must—'

Whatever he wanted to say came to an abrupt stop, because the Englishman had reached into a pocket and produced a rough-cut diamond the likes of which the man with the ledger had only seen once or twice in the five years he had been buying stones from the diamond fields.

'I really must apologise, sir. I rather think we got off on the wrong foot.' Composure and grace replaced snobbery in an instant, and the man stood up properly, offering his hand, the crimson flush spreading across his face and neck one now of embarrassment rather than ire. 'My name is Smithers. May I ask who I have the absolute pleasure of addressing?'

The Englishman snorted at the sharp change in the man's demeanour.

'Lark. Jack Lark.' He turned to usher his companion into the conversation. 'I have the pleasure of introducing Anna Baker. You may have heard of her uncle, Sir Samuel.' He dropped the name without hesitation, then leaned forward. 'Now, you are going to offer us both a cup of tea, and then you are going to provide us with the best price you have ever given for a diamond like this, one that we might or might not accept. Am I being clear enough, Mr Smithers?'

'Yes, yes indeed.' Smithers bowed, his entire stance transformed from one of supercilious disdain to grovelling obedience.

It was enough to make Jack smile.

For he knew he would get a fine price for the stone now lying on the ledger.

And he had Anna at his side.

Finally, he had it all.

Author's Note

This is perhaps the first occasion when I have not had to use a historical note to apologise for my blatant manipulation of history. Life in Du Toit's Pan was largely as described in this novel, and it was just as hard and remorseless as I have tried to portray. Thousands of hardy and hopeful souls were drawn to the dry diggings by the lure of finding diamonds, but few found more than a handful of tiny stones or some of the cursed carbon that sustained many a digger for a while at least. For those wishing to learn more of this time in the diamond fields, I heartily recommend *The Diamond Diggings of South Africa: A Personal and Practical Account*, by Charles A. Payton, published in 1872. The account is as close to a guidebook of the period as I have found, and it proved to be a fantastic guide to the daily life of a digger at Du Toit's Pan.

Of course, this would not be a Jack Lark novel without some embellishment. There is no record that I found of any fighting between the Boers and diggers from either the Cape Colony or further afield. There was certainly tension, and I believe it is true to say that the boundaries of the British-controlled Cape Colony and the twin Boer republics – the Orange Free State and the Transvaal Republic – were fluid, to say the least, and most certainly added to the antagonism between the Boers and the rest of the diggers. The dispute touched upon in this novel regarding the ownership of the diggings themselves and the wider tract of land around, claimed by Captain Nicholas Waterboer, chief of the Griqua people, is just one of many of that period. For those who are interested, it was later deemed that the land did indeed belong to the Griquas and it was officially awarded to them by the Keate Committee in October 1871, after Jack's time in the diggings.

I should also mention that Anna Baker and her father are fictitious. There is a wealth of excellent histories that cover the life and expeditions of her supposed uncle, Sir Samuel White Baker, and part of his story is told in the ninth Jack Lark novel, *Commander*.

We are still a good few years away from the start of the First Boer War, but I needed Jack to face a new enemy, and so the Boers became the foe of the English – or of Jack Lark, at least – well before the real hostilities broke out late in 1880. De Klerk, Oom Joost and their gang were all drawn from my imagination, and of course bear no relation to any real Boer family. We may see more of the conflict between the Boers and the British, but that is certainly far in both my future and Jack's!

So, what *is* next for Jack?

Well, he and Anna survived a torrid time in the dry diggings.